A GENTLEMAN'S SEDUCTION

"Do you know," he said, his voice only slightly thickened from the whiskey, "you're absolutely the most beautiful gentleman I've ever had a drink with."

She tipped her glass in a toast. "Same to you."

"And you make a cutaway and a shirt look more feminine than the most beruffled gown ever created by Mr. Worth of Paris."

She didn't know what to say to that, so she sipped her drink. "Brandy?" she asked as she tasted it.

"A gentleman can't very well seduce a lady with Kentucky bourbon."

She coughed on the brandy. "Are you going to? Seduce me?"

"Oh yes, ma'am, I certainly am."

And she knew, from her curling hair to her suddenly curling toes, that he was right.

All The Time We Need

Megan Daniel

LOVE SPELL  **NEW YORK CITY**

LOVE SPELL®

October 1993

Published by

Dorchester Publishing Co., Inc.
276 Fifth Avenue
New York, NY 10001

Cover Art by John Ennis

The name "Love Spell" and its logo are trademarks of Dorchester Publishing Co., Inc.

Printed in the United States of America.

Chapter One

"Hunh! Hunh! Hunh!" Charli Stewart opened her mouth and let the sound explode out of her, putting her guts into it as first her left fist, then her right, then her left again shot out, board straight and iron steady. Her white karate *gi* was soaked through and sticking to her flushed skin, her almost-black hair was pasted to her skull, sweat ran down her neck in small streams, and she felt great.

"Again, please," said the instructor, *Sempai* Joe, in a voice that never rose above a polite murmur, and Charli did it again. And again. And again, until the *Sempai* was satisfied.

They moved on to front snap-kicks. She gathered herself within herself before each one, an instant of perfect stillness, before . . . "Haaahh!" She pulled the sound and the power up together

7

from deep inside her, stepped forward on her left leg, and threw out her right, hard and fast and high, straight into the solar plexus of her invisible attacker. "Haaahh!" And another, "Haaahh!" And another, "Haaahh!"

When it came time for sparring, Charli, as usual, picked the biggest, brawniest guy in the room as her adversary. It was so satisfying keeping him on the defensive.

She loved karate. Six days a week, Charli came to the *dojo*, gently bowed her respect to the room, the other students, and *Sempai* Joe, then kicked, punched, and yelled her way through the next hour and a half, her taut five-foot-two body fending off much larger would-be assailants by focusing all her force, both mental and physical, in every kick and punch. Just as important, she'd learned how to see a blow coming and use her opponent's own force against him, by stepping back and then going with his energy, making it work for her instead of against her. In another month she'd be tested to see if she was worthy to wear the coveted black belt. She was determined to be ready.

Charli had been studying karate for nearly two years, ever since the night she'd become another statistic on New York's Sixth Precinct police blotter—just one of many Manhattan mugging victims. It had changed her life, leaving her with an overwhelming sense of vulnerability and anger that had paralyzed her. Desperation had carried her to the *dojo*, a mad grab to regain some semblance of control over a life she feared she was losing her grip on. She had hoped karate could give her back that sense of control that was so essential to her. But she hadn't expected to love it so much—the power, the strength, the sense of herself she got when she threw a perfect punch or blocked a deadly blow. And the inner calm that came from knowing that because she could defend herself, it was less likely she would ever have to. Never again.

Finally the class was over. She bowed once more to the *Sempai* and headed for the shower, exhilarated, every muscle quivering with a combination of fatigue and precision tuning. The hot water attacked her overworked body, pounding relaxation into it, soothing her sweaty skin, throwing her mental Alert switch back to At Ease.

She felt so good she laughed out loud, and the sound turned to a gurgle as her mouth filled with water. Even the lunch she'd had earlier that day with her mother couldn't dampen her spirits, at least not too much.

The setting, of course, had been Mortimer's, her mother's favorite haunt—the table by the window when no one more important was in attendance and she could get it. And the conversation had been just as predictable.

"Charlotte," Victoria Stewart had said to her daughter, "how much longer is this silly downtown game going to go on, pretending you have to work for a living, hanging around with musicians in God knows what sort of dives, and refusing to even try to meet a really nice man who will take care of you? I know I don't have to point out that at age twenty-seven the number of men available to you is definitely dwindling."

Charli had smiled over her radicchio and mandarin salad. "Well, there's still Bobby Dibbs-Kent. I'm sure he'd be willing to ask me again, and I suppose I shouldn't mind being married to a drunk as long as he got there only on Chivas and champagne."

Her mother stabbed at her warm chicken and tarragon salad—no dressing—and frowned. "That is precisely the attitude I'm talking about. I really don't understand you."

"I know you don't, Mother."

No, Chàrli knew very well that Victoria Wainwright Stewart did not understand her only daughter, the girl who had once been so sweet and clever, such a pretty debutante, so popular with the right kind of boys—and so easily controlled. The daughter who was now a mystifying mix of rock-rigid independence and fierce stubbornness and plain hard work. And who seemed manifestly uninterested in settling down with a nice man in a nice house and raising lovely grandchildren for Victoria to spoil with lovely designer clothes and extravagant toys from F.A.O. Schwarz.

She sighed and flecked a crumb from her so-correct Pauline Trigere luncheon suit. "After what happened to you down in that neighborhood, I'd think you'd want to move back uptown where you belong."

"I could just as easily have been mugged on Park Avenue, Mother, and you know it." Charli stabbed fiercely at an onion ring, hating to remember the vulnerability and the pain of lying in an alley with a broken arm, a missing tooth, and no wallet. "And it won't happen again. I've seen to that."

"I suppose you mean that judo of yours."

"Karate," Charli corrected. "And yes, that's what I mean. I can take care of myself now."

"But why on earth should you want to take care of yourself?" her mother wailed. "That's what I don't understand."

"I know," she said again, sad that her mother would never understand and never approve of much of anything about Charli. She had stopped understanding some years ago, back when Charli decided to stop being her mother's remote-controlled doll and take over the management of her own life. Charli knew her mother did not want her throwing punches and yelling till her throat hurt, she did not want her living alone downtown in—the woman could hardly bring herself to say it—Greenwich Village, and she certainly didn't want her sweating. Victoria Stewart wanted her daughter Charlotte perfectly dressed and manicured, presiding at teas, sitting on charitable committees, and preparing to take her rightful place one day as co-chairwoman of the Metropolitan Museum's Spring Fling fundraising ball. She wanted her uptown, where she belonged. And dammit, she wanted her married.

"Sorry, Mom," Charli muttered now as she turned off the shower. "Sometimes we just don't get what we want."

She stepped out onto the cold tile floor, reached for a big, rough towel, and rubbed her skin pink with it. As the thumping sounds of the next class echoed through the *dojo*'s thin walls, she toweled her hair—in its second year of growing out from what Charli described as "about an Irish inch

11

longer than a Sinead O'Connor shave"—fluffing it into a halo of damp black curls. Then she reached into her locker for a pair of hot-red Lycra leggings.

"Whew!" said a blonde just peeling off a *gi* as soaked with sweat as Charli's had been. "Some class. He doesn't let up, does he?"

"Would you want him to?" asked Charli.

The two women looked at each other, then said in unison, "Nah."

"Want to go over to the Waverly?" asked the blonde, reaching for a towel. "That new Kevin Costner film starts in twenty minutes."

"Thanks, but I've got a date with a contract. Hot negotiation in the morning." She stepped into black half boots and pulled an oversize silver lamé shirt from her locker. "Besides, he's not my type. I'm more into the dark, smooth ones. You know, Gable, Flynn, like that."

"You're about fifty years late, babe."

"Kevin Kline?"

The blonde nodded. "You could do worse."

Charli laughed. "Don't I wish." She stuck her arms into the sleeves of a wide-shouldered leather jacket and slung her oversize bag across one shoulder. "See you tomorrow," she called before she bounced down the stairs and swung out the door onto Sixth Avenue and into the whirl of New York City.

She breathed deeply of the gas- and garbage-scented air, glassy now with a late February chill, and smiled. This was her city and how she loved it—the energy, the talent, the ambition, even the gaudy ostentation. She loved the buzz of it, the demands it made. The knowledge that "if you can make it there, you'll make it anywhere." And how she hated it—the dirt, the crime, the vulnerability it made you suffer and fight against, the always looking back to see who was gaining on you. The merciless cold shoulder that said if you couldn't make it there, you were nothing.

But Charli was making it, at least she had a decent start on it. And she was doing it her way, on her own. She was in control of her own destiny.

Few of her friends had any idea Charli had once been an uptown girl, a white-dress debutante. And all of them would have been sucker-punch surprised to hear that she was a "Trust Fund Baby." All they knew was that she was blade-sharp, funny, independent as hell, and a soft touch for a hard-luck story. They knew she was impetuous but that you could trust her with your life or your last dime; if Charli Stewart made a promise, the thing was done. And they knew she worked at least as hard as any of them.

She had long since come to her own rather tortured decisions about her family's money and what she would allow herself to do with it. The income from her trust fund was for things like giving large sums of money to worthy causes, from Big Sisters and the struggling local rape crisis center to the Lady Bird Johnson Wildflower Fund. It was for fun, too, like buying the sort of funky, trendy clothes she looked good in, or treating herself to a complete facial and massage once a month just because it felt so great. But none of those things was essential to Charli. The necessities she paid for with money she made herself—her apartment, food, business expenses, gifts to friends, books, her karate classes. And always music. The important things in her life, the things without which she would be empty, she was determined to pay for with money she earned.

And music was how she did it. Jazz was paying her way.

She'd first started her downtown life as a jazz singer, showing up for open-mikes in the smoky basement clubs on MacDougal and Bleeker and Sheridan Square, playing piano-bar gigs when she could get them and waiting tables or doing temp office work when she couldn't.

But as much as she loved to perform, it didn't take Charli long to realize that it was never going to give her the kind of success she wanted, the kind she could hold up to her mother and say, "See!" She had to find something else, and she did—almost by accident. She'd always known she had a good business head and she understood people. She started informally advising her performer friends about how to stand up for themselves with club owners and record producers, and before long they started giving her commissions for it. Pretty soon, she stopped performing altogether.

In the last three years, she'd built a solid business as a musicians' agent, specializing in jazz performers.

It had been a rough climb. Jazz was a man's world. Women were welcome to stand behind a mike and wail out the blues about being done wrong before they went home to the bass player's bed. They were far less welcome on the other side of the stage, negotiating contracts, arranging gigs, and standing up to hard-drinking club owners who, faced with Charli, would rather cop a feel than seal a deal. But she was sticking with it and it was working. At last.

Dodging Sixth Avenue traffic and the slush of melting snow piled up in the gutters, she crossed to the Korean greengrocer for a pound of tangerines and a Butterfinger—"I'll work it off tomorrow at the *dojo*," she told herself—then turned onto Washington Place. She had her keys in her hand before she reached her building, by now an instinctive precaution, and she pushed open the front door with her shoulder, turning to scan the street to be sure no one was following her inside. It didn't take a mugging to learn to be careful in New York. And once you had been mugged right into a hospital, you were doubly wary. When she'd first seen the apartment a year ago, she had almost turned it down because it lacked the safety of a doorman. But she'd fallen in love with the big, raw loft space, instantly envisioning the home she could create there, so she had closed her eyes, said a prayer, and signed. She hadn't been sorry.

Waiting for the old elevator that sounded like a dying washing machine to inch its way down to her, Charli flipped through her mail and whistled a variation on a Sonny Rollins sax cut she'd heard recently. When the car arrived, she carefully checked out the interior for lurking strangers before stepping in and creakily making her way up to her downtown penthouse.

As she triple-locked her heavy metal door behind her, she smiled. She was home.

15

The apartment had Charli's stamp all over it. White walls, starkly modern white furniture— and not much of it. Plump cushions of poppy red, buttercup, and cobalt thrown here and there and a dense forest-green rug that felt like new-mown grass under bare feet. A century-old Bechstein baby grand filled one corner, a gift from her father on her 18th birthday, the year before he died. A wall of windows showed off a Woody Allen-perfect view of the Empire State Building, now kissed silver by the lowering sun.

She tossed her bag on a sleek chair, kicked off her shoes, and punched a button on a state-of-the-art sound system. Miles Davis' "Sketches of Spain" immediately filled the room. In the kitchen, she hummed along as she tossed a Lean Cuisine in the microwave, popped the top on a Diet Coke, and peeled away the slippery yellow wrapper of her candy bar. Then she reached toward the winking light on her answering machine and hit the playback button.

"Hello, Charlotte Victoria, my sweet," said a disembodied voice. She grimaced, then laughed. Glen Odens was the only person in the world besides her mother who could call her Charlotte without instantly becoming an active enemy. And then only because he did it with such flair. "I call merely to remind you, my dove, that the entire future of my career, not to mention the maintenance payments on my co-op and the bills to my plastic surgeon, rests on the incomparable negotiating skills which I know you shall bring to bear on the morrow. In other words, sweet cheeks, I'm trusting you to screw them to the wall, as I have reason to know you can do so well. I thank you,

16

my piano thanks you, my co-op board thanks you. Call me when it's over." Beep. She laughed again. Glen was a case, but he played piano like he was God's sideman.

She licked some chocolate from her lower lip. "Charli?" came the next voice. "Janet here. I've got a question on the Minneapolis gig. Call me as soon as you get in, okay?" Beep.

She chugged some Coke and watched the winter sunset as the tape spun to the next message. "Yeah, this is Rob Sams." She snapped around like a top. She'd been trying to get to Sams for weeks, ever since she'd seen him play an open-mike spot at the Black Cat and he'd made his soprano sax do things she didn't think were possible. The guy was a genius on that horn. She'd caught him backstage that very night, practically shouted "Hallelujah" when she found out he didn't already have an agent, and thrust her card at him with a confident "I can help you." To which he'd shrugged a nonchalant "I don't need help" and walked away. Luckily, the club owner had a number for him, a number she had dialed at least fifty times, leaving message after message. She wanted this one, bad.

"I'm not sure I ought to have an agent yet," Sams said now on the tape, "especially a woman, but I asked around. I hear you're pretty good, that you don't take any bull off anybody and that nothing much gets past you."

"Oh, please please please please," she muttered as he went on.

"But the music's the thing, see, and you haven't heard me play, not really, not to know what I can do. That Black Cat gig was nothing."

17

"Nothing?" she said as he paused. "Only enough nothing to have me salivating over what I could do with your career."

"So anyway, you gotta hear me do it right and I gotta see you while you're hearing me. Then I'll know. I'm playing a Mardi Gras gig tomorrow night at Jimmy's Bourbon Base, you know it? I'll leave your name at the door. If you're serious about this, about me, you'll be there." Beep.

Be there? Damn straight she'd be there. She'd been waiting for a Rob Sams to come along for years, ever since she'd started her own shop. She could put him in the big time, and he could do the same for her.

She grabbed her bag, shook it upside down, and fished her Filofax from the unimaginable pile of junk that spilled out onto the table. "Tomorrow, tomorrow, tomorrow," she muttered as she flipped it open. Tuesday—well, she had plans to catch the hot trumpeter playing at Sweet Basil, but she'd cancel. Hell, for this guy she would have canceled an audience with the pope. "Rob Sams," she wrote in big letters with a giant exclamation point, then she added, "Jimmy's Bourbon B—"

Her hand froze. She knew about Jimmy's even though she'd never been there or booked anyone there. It was a good gig. It was a step in the right direction.

But it was, God help her, in New Orleans!

Chapter Two

After the slush and freeze of New York, New Orleans was practically tropical. Outside Charli's hotel room window there rioted a profusion of the sort of green and growing things she hadn't seen in months. And the air, even on a February evening, smelled like cheap perfume sponged on with a too-heavy hand—an exotic blend of over-blown flowers, roasting coffee, and river mud.

She tossed her bag on the bed and looked at herself in the mirror. "Not a pretty sight, Charli," she told her image, leaning closer to peer at the dark circles under her blue eyes. "Regular shiners," she muttered, not surprised that she looked like a hag. The last twenty-four hours had been grueling. "I just hope Rob Sams is worth it," she said. Then she straightened. "He is," she stated flatly. "He is definitely worth it."

Megan Daniel

Thanks to Sams's phone call, last night had entailed about a hundred phone calls to reschedule her life and a couple of hours at her computer to sort out work for her secretary to handle while she was gone. Then the seemingly impossible task of booking a room—any room—in New Orleans during Mardi Gras on a few hours' notice. That had required calling in a lot of markers and handing out many a promise of future favors before she came up with the assurance that she'd have a place to lay her head in The Big Easy. By the time she started checking for flights, she was blessing the god of 24-hour reservations lines.

And then she'd still had to pack, after doing a load of laundry and ironing so she'd have something to pack.

Come morning, a cold shower, three cups of coffee, and a large handful of vitamins got her through the meeting on Glen Odens's new recording contract just before she headed for the airport.

Now, numb from lack of sleep except for an hour's catnap on the plane that had done nothing but give her a crick in her neck, and with two airplane meals feeling like half-solidified concrete in her stomach, she kicked back and sipped a cup of strong coffee laced with chicory that she'd ordered the minute she got to the hotel.

She would have killed for half an hour in a Jacuzzi, but her contacts hadn't stretched to a room at the Hilton Riverside or the Marriott, with their high-tech pampering and their high-perch views of the curve of river that gave the Crescent City its nickname. She'd had to settle for this renovated Creole mansion in the French Quarter.

It was the sort of place the travel mags wrote up with adjectives like "quaint" and "intimate," full of claw-foot furniture, lace curtains, and giant urns overflowing with exotic blooms. Charli's room was in one of the former slave cottages overlooking a brick-paved courtyard dripping with wisteria vines and hibiscus and fringed with banana palms around a fountain. It was very pretty, but it wasn't at all Charli. The stark modern angles and clean black-and-white of an Andrée Putman design were more her style.

She gave herself five minutes to enjoy the peaceful view and the downright heavenly coffee before, with a groan, she had to start moving again. Rob wasn't a headliner—not yet, she told herself, but soon!—so he was playing only the early set, a warm-up to the main event. She had less than an hour to get to Jimmy's Bourbon Base. Five minutes in a hot shower topped off with another five under the icy needlelike spray perked her up a bit. Ten minutes to dry and mousse her hair into a spiky black aureole. Five more for makeup. Then dress.

In the middle of packing last night, she'd had a terrible realization. Mardi Gras in New Orleans meant she needed a costume! At three o'clock in the morning, it had seemed hopeless. But she'd rummaged around in her cavernous closet until she came up with something that suited her sense of the ridiculous. Now she grinned as she stepped into a black Donna Karan catsuit and zipped it up the front only far enough to keep from getting arrested. She stuck her feet into droopy yellow cuff-boots she'd found in Milan's Galeria during the Italian jazz festival last year, put on a wide leather belt that showed off her tiny waist, and added bright plastic earrings that almost brushed her shoulders. For the coup de grace, she swung a hot pink cape lined in canary yellow around her shoulders. It had been the gift of a matador she'd dated once, and only once, in Barcelona.

She turned to the mirror and struck a pose. "Not bad," she said out loud. "Puss in Boots with attitude." She gave the matador's cape a rakish toss so it flipped back over one shoulder, then grabbed her purse and a big empty shoulder bag of yellow vinyl. She looked at her watch.

"Damn!" she muttered. She was going to be late if she didn't hurry, and one of Charli's unbreakable rules was that she was never late for business appointments, even jazz gigs in New Orleans on Mardi Gras on twenty-four hours' notice. There was no time to sort out the jumble of stuff in her purse and take just what she needed for the evening, so she simply upended it, spilling everything into the yellow bag—an incredible collection of absolute necessities, maybes, and probably-not-but-who-knows items mixed with what she was sure was a lot of junk.

Then she zipped the yellow bag shut with its Ziploc-type closing, slung it around her shoulder, bandolier fashion, retied the cape over it, and ran out the door.

The streets were thronged with Mardi Gras crowds. She was only a few blocks from the club, but in that short distance, she was jostled by one Beast without his Beauty, three clowns, and an Abraham Lincoln in a dented stovepipe hat and a beard that had been knocked off-center by the beer he was swigging from a plastic cup.

A Harlequin jabbed an elbow into her right side; a Mexican in a molting Zapata mustache got her from the left.

"Where y'at, darlin'?" he cried in a distinctive New Orleans twang that sounded exactly like Brooklynese. "C'mon an' dance, *cher,*" he added. She laughed and turned the corner.

On Bourbon Street, neon pierced the night and music spilled from every door—ragtime and blues and the syncopated accordion and *frottoir* washboard rhythms of Cajun-zydeco. She found herself changing her step in time to each new beat. Devils, angels, gypsies, and queens (both fairy and drag) poured past her. A gorilla danced by with a rhinestone cowgirl. A Rebel soldier stood on the corner giving out a series of lusty Rebel yells between swigs of Dixie beer. By the time she got to Jimmy's, she was laughing but sweating and glad to get out of the madness.

With most of the city's revelers out in the streets waiting for the torchlit Comus parade to start—the climax of the two weeks of madness that was Mardi Gras—the club was half-empty. Though thankful for the relative quiet, Charli was sorry Rob wouldn't have a full house.

She hadn't been there five minutes before Rob walked onto the stage, nodded to where she sat at a front table, lifted his sax, and made Charli Stewart and everyone else in the little room forget all about Mardi Gras, sleepless nights, empty seats, and everything else in the world.

She'd been right. This guy could play! He had everything he needed except the right contacts to become a breakout star, a world-class reedman.

23

And she had the contacts to finish the job.

He was in his mid-twenties, with the ivory pallor of so many musicians who spend their nights in smoky clubs and their daylight hours asleep. Dressed all in black and so thin he looked like a Sobranie Black Russian cigarette, Rob had a big, round, gorgeous sound that flowed from his horn like lava or erupted like a volcano. Charli's drink sat untouched as she watched him make love to his saxophone. There was no other way to describe it. His long, slender fingers caressed the valves, his full lips kissed the reed as sensually as any man ever kissed a woman he loved. He blew the notes out so they stroked the air.

He was on a stage the size of a postage stamp, and he made it seem as big as Madison Square Garden. He was backed by an uninspired house rhythm section, the worst backup a player could have, and he made them sound like angels. He played the old standards—"Perdido," "Body and Soul," "Take Five"—and they sounded like no one had ever played them before. His "Harlem Nocturne" was so fresh it could have been written yesterday, rounded out with a bossa tempo and the kind of passion the song deserved but seldom got. She couldn't help comparing him to Coltrane, that mystic knight of the soprano sax, though of course he had a long way to go to reach Trane's mythic proportions.

He hadn't learned to pace himself. He played every tune with a swaggering intensity, punching out the notes as if they were words in an argument he had to win or die trying. If he kept it up, after a few years he'd burn out like a Fourth of July sparkler.

He finished a scorching "Donna Lee" and glanced down at her. His dark hair was damp with sweat, his eyes as hooded as a lover's. He'd come out of the music long enough to really look at her, and she immediately knew she was going to have trouble with him.

Charli had been in the business long enough to recognize the signs. As soon as he got off the stage and mopped the sweat from his face, Rob Sams was going to come on to her. And she was going to have to find a tactful way to turn him right off again without making him angry.

Not that he wasn't attractive, in a dark, reedy sort of way, with the hungry look of so many musicians. But Charli had made a decision about this sort of thing right at the start. Business was business; love—and sex—were something else entirely. She refused to get involved with anyone she did business with, or might someday. She only dated guys outside the music world. Trouble was, she hardly ever met anyone outside the music world, except for the pathetic Bobby Dibbs-Kents of her mother's world.

Rob Sams was giving her the look that said he wanted her. She hoped he wasn't going to make it a prerequisite to a representation agreement, because she wanted him, too, but not in that way. She sipped her Perrier and studied him as he swung into his rapid-fire version of Bird's "Now's the Time."

It had been a long time since she'd had someone to care about, someone to hold her, to celebrate her successes and listen to her gripe when things went sour, to laugh at her when she was dumb and with her when she was clever, to fix her coffee when she was too tired to do it herself. Someone to make her body feel alive and her heart feel safe.

But she had learned to do those things for herself. She didn't have to break her own rules or settle for less than what she wanted from a man. She was thankful that, unlike her mother and so many mothers before her, she didn't live in a world where a woman had to marry—whether she wanted to or not, whether she was in love or not—just because there were no viable options open to her. She was grateful to live in a world where a woman could control her own life and her own destiny.

At the song's end, she gave Rob a brilliant smile. She'd turn him down, but she'd do it gently and start talking business. Experience told her that when dollars, contracts, and gigs were at issue, musicians' attention could pretty quickly be turned from their libidos to their careers.

The set finished and a few minutes later Rob appeared at her table, ordered a bourbon and branch, lit up a Camel, and leaned back in his chair.

"You liked it," he said matter-of-factly, smoke oozing from his mouth in a thin blue line.

"You know I did. I'd be crazy not to."

He nodded and said, as if to himself, "Yeah."

"You play polyrhythms as easily as I play 'Chopsticks.'"

He shrugged. "The rhythm's always been in me."

She watched him take a drag of his cigarette and a mouthful of his drink and hold them together in his mouth. He closed his eyes a moment to enjoy the taste. He looked almost as gone as he did when he blew his horn. "You lose yourself when you play, don't you?" she said.

He sat up straighter and opened his eyes. "How'd you know that?"

She just shrugged. Get him talking about the music, Charli, she told herself. Turn him on to the music more than he's turned on to you. "I've seen it before. And I can hear it when you play. You go away, and the music's the only thing left."

"Yeah," he said again. "I gotta be gone, or the music doesn't work, you know? I can't think when I play. If I see myself thinking, then I lose the picture I'm trying to make with the music. So I just make my mind real empty and let the music in." He took another long drink and looked right at her. "You know, like with sex."

Uh-oh. It wasn't working. She tried the direct tack. "Are we going to have a deal?" she asked.

"Are we going to make it together?"

"Depends on what you mean."

"You know what I mean." He let his gaze roam over the catsuit, the tiny waist, the spiky hair and catlike eyes. She felt him cataloging every item.

"Why don't we talk about what I can do for your career?"

He ignored the comment and continued checking her out. "I like cats," he said in a smoky voice. "I like to make them purr."

She had to stifle a groan at the ridiculous line. Why were the talented ones always the biggest jerks? As a woman in a man's business—especially one as sensual and hedonistic as jazz—she knew it went with the territory. She could almost never come to a business agreement with

27

a guy without having this stupid conversation. But the pushing, the testing, really pissed her off. He certainly wouldn't be coming on to a male agent here.

She put down her glass, set both elbows on the tiny table, and clasped her hands. "Okay, straight ahead. Here's the way we're going to play it. What you're going to do for me is make me a lot of money and put my agency in the top ten. What I'm going to do for you is make you even more money and put you on the charts and in the record stores and in the history books. That's all we're going to do for each other, and if you're as smart with your head as you are with a horn, that'll be enough."

He crossed his arms and tipped his chair way back, looking at her from under lowered eyelids. He stayed that way a long time. Finally, he lowered his chair, took a gulp of his drink long enough to worry her, then set down the empty glass. "Okay," he said, nodding to himself. "Okay, we got a deal." As simple as that.

Charli breathed again, realizing she hadn't been doing it for the past full minute. She had him. She had Rob Sams!

Chapter Three

All New Orleans was celebrating and Rob and Charli celebrated with it.

"Tomorrow," said Rob, as they shook hands on their deal, "we sign the paper, cross all the *t*'s and dot all the *i*'s. Tonight, it's Mardi Gras and I'm going to show you my city."

"You're from New Orleans?"

He grinned a real Big Easy grin. "You betcha, *cher.*"

He hauled her up from her chair, and she grabbed her bag. "Why not?" she said with a laugh. "Why the hell not?" And they swung out into the Mardi Gras madness of Bourbon Street.

The Comus parade was just passing by and the crowds were unbelievable, a roiling mass of monks and magicians and Mad Hatters, pushing, elbowing, reaching up toward the gaudy floats and calling frantically, "I want the pearls! I want the pearls!" as the masked men on the floats tossed strings of gaily colored plastic beads into the crowd. Charli was sure they wouldn't be able to get through. They couldn't even move. But Rob took control and elbowed and pushed until they were at the curb.

Soon Charli was into the spirit of the thing, yelling with the best of them, and in no time she had a red necklace and a green one slung around her neck.

After the parade was over, things quieted down a notch—though you had to be a New Orleanian to notice—and they were able to move again. It was nearly midnight, and her lack of sleep and frantic day were catching up with Charli. Her eyelids felt like sandpaper had been Krazy-Glued inside them.

"Rob," she began, "I've got to—"

"We're going to Tipitina's," he interrupted. "The Neville Brothers are playing," he said, pulling her through the throng. "And when the Nevilles play Tip's, they own the place."

That got her attention. She adored the Brothers' funky blues and had never seen them in person. But she was so unutterably exhausted. "Rob, I can't. I—"

"Aw, c'mon, *cher*. It's Mardi Gras." A sly smile took over his face. "And you do want me to sign that paper tomorrow, don'tcha?"

It was blackmail, pure and simple, but to keep Rob Sams she'd have to keep her eyes open at least another hour. Hopefully the music would help. She dragged off behind him, one very tired pussy cat.

Tip's did its job. The honky-tonk atmosphere woke her up some and the music did the rest. Brother Art pounded the piano like it was an enemy or a lover or both and Cyril hammered his drums till his dreadlocks writhed like Medusa's snakes. They swung from pop to funk to soul to a rap anthem that became a soulful lament before booming out a gospel number that made the plaster ready to repent.

Everybody, including Charli and Rob, danced. And everybody, including Rob but not Charli, drank. Rob was putting away the bourbon and branch like it was Perrier and lime, but he was holding it well, she thought. Well enough to keep dancing as long as the Brothers kept playing, which was until well past three.

Finally, they moved with the crowd out into the cool night air, and Rob pulled her toward the levee.

"Rob, my hotel's the other way," Charli said.

"Got a friend with a boat," he replied, his voice finally showing the effects of the drinks he'd been downing like 7-Up. "Taking it out on the river in ten minutes. Said we'd be there."

She dug in her heels. "Rob, I can't. I'm dying on my feet here."

"Sure you can, agent lady. You're a cat. Cats are night animals, just like jazz nuts."

"Well, this kitten is cashing in, Mardi Gras or no."

He leaned back a little shakily and looked down at her through eyes held at half-mast. "They didn't tell me you're a quitter. Don't think I want a quitter working for me."

Damn! More blackmail. Just how bad did she

31

want this guy? she asked herself. Much as she needed him, at this moment she wondered if she could afford him.

While she stared and thought, Rob walked off, up onto the levee. She followed. At the top, she looked out at the black water, glistening with a thousand colored reflections. A giant stern-wheeler—a reproduction from the glory days of New Orleans's past—eased slowly past, strung with lights like tinsel on a wedding cake and with Dixieland pouring from its decks. Rob was already down at a dock, climbing aboard a beautiful small yacht strung with more lights. At the top of the gangway he stopped and turned back to her. Drunk or not, he managed to plaster an unmistakable challenge on his face. Come with me or go back to New York—without a contract.

She went aboard.

As the boat pulled out onto the river, Charli was numb, totally operating on automatic pilot. Someone handed her a drink; she drank it. Someone handed her a plate of oysters; she ate them.

The decks were crowded. Everyone was singing, laughing, drinking. Everyone was drunk. She wondered idly if there was a cabin someplace where she could go to sleep. She did manage to find a quiet corner, just at the stern, looking out over the twinkling waters. She closed her eyes. Maybe she could sleep standing up.

She felt a hand reach under her matador's cape and snake around her and she looked up. It was Rob. Numb with fatigue, she watched his hand slide around her and begin slowly inching the long zipper down the front of her catsuit. She woke up enough to bat it away like it was a pesky fly.

"Aw, c'mon kitten," he whined. "After all, we're in business together now." He reached for the zipper again, taking another swig from the cup in his other hand. "Aren't we?" he added slyly.

Her head snapped up; she was fully awake now. "That's it! That's enough manipulation, cowboy. In the last thirty-six hours, I've turned my life upside down for you. I've pissed people off with rescheduled appointments, I've missed a night's sleep, I've flown halfway across the country and dressed myself up like a fool. But there's one thing I don't do for you or anybody unless I really, really want to. And all I really, really want to do right now is get off this damn boat and get some sleep." He was still leering. "Can you hear me?" No response. "Earth to Rob. Earth to Rob."

Something happened behind his eyes, but it wasn't clear what until he moved. Actually, he lunged straight at her. With her mind so clouded with sleeplessness and the drink she had mindlessly downed, she reacted instinctively. Two years of karate training came to the fore and she dodged. She stepped back and to the left, twisting away from him. Just at that moment, the boat tilted into a turn, combining with Rob's momentum and his bourbon-wobbly footing to send him lurching right over the rail and into the ink-black Mississippi.

Charli gripped the railing and peered into the dark water, trying to see where he'd sunk. For a terribly long moment, she couldn't see anything. Finally, he surfaced off to the left. Incredibly, he still had his cup in his hand. But that hand was flailing wildly, slapping at the water as if he could grab it and lift himself out.

Obviously the guy couldn't swim. While she, Charli Stewart, had been her prep league all-star in the breaststroke. Great! What else was she going to have to do to get this guy signed to a contract and make him rich? She looked around. Everyone was gathered at the front of the boat, singing raunchy, drunken songs. No one else had even seen Rob go in, and not one of them was in any condition to help anyway.

She struggled to untie her cape, but it had knotted. Her feet had swollen and she couldn't yank her boots off. No time to fuss with them. Rob went under again, and she pulled herself up over the railing, took a deep breath, and launched herself into the Mississippi.

Cold! The water was incredibly cold. It took her breath away so that when she surfaced she had to gasp to fill her lungs. At least it woke her up. She started stroking toward where Rob was bobbing in the water, but the current was much stronger than she'd expected. Her waterlogged cape dragged at her, and under it, her heavy shoulder bag added its weight. It seemed like every stroke toward Rob and the boat actually carried her farther away.

Her trendy boots felt like cement blocks on her feet; the cape wrapped around her legs like seaweed. And she was cold, so god-awful cold. She tried to breathe and instead gulped in a mouthful of river water. It tasted like gasoline and garbage. She coughed and barely managed to get a breath before she was sucked under again.

For the first time in a very long time, Charli was

scared. Was this it? Was this going to be how it
ended? she wondered. No! She wouldn't die in a
dirty river dressed in a catsuit. She wouldn't! She
clawed her way back to the surface and looked
for the yacht. It was much farther off now, hardly
more than a few lines of twinkling lights. And no
one on it even knew she was in the water!

She heard a booming in her ears, a thunderous
chug-chug with a bright underlayer of Dixieland,
and she turned her head. The giant stern-wheeler
she'd seen from the levee was practically on top
of her. Its fairy lights flashed like sparklers in her
eyes. She heard a giant boom, and a bright flash
of color burst over her head. They were setting
off fireworks from the riverboat, and with each
flash and boom, the huge boat came closer, its
giant stern wheel sucking her toward its chug-
ging, splashing blades. From her position in the
water, the wheel looked as big as the Metropolitan Opera House, the spaces between the churning paddles gaping like hungry mouths waiting to
devour her.

Frantically, she kicked, trying to disentangle
her legs from the intractable folds of the cotton
cape that had once enticed a bull to its death.
Desperately, she stroked away from the hungry
behemoth, but her arms were numb with cold
and exhaustion and she made no progress at all.

The boat came closer and closer, till the churning sound was all around her. Another firework
flower burst overhead—magenta and purple petals of fire floating down toward the water—as she
said a prayer. A snatch of music struck her ear
as she went under again. Her lungs felt like they
were bursting.

Megan Daniel

Once more she surfaced, very near the splashing wheel now. The prayer turned into an apology. Something hit her leg, hard, and she opened her mouth. Just before the Mississippi rushed in to fill it, she said aloud, "I'm sorry, Mama." Then she went under again.

She almost relaxed then, merely hoping it wouldn't hurt too much to die, that she would pass out before the stern-wheeler ate her to pieces. She felt something hit her arm, and instinctively her body twisted away from it. But she immediately felt it again, encircling her arm like a clamp. She felt her body moving through the water and assumed it was the power of the wheel sucking her into its jaws. She tensed.

Then suddenly she was out of the water. The vise on her arm had pulled her free. Vaguely, she was aware of other grips holding her, hands grasping her arms, pulling her up, away from the hungry jaws, away from the ink that was the Mississippi. Dimly, she was aware of being hauled over a railing and laid down on something smooth. Hands were pushing down on her chest like stone weights. Water poured from her mouth. She coughed.

"She's alive," someone shouted, a long way away. "Turn her over." Someone did.

She hurt. She hurt all over. And shivered. A hand stroked her face. It felt like warm silk. She opened her eyes and looked up into the darkest eyes she'd ever seen. He was leaning over her, staring at her with a mixture of concern and stupefaction. He had wavy dark hair; one lock had fallen over his right eye. He had a small scar over his left eyebrow and a thin, dark mustache.

36

He was wearing a pearl gray Victorian coat with velvet lapels and a flowing black bow tie with a diamond stickpin.

All this she noticed in a moment, wondering if he was real, or if she was still in the river and hallucinating. Or if she were dead.

Then he grinned, and it was a very real grin that lifted his mustache, with a dimple beside it. Oddly enough, she felt herself grinning back.

She tried to speak, coughed, spat out another mouthful of water, and tried again. "Cap'n Rhett Butler, I presume," she said.

He smiled even more, and there was relief on his face as well. "Sorry to disappoint you, ma'am," he said in a voice as velvety as the night. "But perhaps I'll do until he comes along."

She nodded. "Oh yes. You'll do," she said.

And then she passed out.

Chapter Four

When consciousness eased back into her mind, Charli figured she must be alive because she hurt. Her chest hurt like it had a too-tight Ace bandage wrapped around it; her foot stung where it had struck the boat; her arm ached where a strong hand had clasped it tight and hauled her from the river. Her mouth tasted like rusty tin cans and dead animals. And her head felt like a flamenco troupe was stomping away for all it was worth while the entire Polish Army marched an accompaniment within the confines of her skull. She didn't dare open her eyes for fear of inciting the lot of them to a full-scale riot.

She must not have been unconscious long, since water was still running in streams from her hair and she was still shivering violently. But she'd been out long enough for someone to pick her up, because she could feel herself being cradled in a pair of steely arms, nestled against a solid chest. She was being carried somewhere by someone, and at the moment she didn't care where or by whom. She snuggled closer to the warm chest and made a sound that might have been a moan or a purr, before it turned into a racking cough.

"She's coming around again," said a voice as rich as the music being played nearby, not the Dixieland she'd heard in the water but a lilting Strauss waltz. "Bring that blanket," the voice demanded. "Now!"

She was set down on something padded and instinctively rolled onto her side and started to curl into a ball. But a hand, gentle though firm, stopped her. "No, you've got to sit up, ma'am. You'll breathe easier that way," the voice said as he lifted her into a sitting position, tucking a blanket about her as he supported her shoulders. She didn't want to sit up. She wanted to sleep, maybe forever. But it was somewhat easier and less painful to grab the air and suck it into her aching lungs as he propped her up. "That's a good girl," the voice encouraged. "Now open your eyes. I know you can do it."

"You don't have to talk to me like I'm six years old," she said between coughs, still not opening her eyes.

The voice chuckled, the sound warm and smooth as VSOP brandy heated over a candle. "Then open your eyes. Come now, you have to wake up."

"Oh, all right . . . bully," Charli said, and heaved her eyelids up. And there he was again. She had figured probably the handsome Gable look-alike

in the antebellum frock coat was a figment of her
near-dead imagination, but Clark/Rhett was still
beside her and still grinning down at her. And he
was still, by God, gorgeous.

"Good," he said. "You feeling better now,
ma'am?" She couldn't believe anyone still said
ma'am, not even in the South. She'd thought the
only woman who was still regularly honored with
the epithet was the queen of England. But when
this guy said it, it sounded pretty delicious.

"Yeah, I think so," she answered, then added,
"sir." She drawled it into a "suhhh."

Even that small effort cost her. Her head felt like
it was made of steel-girded cement, about three
tons of it, and she let it fall back against the wall
behind her. Her eyes, almost as heavy, wanted to
droop, but he made her open them again and keep
them open. She felt slightly nauseous.

Trying to focus on something, she looked
around and zeroed in on the strings of lights
she'd noticed when she was in the water. She was
astonished to see that they weren't electric. They
seemed to be oil-fueled, judging by their greasy
smell, which didn't do her uneasy stomach any
good. And the light they put out was as feeble as
a forty-watt bulb.

A knot of people had gathered in a brilliantly
lighted doorway nearby, watching her as if she
were about to expire on the spot.

"Guess I'm the floor show, huh?" she said to
Rhett Butler.

"They're concerned," he reassured her, but he
moved away a few steps and spoke to a man on
the edge of the group, and the lot of them disappeared like morning mist when the sun came

out. She was alone with her hero.

She reached up and ran a hand over her sodden hair. Something stringy was caught in it, something the Mississippi must have coughed up just for her. She was afraid to think what it might be. "If I had to hazard a guess, I'd say I probably look a fright," she said. "Definitely Halloween material."

"And I'd say you look like a slightly soggy but altogether charming water nymph." She loved the words even if she didn't believe them.

He reached down toward the once-jaunty yellow boots peeking out from beneath the red wool blanket. They were black with slime and squishy with water. He knelt and pulled them off, and it struck her as an amazingly intimate action. He poured gray water from them like champagne from Cinderella's slipper, and she tucked her feet up under her to warm them. The movement started another coughing spasm.

He grabbed another blanket, which he quickly wrapped around her, holding her close with one arm. The shivering lessened. But still she coughed, and it hurt so much she tried not to breathe.

"I know it hurts," he said, as if he'd just read her mind, "but you have to get fresh air into your lungs. Breathe in through your nose."

She did and the coughing spasm passed. Still, he held her close to him and she relaxed. "Sorry," she said. "I'm not being very gracious, am I? After all, you're my hero. I really do think you just saved my life. Thank you."

"Think nothing of it, ma'am," he said, and gave her that devastating grin once more. "I'm glad I was available. I've ordered the captain to turn about and put in at once. My carriage will be waiting at the wharf, and I will escort you home."

Charli remembered seeing the old-fashioned horse and buggies lined up around Jackson Square waiting for tourists—pretty much like the hansom cabs back home that ferried tourists and lovers through Central Park. Quaint, of course, but she didn't feel up to the jostling just now, so she said, "Thanks, but a cab will do nicely. Less picturesque, but quicker. And smoother."

He drew his eyebrows together, looking at her as though she'd said something odd. But all he said was, "Where do you live, ma'am?"

"I don't."

"I beg your pardon?"

"I mean I don't live in New Orleans. Just visiting. I'm staying at a hotel, the . . ." She had to stop and think a minute. "The Maison du Carré."

He frowned. "I thought I knew every hotel in New Orleans, but I'm not familiar with that one. Where is it?"

"In the Quarter. Toulouse Street, just off Bourbon."

His frown deepened. "Are you certain, ma'am? I know that neighborhood well—I live quite near to it—and I know of no hotel there."

"Of course I'm sure. I may have almost drowned, but I didn't go crazy. It's . . . just a minute, let me think." She switched into her memory mode, running through the Rolodex in her brain where she efficiently stored bits and pieces of information most people either never noticed or quickly forgot. "Number 787. That's it. 787 Toulouse Street. Pink house. Dripping with wrought iron. Lantana vines and wisteria out front. You know, one of those quaint, converted antebellum places."

"Antebellum?" Now he looked genuinely confused.

"Yes," she answered, wondering if he was retarded or just uneducated. "As in, before the war?"

"Which war?"

"The Civil War," she said, enunciating the words now as if talking to a child. "Or as you Southerners prefer to call it, The War Between the States."

He tucked the blanket more firmly about her, shaking his head as if puzzled or concerned or both. "I think I'd better get you inside someplace warm and dry as soon as possible. You must have taken a blow to the head when you were in the water." He peered closely at her. "Do you know your name?"

A standard question, she knew, in possible concussion cases, but still it annoyed her. She made herself sit up straighter. "Charlotte Victoria Wainwright Stewart. Agent. Social Security number 547-64-4390. Name, rank, and serial number. Torture me if you must. That's all you'll get out of me." She gave a salute.

He stood up and looked down at her, and she felt icy again as soon as his arm left her shoulder. "Where am I to take you?" he asked, almost to himself. "I certainly can't take you to 787 Toulouse."

"Why not? It's where I'm staying."

"There is no hotel at 787 Toulouse. I know the house in question, the home of Dr. DuPrée. I had dinner there with him only last week, as a

43

matter of fact. He bragged to me about a revolutionary new system of indoor plumbing he was installing."

She laughed and it brought on a spasm of coughing that made her chest and head both hurt. "Don't do that," she scolded when she could speak again.

"Do what?"

"Make stupid jokes. It hurts."

He put one finger beneath her chin and lifted her face to his. "Are you perhaps a houseguest of Dr. DuPrée?"

"Never heard of the guy."

He shook his head, in exasperation she thought, though she couldn't imagine why he should be exasperated. She was the one who'd fallen in a filthy river, almost drowned, and would be lucky if she didn't catch pneumonia or hepatitis or both.

He stood. "If you'll excuse me for a moment, Miss Stewart," he said, "there are a couple of arrangements I must make. Will you be all right by yourself?"

She swallowed a sudden surge of disappointment and fear, which she immediately put down to delayed reaction to her trauma. She nodded. "Of course."

He snapped his fingers, and a black sailor appeared. "Stay with her," he ordered, then strode off. She was awake and aware enough to notice that he wore his nineteenth-century Mardi Gras costume as if born to it, the frock coat sitting easily on broad shoulders, the pants tapering down long, lean legs before being tucked into black half boots. Then he was gone.

She was freezing and she pulled the blankets closer, but she shivered even more. The cold seemed to be inside her. Maybe if she moved. On your feet, Charli. Get the circulation going again.

Everything hurt when she stood up; everything seemed to weigh several tons. She started coughing again so hard she had to grip the boat's railing and hold on till the spasm passed.

"Ma'am?" asked the sailor at her elbow.

She waved him away and peered toward the shore.

But something wasn't right. New Orleans, which had been lit up like a Christmas tree and Disneyland and the Fourth of July all at once when she'd boarded the yacht with Rob less than an hour ago, was now almost completely dark. She couldn't see the bright red *H* atop the Hilton, or any of the lights from the huge waterside convention center or the brassy Riverwalk Mall or the converted Jax Brewery. The towers of the downtown skyline were all dark, too, and the sky held none of the amber glow that hung over virtually every major city in the world, the product of thousands of high-tech streetlights. There must have been a blackout in the last half hour, she thought. There were some lights, but they were pale and low and they seemed to flicker, as if the emergency power that ran them was weak and unreliable.

She shrugged and turned away from the water and the mysterious darkness on the shore as the orchestra inside struck up another waltz. The music, as always, drew her. She walked, albeit slowly and painfully, to an open door, then blinked at the brightness within.

Under the light of a magnificent chandelier lit with dozens of candles, at least a hundred couples circled the floor of a ballroom gaudy with red draperies, mirrors, and gilt trim. Flowers—orchids and gardenias and roses and other blooms she couldn't name in red and white and lavender— were banked in incredible profusion throughout the big room. The group, men and women alike, seemed to have all agreed in advance about the proper Mardi Gras costume for this particular ball, and Charli had to admit the result was spectacular. As near as she could guess, the chosen date seemed to be mid-nineteenth century—the men in frock coats or exquisite cutaways with sleek strapped pants, the women in gowns over bell-shaped hoopskirts that swayed gently as they danced. Even the accessories were perfect—the fans dangling from wrists, the elbow-length gloves, the jet-and-feather headpieces, the watch fobs and spats and cravats with glittering stickpins. Even Charli, who had grown up in a world where people thought nothing of spending several thousand dollars on a single ball gown, was aghast at what the entire thing must have cost. Who, in these penurious days, could afford to put on such a show? Who, in the almost Puritan aftermath of the Decade of Greed, would dare?

They were waltzing, but the word hardly seemed to fit. This was a far cry from the waltzing Charli remembered from her debutante balls. For all the dancing lessons she and her kind had suffered through, no one she had ever known danced like these creatures. They twirled and dipped. They covered the floor as if floating. The ladies bent languidly away from their partners as they went into a turn, then came up again as gracefully as a palm tree swaying in the wind off the Gulf. She hadn't known there were people left in the world—or at least not outside Vienna—who remembered how to waltz like this.

She found herself swaying to the music, and it seemed to make her feel better.

"Miss Stewart?" She turned. He was beside her, holding a cape over his arm, a top hat in one hand, and a malacca cane in the other. He'd really gone all out to look the part and, she duly noted, he looked it splendidly.

Only now did she notice the increased activity on deck as sailors scurried about, throwing out lines and shouting orders to each other. The boat bumped against the pier. The great paddle wheel stopped its splashing. They were docked. A gangplank was immediately maneuvered into place and he turned her toward it. Then he swept her up into his arms.

"I can walk," she complained.

"But why should you?" he asked, a grin on his face. "What good are heroes if they can't even carry ashore the damsels in distress they rescue?"

It felt very warm and safe in his arms and she didn't really want to have to walk down the rickety gangplank on equally rickety legs, so she said, "None, I guess."

"Fine."

As they waited for the gangplank to be secured, Charli turned for one last look at the magical scene in the ballroom. Standing in the doorway, looking back at her, was one of the most beautiful women she'd ever seen. Thick black hair, piled high in soft curls, gleamed in the candlelight. Skin the color of melted caramel held a delicate peach blush on the high cheekbones. And eyes as brown as Godiva chocolates stared at Charli with undisguised anger.

Then her Rhett Butler whisked her away.

God, she was tired. Tired all the way through to her bones and out the other side. She let her head droop against his solid chest as he carried her back to unmoving ground. But she kept her eyes open.

It was so dark she couldn't see much, thanks to the blackout that had taken out the lights of all the skyscrapers. But as she scanned the harbor, she could easily see that the sleek white cruise ship that had been tied up earlier along with all the tankers and cargo liners—everything she expected to see in the largest port in America and had, in fact, seen just hours ago—seemed to have disappeared, to be replaced by rows of tall-masted sailing ships, flat barges, and paddle wheelers of every size.

I'm getting delirious, she thought. That's it. That dunking in Old Man River hit me harder than I thought. Nothing else to it. Sleep. I need sleep. About a week of it.

She was already nodding off when her rescuer set her down beside a shiny black closed carriage with a pair of equally shiny horses hitched to it. A black coachman in a red jacket with velvet lapels jumped down, opened the door, and lowered the steps.

"No cab?" she asked, looking up at Rhett.

"Afraid not," he answered, gesturing her to climb in. She hesitated, looking about her, feeling a growing confusion. "Miss Stewart?" he prodded, placing a firm hand under her elbow. She climbed in.

As he settled beside her and the carriage moved off, she leaned back against velvet cushions of midnight blue. Sleep, she thought. That's all that's wrong with me; I need sleep. Everything will be fine and normal and everyday again in the morning.

And with that thought, she drifted off.

49

Chapter Five

As the landau clopped through the New Orleans night, Trey Lavande looked down at the bedraggled mermaid he'd pulled from the Mississippi. She was unlike any woman he'd ever seen—and Trey was a man who had grown up with women, dozens of them. But this Miss Stewart was in a category all her own.

She leaned against him trustingly in her sleep, and he wrapped an arm around her shoulders to hold her safe. He could feel her muscles through the layers of cloth, and he wondered at them. She couldn't be more than five foot two or three, thin-boned and delicate, with a neck that hardly looked substantial enough to support her head. Yet that slender frame was as honed and muscled as a boxer's. And he had seen how strongly she had swum through the frigid river before the force of the paddle wheel almost sucked her into its blades. This was no fragile flower he held in his arms.

He reached out a finger and brushed a strand of hair from her cheek. The skin was soft as a camellia petal and, thank God, finally warm. She murmured something and snuggled closer, and he tightened his hold on her. For all her tiny size, he noted that she fit perfectly within his embrace.

Her hair, as black as his own, was also nearly as short as his own—definitely not the thing in his Victorian world. He'd never seen anything like it on a woman. In the front, where it had mostly dried, it curled into feathery wisps that framed her face and made her look like a dark little cherub.

And then there were her clothes. Trey had never seen a more improper garment worn by a woman in public. Though he had to admit that, once he was certain she wasn't dead or dying, he'd thoroughly enjoyed the view the ensemble so perfectly showed off; the sight of the small but perfectly shaped breasts, tiny waist, and nicely rounded bottom was delightful indeed.

The blankets he'd wrapped around her had fallen open, and he stared again at the odd outfit she wore. The basic garment looked for all the world like a pair of black wool long johns. They fit her like skin and were decorated down the front with a sort of trim made of tiny silver metal teeth. A fuchsia cloak that was probably once lovely but was now matted with mud and other river detritus was wrapped around her waist. And across her chest was slung a bag of some sort of shiny material like rubber, but not quite—and it was a bright yellow beneath the mud and slime that stuck to it. He stroked it, intrigued by the unknown material, his naturally curious mind wanting to examine it further.

But what the devil was he to do with his sodden siren? Having gone to the trouble of rescuing her, he could hardly leave her on the street to fend for herself—something she was clearly in no condition to do, in any case. He also couldn't take her to Dr. Duprée's house, at least not without speaking to that gentleman first. Particularly since the woman admitted she had never met the man, though she claimed to be staying in his house!

He wouldn't take her to his own house. If she was a lady, it would be highly improper since there was no woman there to act as her chaperon. She would be so compromised he would have to offer her marriage. And if, as her clothes suggested, she was not a lady, his house, where he strove so hard to create the proper reputation for himself, was definitely not the place for her.

But he had to take her somewhere. And the only other place he could think of was to his mother. He chuckled to think what Lisette Lavande would make of his water nymph. From the look of her, Lisette's house was exactly the sort of place she belonged.

They hadn't far to go through the gaslit streets of the Vieux Carré, and within minutes the coach pulled to a stop.

The lovely house, painted a pale moss green with darker green shutters, was still ablaze with lights, even though it was past four in the morning. Trey lifted his burden gently from the coach, strode up the steps, and tapped at the door with his booted foot.

"Mister Trey!" said the tall black butler who opened it.

"Evening, Jacob. Where is my mother?"

The butler quickly regained whatever equanimity he'd lost at the sight of the young master standing in the hall with a dripping bundle of female flesh in his arms. "I'll fetch her, sir."

"Please," Trey agreed. He couldn't sit with Miss Stewart in his arms, and he didn't want to put her down, so he stood there, waiting a moment, listening to the soft murmurs of conversation and the strain of a Chopin nocturne coming from the nearby drawing room, mingling with the smell of fine old brandy and good cigars. After a moment, a magnificent woman walked into the room.

Lisette Lavande was extremely tall, nearly six feet, and generously endowed. She was also wonderfully preserved for a woman just barely on the sunny side of sixty. The auburn hair piled high on top of her head added even more to the awesome impression she made. She was exquisitely gowned in a dress of deep rose peau de soie fringed with silk floss. It practically screamed of Paris. While perfectly decorous, it hid none of her considerable charms.

She snapped shut her fan of pierced ivory and looked at her handsome son, standing there like a penitent with a sacrificial offering.

"Oh, Trey," she said with a sigh. "Not again!"

An hour later, with Charli comfortably tucked into a four-posted feather bed in the best guest room, mother and son sat over balloons of aged cognac in her private sitting room.

"Well, I could hardly leave her to drown in the river, Mother," said Trey, sipping his brandy.

"I know, dear, but I do wish they would not involve you in these horrid theatrics just to get my attention. There was that Creole girl last year, Marie-Claire I think she said her name was, who threw herself in front of your curricle. Lucky you didn't kill her. And then that awful Roxanne— though how the girl ever managed to come up with such a classical name for herself when I'm certain she couldn't read a word is beyond me. When she bribed your parlor maid to let her into your house in the middle of the night and woke you up in that highly distasteful fashion. Well!"

"Was it distasteful?" he asked with a chuckle. "I don't remember."

"Of course it was. Why, the girl was nothing but a street slut." She sipped at her drink. "Trey, she had dirty fingernails!"

"True," he agreed, and smiled into his brandy. "But what are we going to do with this one? You might consider her, you know. She's quite pretty, in a delicate sort of way."

Lisette made a sound almost like a snort. "You know I require far more than mere looks, my dear. I did not get my reputation for running the finest house in all New Orleans with such shallow values as that."

And Lisette did, indeed, run the finest house in New Orleans, the classiest bordello in the Crescent City. Everything about it bespoke Lisette's perfect taste and even better business sense. The wines were the finest vintages available. The chef had been summoned directly from Paris. The decor was refined, elegant, and rich.

And the girls! They were all beautiful, well-spoken, well-mannered. They wore the newest Paris fashions. They could converse with wit and intelligence on the latest literature, what was playing at the opera, or even the current price of cane and cotton.

Lisette had taught her girls the secret of her success—the ideal male fantasy: to be perfect, lively, intelligent ladies in the drawing room . . . and perfect whores upstairs in the bedrooms. What her customers didn't know was that it was very often a female fantasy as well—to be treated exactly that way by a man who knew how to be a gentleman in the parlor and a lover in the bedroom.

Though she was no longer actively involved in that side of the business herself, Lisette had learned a large number of clever bedroom tricks during her career, and she now taught them to her girls. She prided herself on the fact that no man had ever left her house less than fully satisfied—and not one of her girls had ever been molested in any way, either. Many of them had worked only long enough to make their fortunes before moving on, often to a respectable life in another city. A few had even married men they had met right there in Lisette's house. And since her clientele was as select as her girls, they were assured of living in comfort for the rest of their lives.

Her girls were grateful. There were more than a dozen children spread across the United States who called Lisette godmother.

To maintain such high standards, Mme. Lavande was extremely particular in choosing her girls. For every one she hired, fifty were turned away. With such fierce competition, many an ambitious young woman had resorted to some devious strategy to attract Lisette's notice and increase the odds in her favor. And one of the favorite ways of doing it seemed to be by attracting the attention of her son.

And this Miss Stewart had certainly captured his attention!

He wondered why the thought of her—a woman he knew virtually nothing about except that she wore outlandish and improper dress, had an odd sense of humor, and could swim—why did picturing her working as a prostitute in his mother's house seem to make him sick to his stomach?

Shaking his head to shake away the thought, he gulped the last of his brandy, retrieved his cloak and hat from Jacob, and bid his mother good night, promising to return in the morning to check on the progress of the mysterious Miss Stewart.

Charli woke up with a headache that shamed such a pitiful word.

The sun poured through the windows like white heat and pounded the backs of her closed eyelids. Her throat felt raw and scraped, like someone had just pulled her tonsils out without an anesthetic.

A grating noise nearby made her open her eyes. Mistake. Pain sliced across her brow and she slammed them shut again, but not before seeing a young black woman setting a silver tray on a nearby table.

It was a minute before Charli could remember where she was. New Orleans. Rob Sams. Right. She'd come here to get him and she'd got him. Now she could go home.

The black girl hummed softly, and Charli slowly peeled one eye open to look at her. She wore a full-skirted blue dress that fell to the floor under a ruffled white apron. Her head was wrapped in a snowy white kerchief with the ends pointing up—just like Butterfly McQueen in *Gone With the Wind.*

Quaint, Charli thought as she rolled over and groaned into the feather-soft pillow. These restored mansion-hotels just loved to be quaint, even to the point of putting the room service waitresses in period costume. But she hadn't called room service, had she?

"Missus says you're to wake up now, miss," said the maid, lightly touching Charli's shoulder. "Here's café au lait and beignets to help."

Charli couldn't imagine who "Missus" was or what gave her the right to have Charli awakened, but the coffee and beignets sounded like heaven. She remembered having the delicious, sugar-coated pastries once at the Cafe du Monde on an earlier visit. Beignets alone made New Orleans worth the trip. And she realized she was starved.

With a groan, she pushed herself up in the bed and opened her eyes. Then she blinked. Then she rubbed her eyes and looked again. This was not her hotel room at the Maison du Carré. Was it?

Surely she would have remembered this massive mahogany bed with the posts carved into

57

spirals. She would have remembered the crimson hangings of silk damask that draped it as well as the windows. And she definitely would not have forgotten those ridiculous cherubs cavorting around the huge white marble fireplace. Hadn't hers been rather small and made of painted wood? And this one had a coal fire merrily burning in it. A coal fire?

She felt like a stupid cliché even as she opened her mouth to ask, "Where am I?"

"Why, at Missus Lavande's house. Mister Trey brought you here, miss. Don't you remember?"

Remember. It hurt to think, but she gave it a shot. She closed her eyes and immediately remembered the feel of cold water closing over her, the pain in her lungs, the absolute certainty that she was about to die. But she hadn't died. Right, she did remember. A hunk with a mustache, a Clark Gable look-alike dressed in a Victorian-style Mardi Gras costume, had fished her out of the river, wrapped her in a blanket, and put her in a horse-drawn carriage of all ridiculous things. She looked down. Someone—the hunk?—had dressed her in a white lawn nightgown, high-necked and long-sleeved with tiny pin-tucks on the cuffs and embroidered flowers all over. It was pretty, but she was used to sleeping in the nude.

"Could you get me an aspirin, please?" she asked.

"An asp . . . a what, miss?"

"An aspirin. An Excedrin. Tylenol. Whatever. My head feels like it's ready for a size forty-two long."

The black girl just stood there, looking puzzled. Charli caught sight of something yellow out of one corner of her eye. "Never mind, I've got some in my bag. Would you hand it to me?" she said, gesturing to where her yellow vinyl tote lay on a chair.

Hesitantly, the maid picked it up, holding it away from her as though it might bite her at any second. She dropped it on the bed. Charli slid open the plastic Ziploc-type closing—silently blessing the inventors of waterproofing—rummaged around till she found a bottle of Advil, popped two into her mouth, and gulped them down with some of the delicious coffee. Then she fell back against the pillows.

"Mister Trey, you said. Is this his house?" she asked.

"Oh, no, miss. It's his mama's house."

"His mama," she began, but before she could say more the door opened and a startling woman entered. The size of a Valkyrie, with a mass of auburn hair flowing halfway down her back, she was dressed in a magnificent brocade robe of ivory damask embroidered all over with peacocks in full plumage. Large eyes of a startling blue took Charli in at a glance.

"Good, you're awake," said the Valkyrie. "The doctor will be here soon."

"I don't need a doctor. I just need to get home. Maybe you could call me a cab?"

"That was a stupid trick, you know," she said, as if she hadn't heard the request. "You might well have died. But now that you're here, I can't let you go until I know you are quite recovered."

"Stupid trick?"

"You could easily have drowned for real, and you still might take a fever." She came over to the

59

bed and sat beside Charli. "I am Lisette Lavande, though of course you already know that, don't you?" Charli was about to ask how she could possibly be expected to know who this amazon was when the woman reached out and tilted her face toward the light. "So," said Lisette, eyeing Charli like a cook judging a piece of fish she thought might well be off. "You want a job, I imagine."

Charli frowned. "I already have a job. Or rather, I work for myself."

"Oh? You've been out on your own? That's a hard life for a girl. How long have you been at it?"

"Three years," Charli answered, wondering why she did and what made the woman think she had the right to ask.

"You don't look it. In fact, you still look quite fresh."

"Considering what I've been through in the last forty-eight hours, I guess that's a compliment. I thought I probably looked like Attila the Hun on the day he finally lost a round."

Lisette laughed, a rich contralto sound full of life. "You just might do at that," she said, shaking her head. "You would be a novelty, certainly." She reached out and lifted Charli's left hand and studied it, for all the world as if she expected to find dirty fingernails or something. Apparently satisfied, she dropped it again. "What did you do to your hair?"

"My hair?" Charli said, feeling out of her depth.

"I've never had a girl with short hair." She touched a curl and rubbed it between her thumb and forefinger. "Though it does suit you."

"Thank you," Charli answered, lacing the words with sarcasm.

"You needn't take that tone, you know. I'm seriously considering giving you a chance. Even though I frown on anyone trying to get to me through my son."

That was enough! Charli batted the woman's hand away. "I don't have a clue what you're talking about, but if you'll excuse me, I'll get dressed and get out of your hair and out of your house. I've got a plane to catch."

"Spirit, too," Lisette murmured. "Good." She laid her hand on Charli's forehead. "But I fear you're developing a fever. You're quite warm. Wouldn't you like to sleep some more, just until the doctor comes?"

The truth was that Charli wanted to play Sleeping Beauty. The way she felt, she wasn't sure even a hundred years would do the trick. Not to put too fine a point on it, she felt like hell. The amazon stroked her brow, and her hand was cool and smooth. Charli lay back against the pillows and closed her eyes.

"Maybe just for a minute or two," she muttered. "But no doctor." In no time at all, she was asleep.

61

Chapter Six

It might have been minutes or hours later that she was awakened much more rudely than the first time.

"Where did you get this?" shouted a voice in her ear. She would have sat up on her own if she hadn't just been pulled up by a viselike hand on her right wrist. She was staring once again into the dark eyes of her Gable look-alike, and this time there was no captivating grin. In fact, he looked mad enough to kill.

"Pleased to meet you, too," she muttered as she tried to struggle out of his grasp.

He wasn't having any of that. "Where did you get this?" he asked again, and she could hear the fury in his voice.

"What?"

"This ring."

She looked down at the ring on her right hand. It was an heirloom, a beautifully ornate design in silver and amethyst. "Not that it's any of your business," she said, "but it's been in my family for generations. My grandmother gave it to me because I was so much like her. She was a rebel, too. And she got it from her grandmother—another rebel, or so goes the family legend."

"Take it off," he said, his face rigid.

"I will not! Why should I?"

"Take it off. I want to see the inscription."

"How'd you know there was one?" she asked, but she slipped the ring from her finger and turned it so that he could see the inside. An intertwined *T* and *C* and the word Forever— worn nearly smooth by generations of fingers— were faintly visible.

"Where did you steal this?" he demanded.

"Steal it? Now wait just a minute, mister. I told you, this ring has been in my family for well over a hundred years, ever since my great-great-grandmother Charlotte."

"Charlotte?"

"Charlotte DuClos. I was named for her. She died in 1882."

He dropped her hand as if it were about to explode and stared at her like she was mad. "I don't know what game you think you're playing, Miss Stewart, but it's not going to work. There is only one ring like that in the world. I should know; I designed it myself, and I put that inscription in it. For my fiancée." Despite her shock at this inane statement, she couldn't help noticing the look of pain that crossed his face.

"Fiancée?"

"Corinne," he said softly. "Corinne DuClos. And when she died shortly after I gave it to her, her sister Charlotte took the ring and moved north. That was two years ago."

Charli laughed and held out the ring. "Does it look like it's two years old? The design is clearly Victorian, it's worn practically smooth here at the edge, and the inscription's almost invisible."

He took it and studied it more closely, a perplexed look on his handsome face. It did look worn. "I don't know what you've done to it, but that does not alter the fact that this is Corinne's ring. I would know it anywhere. And I know Charlotte would never have considered giving it up. You can forget ever working for my mother, Miss Stewart. She does not hire thieves or lunatics."

"I am not a thief!" she exclaimed, snatching the ring back even as he tried to drop it in his coat pocket. He was once again dressed as a Victorian gentleman, this time in buff-colored breeches tucked into glossy boots and a long-tailed coat of russet wool over a creamy white shirt and an elegant black cravat. "And who the hell are you?"

"Trey Lavande," he said with a brusque little bow.

"Well, Mr. Trey Lavande, if you want to talk about crazy, it seems to me there's only one Looney Tune in the room, and it sure ain't me. You want to explain the outfit? Mardi Gras's over, you know."

He puffed up like a peacock, and she saw that he was quite tall, at least six feet. "I am not the one who will do the explaining here, Miss Stewart. I want to know—"

"All right, that's it!" she said, swinging her feet over the side of the giant bed. "If this is an example of your famous Southern hospitality, I'll take Manhattan. And I think I'll do it now." The bed was so high off the floor she had to hop down to stand up. When she did, she was dizzy and had to grasp one of the bedposts to keep from falling. Immediately, she felt his arms around her, easing her back into a sitting position on the bed. His hand was warm through the thin cotton of the nightgown. She was grateful for the help and hated him for offering it.

"Get back into bed," he said sternly, his hand still resting on the small of her back. He didn't seem to want to remove it. "The doctor said you are to rest. You're as weak as a kitten."

"All part of the Puss in Boots act," she said, but she didn't try to stand again just yet. His hand started making a small, slow circle up her back, a comforting gesture. Give me a minute, she told herself. I'll be fine in a minute. God, her head hurt. She would have liked to ask the doctor for something stronger than an Advil, but apparently he'd come and gone while she was asleep—or perhaps unconscious.

She had to get out of here and go home. She looked around for her clothes but saw nothing familiar except for her yellow tote bag and her boots, cleaned of the river slime that had covered them last night. "You have my undying gratitude for saving my life, I'm sure, but now if you'll just get me my clothes I'll take off."

"I had the maid burn the garments you were wearing."

"Burn them? You had her burn my clothes! What right—"

Megan Daniel

He removed his hand from her neck. "They were ruined beyond repair."

"Oh," she said, chastened a bit, though she still would have liked to make the decision herself. That Donna Karan catsuit had cost her a bundle, and it was amazing what her French cleaner on the Upper East Side could do. It might have been salvageable.

"And I would not have let you leave this house in them in any case."

"Why not?"

"You clearly care nothing about your reputation, or you wouldn't go out in public in the most outrageously improper outfit it has ever been my misfortune to see on a female. But my mother has worked long and hard to establish a reputation for taste and elegance in her house. I'm not about to let you destroy it by being seen so tawdrily garbed."

"I think I've fallen through the looking glass here," Charli muttered. "Don't tell me, you're going to turn into the White Rabbit any minute, right?"

"White Rabbit?"

"Never mind." She brushed her hand before her eyes like she was batting at a fly. "So, having burned my clothes, I assume you've got something else for me to put on? I can't very well go through the streets of New Orleans in this."

He looked down at her. She'd been around enough men in her life to tell from the look in his eyes that he liked what he saw. The cotton nightgown, after all, was close to transparent. She crossed her arms in front of her.

"I'll have Betsy bring you something at once."

"Great. In the meantime, I'm going to take the longest, hottest shower ever invented."

"Shower?" he said, with the odd, puzzled look again.

"Great. No shower. I should have guessed as much in a museum like this place. So okay, I'll settle for a bath. You do have a bathtub?"

"Certainly." He walked over to the fireplace and pulled on a fringed, embroidered strip of fabric hanging there. Charli knew from watching historical movies that it was a bell pull. These New Orleanians certainly took their history seriously!

The maid appeared almost instantly and dropped a curtsy to the mysterious Mr. Trey Lavande. "Miss Stewart would like a bath," he said.

"Yessir," she replied, and dropped another curtsy.

"My mother would kill for a maid that well trained," said Charli.

"My mother's slaves are all properly behaved."

"Slaves?"

"Most of them. Some have been freed, but of course they chose to stay."

Charli passed a hand over her eyes. She was beginning to get seriously scared. This guy was most definitely whacko. Seemed to think he was living before the Civil War. Might even be dangerous.

"Uh," she started, "d'you think maybe you could leave me to my bath?"

He bowed, a truly elegant gesture that made Charli regret the present for a moment. "Of course," he said, and left the room.

As soon as the Lavande loony was gone, Charli went into high gear. She rummaged through her vinyl tote until she came up with the key to her hotel room. The name and phone number were printed on the heavy tag. She'd call them and have them send a cab for her. She wanted out of this place just as fast as possible.

She looked around. No phone by the bed. None on the ornate Victorian bureau or on the pretty little table drawn up before one window. Great. As long as she was in this room, she was incommunicado. And stuck until someone brought her some clothes.

Well, at least she'd have her bath. She looked around again. There was only one door, the one through which her rescuer had disappeared into the hall. So, no private bathroom. Which meant she'd have to wander through the house in her cute Victorian nightgown looking for it. Right. Who cared? She'd be out of here within the half hour anyway.

Just as she reached for the brass doorknob to begin her search, the door opened again and the pretty black maid appeared, followed by three men, also black, carrying a good-sized hip bath and several large canisters of steaming water. As she watched, so astonished she couldn't even comment, they set the tub up in front of the fire, arranged an embroidered screen around it, filled it with the water, set out towels and soap, and left the room—all but the maid.

"Your bath's ready, miss," she said.

Charli stared at her. Finally she said, "It's Betsy, isn't it?"

"Yes, ma'am."

"Well, Betsy, I really think it's time for some explaining. What the hell is going on here?"

The girl looked momentarily shocked, then confused. "Miss?" she asked.

"I mean, why is everyone dressed like they work for Disneyland? Why does that guy out there drive a horse-drawn carriage? And why the bath-by-the-fire routine? Where's the bathroom?"

"Bathroom, miss?"

"Does this place even have indoor plumbing?"

"No, miss."

"Great. Just great!" She paced the room, running her fingers through her short, tangled hair. Then she gave an ironic laugh. "I've fallen through a time warp here, right? One minute I'm in 1993 and the next I'm in . . . what year do you think this is, anyway?"

The maid was beginning to look at Charli like she was crazy.

"1858, miss."

Charli laughed. "Right. 1858. How could I not have guessed?" She peered at the maid. "Well, I have to say this for them. They've got you all well trained. Everyone seems to play the part to perfection."

Betsy fidgeted with a towel. "You . . . your bath'll get cold, miss."

"Right," said Charli. "As long as it's here, I may as well take advantage of it. Then, I got to tell ya, I'm outta here." She turned and stripped off the fine lawn nightgown, then turned back toward the tub. Betsy was still there. And Charli was naked. She snatched up a towel and wrapped it around herself. "You may go," she said.

"Oh no, miss. I'm to help you with your bath."

"I don't need any help," she cried. "I've been bathing myself for more than two decades, and

I'm sure I can manage one more time. Go."

"If you're sure, miss . . ."

"I'm sure. Just go." The maid still stood there. "Go. Go, go, go!"

Betsy curtsied and left the room, shaking her head and setting the ends of her headscarf bouncing.

Alone at last! Charli eased herself into the hot water. That, at least, felt familiar. In fact, it felt like heaven, even though she couldn't stretch out like she wanted to in the small tub. But when she bent her knees and scrunched down, the blessed liquid came almost to her chin. The warmth penetrated her aching muscles and eased the tension knotted there. She folded one of the towels, luxuriously thick and soft, and put it under her head, then leaned back.

What had she gotten herself into here? she wondered. Just her luck to be fished out of the river by the best-looking man she'd seen in donkey's years and then have him turn out to be a case for the nuthouse. She'd heard that there were Southerners who, even today, had never accepted the fact that they lost the Civil War, but this guy was carrying his obsession to pretty fantastic extremes. Though there was a certain sort of crazy logic to it, she guessed. If you could believe it was 1858, then the war hadn't happened yet, so you couldn't have lost it.

Apparently, he'd convinced his mother to go along with the charade. And even the servants seemed to be convinced, or at least frightened enough to act like they were.

Well, the sooner she was out of here the better. A few more minutes in this heavenly hot water, and then she'd make Betsy bring her something to wear. Pick up her luggage at the hotel, and in less than an hour she'd be on a plane out of this crazy city.

A thought struck her and she sat up abruptly, sloshing water over the rim of the tub and onto the beautiful Persian carpet. Rob! What had happened to Rob? Had someone pulled him out of the river, too? Was he okay? Was he even alive? She had to get to a phone. She'd have to call from the hotel.

Quickly now, she scrubbed, washed her hair, rinsed it till it squeaked, and stepped from the tub. She toweled her hair into its usual fluffy black halo. Just as she was heading for the bell pull to ask Betsy to bring her something to put on, the girl reappeared, arms laden with what looked like about twenty pounds of garments. Carefully, she laid them on the huge bed while Charli watched, her astonishment and indignation growing with every garment. First, a long dress of peach-colored cambric with a waist the size of an ant's middle. Then petticoats, at least three of them, embroidered all over in white on white and with rows and rows of ruffles. A camisole with a ribbon tie at the neck. Ruffled pantalets. And finally, a corset that looked like something Madonna might wear in one of her weirder videos.

The door opened and another servant entered carrying what looked like a giant birdcage. She dropped it on the floor—where it stood by itself—curtsied, and left the room.

Charli, fearing she already knew the answer, asked, "What is that?"

"Why, it's your hoop, miss."

"No way, José! I am not walking through New Orleans inside a birdcage. And take the rest of these things away, too. There's got to be someone in this house with a simple dress, a pair of jeans, even a sweatsuit. Anything to get me back to my hotel."

Betsy, so friendly this morning, was now eyeing Charli as if afraid she might attack at any minute. "This was the best I could find, miss. They're Germaine's. She's the only girl in the house that's your size."

Charli eyed the pile on the bed. She had to get out of there, and if this was the only way to do it, so be it. "Oh, all right," she said, reaching for the pantalets, "but I'm not wearing the corset, nor the hoop either. Not on your tintype."

Warily, Betsy helped her dress, tying the waist tape of the pantalets, buttoning up the camisole, smoothing the stockings and tying the garters that held them up. Charli muttered throughout the elaborate process. "How dare he burn my clothes?" The first petticoat settled into place. "He had no right." Then the second. "I ought to sue the guy." Then the third. They were so long she had to pull them up to just below her breasts to keep them from dragging on the floor. "Aargh!" Charli shook a fist at the ceiling. "I want my clothes!"

"Miss?" said Betsy. "I didn't burn them all, though Mister Trey told me to. I saved two pieces." She looked around the room as though someone might be watching, then pulled two minuscule bits of silk and lace from the pocket of her apron. "You was wearing them under your other things,

72

miss. Didn't seem right proper, but they was so pretty, I didn't have the heart to burn 'em."

Charli grabbed the dainty bra and bikini panties with a smile. "My underwear! Thank you."

"They . . . they be so tiny, miss."

"Big enough to do the job."

"I washed them for you," the maid said shyly.

"I can't thank you enough, Betsy." Charli wanted to put them on right then, but she was already more than half dressed in the layers of silliness the house seemed to demand, so she stuffed them in her tote bag to take home with her. "So what's next?" she asked the girl.

Betsy lifted the peach-colored gown and dropped it over her head. It fit nicely in the bust and waist, molding her trim figure perfectly. But the skirt dragged a good six inches on the floor.

"The hoop's supposed to hold it up, you see, miss," said Betsy.

Well, she couldn't very well walk down the street tripping on her skirt every step, so she reluctantly stepped into the steel construction, feeling like a newly housed canary. "I'm only a bird in a gilded cage," she warbled, trying to convince herself this was funny.

When Betsy was finally finished with what must have been a dozen tapes to be tied and a hundred tiny hooks-and-eyes up the back of the dress, when she had smoothed the skirt over the layers of hoop and petticoat and fluffed out the full bishop's sleeves, she turned Charli toward a tilted cheval glass.

Charli gasped. Yes, she thought, there is a certain charm to living in the past. She looked lovely, if she did say so herself. The dress was so tight

73

she could hardly breathe, and so long she was afraid to walk, and the hoop tended to sway like the Liberty Bell in full spate whenever she tried to take a step. But she did look like a particularly delectable wedding cake.

The peach of the dress gave her complexion a nice glow, and the cut of the bodice made her bust look better than it ever had. She even looked like she had a bust. The gown's low neckline was demurely filled in with ecru lace so fine it was almost transparent. The skirt was swagged and caught up here and there with rust-colored bows beneath embroidered rust flowers with green velvet leaves.

She inspected the stitching. It was done by hand! She turned up the hem of the skirt. Also hand-stitched, and it must have been twenty yards around! This dress must have cost hundreds, maybe thousands, of dollars to make. She'd bet it certainly cost more than her mother's favorite Carolina Herrera evening gown.

So, okay. If she had to go through the streets looking like a Southern belle, at least she'd be a pretty one. She'd be as lovely as Scarlett O'Hara for an hour.

"Bring my bag, please," she said to Betsy as she picked up the edge of her skirt and left the room.

At the end of a short hall was a stairway she assumed would lead her where she wanted to go. But she stood at the top a moment. It was a perfectly ordinary stairway, with turned newel posts of polished mahogany and a flowered runner down the center, but it looked very long and steep when you were wearing a hoopskirt that brushed the ground and just might send you to your death at any moment.

She tried to remember how Scarlett had managed this when she sneaked downstairs after the barbecue to find Ashley and found Rhett instead. She gripped the banister, lifted the hoop and skirt with one hand, and took a timid step down. Slowly, one step at a time, she made her way. She was feeling almost confident by the time she reached the halfway landing. She looked up, and there he was.

Her crazy hero was watching her with an odd look on his face. When he caught her eye, he grinned.

"I thought you'd clean up well," he drawled, "but I had no idea. You look lovely."

To her immense surprise, Charli felt herself blush with pleasure. "And proper?" she asked with a grin.

"Extremely," he agreed. He held up a hand to help her down the last few steps. "Are you hungry?"

"As a bear."

He laughed. It was the first time she'd heard it, and she loved the richness of the sound. "Good. Breakfast is ready."

"What time is it?"

"Nearly one.

"Breakfast? At one?"

He chuckled. "In my mother's house, yes."

He led her into a sunny room at the front of the house. Lace curtains screened the brilliant light from the inside, wisteria vines from the outside. A mahogany table was spread with gleaming embroidered linen, fine china, and museum-quality antique silver. And around it, chattering animatedly, were a half dozen of the most beautiful women Charli had ever seen. She imagined they must all be Trey's sisters or other relatives, since they obviously lived here with his mother. Whatever, they were all in on the craziness, since they were dressed in exquisite antebellum gowns similar to the one she wore herself.

Before she could ask, Trey was making introductions. Desirée, Aimée, Christine, Dominique, Angelique. And Germaine. At that, Charli had the grace to gather her wits and say, "Thank you for the loan of your gown. It is lovely."

"On you," said Germaine with a smile. "It makes me look like an overripe peach. I shall never wear it. You may keep it."

"Thank you," Charli answered, assuming it was the right answer, though she'd have no need for the gorgeous gown in another hour or so. In a daze, she allowed Trey to seat her and pour her a cup of coffee while the women rose as one and made their excuses.

"The dressmaker is waiting," said one, Desirée, Charli thought it was. Another added, "And Monsieur is here for my piano lesson." A third said, "I'm off to shop for a parasol for my new azure silk."

In a moment they were gone, fluttering out like a clutch of exotic birds in search of juicy worms.

Charli picked up the Sevres china cup and sipped at her coffee. She frowned. "No chicory?"

"Chicory?" Trey asked.

"In the coffee. There's no chicory in it."

"Why would anyone want to ruin a perfectly

good cup of coffee by putting chicory in it?"

"But this is New Orleans and—" She suddenly remembered a tidbit of history. She'd read it on the plane just yesterday, in an article on New Orleans in the in-flight magazine. "Oh, right. You, unlike the rest of New Orleans, refuse to put chicory in your coffee because the practice didn't begin until the Civil War, when the blockade made coffee scarce so chicory was added to stretch it. And of course, the war hasn't happened yet, has it?" she asked wryly.

"That's the second time you've mentioned a Civil War, and I still have no idea what you're talking about."

"Of course not," she muttered, drinking the coffee which was delicious even without chicory. She watched him over the rim. He certainly was gorgeous, even in those ridiculous clothes. Maybe because of the clothes. She had to admit the style suited him, showing off as no modern suit would the way his broad chest tapered to a small waist and slim hips. And though his cravat looked even more uncomfortable than a regular necktie, it was undeniably elegant. He wore the clothes with an assurance, almost an arrogance, that suited them perfectly.

While she studied him, Trey studied her. He didn't know what to make of this water nymph that had turned into a perfect little beauty. She would do well in his mother's house, he could see that at once. She'd soon become a favorite with the customers. At the thought, his hand gripped the fine china cup so hard it shattered, shards flying, hot coffee scalding his hand, a stain spreading on the snowy linen tablecloth.

Megan Daniel

"Damn!" he exclaimed. He jumped up, dried his burned hand on a napkin, and stalked to the window. He looked out a moment, turned back to glare at her with a fierce frown, then looked away again. What he ought to do was report her to the police for theft. Her explanation of how she had come by Corinne's ring was ridiculous. It wasn't even very clever. She had clearly stolen it. But the image of her behind bars was almost as disturbing as picturing her working in his mother's house. He brought his fist down on the windowsill.

Charli was mystified by the man's behavior, but having already determined that he was bonkers, she supposed she shouldn't try to figure out anything he did. Best thing she could do was to get the hell away from him.

"I'm not hungry after all, I guess," she said, standing so quickly she set her hoop swaying like a puff ball in a cyclone. "I'd like to go back to my hotel now."

"Fine, if you'll tell me where it is."

"I already did."

"Miss Stewart, you cannot possibly expect me to believe—"

"Look," she cut him off. "I don't give a rat's behind what you believe, mister! I'm out of here." She swung toward the door, helped along by the momentum of the skirt, and stepped into the front hall. She spied her yellow tote bag on a chair near the door. "Thank God," she murmured, scooping it up and heading out the front door.

He stopped her on the stoop. "I shall escort you."

"Thanks but no thanks. I can find the way."

"Nonetheless, I shall escort you," he repeated. There were things he intended to learn about Charli Stewart, and he wasn't about to let her slip away just yet. He took her bag from her, winced at the weight of it, and set it down with a word to the butler. She was already halfway out the door.

Chapter Seven

Outside, the sun was a brilliant white, and Charli blinked. As Trey led her down the path, she had to concentrate on controlling the vagaries of her skirt. It seemed to have a mind of its own.

"Stupid contraption," she muttered as a ruffle caught on a piece of wrought-iron railing. "Why did women ever allow themselves to be subjected to these things?"

She didn't look up until they had reached the sidewalk—or the banquette, as she had heard New Orleanians call it. As she dropped her hoop and stood up straight, she looked around. Then she wished she hadn't. Her whole body froze, totally motionless except for her eyes, which frantically swept the scene before her.

Where were the cars? Where were the window-shopping tourists in too-tight polyester who haunted the French Quarter at all hours? Where were the neon signs in the jazz joints, the topless bars, the music that poured from open doors and windows, the leftover Mardi Gras drunks with their empty cups of Dixie beer? *Where was the world she had walked out of just last night?*

Oh, there were people, all right, but every single one of them was dressed like she and Trey Lavande were dressed, in nineteenth-century style. And there was traffic—the street was crammed with horses and carts and fancy carriages of every size and style, driven by black coachmen in full livery. Instead of the confetti, broken beads, and smashed plastic cups she expected to find littering the streets after last night's revels, there were horse droppings, orange peels, and a thin river of something that smelled of sewage and dead fish. A fat black woman in a long red skirt waddled past, balancing a tray on her head and calling in a sing-song voice, "Pralines! Sweet as love, gold as honey. Buy my fresh pralines!"

Charli couldn't move except for the trembling that suddenly attacked her. Something was very wrong here, and she was having a lot of trouble figuring out a way to make it right. She sucked in a mouthful of air, and it came in ragged, as if she'd been running or sobbing or both. She tried to take in another gasp, and then another, but without breathing out. She couldn't get any air!

"Miss Stewart?" said the man beside her.

At the sound, she finally moved, wrenching her hand from his arm and stepping back. "Don't touch me," she whispered frantically, her eyes huge as they stared at him.

"Are you all right?" He sounded genuinely concerned.

"No," she whispered. She looked back at the busy street scene. "No, I am not all right. I think I've gone insane." She looked down at the full-skirted gown, at the man beside her, at a dog that loped past. "Or I am dead."

He reached for her hand again. At his touch, instinct and training meshed into a single need to protect herself. Quick as lightning, her left leg dropped back, her knees bent, her left hand pulled in, fist up, and her right shot out. Right into Trey Lavande's gut.

He dropped to one knee with a soft *oooph* and stayed there, gasping for breath.

Immediately, Charli's hands flew to her mouth. "I'm sorry," she breathed behind her fingers. "I didn't mean to . . . I'm sorry."

He looked up. Her eyes were like two enormous puddles of blue ink in her pale face, and she was still trembling. He could see that she was genuinely terrified. He struggled to stand, still fighting for breath, and reached for her hand as slowly and smoothly as he would reach to gentle a skittish horse. Her small hand was icy cold. He took a deep breath and grinned.

"Quite all right, ma'am, but remind me to warn my mother . . . and her customers."

"I . . . what . . . I don't understand what's happening."

"You've had a difficult night and day, Miss Stewart. I'm sure you'll feel better as soon as we can get you home again with your own family." He tucked her frigid hand into the crook of his arm and patted it reassuringly, as he might a child's. He had to take her home, if he could figure out where it was. Perhaps if he walked her through the Quarter, she would recognize it when she saw it. Perhaps it was near Dr. DuPrée's house. "Toulouse Street, you said?" She nodded. "It's just around the corner."

She allowed herself to be led along the banquette because she didn't know what else to do. Her initial shock and immobility had dissipated, and now her mind was racing like a car in the Indy 500. There had to be an explanation for all this, a perfectly logical, sane explanation.

She remembered hitting her head on something just before she'd been pulled out of the water last night. Was this all a hallucination, the result of some sort of concussion? Or was she, in fact, still unconscious in a nice safe bed somewhere and only dreaming this?

But it seemed so real. She could smell the heady perfume of an oleander. She could see the sun sparkling off the broken shards of glass embedded in the top of a garden wall to keep intruders from climbing over it. She could hear the bells ringing in the cathedral towers, calling the faithful to mass. It was all so real. And the most real thing of all was the man beside her—the warm solidity of his arm beneath her hand, the soothing quality of his voice, the tang of the lime-scented cologne he wore.

So what other explanation could there be? For surely there had to be one.

Earlier, she had joked with the maid about having fallen through a time warp. What if she really had?

No, such things didn't happen. Certainly not to Charli Stewart.

But how else could she explain the clothes and carriages, the horse-drawn trolley that clanged past, the lack of anything even remotely modern-looking in the shop windows?

1858, the maid had said. 135 years ago. Could it possibly be?

Trey was talking, gentle soothing nonsense that she could tell was meant to keep her calm so she wouldn't punch him again. But she didn't care why he was doing it, and she had no intention of punching him again. For the moment, he was a lifeline she clung to like one drowning, her only tenuous link to reality.

"Yes, yes," he said, patting her hand again. "You'll be fine when you're home again. You—"

"There!" she cried, pointing. It was her hotel. There was no sign—and she was almost positive she remembered seeing one yesterday—but this was definitely her hotel, with the same rose paint and gray shutters, the same cornstalk-design wrought iron on the upper balcony, even the same magnolia tree heavy with unopened blossoms in front of it, though it was smaller than she remembered.

With a gasp of relief, she ran to it and grabbed the door handle. When it wouldn't turn, she pounded on the door. "Let me in. This is my hotel. Let me in!" she shouted.

In less than a minute, the door swung open to reveal a black butler with a halo of springy gray curls.

"Ma'am?" he asked, jumping back from Charli in amazement.

Trey stepped forward and grasped Charli's arm. "Good afternoon, Rufus. Do you know this young lady?"

"Why, no sir, Mr. Lavande. I can't rightly say I ever seen her before."

"And I don't know you from Adam," she agreed, "but this is my hotel, and I want my things." She wrenched free of Trey's hand and pushed past the startled butler and into the house.

Trey quietly asked the butler, "Is the doctor at home?" The butler nodded. "Will you get him, please?"

In the hall, Charli hesitated. It was different. She was sure there had been a desk there, against the right wall, where she had registered yesterday. A desk with a phone and a computer behind it. And the room opening to the right was the restaurant, but she thought that yesterday it had been set with a dozen or so small round tables with pink cloths and bowls of rosebuds, not this single long table sporting a giant silver epergne.

But the staircase was the same and so was the hallway behind it that led to the back of the house. She moved down it and out into the courtyard.

Yes! This was right! Atop the fountain where water danced, she recognized the pair of wrought-iron herons. The same banana palm swayed in a light breeze. She hurried across the brick paving and gratefully pushed open the door of her room.

At her entrance, four startled black faces looked up. On a cot in one corner, an old man lay smoking a pipe. At the fireplace, a young woman bent to stir something in an iron pot. Two children played on the floor. They all stared at Charli.

85

Her eyes covered the room. It was dark, crowded with three beds and an overabundance of other cheap furniture, the walls streaked with soot. A length of faded calico fluttered at the window.

There was no four-poster with antique quilt, no TV and VCR, no air conditioner in the window. And none of Charli's luggage.

The woman straightened, then curtsied. "Get you something, ma'am?"

"What . . ." Charli began, but it came out a croak. She swallowed and tried again. "What year is it?" she asked, her voice barely more than a whisper.

"Why, it be '58, ma'am."

"No," she whispered. "God, no." She turned and ran back into the house where Trey stood talking to a redheaded man in shirtsleeves with a pipe in one hand and a folded newspaper in the other.

"Dr. DuPrée," said Trey, "allow me to present Miss Stewart. She—"

Charli stopped him by ripping the newspaper from the doctor's hand. Her eyes flew to the masthead—*The Daily Picayune*—and the date: February 28, 1858.

"No," she said again. Then louder. "No! No, no, no. It can't be. I won't let it." She stared at Trey, at the doctor, at the butler, her eyes as wild as a banshee's, then she dropped the paper and started running, out the still-open door, down the steps. She wanted only to get away from whatever it was that had happened to her, get back to her own world, her own life.

She tripped on the awkward skirt, almost falling, and hiked it up to her knees. She kept running, down the street, through the crowd. She hadn't gone more than twenty yards when her boot heel caught on a hoop wire and down she went in an ungainly flutter of ruffles, wire, and peach-colored cambric. And there she stayed, her head in her hands, trying to make sense of what made no sense, until Trey came and lifted her very gently to her feet and led her toward Jackson Square.

There, he found an unoccupied bench and sat her down, then seated himself beside her, still holding her hand. A black nanny pushed a wicker baby carriage past. A little girl ran by, rolling a hoop with a stick. The hooped and crinolined skirts of ladies brushed the walkways with a soft *shush*, and men tipped sleek top hats to one and all.

She looked at Trey. "It's really 1858," she said, certain now that this was not a dream.

"Of course. What year did you think it was?"

She laughed, though it had an edge of hysteria to it. "Stupid me, I thought it was 1993."

"1993! Why would you think that?"

"Oh, just perverse, I guess. Or crazy." She studied his face. His expression was a mixture of concern, confusion, and disbelief, but it was nothing compared to the roiling stew of emotions she was feeling herself, she thought. "It is me that's crazy here, isn't it? And all along I've been thinking it was you." She shook her head. "1858." She laughed harder.

"Would you care to share the joke?" he asked.

"Why not? It's certainly a good one, and it's all on me. History has never been my strong suit. For me, history starts with Billie Holiday and Charlie Parker. I'm a woman who can't balance

Megan Daniel

my checkbook without a calculator or heat up a cup of coffee without a microwave."

"Microwave?"

"It hasn't been invented yet."

Now he was really looking at her like she was crazy, and that made her laugh harder. She remembered the classic question psychiatrists used to determine if their patients were in touch with reality. "Who's the president of the United States?" she asked.

"Don't you know?"

"Yeah, do you?"

"President Buchanan."

"Buchanan?" She giggled. "Buchanan!" Then she really started to laugh, great big whoops of sound that brought the air pouring into her lungs. It might be hysteria, but somehow it made her feel better.

Chapter Eight

There was no question about it, Trey thought as he watched her laugh. She was the oddest female he'd ever met. And what was he to do with her? As he pondered the question, she asked one of her own.

"How did I get here?" It came out hardly more than a whisper, and she shook her head in accompaniment.

Gently, he held her hand, remembering that awful bump on the head she'd sustained. "Don't you remember how you got to New Orleans?"

"Oh, that I remember perfectly well. I flew."

"Flew?"

"In an airplane." She looked up at him with a rueful grin. "But you wouldn't know about that, would you? Amazing, how many really vital things haven't been invented yet."

Megan Daniel

"You're not making any sense."

"None of this makes any sense!" She looked up at him, and for a minute he felt himself drowning in the confusion he could clearly read in her huge blue eyes. "You still don't understand, do you?"

"Understand what?" he asked gently.

"That yesterday morning, when I woke up in New York, the year was 1993. I made phone calls and printed out a contract on my computer. I took a cab to the airport—not a horse-drawn carriage, a car with an engine. I flew to New Orleans and checked into the hotel that Dr. DuPrée's house has been turned into. I went to a club, listened to music, danced to the Neville Brothers. And when I jumped into the river after Rob Sams, it was still 1993. But then you pulled me out, and somehow I got yanked back into the past."

He dropped her hand. He'd been feeling sorry for her, and somehow responsible, but this story was ludicrous. Even with a head injury, she had to be making this up. "That's preposterous."

"I know," she said softly. Again, her eyes caught him, and now what he saw in them was fear, genuine, terrible fear. "I don't want to be here," she said softly. "I don't know how I got here. I want to go home." He felt himself being pulled into those magnificent eyes that now shimmered with unshed tears. He felt like he was drowning in them, like he wanted nothing more than to comfort her, to make everything in her world all right again. With a jerk, he pulled himself out.

"You're good," he said softly, no longer smiling. "One of the best I've seen. My mother will hire you in an instant. Such clever actresses always do well for her."

90

She gulped in a sob and sat up straighter. "Damn you! I'm not acting." She caught another breath and he could almost see her marshaling her arguments. "I know this is difficult to believe, but it's even harder for me than it is for you, and if I believe it I don't see why you can't. There's too much evidence to explain it away."

"Such as?"

"Well, look around you. There are . . ." She realized then that when Trey Lavande looked around him he saw only the world he expected to see, the world he was used to seeing every day of his life. His world hadn't been turned upside down. Then she remembered. "My bag! Where's my bag?"

"Do you mean that shiny yellow thing?"

"Yes, of course, where is it? You said you'd bring it."

"Miss Stewart, I am not a pack animal. I am not accustomed to carrying loads heavy enough to sink one of my own boats. What on earth did you have in that thing?"

She smiled, and once again he was pulled toward her almost against his will. She did have the most engaging smile. "Proof!" she explained, an unmistakable note of triumph in her voice. "Proof. Where is it?"

"At my mother's house. I told Jacob he could have it delivered when we knew where you lived."

"C'mon," she said, jumping up so fast her massive skirt again swayed like a flower in a high wind. She reached for his hand and pulled him to his feet. He was astonished at her strength. At the banquette, she stopped. "Which way?"

He grinned, oddly charmed by her quick enthusiasm, and offered his arm. "Come with me," he said, "but we will not run like a pair of hoydens. We will walk, like ladies and gentlemen."

She grinned back. "Right. But we'll walk like ladies and gentlemen in a hurry, okay?"

Her big yellow tote was sitting on a side table in Lisette Lavande's front hall. With relief, Charli ran for it. A parlor maid passed through the room with a pile of linens, heading for the stairs. Two of the girls, chatting in the front parlor just off the hall, looked up and smiled at Trey. Jacob stuck his head around a door.

"This place is as busy as the riverfront," Trey muttered, grabbing Charli's arm. "Through here." He led her down the hall and into the back parlor and seated her on a damask-covered settee near a baby grand piano. "All right. Where's your proof?"

"Right here," she said, holding up the bag like a trophy.

Once again it caught his attention, as it had last night in the carriage. He reached out and stroked the smooth, shiny surface, not surprised to find it cool to the touch. "What is this material? I've never seen anything like it."

"Of course you haven't. It hasn't been invented yet. At least, I don't think it has."

"You keep saying that."

"Because it's true. This is called vinyl. It's a kind of plastic."

"A what?"

"The twentieth century's answer to beauty," she said. "It's made from oil, I think."

"What kind of oil?" he asked, examining the slick surface.

"Petroleum." She slid open the watertight Ziploc closure as he watched, fascinated.

"Do that again," he commanded. She did. He took the bag and examined the plastic zipper intently, sliding it open and closed, open and closed several times, testing the tightness of it with one manicured fingernail, holding it to the sunlight, even smelling it. "Fascinating," he said, finally. "Very clever, that."

She grinned. "Buddy, you ain't seen nothin' yet."

Once again, she opened the bag. She rummaged for a second or two before pulling out a brochure, slick and colorful. Big red letters spread across the cover; *Welcome to the Big Easy—The City that Care Forgot,* it read. She opened it up and pushed it toward him. It was covered with bright photos—the riverfront, where a few restored paddle wheelers moored beside oceangoing tankers and cruise ships; the nighttime skyline, with skyscrapers all atwinkle; black jazz musicians in Bourbon Street joints; the concrete hump of the Superdome. He studied the brochure as minutely as he had the zipper.

"A very clever artist created this," he finally said, still studying it. "And a very imaginative one. I wonder how he managed to think some of these ideas up." He handed the brochure back to her.

"They're not paintings; they're photographs. Of real places."

"As I said, Miss Stewart, a clever and imaginative artist. But he overstepped himself."

"What do you mean?"

"Look there," he said, pointing to a photo of tourists window-shopping in the French Quarter.

She didn't see anything unusual about it and said so. He laughed. "He gave himself away when he put those women in trousers! Bloomers I would have bought, but trousers?"

She sighed. "Right," she said as she grabbed it back, muttering, "and how I wish I had some right now." She rummaged in the bag some more, then started pulling things out at random, like a magician pulling rabbits from a hat. She piled them up on the settee beside her, naming each one as she set it out. "Room key—note the name on the tag, Maison du Carré, 787 Toulouse Street. A fax from my secretary that was waiting for me at the hotel yesterday—note the date. My plane ticket, also dated. Ballpoint pen . . ." She clicked it a couple of times in his face. "One plastic spoon. One paperback book. My Filofax."

His expression grew more and more bemused with each item. No sooner did he pick one thing up to examine it than she was thrusting another in his face. The thing she'd called a fax was merely a piece of thin, slippery paper with some printing on it, though he did see the date, February 27, 1993, printed across the top. Easy enough to fake, however, though it did seem like an enormous amount of trouble to convince him of such a preposterous story. Same with the piece of paper she'd called a plane ticket. The pen was certainly interesting, and he clicked it several times, making the tip appear and disappear, reappear and disappear again. He scribbled his name on the fax and was amazed when ink came from the pen's tip. How clever!

The book was merely a book, though he'd never seen one with a paper cover. Didn't seem very practical to him. And she had carelessly bent over several page corners, an unforgivable sin to a book lover like Trey. Books were too precious to be treated so cavalierly. The leather thing with a snap clasp seemed to be a sort of appointment book and notebook combined, of rather good quality, he could see, though far too bulky to be really useful.

"Uh, no," said Charli, as she pulled out the small, pink plastic compact that held her birth control pills, then thrust it back in again. "You don't need to see that."

She rummaged some more in the bag's seemingly unfathomable depths. "Aha!" she exclaimed, as she thrust a small blue booklet at him.

"What is that?" he asked.

"My passport." She flipped it open and shoved it under his nose. Inside was a photograph of her—tinted and not very flattering, he thought—and some printing. "Read the dates," she commanded.

He did. According to the document, Charlotte Victoria Wainwright Stewart had been born in New York, New York on August 5, 1965. It also said the document had been issued in New York in January of 1988.

He looked back up at her. "As I said before, Miss Stewart, you know some talented artists—or one might say forgers."

"Why on earth would I go to so much trouble?"

His mouth thinned. "That remains to be seen."

"Oh!" she exclaimed, tossing the passport onto the growing pile beside her. "All right. I wasn't going to show you this yet, because I was afraid you'd accuse me of using voodoo or something, but here goes." She pulled a flat black-and-gray box from the bag. Trey watched as she flipped it open and it took on an odd, triangular shape. She lifted it to her eyes, said, "Say cheese," and touched a button on the top. A bright light flashed in his eyes, temporarily blinding him.

"What the devil . . . !" he exclaimed, rubbing his eyes.

"It's a Polaroid," she said. "A kind of camera."

"Don't be ridiculous," he said as he tried to get his eyes to focus again. "I've seen cameras before. They are large. And black. And set on a stand. That little thing couldn't possibly be a camera." As he spoke, a small, white card emerged from the bottom of the box. She pulled it out and handed it to him.

"There's nothing here," he said, looking at the blank card.

"There will be," she said with a smug smile. "Just wait a few seconds. Keep looking at it."

As he watched, something amazing started to happen. Slowly, and very faintly at first, then with growing clarity, an image began to appear on the small square in his hand. As he watched, the edges became more and more defined and the color deepened. In less than a minute, he was looking at a picture of himself. In color. He had a startled look on his face, but he couldn't deny that it was him. In the picture he was sitting right there on that settee, in those clothes, with that particular potted fern growing just behind him, with the pile of unusual articles she'd pulled from the bag clearly visible on the settee beside him.

He turned the card over, expecting a silvered backing. It had to be a clever sort of mirror. But it was only paper after all. And when he moved, the image remained static. It wasn't a mirror. It was, just as she had said, a photograph. And she had just made it with that ridiculous little flashing box!

"I don't believe in voodoo," he said softly, staring at the picture, then back at her. "But I just might be convinced that there are still witches in the world."

She had him now. She couldn't tell if he actually believed she was from the future, but he knew she was not your ordinary, everyday French Quarter Victorian miss. She wanted him to believe her. Somehow it was terribly important that he did. She wasn't sure why. It just was.

"It's the truth, you know. I really am from the future."

"And I'm George Washington," he said, but he grinned, a dazzling white smile.

She returned a rueful one. "Not even close. Not with teeth like that. His were false, you know. Wooden."

"Really? No wonder he looks like he's in pain in all those portraits."

"I always thought so too," she said, inordinately pleased at sharing an opinion with him. "I wonder if Lincoln did too. He always looks a little pained in his photographs."

"Lincoln who?"

"Abraham Lincoln."

"You mean that fellow who's been debating with Douglas?"

97

She thought a moment. From her tiny reservoir of historical knowledge the term "Lincoln-Douglas Debates" rang an even tinier bell. "Is that happening now?"

"Yes. Preposterous fellow. Looks like a skeleton with mange. He's running for senator in Illinois."

She chuckled. "I know as a Southerner you won't like to hear this, but in a couple of years that mangy skeleton is going to be president of the United States."

He laughed then too, a rich, round sound that made her feel warm. The girls in the front parlor glanced around at the sound. "Well, if you believe that, Miss Stewart, I've got some swampland a ways up the bayou I'd like to sell you."

So she reached into her bag once more, fumbled in her wallet, and pulled out a five-dollar bill. "Have a look," she said with a triumphant smile, thrusting the bill at him. "Except for Benjamin Franklin, I think we only put presidents on our money."

He took the bill and studied it, not only the face of the skeletal, bearded Lincoln but the whole design, the *E Pluribus Unum*, the signatures. The date: 1990.

"It's real, you know," she said, willing him to believe.

"I'm more inclined to think this proof of your insanity than of your story of being from the future. I've read about your Mr. Lincoln. I know what he and his Republicans stand for, and I know no sane person would vote for him for president. It would mean immediate war between the North and the South."

"It does," she said sadly, thinking of the horror depicted in the PBS series she'd seen about the Civil War. "The bloodiest war imaginable."

He handed back the bill. She stuffed it into her bag, and when she looked back up, he was staring at her with a new intensity. "You have the most expressive face," he said. His voice held a kind of huskiness she'd heard before. In fact, she'd heard it just last night, in the voice of Rob Sams. It was the sound of a man who desired her.

But, unlike with Rob, her first thought was not of how to put him off, change his mind, get him onto another subject. Her first thought was that he looked like he was about to kiss her and she wished he'd get on with it.

He did. Gently, with one finger, he lifted her chin and brushed his lips lightly against hers. They were warm. They tickled and teased. Then, a little less gently, they insisted. His tongue emerged to trace the seam of her lips, coaxing them open. Her tongue answered.

The kiss went on a long time, or maybe it was just that everything seemed to shift into slow motion. Warmth oozed down from the fire-point of his lips, down her shoulders, across her breasts, right down to the pit of her stomach and beyond. If she hadn't been sitting, she probably would have fallen. But by this time, his arms were around her, and they were so strong, almost fierce, that she knew he wouldn't have let her fall. Her hands gripped the soft wool of his lapels, holding on for dear life—or perhaps to stop him should he decide to pull away.

Suddenly, it seemed much less important what year it was or how she had got here. She was just glad she had. She couldn't remember the last time she'd been so expertly kissed. Maybe never. His tongue kept up its assault, probing, entwining itself with hers. His hands moved up her back, massaging her shoulder blades through the fabric of her gown and the chemise beneath it. The thought struck her that if she were dressed in her usual fashion—a silk T-shirt or an oversize sweater, often without a bra—he could just slide his hands right up under it to her bare skin, to her breasts, to her nipples, now puckered merely from the thought.

Her fingers loosed their hold on his coat and crept over the fine cotton of his shirt while his moved around her rib cage only to encounter stiff whalebone. This stupid dress!

The intensity of her reaction to this man she didn't even know astonished her. She wanted to swallow him, take him right into her, become part of him. Deep inside her, something moved, like a hungry animal waking up and demanding to be fed. Her skin burned. Her stomach felt like it had been snap-kicked by a black belt. She, who prided herself on the rigorous discipline she'd imposed on her body, had lost all control over it. It frightened her. She pulled away, breaking the clinch like a deep-sea diver coming up for air. She thought she might need a decompression chamber.

Holding her at arm's length, Trey stared at her with a passion as burning as his kiss had been. He looked almost as flustered as she was. "Who are you?" he whispered.

"Just Charli Stewart," she answered.

"And who is Charli Stewart?"

"Someone who doesn't know how she got here or why." She jumped up. She needed to cool off and she needed to think, and to do both of those things she needed to put some distance between herself and Trey Lavande.

She was more shaken by his kiss than she cared to admit, even to herself. She felt totally out of control of her reaction to him, of the situation she was in, and nothing in the whole world scared Charli more than feeling out of control. It made her vulnerable, and vulnerability was the enemy. She had structured her whole life so she would never again have to suffer from that particular emotion. And now here it was, swamping her. So she reacted in her usual way. She became brisk and busy.

"The point is," she said, starting to pace between the fireplace and the piano and willing her breathing and heartbeat to return to normal at once, "I am here. Now I've got to figure out what to do about it."

He leaned back, his arms stretched along the top of the settee and his long legs thrust out in front of him, crossed casually at the ankles. But his face was not casual. She thought he looked like a raptor eyeing a fat cottontail.

"But where do I start?" she went on, trying to ignore the fierceness of his gaze and the odd things it did to her insides. "All my friends are in New York in 1993. I don't have any money that anyone here will accept. I don't have any clothes or anyplace to stay. I can't even begin to guess how a nineteenth-century lady ought to behave. I'm sort of like a stray dog who doesn't know the way to the pound." She tried to laugh

101

as she said it—the universe had certainly played a good joke on her—but her anxiety must have come through, because when he answered, his voice was kind.

"You are not without friends in New Orleans, Miss Stewart," Trey said. "Or people who will help you." He grinned. "I did save your life. Perhaps you've heard of the Oriental belief that if you save someone's life, you are forever after responsible for that person."

"I've heard it," she replied, spinning to face him, "and it's a noble thought, but completely untrue. No one is responsible for my life except me. No one."

"An unusual sentiment for a woman."

"Not anymore." She paced some more, turned, and took a deep breath. "Okay, I'm here. We take that as a given. I don't know how to get back, at least not yet. I'll figure it out, because I have to. In the meantime I have to eat, which means I need a job."

His reaction to that puzzled her. He sat up abruptly, closed his eyes, and sighed. She would have sworn he looked disappointed, though she couldn't imagine why he should be. "So," he said, "we come to that at last."

"At last? What do you mean?"

"You almost had me fooled." He opened his eyes and gave her a look no less powerful than it had been a minute ago but entirely different. Now he looked disgusted. "I even found myself hoping you were telling the truth, preposterous as it is. But then, as I said earlier, you are very good. Better even than I imagined. I'm certain my mother will be happy to take you on."

"You mean you think she'll give me a job? What sort of job?"

"Exactly the sort you are best suited for, Miss Stewart," he said, rising. His voice was suddenly icy. "Pretending." He spun to face the piano and brought his fist down on it hard enough to shake the sheet music lying there and set the strings inside to vibrating with a discordant sound.

His behavior mystified Charli. She was beginning to get used to feeling confused all the time. She certainly didn't like it, but it was starting to feel familiar. What did he mean by pretending, and why was he so upset to think that his mother might give her a job?

While she tried to figure it all out, the clock on the mantel, a delicate porcelain thing encased in a bell jar, gave four shivery chimes. They were followed almost immediately by the more resonant chime of the doorbell.

A moment later, through the archway, Charli saw a tall, well-dressed gentleman enter the front parlor. Both Aimeé and Felicité rose eagerly to greet him. He gave the first a familiar squeeze and the second a kiss on the mouth. They hung on him, one to each arm, chatting animatedly. Charli wondered if he were yet another relative in what she was beginning to think must be an enormous and extremely affectionate family.

Just then he looked up and caught her staring at him. He stared right back, one eyebrow cocked, and smiled. He excused himself to the two girls and strode directly into the back parlor.

"Looks like Lisette's found a new treasure," he said, smiling at Charli with evident admiration. He let his eyes roam over her, taking in every

Megan Daniel

inch and curve from her head to her feet, astonishing Charli with such blatant rudeness. Then he
turned to Trey. "Aren't you going to introduce me,
Lavande?"

"No," he said. Charli was even more amazed
at the surly tone in Trey's voice as well as his
shockingly bad manners. She never would have
guessed it of him.

But the gentleman just laughed. "Hoping to
keep her for yourself, eh? Sorry, old fellow, not
a chance, not with one who looks like this." He
turned to Charli. "Since this bad-mannered lout
refuses to do the honors, ma'am, I'll have to do
them myself. Remy Sauvage, at your service."
He made a smooth bow. When she offered her
hand he took it, but instead of shaking it, as she
expected, he kissed it lightly. Right, she thought,
she was going to have to get used to that.

"How do you do, Mr. Sauvage."

"Very well, thank you, and with your help I'm
certain I shall do even better shortly. Are you
available just now?"

"No, she is not." Trey bit out an answer while
Charli was still trying to figure out what the question meant.

Sauvage grinned down at him. "I'd heard you
like to break the new ones in yourself, Lavande. I
wasn't sure it was true until now." He turned back
to Charli. He was still holding her hand, stroking
his thumb slowly across it, an amazingly intimate
gesture from someone she'd just met. She pulled
away. "Too bad. Perhaps later, my dear, when
you're tired of this fellow's ill humor, you will
enjoy spending time with someone more entertaining. I think I can guarantee you'll enjoy it.

In the meantime, I suppose I will have to make do with Felicité." He winked. "But don't tell her I said so. She likes to think she's the house's main attraction for me rather than being only one of many. Nothing like a little variety to keep a house lively."

She watched him stroll back into the front parlor. He kissed Felicité again, took her by the hand, and led her off toward the stairs. She glanced back at Charli with what could only be called a triumphant smile.

Suddenly, as clearly as if a lightbulb had gone on over her head like in a cartoon, Charli realized where she was, what Lisette Lavande's house was. How incredibly stupid she had been! How unforgivably dense! And now she knew what Trey had meant when he said his mother would give her a job.

She spun around and glared at him. He glared back. And then she did something she'd never done in her life, and had never even seen anyone do except in bad movies.

She swung her arm back and slapped Trey Lavande across the face as hard as she could.

Stunned, he watched her scoop up the big yellow bag, swing about, and stalk through the front parlor. He heard the street door slam with a resounding thud. Inside him churned a rich brew of emotions: anger, frustration, confusion, disappointment, guilt. And hope.

Chapter Nine

Charli stormed out of Lisette Lavande's house,
propelled by pure rage. She headed down the
street with an angry stride, pushing her way
through the crowds, oblivious to people, horses,
indignant stares. She didn't know where she was
going and she didn't care, as long as it was away.
Away from Lisette's beautiful house, away from
her own blind stupidity in not recognizing it at
once for what it was, away from Trey Lavande
and his sly, smug smiles.

How dare he think that of her! That she would
prostitute herself for money or any other reason.
She would never be that desperate.

Was that why he kissed her—testing the merchandise, so to speak? The thought hurt more
than anything else. She had felt so close to him
in that moment, so connected. And he had been
thinking *that*.

So, okay, let him! She didn't need him. She didn't need anybody. She'd been making her way in strange countries since she was eighteen. She was a success in a man's business. She lived in one of the toughest cities in the world, for heaven's sake, and it hadn't gotten her down. She could handle this, and she could handle it alone.

As the first flush of her rage abated somewhat, she noticed that she was attracting more than a little attention as she marched down the street. Men stared. Ladies in fine gowns stepped aside and looked shocked. A few children giggled. She stopped and looked around, studying her environment.

She saw black women going about on various errands, generally alone, while simply dressed white women with baskets looped over their arms headed to and from the market. Men of every color and class strode up and down, dodging in and out of the heavy traffic, alone or in pairs or groups.

But Charli quickly realized that she was the only woman dressed in a fashionable and clearly expensive gown who was alone on the street, neither accompanied by a maid nor walking with another fashionable woman or man. These other ladies walked with small, almost mincing steps, leaning on the arms of their escorts if possible, while Charli strode down the street as if she were back in New York and wearing a pair of blue jeans. They carried tiny lace or beaded reticules, not bright yellow vinyl totes big enough to carry home half the market and heavy enough to sink the *Titanic*. They shaded their faces from the Southern sun with delicate parasols. Not a single woman she could see anywhere, of any class, was bareheaded. And none of them, as far as she could tell, had short hair. Charli's uncovered and boyish black curls rioted around her head and danced in the breeze.

At first, the reaction of the people around her made her laugh. In modern New York, it took a certifiable crazy, someone cursing the sky with shaking fists or punching out a bus, to attract any attention at all, and then it was rarely more than a slide of the eyes to check out the danger level before moving out of the way. But in nineteenth-century New Orleans, a woman alone without a hat seemed to be a bonafide tourist attraction.

Maybe I ought to buy myself a bonnet, she thought, and then remembered that she had no money—and she figured her credit cards weren't going to do her a whole lot of good here. She hadn't lied when she told Trey she needed a job.

But what could she do? She could negotiate a contract. She could find her way around a computer and put together an impressive spreadsheet. She even knew a bit about the technicalities of sound mixing and recording dynamics. She knew just about everything there was to know about jazz. And she could fend off a determined man three times her weight.

Great, she thought. Everything I'm good at hasn't been invented yet!

She had waited tables once or twice, back in her singing days, and she'd be willing to do it again. Even as the thought struck her, she came to the front door of Tujague's. Amazing, she thought. She'd eaten in this very restaurant last year, in

1992, and here it was 135 years ago! She even remembered that its name was pronounced "Two-jacks." It had to be a good omen.

She pushed open the door and was inundated by the wonderful and familiar pungent smells of gumbo and jambalaya and dirty rice. It was dark inside, and she peered into the gloom, just making out a few tables topped by unlit lamps with green glass shades and a shiny brass spittoon not far away. Several faces turned towards her.

"Ma'am?" came a voice from behind her.

She spun around. "Oh, yes, good afternoon. I was wondering—"

"I am sorry, madam," said a very stiff man in a very stiff black suit. "We do not serve unescorted ladies at Tujague's." He swung the door open again and all but pushed her back out into the sunlight. Well, she had her answer, anyway. She'd seen enough to know that there wasn't a single waitress in the place—only sour-faced and stiff-backed waiters.

She poked her head into a couple of other places, including a tea shop she thought might be more promising, only to come up with the same result. No women need apply.

So, waitressing was out. What did that leave her?

She watched an elegantly dressed pair of ladies come out of a shop and climb up into an open carriage to be driven off. She looked back at the store. The window displayed several bolts of fabric and loops of ribbon along with fashion plates propped up on a stand that looked like a music rack. A dress shop!

Well, if there was one thing Charli knew about, it was clothes. She went in.

A bell tinkled over the door as she opened it, but the shop was empty. She looked around. There were no racks of dresses as she expected, only some little gilt chairs and a settee grouped around a table covered with fashion plates. Shelves of fabric bolts lined two walls. So, it was the nineteenth-century equivalent of a couturier house—everything made to order.

A rail-thin woman in a black silk gown appeared from behind a blue velvet curtain and approached. The woman looked Charli quickly up and down and frowned at her uncovered hair, but hid it quickly with a tight smile.

"May I be of service, madame?" she asked politely, her hands clasped together in front of her stomach.

"I hope so. I'm looking for a job."

The woman was clearly taken aback. "What sort of a job?" she blurted out.

"Any sort at all. I'll do anything."

The woman frowned. "Sewing?"

The truth was that Charli could hardly remember the last time she'd sewn on a button, badly at that, and it wasn't in her to lie. "Not really, though I suppose I could try. I'm a quick learner." She paused. "But actually, I thought maybe I could sell. I'm good with clothes and I can be very persuasive."

The woman sniffed then; she actually sniffed. "Young woman, I cater to the finest ladies in New Orleans, ladies of great refinement and discriminating taste. And they expect to be served by ladies of equal refinement." She had moved toward the door as she spoke. "They do not expect to be met with women of lax standards in my establishment." She looked pointedly now at Charli's bare, shorn head. "Good day, miss," she said and held the door open. The little bell tinkled as it closed behind Charli.

She did no better in the dozen or so other shops she tried, whether the perfume shop, several jewelers, a candy shop, even a furniture maker. Few of them had female employees at all, and those that did had no need of extra help—particularly a young woman without a hat.

She slumped on a wrought-iron bench in front of the French Market. Apparently, the bench was the 1858 equivalent of a bus stop, since a number of other people waited beside her before boarding one of the horse-drawn omnibuses—huge coaches pulled by two horses and carrying more than a dozen passengers—that regularly clip-clopped to a stop in front of her.

She was exhausted. She'd been walking for hours. Her leather boots, stiff from their dunking in the river, had rubbed a nasty pair of blisters on her ankles. The mist rising from the river was damp and very soon now it would be growing dark.

The fight to keep her optimism up was getting the better of her at last. She was confused. She was scared. And she was alone in a world she knew less than nothing about. Except for the odious Trey Lavande and his madam of a mother, she knew no one. It was worse than the time she had traveled on her own through Turkey without speaking a word of Turkish. That had been a lark, an adventure, because she had always known that

111

she could go home whenever she wanted.

Well now she wanted. But since she had no idea how she'd gotten pulled into the past, she had even less idea of how to go about getting back to the present. Her present.

She shivered even harder, and she knew it was as much from anxiety as from the cold, since it wasn't really all that chilly. Though the February slush still swished in the gutters of New York, it was already spring in New Orleans. She wrapped her arms around herself, but she shook all the harder.

And she was hungry. Starving, in fact. All around her, the offerings of the French Market reminded her that she hadn't eaten anything since the single roll she'd nibbled for breakfast. The rich blend of smells—of fish and oysters, sweet pineapples and bananas, braided strings of garlic, ripe tomatoes, and fresh baked bread—made her almost faint with longing.

And the coffee! The smell of fresh roasted coffee made her want to scream with craving it. She had dreamy visions of the shiny brass cappuccino maker back in her New York apartment; she could almost hear it sputter, could almost taste the rich black espresso, the foamy steamed milk, the flecks of cinnamon. And now here was great coffee right in front of her nose, offered for sale, and she didn't have even a nickel anyone around her would recognize as legal tender.

She felt someone sit beside her on the bench and turned. It was a man, rather nondescript in a dark coat over a green-and-white striped waistcoat. He was staring at her and the look on his face was definitely a leer.

"Mademoiselle?" he said. She raised one eyebrow as his gaze dropped to the neckline of her gown, then lower. "You are alone?"

Was the fellow blind? Of course she was alone. "No," she lied.

He looked past her, grinned, and said, "You are alone. I will see to it that you do not remain so." He paused, then added. "How much?"

To his surprise and her own, she laughed. It really was too funny, she thought. Here she had turned down a job in what was clearly one of the classiest bordellos in New Orleans, only to be propositioned at a bus stop! She couldn't stop laughing; she wrapped her arms around her waist and rocked with it.

The man, openly insulted, rose, glared at her, and walked away muttering something under his breath she was sure her mother would not have approved of.

Good, she thought, at least she wouldn't have to fight him off—if she even could in these ridiculous clothes. She was still livid at herself for that punch she'd thrown at Trey earlier in the day. She had panicked, and her reaction was to hit out at the nearest object—going against everything she'd learned in two years of karate training. It represented an inexcusable loss of control. *Sempai* Joe would have been disappointed in her.

She caught her breath on a gasp and made herself stop laughing. She had to get hold of herself, reestablish control. Now! That was the important thing, to stay in control. Anything could be dealt with if she just didn't lose control.

Okay, Charli, she told herself, think this thing

through. Having that man offer her money was just another reminder that she had none and she needed some. So what resources did she have?

And then it struck her. In the massive depths of her tote bag she had any number of things no one else in New Orleans had. Trey had been fascinated by several of them. Surely someone else would be too. She could sell them.

Mentally, she flipped through the catalog of shops she'd been in that day. The dressmaker—no luck there. A praline shop—nope. Two yard goods stores, the furniture-maker, a druggist—not likely candidates. But wait! There had been a perfumer and she had an almost full bottle of Poison in her bag. And there had been that jeweler/watchmaker. He might give her something for her Swatch watch.

Driven by the thought of a cup of thick black coffee, she jumped from the bench and headed up Decatur Street.

An hour later, she sank gratefully onto a big comfortable bed in the St. Charles Hotel with a coal fire glowing merrily in the fireplace. The jeweler had been happy to give her fifteen dollars for her Swatch—not bad, she thought, since she hadn't paid much more than that for it—and the perfumer, after a very suspicious sniff, had bought her bottle of Poison for another ten, begging her to come back with more. Twenty-five bucks! She figured by 1858 standards, she must be rich. She got a room at the best hotel in town for only two-fifty a night, though she'd had to con her way into it. Unaccompanied women without luggage and without hats did not fit the establishment's high-class image. But Charli called on her fertile imagination and came up with a story of broken-down carriages, delayed luggage, and an ill family that had done the trick. The fact that she was nearly in tears of hunger and exhaustion had added to the verisimilitude of her tale and gotten her in.

I'm okay, she told herself, chanting it over and over again in her mind like a mantra. I'm okay. I've got a bed. I've got money so I won't starve. And soon I'll find a way to get home. I'll find my very own pair of ruby slippers and I'll click them together for all they're worth and I'll really, really believe the words when I say "There's no place like home." And then I'll wake up in New York with Glen Odens talking into my answering machine.

And in the meantime, tomorrow she would buy a hat.

"Where the devil could she have gone?" Trey Lavande roared at his mother the next morning. He'd spent most of the day before and the entire night wearing holes in his leather soles combing the streets in search of the mysterious Miss Charli Stewart. "A girl can't just disappear in New Orleans."

"Of course she can," Lisette replied, smoothing the skirt of her latest violet silk faille from Paris. "It happens all the time. New Orleans is absolutely filled with places in which to disappear, either by choice or otherwise."

"That's exactly what I am afraid of."

"And so you should be. Whatever did you say to the poor thing, Trey, to make her run out like that? From my vantage point on the stairs, I'd say she looked as though the Furies themselves were after her."

"All I did was tell her you would offer her a job here."

Lisette shook her head, though not hard enough to dislodge her gloriously curled coiffure. "Well, no wonder, dear. Really, Trey, I hadn't thought you dense, or blind."

"What do you mean? It was what she wanted, wasn't it?"

"Well, I thought so too at first, but it didn't take long to disabuse myself of that notion. Why, any fool could see that girl was no common whore. Nor even an uncommon one, if it comes to that. Pity, because I think she would have done very well. But it is not what she is."

"Are you certain?" he asked, an unmistakable tinge of hope in his voice.

She raised an eyebrow. "Really, dear, you might give me a little credit. After all, I am reputed to have the best eye in New Orleans."

"You might have told me."

"You might have seen it for yourself if you'd taken the trouble to really look." She peered at her son, who was pacing before the empty grate and running his fingers absently through black hair that was falling every which way since he'd been finger-combing it for most of the last twenty hours. His jaw, normally immaculately shaved, was shadowed with a dark stubble. His dark eyes were tired. It had been a long time since Lisette had seen him so agitated over anything—even longer since it had been over a woman. The situation had very interesting possibilities!

She rose in a rustle of beruched and beribboned

silk faille. "Well, the thing now is to find her. You say she has no family in New Orleans?"

"She said quite specifically that they were all in New York."

"Might she have gone back there, then?"

"She has no money." Suddenly, remembering the preposterous five-dollar bill with the even more preposterous picture of that upstart Lincoln on it, he chuckled. "At least none anyone will accept."

"Friends, then?"

"Not now." Lisette thought it an odd answer but she let it pass. She was more interested in watching the very intriguing play of emotions on his handsome face.

"Where have you looked?"

"That's just it, *Maman*. I have no idea where to look. I've just been wandering the streets all day and all night with no plan, looking for her face under every parasol and bonnet. I've even accosted two perfect strangers only because they wore peach-colored gowns and had dark hair."

She smiled. More and more interesting! Lisette knew men and, more particularly, she knew her son. She was looking at a man who had been struck by lightning. He had not been so agitated even over Corinne, the pale and timid little thing he had wanted to marry. And about time, too. But who would have thought an oddly behaved, dark-haired, outspoken thing like Charli Stewart would have been the one to do it?

But if she was the one, Lisette would encourage him. She wanted desperately to see her son happily settled—loath though she was to imagine herself a grandmother. She reached out and took his hand. "She must be out there, Trey. Go find her. Find her and bring her home."

He straightened. "I intend to." He grabbed his low-crowned beaver hat, jammed it on his head, and plunged back into the streets, still with no definite plan in mind but fired with determination.

Chapter Ten

Charli was having quite a time.

With a good night's sleep behind her, she felt reborn and ready to take a look at this past she found herself in. She became a sightseer in time, and the sights were certainly worth seeing. She couldn't help but think of the old party conversation of "If you could go back in time, where/when would you go?" She'd always thought the Twenties would be her choice, when jazz was pouring out from behind the walls and into the mainstream. Or maybe the Fifties in a vain attempt to prove that her mother had once been a young, carefree girl with dirty knees, who dared now and then to break a rule.

She would certainly not have picked this particular here and now. But since she was here now, she figured she might as well have a good look.

It was difficult to get past the feeling that she was on a movie set, to convince herself that this was all quite real. She was astonished at how vivid everything seemed, how colorful and bustling and alive, until she realized that the only images she had of this part of the past were from faded and rigidly posed black-and-white or sepia photographs and old etchings. But the world that surrounded her now was filled with color and movement and sound.

The racket of horses and carts rivaled anything a fleet of New York cabbies could produce. The clothes were as colorful and eye-catching as anything on Fifth Avenue. The bustle on the banquettes matched midtown at rush hour.

The first thing she did that first morning on her own in the New Orleans of 1858 was to go shopping. It wasn't exactly like doing the floors at Bloomingdale's or cruising the mall, but it turned out to be something of a kick. First she bought herself a hat—she was tired of being stared at. It was a ridiculous little confection of straw and lace and ribbon with a handful of fake cherries tucked jauntily under the brim on one side. When she looked at herself in the mirror, it looked so incongruous on her tousled curls that she fell in love with it at once. At two dollars and a quarter, she did think twice, but by the time she got to thought three, it was perched at an impish angle on her head and she was on her way out the door.

Next, she bought some underthings. With just the one dress to her name and the impossibility of hopping into a hot shower at will, she needed fresh underwear even more than usual.

Eating turned out to be an unanticipated problem, though she might have expected as much from her job-hunting forays. "No unescorted ladies," was the refrain she heard over and over from doormen and maitre d's with their noses in the air. If it hadn't been for the stalls at the French Market, for the wandering fruit and praline sellers, for the stands that would condescend to sell her bowls of fiery gumbo and cup after cup of delicious French roast coffee, she would have starved.

The novelty of her situation kept her going for a while, but by the end of the third day, Charli strolled disconsolately along Bourbon Street, worrying about money. What little she had was disappearing at an alarming rate.

The jeweler who'd bought her watch had given her another dollar that morning for her big plastic earrings and one for the pair of cheap plastic necklaces she'd caught off the Comus float at Mardi Gras. But the money wouldn't stretch far. He'd offered her fifty more for her amethyst ring, but she pulled her hand away as if he'd bitten her. She would never sell Grandmother Charlotte's ring.

But the man's interest in the ring had served to remind her of Trey Lavande. Actually, she didn't need much to remind her of her rescuer. He popped into her mind with disgusting frequency. He may have been way too cocksure of himself and stupid as a board to imagine she'd work as a prostitute, but she had felt strangely safe with him. And that kiss! Charli was definitely not a girl who'd never been kissed, but she'd never been kissed quite like that. Or at least it had never felt quite like that. The man had something special, that was for sure. And she couldn't deny she would like to have sampled more of it.

Maybe his special ability came from growing up in a brothel. He must have had all the opportunities in the world to practice!

"Bels calas, bels calas, tout chauds," cried the cala woman as she rounded the corner with her big covered wooden bowl of hot calas balanced on her head. Charli had developed a taste for the fritters made of rice, eggs, butter, sugar, and she knew not what else, then deep fried. She gave the immense black woman a nickel for two of the delicacies and nibbled as she walked.

Okay, Charli, she told herself. Bottom line. Money's going out and none is coming in. You can move to a cheaper hotel tomorrow, or even find a rooming house of some sort, but you still need a job. But doing what?

In her own world, one of Charli's personal emotional safety valves was that she would always be able to work. She could type, do word processing, wait tables—she'd done them all at one time or another. She could judge the viability of a singer and choose the best lineup of songs for an album, none of which did her even the tiniest bit of good right now. She was seriously overqualified for this world.

But wait! She stopped so suddenly a man behind her collided with her, apologizing profusely. She brushed him away. She could get a job; she'd already been promised one. She would make Trey Lavande stick to his word to convince his mother to hire her. But not as one of her girls.

She could provide a different sort of entertainment for Lisette Lavande's customers. She remembered the beautiful Bechstein piano in the back parlor. She had itched to get her fingers on it when she first saw it. It would be her ticket. She would convince Lisette to hire the newest New Orleans singing sensation—Charli Stewart!

Trey walked until he ached all over, and with nothing to show for it. He still hadn't found the damnable Miss Stewart. She might have simply melted into the pavement. Or fallen into the river again, perhaps to return to the mysterious future she claimed to be from.

He had even gone down to the levee. He stood there like a pillar staring at the spot in the river where he had fished her out of the water. Had she jumped back into the river in an attempt to get back?

He shook himself at such a ridiculous thought. The woman almost had him believing what was totally unbelievable. She was certainly odd—and she had some even odder things in that big bag of hers—but she couldn't possibly have traveled back almost a century and a half. It wasn't possible!

But what if she had jumped back in the river? And what if she had drowned this time?

He didn't know quite why his stomach clenched at that idea, or at the image of her lying dead—or worse—in an alley somewhere. He knew better than most that New Orleans was no safe place for a young woman alone. And she didn't know her way around this town. If he could believe her crazy story, she didn't even know her way around this century! Anything could happen.

But why the hell did he care so much? He barely knew her.

You know damn well why you care, he told himself. You care because after that kiss, you want her more than you've ever wanted any woman in your life. More than you ever wanted Corinne, the woman you planned to marry.

He didn't know why he'd kissed her. He hadn't planned to. It just sort of happened. And once it started, he hadn't been able to end it. She had the most delicious mouth he'd ever tasted—so soft, so pliant. The way she had kissed him back lit a fire in him that burned still. His guts twisted every time he thought of touching her. His loins turned to fire at the idea of bedding her.

It was lust, pure and simple. As a man who'd grown up in a brothel, he certainly knew about lust. And he knew how to slake it. He had to find her. Then he had to bed her. Only then would he be able to forget about her. He hoped.

He had tried earlier in the evening to rid himself of this possession by visiting Justine, the lovely quadroon mistress he kept in a cozy cottage in Rampart Street. But, much to Justine's confusion and disappointment, he left after less than an hour, having done little more than drink her brandy and gaze into her fire.

He wanted Charli Stewart more than ever. But he'd been looking for her for three days with nothing to show for it but a hole in his shoe and a haggard look on his handsome face. How much longer could he look?

It was nearly two A.M. when he reluctantly gave

up the search for the night and turned his steps toward home. But when he reached his own love-ly new house on Chartres Street, he couldn't bring himself to go in. It seemed so empty somehow. He'd sleep at his mother's again. Maybe he'd even let one of her girls take the edge off this absurd need for Charli Stewart. Aimée was a lovely hand-ful and always willing.

"Evenin', Master Trey," Jacob said as he took Trey's hat and cane at Lisette's door. "Full house tonight."

"So I see," Trey answered, peering into the front parlor. At least two dozen men lounged there, sip-ping good brandy, smoking good cigars, and talk-ing to beautifully gowned women who they knew would, at their command, lead them upstairs and become just as beautifully naked and as eager and innovative as any man could desire.

Music drifted down from the piano at the far end of the room, a song Trey didn't recognize. Soon a voice joined in.

"You can cry me a river, cry me a river," came the song in a rich, sultry voice. It was like nothing he'd ever heard before. The voice caressed the words and sent them straight through him. His body reacted as though he had been stroked in a very sensitive spot.

He strode down the room, elbowing his way through the throng of men crowded around the piano. One of them was Remy Sauvage, he noted, and the man had a look of blatant desire on his face.

And there, at the piano, almost ethereally beau-tiful in a low-cut gown of emerald green silk, was Charli Stewart.

125

She looked right at him.
"I cried a river over you."

Charli was feeling happier than she had in years. Since leaving performing for the more certain fortunes of agenting, she'd forgotten just how much she loved singing for an audience. And what an audience she had!

Since her nineteenth-century listeners knew none of the twentieth-century music she sang, had never heard of jazz or country or rock-and-roll, she had complete freedom to roam through her dream repertoire. It was a fantasy come true. In her performing days in New York, she had always been stuck with a label—she was a jazz singer—and club owners didn't want the music polluted with country or rock or anything else. But tonight she could, and did, swing easily from Cole Porter cabaret to a torchy version of Sondheim's "I Think About You." She'd done a perfect Patsy Cline, sobbing through "Crazy," followed by some scat à la Ella, then segueing into a smoky "Tenderly." She even pounded out a rousing "Great Balls of Fire," though not quite with Jerry Lee Lewis's abandon. She had them in the palm of her hand all night long.

She loved it. So much so that she wondered if perhaps this was why she was here, in this time and place. Could the universe somehow have known how badly her soul needed this, the chance to really do what she'd always thought she was born to do, but which few New York bookers or record execs realized she was born to do? Had she been pulled out of her time so she could realize a dream? An interesting question, but right then, as the music poured out of her, she wasn't going to stop to analyze it. She was too busy loving it.

And then Trey Lavande had walked in, and he was the icing on the cake. He certainly looked good enough to eat, even though he obviously could use a night's sleep. He was clearly one of those men who would be gorgeous in a tux or in blue jeans. Too bad she would never see him in them, she thought. He'd look edible whether freshly barbered or with a two-day growth of beard.

Charli knew she didn't look too shabby, either, and she thanked the stars and Lisette Lavande for ensuring it. The green dress Lisette had given her, complete with whalebone stays at every seam, pushed everything in exactly the right direction, taking what she'd always thought was pretty insignificant and maximizing it into downright shapeliness. No wonder women opted for boning in those days. Even Charli would give up a few hours of comfort in exchange for a measurable bustline to flaunt in front of Trey Lavande.

The look on his face when he first saw her was priceless. She wanted to frame it and take it home with her—if she ever found a way to get home. Then, whenever she looked at it, she could feel again the electric jolt that shot through her at the sight of him. Lord, she'd only kissed the man once, but it had been such a memorable kiss, such a soul-jarring kiss, that just looking at him set her to trembling again. She wanted another one just like it. And then she wanted him to do what came after that.

The thought surprised her so much that she faltered on the opening bars of "Evergreen." When she mentioned love, soft as an easy chair, she

Megan Daniel

remembered the soft touch of his lips and wanted more. Her eyes kept leaving the keyboard and wandering to his, sky-blue locked with onyx, and she was almost scorched by the smoldering energy in his gaze. When she swung into "All of Me," the intensity only increased, till she thought her body might ignite from the fire in his eyes. He obviously wanted very badly to take all of her.

She wondered if her own eyes were mirroring his, at least a little, because when she sang Fats Waller's "Ain't Misbehavin'" she realized that that was exactly what she wanted to do. Oh boy, did she want to misbehave with Trey Lavande.

Well, okay, it was only natural. He was beautiful to look at and he kissed like the devil himself. And it had been a very, very long time since Charli had been with a man. But, though she'd had time to get over her first shock of offense at his assumption that she was a prostitute, the fact was he probably still thought so. And as long as he did, she wouldn't let him touch her again. She had far too much pride to sleep with a man who would think such a thing of her.

With an effort she wouldn't have believed if she hadn't experienced it, she pulled her eyes away from Trey's. She was exhausted. She'd been singing for hours, and her throat was raw. One more song, she told herself, one more, and I'm going upstairs to bed. Alone. To sleep.

For a finale, she tried to think if she knew any song at all that her audience might be familiar with. For a long moment she drew a blank, then she remembered Stephen Foster. With a grin, she gave them an "Oh Susannah" such as they'd never heard before—a blues lament that had more than one eye tearing. Then, with a sigh, she lowered the lid on the piano and accepted her ovation.

"Encore! Encore!" yelled the crowd of gentlemen pushing around the piano.

"Never heard anything like it," said a man at Trey's right. "That girl sings with her whole soul."

"Where do you suppose she learned such songs?" asked another.

"You can always trust Lisette to come up with something different," said a third. "Wonder if she's as good upstairs as she is down."

Remy Sauvage rolled his thin cigar to one side of his mouth and grinned. "I intend to find out," he said.

Trey's fists clenched involuntarily, while an almost overwhelming urge to floor the man rippled through him.

As Charli rose, Remy stepped toward her. "You're a true original, darlin'," he said, laying his hand on her bare shoulder by way of punctuation. "I like originality in a woman." His look was close to a leer. "Originality and imagination." He gestured toward the stairs. "Shall we?"

"I thought I told you once before, Sauvage," came Trey's voice, like ice in January. "The lady's taken."

"No, she's not," said Charli pointedly but with a smile, looking directly at Trey. "Nor will she be. Gentlemen, thank you for your attention. I hope to see you again at Chez Lisette. Good night." She made what she hoped was a creditable bow, considering the restriction of her clothes, and swept out and up the stairs. Alone. No one followed, including Trey, and she wasn't sure if she was disappointed or not.

Chapter Eleven

Trey slept badly. Every time he closed his eyes he saw her. He heard her. He even smelled her, a rich, spicy perfume like nothing he'd ever smelled before. By eight he was up, washed, and shaved. By nine, he was strolling from his house toward his mother's. It was crazy. No one in Lisette Lavande's house was ever up before noon except the slaves.

She was sitting at the breakfast table, alone, sipping coffee and reading the *Picayune*. With her back to the door, he almost didn't recognize her, and he wondered if Lisette was letting the customers stay overnight now. But then he heard her humming one of those outrageous songs she'd sung last night.

"What the devil . . . ?" he exclaimed as he strode into the room, grasped her shoulder, and turned her around. "What are you wearing?"

Charli looked down at the tan twill breeches and full-sleeved white cotton shirt that fit her better than she could ever have hoped. "Pretty nifty, huh?" she said with a smile. "Jacob got them for me."

Trey did not smile back. "And just what do you intend to do in them?"

"Go out. Walk around. See New Orleans without having to trip over a hoop or worry about a stay puncturing my ribs."

"That's ridiculous. Out of the question."

Charli lost her smile and slowly lowered her cup. "Out of whose question?" she asked. Had he known her better, he might have been wary of the cool calm in her voice.

"Mine. I won't allow it."

She stared at him a minute, breathing tightly through her nose to calm herself, then said, "Well then, isn't it lucky that you don't have anything to say about it?"

That stopped him. Much as he hated to admit it, she was right. What possible right did he have to tell her how to live her life? But still, dressing as a man! He wanted to wring her long, slender neck.

The idea of having Jacob find her a man's outfit had come to Charli last night, just before she drifted off into a sleep so deep she'd swear she hadn't even twitched all night. In that last moment of semiconsciousness, an image, clear as springwater, popped into her mind—George Sand, the nineteenth-century female author, strolling around Paris in men's clothes and getting away with it. And that was in the 1830s, well before her new present.

"Besides," she said now to Trey, "I don't really see how you can complain. There are precedents, even in this backward time."

"What the devil does that mean?"

"George Sand did it."

"George Sand was also famous—or I should say notorious—for her torrid love affairs."

"True. But who wouldn't swoon over Chopin's music. And from the pictures I've seen of him, he was some dish."

"And," he added, "she wrote execrable novels."

She grinned. "They were pretty awful, weren't they? And so many of them, too! I guess even notoriety and industriousness together aren't enough to guarantee true literary talent." She raised her right hand. "I hereby promise never to dip a plume in an inkwell and pen an execrable novel."

He had to laugh. The woman had a delightful sense of humor that matched his own.

She gave him a sly grin. "But there's more," she said.

"What do you mean?"

"A little birdie told me that the infamous Lola Montez—and even I've heard of her—walked around New Orleans in men's clothes not five years ago, and that you, Mr. Lavande, were one of her favorite escorts when she did it."

One of his dark eyebrows shot up. "My mother has never known when to hold her tongue. Lola's a minx, and even more notorious, I imagine, than George Sand. Is that the sort of reputation you want for yourself?"

"Why not?" The answer took him aback. She really didn't seem to care what people thought of her any more than the outrageous Lola had done, and briefly he wondered why that fact bothered him so much. He hadn't given a whit with Lola. In fact, he'd enjoyed squiring her about and, if truth be told, had even goaded her into one or two of her more outrageous stunts.

"You really don't care?"

"No. Even if I planned to hang around this century for long, which I don't, I gave up worrying about what people thought or said about me a long time ago. I decided it's really only important what I think of myself." She carefully wiped her mouth on a snowy linen napkin and got up from the table. "Though I must admit I was furious when you thought I was some cheap hooker."

Trey cleared his throat. "I believe, Miss Stewart, that I may owe you an apology."

"May?" She raised one eyebrow.

"Very well, I do owe you one, and I hereby tender it. I should have known that you were not, well, not suited to my mother's house."

"Actually, I'm very well suited to it, as it turns out," she said with a grin. "Just not in the capacity you expected."

"Quite."

"Apology noted and accepted," she said, feeling inordinately pleased that he had made it, and with such unexpected grace.

Trey watched her shrug gracefully into a chocolate brown cutaway coat. Whoever Jacob borrowed the clothes from had good taste.

"Though you must admit," he said, "that you didn't seem to mind when I brought you here. What was I to think?"

Megan Daniel

"Well, how was I supposed to know it was a brothel? It doesn't look like one," she said, gesturing to the light and airy room with its elegant furnishings in perfect taste.

"And just exactly what does one look like?"

"Oh, you know, like something out of a Victoria's Secret catalog, with a lot of red and paisley and things like flocked wallpaper. And heavy, dark furniture everywhere, settees draped with shawls, Chinese urns full of peacock feathers. Marble statues of lovers in sexy poses and paintings of naked ladies. Claw-foot tables with red glass lamps and potted palms in the corners and fringe and tassels hanging all over the place."

"Sounds ghastly," he said.

"God-awful," she agreed. "They are definitely not supposed to look like something out of a slightly dated back-issue of *Architectural Digest*."

She stepped to the mirror that hung over the fireplace and began knotting the rust silk cravat that had been hanging loose at her neck. By the third try, she was *hummpphing* audibly.

"Here," he said, rising to go to her. "You'll have it looking like a cleaning rag in a minute." He reached out and began expertly wrapping and knotting the silk.

"Well, how am I supposed to know how to tie a cravat or an ascot or whatever this thing's called? My father's Windsor knot was the most I ever had to manage before, and that was years ago." When he was finished, he stood back and looked her over. What he saw made him draw a very deep breath. Last night, in that green silk gown, she'd been the most desirable woman he'd ever seen. Today, seeing her in tight-fitting breeches and a cutaway coat, he was afraid he was going to lose all control and take her right there on his mother's breakfast table.

"You need a hat," he said in a rough voice.

"I've heard that before. Doesn't anyone in this day and age ever go anywhere without a hat?"

"Never. It would be most improper."

"Not even to bed?"

He grinned. "I could arrange for you to discover that for yourself."

"I just bet you could," she said, returning his smile, "but I think I'll take your word for it."

Jacob was sent to find a hat from one of the coachmen or grooms, and soon Charli was setting a high-crowned brushed beaver on top of her curls in front of the hall mirror. "In my time, a hat is a fashion statement, not a badge of propriety," she grumbled.

"You keep saying things like that. Do you still hope to convince me that you're actually from the future?"

"You mean you still don't believe me? After all the things I showed you from my bag?"

"I'll admit you had some odd items, but it's just too preposterous. Who could believe such a thing?"

"I don't have any choice but to believe it. It's happening to me. And if I can believe it, I don't see why you can't."

"That is not a rational answer."

"This is not a rational situation!" she cried. "Besides, I hate reason. I always have. Too much like my mother." She reached down to her yellow bag, propped on the floor by a chair, and rustled around till she found a roll of candy, popped

135

one in her mouth, and held the roll out to him. "Lifesaver?"

"What on earth . . . ?" He took the brightly colored little package and examined it, fascinated by the metallic paper on the inside.

"Wintergreen," she said. "Try one."

He lifted one of the white candies with his thumb and popped it into his mouth. Yes, wintergreen. Quite sharp, but delicious. And such a cunning way to package candies.

Charli was already digging in her bag again. She pulled out a modern map of New Orleans. "Things have changed, of course, but I still have to find my way around and it'll be better than nothing." As an afterthought, she also took out the brochure with so many pictures of the modern city. "You coming?" she asked almost casually as she moved toward the door.

He grabbed his hat and followed her.

"I've got a great idea," she said. "You show me your New Orleans and I'll show you mine." She waved the brochure at him. "I'll show you what it's going to become."

Ahhhh! Charli thought as she took long strides down the banquette beside Trey. It felt so great to finally be able to walk the way she was used to, instead of mincing along with baby steps to avoid tripping on her hoop. As they turned into Chartres Street, she let her arms swing easily, her joints loose. For the first time since the night she'd jumped in the Mississippi, she felt truly comfortable. Jacob had even oiled her boots for her, and they were supple and soft again—no more blisters. He had also dyed them brown to match her outfit. Oh well, who really needed a pair of yellow cavalier boots, anyway?

Matching Trey stride for stride—a bit of a stretch with his long legs, but her pride demanded it—she breathed deeply. The air was rich with smells, both good and bad, but at least there were no diesel fumes to choke on. A milk wagon went past, the mule pulling it plodding steadily along and the brass-bound milk cans clattering. As they turned into Conti Street, they passed Arabs with gold rings in their ears, soldiers in uniform, street urchins in rags, and fine ladies in elegant gowns. A pair of Ursuline nuns glided past in their gray habits, their white headdresses nodding and their beads swinging. Actually, it wasn't all that different from Greenwich Village, Charli thought. Both neighborhoods seemed to have an ever-changing, never-boring street show going on.

Much to her surprise, she didn't seem to attract much attention on the street, despite her unconventional garb. In fact, she got fewer stares than she had simply by going about dressed as a lady without a hat. Could it be that they really thought she was a man?

It had never really occurred to her that they might. No one in New York would think she was anything other than a woman in this outfit. But when she thought about it, she supposed it made sense. After all, most of the people she passed had never seen a woman in pants and never expected to. When they saw someone in trousers and a well-cut coat with a perfectly tied cravat, they expected it to be a gentleman, so that was what they saw.

137

She grinned. This might turn out to be even more fun than she'd thought.

She felt so good, she thrust her arms out as if to embrace the world.

He chuckled. "Are all women from the future so unconventional?" he asked.

"Not to hear my mother tell it," she said, laughing too. "In fact, to her, any sign of eccentricity is considered right up there with devil worship." Then she added, "Let's just say I am not alone. There are lots of others like me—sisters under the skin—who make our own rules. Fortunately, it's a lot easier in the 1990s than it is in the 1850s. Though I suspect you'd be surprised how many women there are around here who would secretly like to emulate your Lola Montez, who would love to live the way I do in New York in my own time— by my own rules."

"And yet they do not walk the streets in trousers."

"Believe it or not, this outfit would be drop-dead fashionable in modern New York."

"It is fashionable in New Orleans. Just not for ladies. I take it you 'modern' women are all disciples of Mrs. Bloomer?"

"You can bet on it. She was a woman after my own heart. Only I would have taken it further than she did."

"You have," he said, looking her up and down.

"Yes, I have, haven't I?" Her voice was full of pride and joy in her freedom. "And why not? Look around you." She gestured to where two women in enormous hoops were gazing into a shop window across the street. "Would you want to have to go through your life stuffed, laced, and caged from the time you got out of bed in the morning until you got back into it at night?"

"No, but—"

"No buts. Of course you wouldn't. You'd refuse to put up with it for five minutes. Why should we be expected to?"

"And yet most women do."

"We'll get over it." She looked at the hooped and corseted women again. "It's ridiculous. They can't take a deep breath. They couldn't run if they had to. They could never defend themselves, fight back."

"Do women of the future often have to defend themselves?" he asked, with a patronizing smile that made her fume.

"Unfortunately, yes," she said, her mouth tight. She looked at the women again. "And we can," she added.

"Doesn't sound very pleasant."

"At least in the 1990s we have a choice about what we wear. We can wear spike heels or sneakers, a Madonna bustier or a T-shirt."

He stopped walking and looked at her. "I know you are speaking English, Miss Stewart, but sometimes I can't understand a word you say."

"I know," she said with a sigh. "I think I'm going to have to approach the past as though I were learning a foreign language."

"Indeed," he murmured. "You know, your bloomers never really caught on here in the South. Too Northern for our belles."

"You don't like Northerners?"

"On the contrary. I like them very much. I went to school in the North."

"Really? Where?"

139

Megan Daniel

"Yale."

She turned to him with an excited smile. "So did I!"

He stopped dead and stared at her, then he burst out laughing. "Really, Miss Stewart. You should be a minstrel comic instead of a singer. You have the most amusing notions."

"What did I say that was so funny?" She was genuinely confused.

"Yale. You went to Yale! No woman has ever graced those hallowed and stuffy halls. And none ever shall, I'm certain."

"Shows what you know," she answered. "I did go to Yale. Literature major, music minor. And graduated cum laude. Class of '87."

"1787? 1887?" he said, his face full of mocking laughter.

"1987, blockhead! Are you from Missouri?"

"You know I'm not. Why ask such a silly question?"

"Because it's called the 'Show Me State,' and I'm getting really bored with your unwillingness to entertain the possibility that I might be telling the truth here."

"But you make it so difficult. Just when I think that perhaps, as hard as it is to believe, you really have come from the future, you come out with something absolutely preposterous, like women at Yale. How can I possibly believe you?"

"So you don't believe that one, eh? Well, I can do lots better than that," she said. "Let's see." She thought a minute. "Okay, how about this? The current governor of Texas is a woman. I can prove that one, because I was reading a magazine on the plane that has an interview with her. It's in

140

my bag. Also the governor of Oregon is a woman. Until a few years ago, the prime minister of Great Britain was a woman. She served more than a decade."

"Really, Miss Stewart—" he began, but she raced on.

"The United States recently fought a war in Saudi Arabia and Iraq, and many of the soldiers and Air Force pilots were women. At least two were prisoners of war. Not so many years from your own time, Marie Curie will win the Nobel Prize in physics. And—"

"Enough!" he cried, holding up his hands in surrender. "I apologize for doubting you."

She could tell from his superior tone that he still didn't believe a word she said, that he was humoring her to shut her up, but she stopped. How could she expect a nineteenth-century macho man to get it? It would take time, probably a lot of time, to convince him. She wondered how much time she had here, how much time she would have with Trey Lavande, and for the first time she felt a slight reluctance to immediately go back to her cozy New York apartment and her clients and her karate classes and her ordered world.

"You still don't believe me," she said, wishing very hard that he did.

"No," he admitted, "but if I agree to at least entertain the possibility, can we enjoy the rest of our day?"

It would have to do for now. She nodded. "Agreed."

And he smiled. The guy really did have a killer smile, the kind that made you smile back whether you really felt like it or not. Without it, he was just another terrific-looking guy. But tack that grin on his face, and the voltage took off to A-bomb proportions, exploded before your eyes, and left you blinded and not caring that you were.

She shook her head, as if to clear it, and they set off again.

When they reached Chartres Street, Charli stopped to consult her map, but Trey was already turning left. "This way," he said.

"Where are we going?"

"To enjoy the best view in town."

She wanted to ask more, but he was grinning like a little boy with a secret and she didn't want to spoil it, so she simply followed him.

As they walked, Charli took in everything around her, noting details she had missed on her earlier forays, such as the sound made by iron wheels clacking on cobblestones or the song of a redbird singing in a nearby gum tree. Many of the people they passed on the street spoke French—New Orleans was still in many ways a French city—but she realized that it was slower, more musical than the language of Paris.

Just as they reached a large brick warehouse, a mule-drawn wagon pulled up and disappeared into it through gaping double doors.

"What's that?" she asked, gesturing toward the building.

"The icehouse."

"Ice?" she asked, surprised. "Where does it come from?"

"They bring it down from upriver. Didn't you know that? Sometimes from as far as Minneapolis. They cut it from the lakes up there. Then they pack it in straw and burlap to keep it from melting."

"Oh. Well, you won't need to bother in a few more years."

"Why not? Won't we use ice anymore?"

"Sure. But we make it ourselves. In my kitchen, I have a giant, double-door, avocado-green, frost-free, super-deluxe refrigerator with an icemaker. It runs on electricity. I can open the door any time, day or night, and pull out a few ice-cubes—or a frozen dinner, or a gallon of ice cream."

He shook his head. "That would be wonderful."

"Yeah," she said, thinking about it. "I guess it is. I sort of take it for granted. I take a lot of things for granted." She looked back at the icehouse they had just passed. "I won't anymore."

A couple more blocks and they were at Jackson Square, where local artists hung canvases for sale on the iron rail fence, just as they would do 135 years later. Trey headed straight for the cathedral. Inside, he approached a priest in a black cassock, spoke a few words, nodded, then herded Charli towards a small door. He looked at her. "Are you up to a bit of a climb?"

"Do I look like I'm not? This isn't one of your Victorian wilting flowers here, you know."

"I'm coming to realize that. Come on then."

They headed up a stairway, up and up and up some more. After four flights Charli wanted to stop and rest a minute, but she'd die before she'd ask him to. "Couldn't they put in an escalator?" she muttered, half to herself.

"A what?"

143

"A moving staircase. You just step on, grab hold, and up you go."

He gave her a skeptical grin. "Right." She kept following him. "They don't usually allow the public up here," he said, "but the monsignor is a friend of mine."

"But of course," she said, and kept climbing.

The staircase narrowed, and she was more than ever grateful not to be stuck in a four-foot-wide swaying skirt. A few minutes later they reached the steeple. Trey pushed open a shuttered window, and Charli was looking at blue sky.

"Don't lean out too far," he cautioned. "There's no railing."

She leaned one hand on the narrow windowsill, holding her hat on with the other to keep it from floating off in the brisk breeze, and looked down on the city. They weren't really all that high—particularly for someone who'd taken the high-speed elevator to the top of the World Trade Towers—but the cathedral was the highest building in 1858 New Orleans. It was like looking down at a toy town.

She gazed down on the top of Andrew Jackson's bronze head as he rode his horse atop its pedestal in the middle of Jackson Square. The trees were a juicy green in their new spring growth, the tulips and daffodils making colorful accents. She could see the lane of trees that marched down the middle of Canal Street, the domes and steeples of churches poking up above the houses, and beyond the levee, the riverboats lined up three deep at the wharves.

She smiled over her shoulder at Trey. "It's glorious."

"I thought you'd like it. Whenever I travel, I always try to get on top of the highest building I can find. It's the perfect way to get your bearings."

"So do I!" she exclaimed, delighted to find something they shared.

"I remember my first day in Paris," he said, "looking out over the rooftops and chimney pots from the north tower of Notre Dame. I'd never seen anything so beautiful."

She spun to face him, her face aglow with excitement. "And did you lean way out so you could get a good look down at the gargoyles?"

"Yes," he said. "Have you—"

"And then did you lie back on that slanted roof thing and look up at the sky?"

"Yes!" he said, smiling hugely now. "I see you've been to Paris, Miss Stewart."

"Yes," she said with a sigh. "And Notre Dame, at least, hasn't changed."

She turned back to the little window. He rested one hand on the sill beside her, leaning forward until his face was next to hers. As he pointed out the Cabildo, the Presbytère, and the sloping red roof of the French Market, she breathed in his warmth and his smell and his nearness.

"And over there, across the river, is Algiers," he was saying, but Charli was hardly listening. If she turned her head only a little, her lips would be right next to his.

But she didn't turn her head. She didn't have to; he did it for her. All it took was one finger, and then his lips were on hers.

This kiss was different from the one they'd shared in his mother's parlor, less fiery, less

145

demanding. But no less thrilling. It was a tender kiss, soft, gentle, his tongue barely brushing across her lips. A melting kiss, turning her mouth as soft and pliant as a ripe berry. A cherishing kiss, she thought, then almost laughed at her own imaginings. He didn't cherish her; he hardly knew her. And besides, she didn't want him to cherish her. She wouldn't be here long enough to cherish him back.

He chuckled, putting an end to such thoughts. "Perhaps we'd better cease and desist before someone looks up and sees me kissing a very fetching . . . young man. You may not care about your reputation, but I care about mine."

"Huh? Oh, right," she said, turning back to the view and seeing nothing. Boy, could this guy kiss! She tried to put her finger on just what it was about his lips that made them so special, then realized she didn't want to think about it too much. She just wanted to kiss them again.

But he was talking. "Tell me, lady from the future, what do you see when you look out at New Orleans?"

She took a deep breath and pulled herself back into one piece. She concentrated once more on the view. "Well, right over there," she said, pointing towards the southern corner of the square, "will be Jackson Brewery, which is not a brewery at all, though it used to be. Now it's full of boutiques and shops and cafes. I mean, it will be. I seem to be having trouble with my tenses here," she said with a laugh because what she was really having trouble with were her senses. They were still reeling. "Next to it will be the convention center." She looked at the brochure. "And, according to my sources, over there, at the end of Canal Street, is the Aquarium of the Americas, complete with, and I quote, 'an Amazon rainforest, a flock of black-footed penguins, several sharks, and a walk-through underwater view of the Caribbean.' Surely you can see it there."

"Of course. I think I can even hear the penguins squawking."

"Of course. It's because the sharks are eating them, one by one."

He laughed, and she realized she loved the sound of it, like the richest bass note on a well-tuned piano.

Except for that laughter and the sound of the wind, it was quiet up here. She looked out at the city again, enjoying its human scale, so unlike New York or any of the many modern cities she'd seen. She looked up at the sky, such a piercing blue, with no pall of the smog that shrouded most cities.

"It's funny about time, and progress," she said. "We've taken a lot of giant steps forward since your time, but I can see now that we've lost some things, too."

"Such as?"

"It's hard to describe. I guess it's a sense of balance, of proportion. We don't always remember what's important anymore. We've grown too greedy."

"Believe me, Miss Stewart, greed is nothing new." He moved to the next window and pushed it open. "Tell me what you see over here."

"The Superdome," she said.

"Superwhat?"

"Right over there. See?" She showed him a picture in her brochure that showed the giant stadium with its huge concrete dome. "Thousands of people will sit inside there and watch a bunch of burly guys knock each other down to get to a small leather ball shaped like a pointed egg."

Just as she had hoped, he laughed again. "And that's supposed to be progress?"

"I guess it's in the eye of the beholder."

She pointed out where the city's skyscrapers would be, showing him photos of them, described the cars and buses and trucks that would one day speed along the road on top of the levee, the giant freighters that would move cargo up the river.

"I wish I could show you New York from the top of the Empire State Building," she finally said. "It's incredible—Central Park, the Chrysler Building, the bridges on the East River, the Jersey Palisades. The view goes on forever."

"It must be very high."

"Well, it's not the tallest building in the city. It's just under a hundred stories, I think."

"A hundred—! Really, Miss Stewart, I've never met a woman with such a lively imagination."

"Oh, I can do better than that," she said in a dry voice. "Later, when I know you better, I'll tell you about penicillin and the space shuttle. I'll describe frozen yogurt and instant coffee. I'll even tell you about my computer."

As she said it, she tried to picture him sitting at a computer in a polo shirt and worn blue jeans and loafers with no socks, with his hair falling in his eyes as he crunched some numbers. Not a bad picture.

Even better, she could imagine him in a slouchy Giorgio Armani jacket, zipping around mountain roads behind the wheel of a red Ferrari. Or in black leather and sunglasses swinging one long leg over the seat of a motorcycle while she climbed on behind. Or even bungee-jumping! She hadn't had the nerve yet to try that one herself, but with Trey Lavande along she just might.

It surprised her to realize how much she would like to see him in her world, sharing her passion for jazz, strolling through the springtime streets of Greenwich Village, sleeping in the big white bed in her airy loft. . . .

And where the devil had that thought come from? Careful, Charli, she silently lectured herself. No point in getting carried away here.

This was not 1993; this was not New York; and this was certainly not the man of her dreams here. This was an autocratic, chauvinistic, uptight Victorian gentleman.

As they came back down the narrow stairway, she glanced back at him over her shoulder. With a sigh, she realized he was a man even her mother would approve of.

Chapter Twelve

They spent the rest of the day wandering through the French Market, eating anything and everything that looked edible and drinking about a gallon of coffee while exclaiming over this and that. Charli was upset by the sight of hobbled goats and sheep, tethered turkeys and ducks, all bound for imminent slaughter.

"Where did you think your last dinner came from?" Trey asked, amused by her reaction.

"From the supermarket," she muttered, "all nicely killed, cleaned, skinned, and wrapped in plastic wrap to make you forget it was ever once alive."

They bought lemons and coconuts, pineapples and pomegranates, then hired a small black boy to carry them to Lisette's house. There was no need to send the *gaufres*—the thin, sweet cookies still warm from the oven—because they were eaten as quickly as they were bought.

Later, they strolled through the streets of the Vieux Carré, talking endlessly and generally enjoying each other's company more than a little.

Charli found Bourbon Street totally charming. Without the tacky atmosphere of the '90s, with no flashing neon, no topless bars or clubs featuring female impersonators, and not a single T-shirt shop in sight, it was a lovely, lively street. She laughed at a hurdy-gurdy player, his box slung around his neck on a strap, squeaking out a pitiful triumphal march from *Aida* while his monkey begged for pennies from the small crowd that had gathered.

She described modern jazz clubs and laughed when Trey pointed out that Bourbon Street was already the heart and soul of the city's musical community, thanks to the opera house on the corner of Bourbon and Toulouse. Shop after shop owed its existence to the opera. There were costume shops and makeup shops, rooming houses with signs reading Singers And Stagehands Welcome. Music floated out many an open door and window: arias from *Il Trovatore, Don Pasquale, Lucia di Lammermoor*. And there were what seemed like dozens of restaurants and cafes catering to the opera workers.

Though it was only early afternoon, people—very ordinary-looking people of every class and color—were already lined up outside the big marble opera house to buy third- and fourth-tier tickets for a quarter.

When she heard a young boy walking along

whistling the overture to *William Tell,* Charli giggled and called "Hi-Ho Silver, Awaaaay!" Trey looked at her like she was crazy. "You hadda be there," she muttered, still chuckling.

At the corner of Bienville Street, they stepped into the Absinthe House, a dark, wood-paneled place, where Charli was the only woman—and she wouldn't have been allowed inside had anyone looked closely enough to see that she was not quite what she seemed. She choked down a tiny glass of the powerful, green, anise-flavored liqueur and they left.

A little while later, Charli was astonished when they walked past Antoine's. She peered in the window of the famous restaurant.

"Now this has hardly changed at all," she said. "Would you believe a restaurant could last 150 years? But I've eaten in Antoine's. Last year—1992, I mean. The Oysters Rockefeller are to die for."

"A quaint expression," Trey said dryly, "but descriptive. And though I've not eaten that particular dish, I can vouch for the fact that the *vol-au-vents* and the *langues du chat* are definitely 'to die for.'"

"*Langues du chat?* You ate cat's tongues?"

"They are cakes, as light and delicate as heaven." He kissed his fingers as he said it.

"Ooh la la," she teased, mimicking the gesture. "How very Parisian."

"Antoine's is as good as any restaurant I sampled in Paris, perhaps better. I will take you to dinner there one night."

"Will you really? I'd love that."

"If you promise to wear a gown."

"Oh, rats, you spoil all my fun."

"I think I can guarantee that you will enjoy yourself . . . even in a gown."

She smiled at him. "I'm sure of it."

As they turned into Royal Street, Trey had an idea. He turned to Charli.

"May I have your ring for a short while?"

"My ring?"

"Only for a few minutes."

"You tried to keep it the last time," she said with a suspicious frown.

"Miss Stewart, I don't claim to understand where you got that ring, but I no longer think you stole it, and I promise to give it back. Please, trust me."

She wanted to, badly. She looked up into his dark eyes and read sincerity there. She slipped the ring from her finger and handed it to him.

"Thank you."

"Where are you taking it?"

"Come with me and see."

He turned into an elegant shop, where a few discreet display cases held fine jewelry.

"Mr. Lavande," said the proprietor, a small, dapper man in a shiny black coat, as he came out from behind his counter to heartily shake Trey's hand. "How nice to see you again."

With a grin, Trey introduced Charli as "Mr. Stewart," and the jeweler shook her hand and said, "Welcome, sir."

She had to choke back a laugh. Trey held her ring out to the jeweler. "Mr. Blackstone," he asked, "is this the ring you made for me a few years ago?"

The jeweler took the ring, stepped behind the

counter to where a reflecting oil lamp burned, and picked up a magnifying glass. "Yes, of course, you designed it for the lovely Miss duClos," he said, studying the ring. "I'd know it anywhere. There is no other like it." He frowned. "But what have you done to it?" He looked up at Trey, then back at the ring. "If I didn't know better, I would swear this ring is quite old. It has the patina of age, as though it had been worn by several generations of hands. It is worn smooth in places."

Charli gave Trey a look of triumph as the jeweler went on. "Sir, you have destroyed my handiwork . . . or . . ." He rolled the ring in his hand, as though savoring its warmth. "I don't know what you've done to it, sir, or how, but it is even more beautiful than it was the day I made it. It has a spirit about it now, as though it had been imbued with the memories of the many people who have loved it."

"Thank you, Mr. Blackstone," said Trey, taking back the ring.

"If you could tell me—" began the jeweler.

"Another time, perhaps," Trey said as he went out the door with Charli right behind him, leaving the little jeweler completely puzzled.

"Now do you believe me?" she asked, taking the ring and putting it back on her finger.

He shook his head. "I don't know. I just don't know."

By the time they returned to Lisette's house, Charli was exhausted but happy. She couldn't remember when she had enjoyed a day more . . . or when she had enjoyed a man's company so much.

All the Time We Need

Trey was feeling pretty much the same, and he wasn't at all sure he liked it. This dark-haired, blue-eyed, outrageous female was starting to get under his skin. After seeing her to Lisette's house, he spent the next hour idly walking the streets, remembering everything she had said, everything they had done. Remembering the thickness of her eyelashes, the smell of her hair, the curve of her thigh in the revealing breeches. Remembering especially the softness and the taste of her mouth, and longing to taste it again. He was afraid he was becoming obsessed with the little minx.

And that was the last thing he needed right now. He had other things to concentrate on, particularly when his half-brother Laurence was falling deeper and deeper into debt and selling off pieces of Rive Douce at an accelerated clip. And later, when the time to become obsessed with a woman was right, she would be the right woman—someone who was an unassailable member of mainline New Orleans society, someone who could carry her husband along on the high tide of her perfect social acceptance and be the ideal hostess for the impressive plantation home that would soon be his. He had it planned down to the last detail.

In the meantime, he could manage perfectly well with the lovely Justine, with her café au lait skin and ebony hair and the unquestioned welcome of her bed.

Still, he couldn't remember when he had laughed more than he had today, when he had felt so completely relaxed in anyone's company, much less a woman's.

Nor could he remember ever wanting a woman more than he did that evening when he returned to his mother's house and watched her re-emerge into the back parlor, no longer a would-be young gentleman but every inch a woman, enticingly draped in wine-red velvet edged in black.

She took her place at the piano and commenced to entertain the eager customers.

But he didn't want her entertaining the customers, dammit. He wanted her entertaining him, in his own bedroom, in his own house, several blocks removed from every one of the men now ogling her as she sat so poised and lovely at the piano, singing shockingly suggestive songs—sometimes with the demureness of a nun, at other times with a roguish glint in her eye that made him want to carry her off at once and ravish her till sunrise and beyond.

Remy Sauvage, leaning on the piano with his ever-present cigar and his even more ever-present leer, was obviously entertaining similar thoughts. Trey wanted to smash the fellow's face in. But this was his mother's house, and he had her reputation to protect. So he watched in seething silence as Charli Stewart inflamed what seemed like half the male population of New Orleans, then sent them off upstairs for one of the other girls to quench the fire she'd set.

But there was no quenching Trey's fire. If he couldn't have her, he preferred to burn.

Charli enjoyed singing tonight even more than she had last night. Perhaps because Trey Lavande was present for the entire evening, and no longer lurking in the doorway but right up there next to the piano, watching her with eyes that made her skin feel like she was having hot flashes many years too early.

Whenever she took a break from the piano, he was there before any of the other men so eager to gain her attention, handing her a glass of champagne, walking her into the courtyard to cool off, shielding her from the pushier customers. She could have handled that task herself—she'd been doing it for years, after all—but she found it surprisingly pleasant not to have to, to hand the responsibility off to him. She even liked the air of possessiveness he wafted over her—and she hated herself for liking it.

This guy was getting under her skin in a way no man had ever done before, or at least not since she was seventeen and certain she would die if Clark Jensen didn't ask to be her escort to the deb ball. And Trey Lavande was better looking than Clark Jensen could ever hope to become.

So okay, there was chemistry. She couldn't deny it. But surely that was all it was. Wasn't it?

But why, then, when she sat down to play the final set of the night, did the emotion behind "I Loves you, Porgy," make the catch in her throat real rather than merely performed? Why did all the talk of love in "The Rose" make her stomach flutter? And why did "Misty" make her more than a little misty? She couldn't possibly be falling in love with the man. She hardly knew him!

Alarm bells and sirens went off in her head. Get a hold of yourself, Charlotte, she lectured herself. You are still in a very vulnerable position here. You've got to make your way in a totally foreign environment while you figure out how to get back home, and you can't afford to diffuse your focus mooning after a handsome face and body. Reestablish control. Now!

With a mighty struggle she did, but then she lost the battle again when he asked to escort her upstairs once she'd finally finished for the night. With the eyes of Remy Sauvage practically burning a hole in her back, she headed up the stairs on Trey's arm.

They passed Germaine on the stairs, returning to the parlor with a customer on her arm—clearly a well-satisfied one if the huge grin on his face was any indication. But the look on her face gave Charli pause. After a smile at Trey, she looked Charli up and down, quickly but thoroughly, and her expressive eyebrows went up in clear surprise. Then she was gone.

Why surprise? Charli wondered. Wasn't she Trey's usual type of woman? Was he known to like buxom blonde beauties such as Germaine? Or tall, porcelain-skinned types like Aimée? Or perhaps delicate redheads such as Dominique? Lisette's girls were gorgeous, every one, and Charli suddenly felt uncomfortably plain.

They reached the door of her room. She knew well enough that he wanted to follow her inside, all the way to her bed. She wanted it, too, but she knew she couldn't bring herself to make love to any man, not even Trey Lavande, in a whorehouse—for that's what Lisette's house was, no matter how elegant the trappings or how refined the employees and the customers.

As she turned to tell him good night, he raised his arms, backing her up against the closed door and trapping her with a hand on each side of her head. He leaned toward her, staring at her with such intensity that she was surprised the mahogany behind her didn't ignite.

"Trey," she began, but he didn't give her a chance to say more. His lips crushed hers in a kiss as hot and hungry as his gaze had been. She responded with equal intensity, her lips capturing his lips, her tongue encircling his tongue. Her arms went around his neck and held him close to keep him from changing his mind and pulling away.

But he clearly had no intention of changing his mind. One hand moved to the neckline of her velvet dress, so low-cut it presented very little barrier to his questing fingers. They stroked the skin there, tickled across her collarbone, caressed the tiny hollow at the base of her throat. Then they moved lower, reached past the black satin edging, and found their goal. In seconds, one perfect, round breast had been lifted free to rest in the palm of his hand while his thumb stroked insistently across the nipple that pebbled instantly under its pressure.

Oh God, she thought, how was it possible that his touch was even more electric than she had thought it would be? She felt like the neon signs lining modern-day Bourbon Street, pulsing and brilliant and buzzing as the electricity shot through her.

And still he kissed her, occasionally leaving her lips to explore the other planes of her face, her eyelids, her temples, the sensitive skin just below her ears. She let her head drop back against the door, grateful for its solidity, and gave herself up to the incredible sensations this man could elicit from her body.

159

His lips left hers again to trail down over her chin, her neck, her shoulder, heading, she knew, for that spot that was burning with need under his stroking thumb.

Far off, she heard a woman laugh, a deep, sultry sound, followed by an answering male chuckle. She opened her eyes to see Felicité crest the stairs and turn down the hall in the opposite direction. Remy Sauvage was right behind her, but instead of turning to follow her, he stopped, his eyes taking in the sight of Charli's bare breast under Trey's hand and her heavy-lidded eyes above Trey's head. She heard him chuckle again, an unpleasant sound, and he gave her a small mock salute before he finally turned after Felicité and disappeared inside her door.

The spell was broken. She grabbed Trey's collar and pulled his head away from where she really wanted it to stay. His hand left her breast, and that part of her suddenly felt icy cold and abandoned.

While he looked at her in confusion, her right hand fumbled behind her and found the doorknob. She opened it and almost fell into the room, regaining her balance just in time not to have him fall in with her.

"Good night, Trey," she managed to say. "Thank you for a lovely day."

He went on staring at her a moment, then he gave her a half-smile. "Good night, little nightingale," he said, his voice thick. "Sleep well—while you can."

But of course she didn't sleep well. She hardly slept at all.

Chapter Thirteen

By unspoken agreement, they met again the next morning, Trey walking in just as Charli was finishing her breakfast, well before the rest of the household was up.

"Good morning, Charlotte."

She was slightly taken aback at the name. No one but her mother called her Charlotte—she had always hated the name—but on Trey's lips it sounded elegant, musical even. In fact, it sounded altogether lovely.

"Good morning, Trey," she said, pouring him a cup of coffee and adding the precise amount of hot milk she had seen him add yesterday. "What wonders have you planned to show me today?"

When she saw the comically exaggerated leer on his face she had to laugh. "I meant New Orleans."

"Unfortunately, I knew exactly what you meant," he replied.

"So?"

"Do you ride?"

She smiled. "Only since I was seven."

He looked her over from head to foot. She was dressed in the same men's clothes she had on yesterday, the shirt freshly laundered and pressed, the coat perfectly brushed. "You'll want to change."

"Why would I want to do that?"

"Well, you can't very well sit sidesaddle in trousers."

"I can't sit sidesaddle in anything, and I don't intend to try. What a truly stupid idea that was. I'm amazed every woman who climbed up on a horse didn't break her neck."

"But you can't mean to ride astride!"

"Why not? As I said, I've been doing it since I was seven."

He shook his head. By this time, he knew he shouldn't be surprised by any outrageous thing she chose to do. He shuddered to think what she'd come up with next.

"I thought we'd ride out to the lake." He didn't add that he had planned a romantic picnic for two complete with large amounts of cold asparagus—said to be an aphrodisiac—and two bottles of champagne, after which he had planned to take her to one of the tidy little rooming houses facing the water and make love to her for hours and hours. But he couldn't very well lounge on the grass with his head in the lap of what everyone would think was a young man, nor kiss him/her under some shady tree, no matter how discreetly.

162

And he certainly couldn't take anyone in trousers into any bedroom, anywhere. Damn the witch, anyway!

"I'd love to see the lake," she exclaimed. "I've never been out there."

He sighed. "Let's go, then."

It was a hot day for early March, the sun beating down and the humidity inching up, but Charli thought the ride was glorious. It had been some time since she'd been on a horse, and she reveled in it.

Trey was surprised at how well she rode. He'd given her a good, lively horse, but he didn't expect her to hold her own when they reached an open stretch and raced the last mile to the lake.

They pulled up side by side just a few feet from the shore.

Charli breathed in the fresh air, cooler as it blew in off the lake. She let her eyes roam over the endless flat expanse of blue-gray, topped with tiny whitecaps.

The openness filled something in her she hadn't even known was empty. She suddenly realized her soul had been hungry for vistas, for space. In New York, most often when someone looked out the window they saw a brick wall. More than twenty feet was considered a view. True, she could see the Empire State Building and beyond from her apartment, but the feeling of being hemmed in by the city was never completely dissipated. But here she could see for miles and miles.

"This must be about where the causeway comes in," she said, pointing to the shore.

"Causeway?"

"Yeah, you know, like a bridge. Across the lake."

"A bridge? Charlotte, Lake Pontchartrain is more than twenty miles across. No bridge could span it."

"Well, it will, straight across from over there." She pointed toward where the opposite shore disappeared into the haze. "I haven't been on it myself, but I saw it from the air the other day."

"You saw it from the air," he repeated in a patronizing tone.

"Yes, as my plane was coming in to land. I guess that's another thing I'm going to have to explain to you, though I don't know why I should bother. It's just one more thing you won't believe."

He dropped the skeptical look and grew intent. "Do you really mean that people can fly?"

"Since 1912 or something like that." Seeing that he was really listening this time, she gave an excited smile. "Think about it, Trey. When you went to Paris, you had to go on a boat. It must have taken ages."

"Four weeks," he said.

"God, how awful. A few months ago I went to London on the Concorde. That's an airplane that flies faster than the speed of sound. The trip took about four-and-a-half hours."

"Four-and-a-half . . . !" Slowly, he shook his head. "Incredible."

"I went for a long weekend and was back at work on Tuesday morning."

He looked surprised at that, then said, "At work? Yes, I suppose as a spinster, you do have to work for a living in New York, just as you do here."

"Spinster!" she exclaimed. "That's the most old-fashioned, not to say insulting, word I've heard from you yet."

All the Time We Need

"I'm sorry, I meant no offense. But you must be at least twenty-six?"

"Twenty-seven," she corrected, "which in my time is a long way from being a hopeless old maid. Lots of women I know don't marry until well into their thirties, or have kids until their forties. Some of us might never take the plunge— either one."

"But what else can a woman do if she doesn't marry?"

"Anything we want. Dig ditches. Design bridges. Do surgery. Type letters and edit books and run for office. The same sorts of things we do when we do choose to marry. If I ever marry, I will certainly keep running my business."

"I imagine your husband will have something to say about that," he said dryly.

"Very little, actually," she said just as dryly.

"I take you are a suffragist, Miss Stewart."

"Thank God I don't have to be. We won that particular battle over seventy years ago. As they say in the commercial, 'We've come a long way, baby,' though not as far as some of us would like."

As they turned their horses away from the lake, he gazed at her with new interest. "Tell me about your work."

She could see that he was really interested, no longer simply patronizing her. And so, as they rode along the shore of Lake Pontchartrain, as the breeze riffled their hair and the birds swooped and squawked nearby, Charli told Trey things about the modern world and the modern women in it, about New York, about her own work, about jazz.

Megan Daniel

By the time they headed back toward town, she almost thought he was starting to believe her—and maybe even believe in her.

Again, it had been a delightful day, and again, Trey was there to hear Charli sing at his mother's house that night as well as—she couldn't escape the conclusion—to keep watch on her. He was the most effective bodyguard she could ever have hoped for in such a place.

And when the evening was over, he once more moved to escort her up the stairs. But this time she stopped him.

"Why not?" he asked when she shook her head at the foot of the stairs, his eyes smoldering with the power of his desire for her.

"Not yet, Trey," she said gently, one hand resting lightly on his chest. She looked around Lisette's front hall. "And not here. This—you—it's all too much, too fast. I feel like my head hasn't caught up with the rest of my body, either in time or in space. Maybe I never will. Maybe I'll just go *poof!* and find myself back in modern New York."

"Don't say that!" he exclaimed, surprising himself as much as her with his vehemence.

She just shook her head, not saying anything because, inexplicably, the thought of disappearing out of a world with Trey Lavande in it made her feel like crying. She turned to go.

"I'll see you in the morning," he said before he left, and that knowledge brought back a smile as she walked up the stairs.

Charli awoke the next morning infused with a sense of elation and expectation she couldn't remember feeling for years. And all because she knew that she would once again spend the day with Trey Lavande.

It was a little scary, this feeling, and she didn't know where it was going, where it could go, but she had decided that for now, she wouldn't worry about that. She would just enjoy it.

She dressed once again in her men's clothes, though she knew he would rather she wore a dress. But she had to have these few hours of physical freedom every day. Her body and spirit both demanded it.

"Where are we going?" she asked him as they headed down the street. Not that she really cared where they were going. She was simply happy to follow him wherever he went.

"I need to check in with my business office," he said. "I haven't been there in four days. Do you mind?"

"Not at all. I haven't got any schedule. Why haven't you been to work in four days?"

He glanced at her with a dry smile. "I was otherwise engaged."

"Oh," she said, feeling guilty when she realized it was she that had kept him from his work. "What do you do?"

"Do?"

"For a living. Your business." She laughed. "You know, it's amazing that I've known you as long as I have and not asked that yet. Back home it's practically the first question anyone asks."

"Your world sounds remarkably rude."

"Not really. We're just direct."

He grinned. "Just Northern." She shrugged.

Megan Daniel

Just then they reached the levee, and Charli stopped to take in the scene spread out before her. Dozens of huge white steamboats, their smokestacks jutting like a forest of soot-covered tree stumps reaching for the sky, were tied up three- and four-deep along the long plank wharves. Their white paint glittered in the morning sun; names like *Red River*, *The Gypsy*, *Grand Turk*, and *Morgan's Return* were picked out in bright paint across the upper decks and on the wheel housings, many of which were also painted with elaborate scenes—landscapes and beautiful women and scenes from melodramas.

Winches hauled up cargo nets strung from the forward derricks on many of the boats. Drays and heavy vans criss-crossed the area, spewing out goods to go upriver or taking on those that had just come down. Hundreds of burly black stevedores, their chests stripped bare, loaded and unloaded the boats, hefting bales of cotton, tobacco, and grain, barrels of cane syrup, rum, gunpowder, and nails, bunches of bananas, bolts of fabric, crates of everything imaginable. Peddlers peddled and beggars begged. Women sold bowls of gumbo; a medicine man pitched his snake oil.

Before she could get her fill of the sight, Trey headed off along the top of the levee, and she had to rush to catch up. In a few minutes they came to a red brick warehouse with "Lavande & Co." painted across the side in large letters. She followed him inside.

"This is yours?" she said as they strode through a cavernous space piled high with goods of all sorts.

"Yes," he said, and grinned down at her. "This is what I do, or at least a part of it. When I'm finished here, I'll show you the rest . . . the best part."

"Mr. Lavande, sir!" said a young man who came running down an open stairway from what looked like the office area.

"Hello, Johnny." With a grin, he gestured to Charli. "I'd like you to meet Charli Stewart. Charli, this is John Johnson, one of my assistants."

"How do you do, sir," said the young man, shaking Charli's hand, before immediately turning back to Trey. "Sir, Mr. Prideaux, he's been looking all over for you. Says he's got a real important message for you."

While Trey and John Johnson conferred a moment, Charli looked around. Among the mysterious boxes and barrels that might hold anything in the world, she could make out a keg of nails and a pile of furs, crated French furniture, fine English china, Spanish sherry, and German Riesling.

Finally, Johnny said, "Yes, sir, I'll send him over as soon as he gets back."

Trey took Charli's elbow, realized that his assistant was staring at him, and dropped it as though it had burned his hand. "This way," he said brusquely.

"Where are we going now?" she asked.

"Now I'm going to show you what I really do."

He led her back out onto the street and threaded a path through the throngs milling about on the docks—loading and unloading, moving, weighing, hustling, buying and selling, stealing and looking to steal. They went past several of the huge white wedding-cake boats until they came to one of the grandest. *Corinne,* read the name painted across it in gleaming red letters. He strode up the gangway and Charli followed.

She realized almost at once that she had been on this boat before. It was from this very deck that Trey Lavande had fished her out of the river and saved her life.

"Is this a not-so-subtle way of reminding me that I owe you my life?" she asked.

He looked taken aback. "Not at all. You asked me about my business. I wanted to show you my pride and joy."

She gazed around, appreciating in daylight the full magnificence that had been lost on her in the dark and in her bedraggled and befuddled state. "You mean this is yours?"

He beamed. "Yes." He reached out and lovingly ran a hand over a shiny brass handrail. "She got in last night, and she'll be heading out again this afternoon. She's my newest and finest—the pride of the Lavande river fleet."

"Fleet?" she said. "You mean you've got more of them?"

"More boats, you mean? Yes, I own twelve at present. Of course, most of them are much smaller than the *Corinne,* good solid working boats for hauling goods, mostly, although three or four also carry passengers. Would you like to look around?"

"Absolutely," she agreed with enthusiasm, peeking excitedly along the gingerbread-edged deck. Some crew members were at work here and there—burly sailors loading wood, mulatto maids readying the staterooms, porters scurrying about on unknown tasks. But the boat was mostly empty, giving it an almost eerie feeling.

Watching the man show off his lovely boat, Charli could see what the boy had been like. He took an engaging, childlike delight in every detail, from the elaborate scrollwork on the Texas deck to the power of the eight huge furnaces on the boiler deck. He showed her the staterooms, sumptuously yet tastefully appointed, each one with a painting on its door—there seemed to be a special liking for meadows and streams populated by fawns and other big-eyed forest creatures. They went down a corridor lit by prism-fringed chandeliers, and through a saloon draped in wine-red velvet and punctuated by shards of colored light filtering in through stained-glass windows. Along one side ran a bar that must have been thirty yards long and was polished to within an inch of its mahogany life.

He told her the staterooms featured the finest feather beds available. "In the dining room," he claimed, "the food rivals any served at Antoine's."

But his greatest pride and his biggest grin was saved for the ballroom. He ushered her in with a flourish. This was the room where, on that fateful night, Charli had seen couples in what she then thought were Mardi Gras costumes waltzing beneath the glittering chandeliers. Now, totally empty, it looked even larger than it had then. The expanse of highly polished floor glowed warmly in the sunshine that filtered through French doors along the sides. Gilt-edged mirrors graced the spaces between the windows. As they strode down the length of the empty room, their boot heels echoed on the parquet floor.

Charli made a beeline for the most beautiful white grand piano she'd ever seen. Another

171

Bechstein! The man certainly had taste, and obviously the money to support it. The piano's pristine paint glowed. She lifted the keyboard cover and played a chord. The tone was perfect.

"May I?" she asked, gesturing at the instrument.

"Of course," he answered, and she sat. She fingered a few chords, riffled her fingers up and down, then began playing a Chopin waltz. Surprisingly, she heard him humming along.

"You like Chopin?" she asked.

"Very much," he said. "And you play it well," he added, sounding surprised. Then his handsome face broke into a grin. "But then I shouldn't be surprised that an emulator of the infamous George Sand should be a fan of the romantic Pole." .

Charli laughed. "A fan, yes, but I've no intention of getting involved in a torrid love affair with him, like she did."

"That's a good thing, since he's dead."

"Is he? Poor George." She played a moment more. "I do adore his music, especially the waltzes."

"But it is going to waste," he said with a small frown. Then he held out his hand to her. "Shall we?" He began humming the tune more loudly. She put her hand in his, he pulled her to her feet, and they began circling the room in a graceful, sweeping waltz.

She grinned up at him. "Fred and Ginger as I live and breathe," she said, then looking down at her clothes, she added, "or maybe it's Fred and Fred." She laughed, but when she looked at him again, the laugh died. He was looking into her eyes with such intensity that she forgot about her clothes, forgot about Chopin and George Sand, forgot everything except him, the look in his eyes, the feel of his hand on her back, the rhythm of their steps, the soft humming of his melodious voice.

Around and around the huge ballroom they circled, their eyes still locked. He was tall and she was not, but she still seemed to fit perfectly into the circle of his arm, her head tilted back to look up at him. Her hat fell off and rolled under the piano; she reached up and plucked his off and sent it sailing across the room to join its mate. The air between them seemed to grow warmer and thicker, like there wasn't enough of it. Charli was having trouble breathing—and with no corset to blame. He pulled her closer, spun her faster. She grew dizzy, but she couldn't tell if it was from the dance or from the look in his eyes.

He looked hungry. And she was uncomfortably aware that she must look exactly the same way. She wanted this man. Oh, how she wanted him!

Suddenly he stopped dancing. He stopped moving. She thought for a minute he stopped breathing. She had. Then slowly, from so far above her, his beautifully carved lips, topped by that beautifully soft mustache, came down to meet hers, and ignited as they touched.

From soft and inviting, his mouth immediately became insistent, demanding a response she was eager and willing to give. His lips opened; his tongue commanded hers to do the same. When she complied, he ravaged her mouth, leaving no corner unconquered. His arms closed around her, his hands pressing on her back then sliding up under the tails of her coat. Fingers splayed, his thumbs moved forward to tease the bottom curve of her breasts. Then higher. Her nipples strained at the silk of her shirt, aching for the touch of his fingers. At last, he complied. The soft pads of his thumbs reached up, found that ache, and turned it into a flame that shot all the way through her. And all the while his mouth plundered hers in a kiss more powerful than any she'd ever known.

A moan she hadn't intended but had no power to contain came from her. Involuntarily, her arms snaked up around his neck, twining in his black hair, pressing him closer, closer. . . .

"Trey, thank God! I've been looking all over—" A voice broke their reverie, pulled them apart, then stopped short. Through a haze that took a moment to clear, Charli saw a young man with café au lait skin standing a few feet from them. He was good-looking, well-dressed, and obviously extremely embarrassed. "Excuse me, I, uh . . . if you . . . I don't . . . excuse me." He turned to go.

"Robert!" Trey exclaimed, stopping the young man's exit. "Allow me to present Charli Stewart," he said to the fellow's back. "*Miss* Charli Stewart." With that the young man spun around, his mouth open, his eyes popping. And his face wreathed in very obvious relief. "This is Robert Prideaux, my manager and general factotum," Trey added.

Charli had to laugh at the young man's expression as he took in her clothes. "I'd explain, but you wouldn't believe it," she said as she offered him her hand. "How do you do?"

He stammered a response and Trey asked, "What's so important that you've been chasing all over town after me yourself instead of sending Johnny or one of the boys?"

Robert Prideaux found his voice again. "It's Laurence," he said simply.

Trey's hand, still resting lightly about Charli's waist, tensed instantly. "What?" he said softly, his voice like steel.

"Today's auction. Twenty lots at least. I found out this morning."

Trey dropped his arms. "Good. I'll be there."

"I thought you would." He turned to Charli, tipped his hat, and gave her a small bow. "Miss Stewart," he said, then he turned and strode out.

"What was that all about?" she asked when he was gone.

"Just some business I have to take care of." He pulled a gold watch from his vest pocket, flipped open the lid, and glanced at it. "I'll have to go at once, I'm afraid."

"Can I come?" she asked. She couldn't bear the thought of watching him walk away from her just now.

He looked her up and down with a smile that had her cursing Robert Prideaux's interruption. Then he turned, retrieved her hat, and placed it on her head, giving it a gentle pat. "Yes, but only if you keep your hat on and your mouth shut."

She gave him a little mock salute. "Aye, aye, Captain."

"And only if you promise to slap my hand away if I forget where we are and touch you the way I want to touch you."

175

She grinned. "On that score I make no promises."

He grabbed her by the shoulders, kissed her fast and hard, and pushed her away. Then he groaned and said, "Let's go."

Chapter Fourteen

They left the boat and headed back into the French Quarter.

Trey ushered Charli through the streets, his stride long and determined, obviously impatient to reach his destination. As the cathedral bells chimed noon, he picked up the pace even more.

"Hey," she said, hurrying to keep up, "where's the fire?"

"We're late."

"For what?" she asked, but he didn't answer. He just turned into an alley where three-story buildings lined the narrow passage. From the open windows of the upper floors, Charli heard the clink and clash of what sounded like swordplay, followed by bellowed instructions of "riposte," and "parry," and "en garde."

At the end of the alley, they emerged in front of a

huge building that stretched the entire block from
Royal to Chartres Street—the St. Louis Hotel.
She'd noticed it before on her solitary wanderings
about the city.

They entered through the main columned entrance and went directly to one of the most beautiful spaces Charli had ever seen. It was a rotun-
da, its dome some ninety feet high, she guessed.
Frescoes of gods, nymphs, and animals cavorted
around its inner surface, while men and women
milled about on the marble floor below. In the
center of the circular room, a man stepped up to
a podium and pounded a gavel, wood on wood,
with a resounding crack.

"What's going on?" Charli asked under her
breath as the room grew quiet.

"An auction," Trey responded, his voice tight.
She looked up at him. His teeth were clenched,
his square jaw firmer than ever. He looked angry,
or at least extremely determined, though she had
no idea why.

"Gentlemen, ladies," called the auctioneer,
"may I have your attention, please? The sale
is about to begin." He cracked his gavel again.
"First lot," he called, and an assistant carried a
small cherrywood side table to the front of the
podium. Even from a distance, Charli could see
that, though finely made, the piece was in need
of repair. One leg was badly scratched, and the
drawer pull was missing entirely. "From Rive
Douce," the auctioneer went on, "a fine French
table, excellent craftsmanship. I will open at five
dollars."

Immediately, Trey raised his gold-headed cane
an inch, signaling his bid, and the process began.

At every bid from anyone else, Trey moved the cane again, until the table was finally knocked down to him at thirty dollars. She couldn't help but wonder why he wanted it.

The next lot up was another table, similar in design but much finer, and in perfect condition, a piece Charli knew her mother would have killed to show off in her Park Avenue living room. Mirroring the higher quality, the bidding began at fifteen dollars. Charli expected Trey to try for the piece, but he stood still, absolutely still, like an animal waiting to strike. The exquisite little table sold to someone else for twenty-five dollars.

"Why didn't you bid on it?" she finally asked him. "It's much finer than the one you bought, and went for less."

"It isn't mine," he said softly, an answer that made no sense, but before she could ask him to explain, he was lifting his cane again, bidding on a case of wine.

On it went like that for nearly an hour. Trey bid with absolute ruthlessness on some pieces while exhibiting no interest whatever in other, finer offerings. In some cases, he kept on bidding well past what even Charli could tell was a ridiculous price for the merchandise in question. In others, he was practically the only bidder.

There seemed no pattern to his purchases. He bought dishes, bolts of silk, a bad English painting and a very good French one, a tarnished silver epergne, an enormous chandelier that was missing several prisms, even a plow and fourteen kegs of nails. Whenever Charli tried to ask him what he was doing, he answered in monosyllables or not at all. Every bit of his concentration was focused on the auctioneer at the podium.

But there was a pattern to his purchasing, she discovered. By paying close attention, she came to realize that each and every item Trey bid on—and kept bidding on until he got it, no matter the cost—was preceded by the words "From Rive Douce." She also noticed that a young man across the room was glaring at Trey with what could only be called a look of loathing. He was shorter and stockier than Trey, with pale hair and eyes and soft-looking muscles, but there was a resemblance between the two men. Despite his mutton-chop whiskers and dandified dress, something in the cut of the chin, the tilt of the eyes, made her see Trey in his face. Charli saw the man run his fingers through his hair in a gesture identical to one she'd seen Trey use just this morning.

And every time the auctioneer called out "From Rive Douce," the blond man's gaze bored harder into Trey, his blue eyes glistening with hatred. And when Trey looked back, it was with a face of triumph. Unmistakable triumph.

The large volume of goods to be sold had been piled in an untidy heap at one side of the room. But now, as that pile slowly diminished, it was to reveal a sight that at first puzzled Charli and then made her ill. She very nearly gagged when she realized what she was looking at.

At the side of the room, behind a low, wooden barrier, some dozen or more blacks—the women in cotton dresses with *tignons* tied around their heads, the men stripped to the waist—waited to be sold to the highest bidder. They were about to auction off slaves! Even as she realized it, the first man, a huge black with a scar across his chest and his feet chained together, was yanked forward. A red-faced man in a planter's hat stepped up and forced the man's mouth open to inspect his teeth.

"I can't watch this," Charli said, pulling on Trey's arm. "Let's go."

"Not yet," he said, unmoving. She pulled again, but she might as well have been trying to move a giant sequoia.

"How can you stand this?" she asked. She heard the auctioneer listing the attributes of the big black on the block, and she really was afraid she was going to throw up. "I've got to get out of here. Now!" She turned and began to push her way through the crowd.

When she heard the auctioneer call, "Sold for five hundred dollars," her stomach roiled. She was frantic for fresh air. But just as she reached the door, she heard him say "From Rive Douce," and she stopped suddenly. Surely, Trey wouldn't . . . he couldn't . . . ! She had to know.

Near the door was a marble bench. She jumped up on it to see over the heads of the crowd.

She was just in time to see Trey Lavande lift his gold-headed cane and give a small nod. Her eyes flew to the podium. Beside the auctioneer stood a girl, no more than thirteen or fourteen, Charli guessed. She was pretty in a weary sort of way, and she looked extremely frightened. The ends of her *tignon* bobbed with her trembling, and her hands gripped each other tightly. Charli couldn't stand to stay and watch Trey buy a slave, but she couldn't bring herself to leave.

In minutes it was over. He had bought the trembling girl for 365 dollars. Just before she moved, Charli saw the blond man who looked like Trey storm out in the opposite direction. With her stomach seriously threatening to do her in, she bolted for the door.

On the street, she leaned one hand against the building for support and took in huge gulps of cool air, willing herself not to throw up. When she was sure her breakfast would stay down, she looked up. There were people everywhere on the streets, fully a third of them black. Was every one of them a slave? Might any one of them find himself on that block in there, not knowing where he would end up, in whose hands, doing what? At the absolute mercy of whoever had the price of his body? It was disgusting.

Suddenly, Charli wanted very badly to go home to New York, to her loft and her clients, to 1993.

She felt his hand on her shoulder before she saw him. "Are you all right?"

She jerked away from his hand. "You bought her. You actually bought another human being!"

"If I hadn't, someone else would have."

"That is the oldest cop-out in the world."

"But true for all that. The girl is a slave. I didn't create the system; I don't even like it. But it is the system nonetheless."

"And it stinks!"

"Anyone else who bought her might not have been as kind a master as I will be." He took her shoulder again and steered her through the traffic thronging the street.

"That's not why you bought her," said Charli, struggling out of his grasp again but not stopping. "You bought her because she was from Rive Douce."

His face turned to stone. "She was Laurence's. Now she is mine."

She reached the opposite banquette and stopped, turning to him. "Who's Laurence?" She remembered the blond man.

"You look like you could use a drink. I know I need one," he said, avoiding her question and pushing her through the door of a nearby bar. They headed for a marble-topped table in a shadowed corner. "They're not likely to have any drinks suitable for a lady here."

"Are they likely to have a shot of good Kentucky bourbon?" she asked.

"Of course."

"Good, because at the moment that will be eminently suitable for this lady." He stepped up to the bar to place their order, and she reached for a chair. To tell the truth, she was glad to sit down. Her knees were still shaking. Beyond the window, an old black man passed by, bent under a heavy load of something in a basket. Trey returned and sat opposite her. "Robert, the man I met on the boat," she said, "is he another one of your slaves?"

"Don't be ridiculous! Robert is my manager. He's from one of the oldest families in New Orleans. He's a *gen du couleur libre.*"

"A free man of color," she translated. "What a quaint expression. It almost sounds politically correct."

"Look," he said, running his fingers through his hair with the exact same gesture she'd seen the blond man use inside. "I didn't make the rules."

"So you said." He was right, of course. He hadn't made the rules. And what right, really, did she have to judge him? She knew so little about this

183

society, this world she'd been plunged into, while he knew nothing else. He had grown up in a world where slavery was the norm, totally accepted, taken for granted, even. "It's almost over, you know," she said softly, "and thank God for it."

"What is?"

"Slavery. A few more years, less than a decade, in fact. And all it will take to end it is one of the bloodiest wars the world has ever known."

"War? Impossible. We're not that stupid."

"Oh yes we are." She looked back at him. "And we're going to go on being just that stupid for at least the next 135 years. You'd be amazed at the ingenious ways we will think up to kill each other, and the stupid reasons we'll do it over."

A waiter arrived with their drinks. He did a double-take when he got a good look at Charli, recognizing the femininity beneath the clothes. Clearly he was about to protest at serving her, but when he got a look at the potential thunder in Trey's face, he thought better of it and backed off with a shrug.

Charli's stomach was feeling better enough that she was actually glad for the burning sensation as the bourbon slid past her throat and hit bottom. Finally, she put down the glass, placed her hands flat on the table, and asked again, "Who is Laurence, and what is Rive Douce?"

He didn't say anything for a moment. Instead, he lifted his drink, also bourbon, downed it in one gulp, and signaled the waiter for another. Then he looked at her. "Laurence is my brother." He took a deep breath. "My half-brother. And Rive Douce is the plantation that should have been mine."

*   *   *

It took her two hours and several more drinks on his part for Charli to get the rest of the story. Even then, much of it she had to surmise, filling in the details with her imagination. Trey would give only the barest facts.

He was the bastard son—the eldest son— of Arthur Campbell, a wealthy planter with a sugarcane plantation upriver—Rive Douce. After Trey's birth, his father had given Lisette, his mistress, a large sum of money. Against Arthur's wishes, she'd used it to create the finest "house of comfort" in New Orleans, available only to the richest planters, the most successful business-men, so good she could ask 150 dollars for her girls and get it.

Arthur Campbell still came for free. He visited often; he was very much a presence in his son's life. He saw that Trey was well-clothed, well-fed, well-educated. He sent him to Yale and then to Europe on a grand tour. He even loved Trey in his own limited way. But never did he let Trey forget that he was not a Campbell.

Only once in all his growing up years was Trey allowed to see Rive Douce. It had been the summer he turned fourteen. While the fami-ly—the "legitimate" family—was summering in Saratoga, Arthur had brought his bastard son home to ride the cane fields, stroll through the rooms of the plantation house, and see the *garconnière* where the young bachelors of the family lived until they married. Trey had seen the room where Laurence Campbell, Arthur's legitimate son, lived—the rows of toy soldiers, the shelves of books, the outgrown hobbyhorse.

185

Megan Daniel

He had stared at a portrait of Leticia Campbell,
his father's wife, in a demure ruffled gown with
an ivory fan hanging at her wrist. He had walked
between the rows of slave cottages, watched by
hundreds of eyes that couldn't help but notice
his astonishing likeness to "the Massa." Indeed,
no one could look at Trey Lavande and not know
instantly whose son he was.

He had wanted it all. It was the life he should
have been born to, the life he had a right to. And
it could never be his.

But now it could. Arthur Campbell was dead,
taken by the yellow fever three years ago, and
Laurence Campbell was throwing it all away. His
penchant for gambling and pretty women was
costing him Rive Douce. Four times in the last
year he'd been forced to sell off pieces of his
heritage in an attempt to hold on to the land
itself. And each time, Trey had bought every single item he sold. He planned to keep on doing
it until he had it all—every spoon and snuffbox,
every piece of furniture, every slave, every acre.
Rive Douce.

Charli looked at the gorgeous man she'd been
fantasizing about for days and saw a hurt little
boy, and she ached for him. When he spoke of
his father and Rive Douce, it was as though he
were peeking into the window of a candy shop
at all the goodies he couldn't have. But she also
saw the ruthlessness that would lead him to buy
up every last stick and stone of his half-brother's
inheritance, if it took his last penny to do it.

"Why not buy your own plantation?"

"It wouldn't be Rive Douce," he said, as he set
down yet another empty glass. "It should have

186

been mine by right. Instead it will be mine by purchase."

"Doesn't it bother you that your money is ending up in Laurence's pocket?"

Trey shook his head and gave her a grim smile. "He won't keep it long. Laurence doesn't keep anything for long, as it turns out." He stood abruptly, pulled some money from his pocket, and threw it on the table. "Come on."

"Where are we going?" she asked, but she stood too, jamming her hat onto her head. She wondered how steady he would be on his feet. The two bourbons she had drunk had made her slightly dizzy, and he had matched her at least three for one.

"Home," he said carefully.

"Oh," she said. He was already on his way out the door so she followed him, something she seemed to be doing a lot of today.

She was amazed to see that the sun was low in the sky. They had been in the bar for several hours, but it seemed like minutes. It was only a few blocks to Trey's house on Chartres Street, and she really did think she ought to see that he got home safely. Oddly enough, he didn't seem at all drunk—no weaving about, no stumbling, only a rather determinedly careful stride.

His house was a beautifully proportioned, salmon-colored building with cornstalk-design iron railings around the galleries. He rapped firmly on his door with the head of his cane—she was realizing that a cane could come in handy for all sorts of things even if you didn't need it to walk—and it was opened by a black butler who took her hat without so much as a twitch of a smile.

Trey motioned her toward a room which turned out to be a library, a lovely masculine room lined with books from wall to wall and floor to ceiling, with a comfortable leather chair positioned in front of the fireplace, and a solid desk designed for working. It was her kind of room.

A large painting hung over the fireplace—Arthur Campbell, a handsome dark-haired man with wings of gray at his temples. It could have been a picture of Trey in another twenty years, and she found herself fascinated by it, wanting to study it, to see exactly what he would become.

"The first item Laurence sold when he needed money," said Trey with a bitter smile. "I got a good price on it." He strode to a sideboard and poured two drinks, then came back and handed her one.

"Do you know," he said, his voice only slightly thickened from the whiskey, "you're absolutely the most beautiful gentleman I've ever had a drink with."

She tipped her glass in a toast. "Same to you."

"And you make a cutaway and a shirt look more feminine than the most beruffled gown ever created by Mr. Worth of Paris."

She didn't know what to say to that so she sipped her drink. "Brandy?" she asked as she tasted it.

"A gentleman can't very well seduce a lady with Kentucky bourbon."

She coughed on the brandy. "Are you going to? Seduce me?"

"Oh yes, ma'am, I certainly am."

And she knew, from her curly hair to her suddenly curling toes, that he was right.

Chapter Fifteen

He took a step toward her, gently removed the glass from her hand, and set it on a nearby table. Through all this, Charli couldn't seem to move at all. She could only watch him do it, watch him come closer, his hands reaching out, almost in slow motion it seemed, to the knotted cravat at her throat. With infinite slowness, he untied it and pulled on one end till the whole thing snaked around her neck and fell to the floor. Then he started on the buttons of her shirt. His fingers felt like branding irons, burning her right through the silk.

"I never knew removing a young gentleman's shirt could be quite so pleasant," he said, his eyes on hers, his fingers moving inexorably lower. The silk opened at his touch. The air was cool on her burning skin and she shivered. He smiled.

"I did," she said, smiling back and reaching for his buttons. His own smile faded a moment and his hands stilled, but only for a moment. And when they resumed they seemed even more eager, more insistent. His eyes darkened as one hand slid easily past the silken barrier to find the tender skin of her throat and the rounded swell of her breast. When he reached the lacy edge of her wisp of a bra, he stopped, pulled his eyes from hers, and stared down at it. "Delightful," he said, fingering the fragile lace that barely covered her nipples. "A twentieth-century invention?"

"Um-hum," she replied, unable to say more because at that moment he reached in and scooped one breast neatly from its cup, and his fingers stroked that part of her that had been aching to feel them ever since he'd done so outside her bedroom. His touch was like an electric shock that went straight through her, making every nerve tingle with wanting.

"More delightful yet," he murmured, scooping out its mate and thumbing the tips of the nipples that now pointed up at him like silken-textured pebbles.

Never had Charli reacted so quickly or so intensely to the touch of any man. She dropped her head back and let the sensations sweep through her, like waves stroking at the beach, gentle yet insistent and growing in power while a storm brewed on the horizon. That storm picked up considerably when his mouth descended to take one nipple, adoring it with his tongue, teasing it with the soft hairs of his mustache, punishing it with his teeth, while his hand did the same to the other. She gasped.

190

"Yes," he murmured, his breath a fire against her skin. "Let me know."

She couldn't very well not let him know, so quickly had he carried her beyond conscious control of her responses. Her body reacted of its own accord, burning, shivering, trembling at his touch. And she wanted more. She wanted to feel him as he was feeling her. Her fingers returned to his shirt, clumsy now in their eagerness to remove the barrier that separated skin from skin. She struggled with the knot of his cravat until finally it dropped away. Eagerly, her fingers moved lower. One tiny pearl button popped off and landed on the floor with a soft *plink* before rolling away unnoticed.

And there he was, displayed for her hungry eyes. His chest was smooth, the color of burnished bronze, and rippling with muscle. The slightest line of soft black hair ran down the center. Perfect, she thought, for she had never liked hairy men. But then, somehow she had known he would be perfect.

She nuzzled her nose into the beautiful tanned skin and breathed him in. He smelled wonderful; his natural scent was like the finest musk cologne laid over clean soap and salty air. He tasted even better, she realized as she licked at his right nipple, inordinately pleased to feel it jump in response beneath her lips. His hands tightened on her breasts.

Then he pushed her, not roughly but insistently, and she took a step back. Was he pushing her away? she wondered. Please God, don't let him be pushing her away now. But no, as she stepped back, two steps, three, he matched her step for

191

step, until the backs of her knees touched the velvet edge of a narrow upholstered bench she'd noticed earlier. His hands moved to her shoulders and gently pushed her down onto the seat. Then he knelt before her and worshiped her breasts with his tongue and teeth, paying equal attention to each one in turn.

Her fingers went around his head, pulling him even closer to her, tangling in his black hair, urging him to keep doing what he was doing.

He needed no urging, none at all. It seemed like his mouth was everywhere—from her throat, over the creamy hills of her breasts, down, down across her stomach. His tongue tasted her navel, circling it before moving lower still. He bit gently at the tender skin of her abdomen, over and over, until she heard herself making sounds like a hungry kitten.

Her hands released his tangle of hair and slid down, pushing his shirt back over his shoulders to bare his magnificent chest entirely. He let go of her long enough to shrug out of it and let it fall away. Then he did the same with hers, tossing it on top of his on the floor. After a moment of exploring, he found the front closure of her bra beneath its tiny silk rose, and it soon joined the other garments.

They were both completely naked from the waist up, and as he grabbed her and held her close, she relished the feel of skin on skin. His fingers feathered up and down her spine, leaving their imprint wherever they touched, as clearly as a branding iron would do. Then he kissed her, fiercely, almost savagely, plunging his tongue into her, plumbing the depths of her mouth. And she gave back as good as she got, for she wanted to take him in, to encase him, to swallow him.

He broke the kiss, giving her a look of burning desire such as she had never in her life felt directed at her. She knew her own face mirrored it.

She felt bereft when he removed his hands from her bare skin, but it was only to bend over and tug off her boots. When he had them both off, he peeled off her stockings, so slowly she wanted to scream. When her feet were bare, he lifted first one, then the other to his mouth, kissing the tender skin of the instep, nibbling on a toe, circling his hand around an ankle. She had never known that feet could be so wildly erotic. It was as though he were kissing the very center of her.

He moaned, a sound she loved, and stood up. Gently but firmly, he twisted her, then pushed her back until she was lying on the bench. Quickly, his fingers worked the buttons of her trousers and slid the supple fabric down her legs and away. He stopped a moment to grin at her when he caught sight of her bikini briefs—a silly wisp of red ribbon and lace—but then they, too, joined the growing pile on the floor.

She was totally naked, lying on the padded bench, exposed to his gaze. He stared at her a moment like a hungry man at a banquet. Then he yanked off his boots, stripped off his trousers, and threw them away. He swung one leg over the narrow bench so that he was standing on the floor straddling it, towering over her like a granite statue of some gorgeous colossus.

But no, not granite, for as she gazed up at him with wonder at his beauty, that most beautiful part of him, erect and proud and as eager as she was, quivered with anticipation. She reached up and wrapped her fingers around him, loving the feel of him jumping under her touch. Then she raised her head from the royal-blue surface of the bench and kissed the velvety soft skin.

Trey felt a groan begin deep inside him and burst from his mouth. He couldn't believe what this woman was doing to him. He'd had many women, but none who set his blood boiling like this. If he didn't take her at once he was afraid he would explode. And yet the waiting was such exquisite torture. Lightly, her tongue feathered along his shaft, leaving a line of bonfires in its wake.

He could stand no more. Pushing her back down, he lowered himself over her. He buried his face in the lovely mounds of her breasts, pert and round and exactly the size they should be. Her legs opened beneath him, an invitation he'd been longing to accept practically from the first moment he'd fished her out of the river. And now he did.

Positioning himself above her, he paused a moment to look down into her face. Her eyes were half closed, heavy with the passion he had made her feel. A sense of power tempered by tenderness surged through him. And then no more waiting. He had to have her. Now.

He plunged into that soft secret place men had been known to kill for, and he found it sweeter than any honeycomb could be to a honeybee, more beguiling than Titania's bower was to Oberon, heady as drugged wine and welcoming as a down quilt. He felt like he had come home.

Charli's whole body surged up to meet him as he entered her. My God, she thought, how right he felt inside her, like a missing piece of a puzzle suddenly found, like a Siamese twin, once separated and now rejoined, like the warmth of a fire on a cold, lonely night. He filled her and completed her. She felt like she had come home.

For a moment, they just lay like that, joined in hearts and bodies, and then the rhythm that wouldn't be denied reasserted itself. As he began to move, she moved with him, their bodies in perfect harmony. He thrust and she accepted; she rose to meet him and he gathered her in. And the storm that had been waiting on the horizon suddenly descended on Charli with all its fierceness. Within minutes she was buffeted by waves of pleasure, tossing her about at their whim until she thought she would drown in them, not caring if she did. Higher and higher the waves carried her, stretching every muscle and nerve to the breaking point, until she heard herself scream his name, begging for a release from the pleasure that was now too much to bear.

And it came, exploding at her very center, spiraling out, filling every cell, flashing like fire up and down her body, wave after wave, on and on and on, until she heard her name, heard it from Trey's lips, a scream that matched her own, and she felt him tense inside her, every muscle taut. And together they rode the wave over the top and down the other side, landing together in the peaceful trough of still water where they could struggle to catch their breath once more.

Well! Charli thought, as her heartbeat slowly returned to normal. When the man says he's

Megan Daniel

going to seduce you, he doesn't kid around. Never in her life had she experienced anything like it. He had taken her to a land she never knew existed, a land she thought could be found only in the realm of fantasy. The problem was, once you'd lived out the fantasy, how could you ever again be content with reality?

And reality was that it was getting late. It was now dark outside the window, and she had a job to get to. She glanced at her wrist, forgetting for a moment that she'd sold her watch. Conveniently, the little mantel clock chimed seven.

But even as she thought she had to go, he reached toward a nearby chair for a crocheted afghan, dropped it on the floor, and gently pulled her down on top of it. Then he nestled her in the crook of his arm while one hand idly stroked her shoulder, her ribs, her breast. It was a casual yet tender gesture, and oddly, it caused tears to well behind her eyes. Ridiculous!

But her own hand responded, trailing across his beautiful broad chest, wisping lightly across his nipples.

Instantly, he gasped and his hand flew up and grasped her wrist. "That's not a good idea just yet," he said in a throaty voice. "Give me a few minutes."

She chuckled. "That's not what I had in mind." He raised her captive hand to his lips and kissed the palm. His touch there sent a sensation shooting through her that almost made her forget she had to get up. "I have to go," she said with a distinct note of regret.

"What do you mean?" he asked, lazily licking at her fingers.

"Stop that!" she said, pulling her hand away. If she hadn't, she knew she would never get out of there. "I said I have to go."

"Why would you want to do that?"

"I didn't say I want to. I said I have to."

"You don't have to do anything, Charlotte, except stay right where you are and let me go on doing what I'm doing." He took her hand again and sucked gently on her little finger. It felt good, just good enough to make her wish it were not her finger but some other part of her in his mouth.

With a groan, she sat up, pushing him away. "In case you've forgotten, I have to work for a living."

"Work? What work?"

"Wake up, Mr. Lavande. Your mother's expecting me, and I'm already late. And it takes a ridiculous amount of time to get into those dresses you people insist on."

"Oh, is that all?" he said, chuckling. "Don't worry about it. I'll explain to her that she'll have to find herself another singer. We have much better things to do with our evenings." He wrapped his arms around her again and moved to kiss her, but she couldn't let him do that. She knew that once those gorgeous and inventive lips touched her she would be lost. She thrust her hands between them and pushed him away.

"I have to go," she repeated, swinging herself out of his grasp. "I need this job."

He sat up too and ran his fingers through his hair, scowling. "Don't be ridiculous."

"Is it ridiculous not to want to starve? In case you hadn't noticed, there aren't all that many jobs available to women in this chauvinistic century of yours. Having found one, I'm not about to throw it away. I happen to like eating regularly and having a comfortable roof over my head." She rummaged in the pile of clothes on the floor until she came up with her bra.

"You'll stay here with me," he said with irritating confidence, at the same time unfastening the bra she had just fastened.

"I certainly will not!" She laughed and slapped his hand away, then went on dressing.

"Why not? Isn't this roof comfortable enough for you?"

"Of course, but it isn't mine." She grabbed her shirt.

"Neither is my mother's."

"It is when I've earned it."

He smiled, such a truly devastating smile that she had to look away. She reached for her trousers. "You can just as easily earn your keep here with me."

The words froze her, cutting like a knife through the warm, hazy aftermath of their lovemaking. She was astonished at how much they hurt. She dropped the pants she had just picked up and stood to face him, and when she spoke, her words came out like bullets. "That is the second time you have as much as called me a whore. But get this, Trey Lavande. I am not for sale, not at any price or to anyone, including you. Especially you. I'll do honest work for honest pay, on my terms, when and where I choose. And the choice I make is none of your damned business." She scrambled into the rest of her clothes, all the while feeling his eyes on her.

When he spoke, she was surprised to see that he was as angry as she. What the hell did he have to be angry about?

He told her. "I have just offered you something I've never offered any other woman in my life—the comfort and protection of my own home."

"Thanks, but no thanks." She jammed her feet into her boots, shrugged into her coat, and shoved her neckcloth into her pocket. She reached for her hat.

"Damn!" he said, standing and reaching for his own pants. "At least wait while I dress so I can escort you to my mother's house. It isn't safe for a lady to be on the streets alone at this hour."

"No one's likely to bother me, since they won't know I'm a woman. And besides, I'm almost certainly better prepared to defend myself than you are. No, I think on the whole I'll be safer alone, thank you very much."

She headed for the door. The last thing she heard as she went out was the crash of a crystal goblet and another fierce, "Damn!"

An hour later, trussed up, gowned, powdered, and perfumed, Charli sat at her piano singing of love gone wrong. Though her professionalism kept her audience from knowing it, her mind was a thousand miles away. No, not true; it was a few blocks away, in a lovely French Quarter mansion with a very special upholstered bench in its library.

What had happened to her there? she asked herself. How could she have been swept away so quickly and completely? Thank God her doctor had put her on the pill last year to regulate her cycles. Since her rational mind had simply stopped working, if she'd had to remember to use a diaphragm, she could very likely be pregnant right now.

Hardly realizing what she was doing, she played a riff and swung into a misty-voiced version of "Baby Face."

Pregnant. The idea of carrying Trey Lavande's child did have a certain charm to it. They might just come up with a pretty spectacular combination of genes. And if Murphy Brown could get away with it . . .

What was she thinking? The guy was becoming an obsession with her. She pounded out a fierce chord and charged into a foot-stomping version of Bob Seger's "Katmandu," wishing like hell she could go there this minute. The other side of the world sounded like an ideal destination right about now.

Chapter Sixteen

Trey stood in the archway and watched her, just as he had done that first night she sang here, wanting her as he had then, too, and every night in between. But damn! He wasn't supposed to still want her. The plan had been to have her and get her out of his system. Once he scratched that particular itch, he'd been sure it would go away. Instead, he wanted her even more. She had been so delicious in his arms, so sweetly yielding and fiery passionate at the same time. How many times would he have to have Charli Stewart before his body stopped jumping to attention at the sight of her? How many times before he could listen to that velvety voice she was treating all these randy gentlemen to and not want to kill every man in the room? How many times until he'd be free of her?

He didn't know what to make of her. She simply didn't fall neatly into any of his carefully thought-out categories for women. Despite his unconventional upbringing—and maybe to some extent because of it—he held tenaciously to one point of the conventional wisdom of his day regarding women. There were two types, he assumed, ladies and whores. Whores you went to bed with and ladies you married. Whores sometimes liked it; ladies never did.

Charli had obviously liked it. Her response to him had been instant and eager, and there was not a doubt in his mind that it was genuine. He'd had enough women not to be easily fooled, though some had tried, thinking it would please him. In fact, few things irritated Trey more than a woman who feigned a response she didn't feel. Charli wasn't faking it.

And he hadn't been her first, that was certain. She was no blushing virgin, as Corinne surely had been and would have remained until their wedding day. She did things to him that no inno-cent—and no proper lady—would think to do or know how to do. It made him wonder if she had left someone behind in her New York world—a lover, a string of lovers, a husband even. The idea made his gut twist in physical pain.

Yet despite her reaction to him, he couldn't think of her as a practiced whore. She was too genuine in her response, too sincere in the emo-tions she made no attempt to hide. And there was an underlying solid core of self-worth in her, reflected in her independent nature. Rather like his mother, and that thought confused him even more.

As she smiled at one of the gentlemen standing at the piano, his fist curled, and he knew an almost unbearable urge to smash the fellow's face in.

Again, he silently asked the question he had put to her the first time he kissed her. Who are you? he asked over the strains of the music, something about a honeysuckle named Rose. Who are you? And what am I going to do about you?

One thing he knew for certain about her: she was dangerous. Look at what had just happened.

Trey had made one decision early in his life: he would never bring a bastard child into the world. Having lived the experience himself, he refused to inflict it on anyone else. Justine, the quadroon mistress he kept in a house on Rampart Street, had been chosen from the many available to him precisely because he knew she was barren. And with other women, he was always careful. He carried a lambskin sheath with him at all times.

But tonight he had not been careful. Just the opposite. In Charli Stewart's arms, he forgot everything but the wonderful sensations she could arouse in him with nothing more than a look. When she'd finally touched him, he thought he would scream from the pure pleasure of it. When he slid into her welcoming warmth, one startling thought passed through his mind: mine.

And the sheath went unremembered and unlamented.

But what if he had planted his seed in her? What if she was pregnant with his child at this very moment? What then? The only solution would be to marry her, and for all her delectability and intriguing manner, she was not the sort of wife he planned to have. He needed a woman who would be a gracious hostess for Rive Douce, a woman of perfect breeding and impeccable lineage, a woman who would finish paving the pathway into New Orleans society that he had already assiduously begun. He needed a lady. Because his children would be the legitimate heirs to Rive Douce, and they must be seen to be worthy of it.

Corinne duClos would have been just such a wife: sweet, soft-spoken, gently reared—a true Southern belle. If Charli's story about how she came by Corinne's ring was to be believed, the two were related, a delectable irony. In truth, they couldn't have been more unalike. Of course, Charli was descended from Corinne's sister, Charlotte, and truth to tell Charlotte had been a real handful. Independent as hell and with a temper to match. Why, she'd even been a suffragist. Charli Stewart bore a strong resemblance to Charlotte duClos—in more ways than one.

Jacob passed with a silver tray of brimming champagne glasses. Trey grabbed one, drained it, set it back on the tray, and grabbed another. Charli started another song, with a refrain that begged him to please try a little tenderness.

Well, he had, hadn't he? He had invited the woman to move into his house. His house! And that was another thing he couldn't understand. Having her live with him openly would be absolute idiocy, perfectly calculated to destroy whatever reputation he had managed to build up in this city's stuffy society. But he couldn't seem to care.

And then she had refused! She, a woman on her own with no money, no family, virtually no friends, a woman who didn't even know how to talk and walk and think like a midnineteenth-century woman, had actually refused to allow him to take care of her. She had thrown his offer right back in his face with her determination to do it herself. By herself.

Her refusal made him livid. It made him want to curb this independent streak of hers, to bring her to heel like breaking a horse to the bridle, to make her decide that nothing was more important than being in his house, in his bed.

The secret, of course, was to give her no choice. He spied his mother making the rounds of her customers, checking to see that everyone was finding what they came for and was satisfied with it. With a determined smile, he made his way across the room toward her.

A half hour later, Lisette Lavande found Charli in the kitchen, taking a break from the piano and the pleadings of the customers to "Come upstairs, just once, I'll make it good for you, I promise."

Lisette poured them each a glass of very fine wine and sat down beside Charli. She stared at the young woman who was having such an interesting effect on her son. She couldn't remember the last time she had seen him so agitated over a woman.

"My son has asked me to fire you, my dear," she said, closely watching Charli's reaction.

Charli froze, her glass poised halfway to her mouth. "Are you going to?" she asked. From the look on her face, Lisette imagined her emotions were just as poised as her body, hovering somewhere between fear and rage.

"An interesting question. I expected something more along the lines of 'How dare he?'"

"I have a feeling your son would dare a lot to get his way."

Lisette laughed a deep, throaty laugh. "How well you know him already, my dear. Of course he would. And he usually does, you know. Get his way, I mean."

"But not always," Charli said, setting her wine glass on a gleaming porcelain-topped table. "Are you going to fire me?"

"I'm not sure," Lisette answered. "Do you know why he wants me to? He wouldn't tell me."

"Oh yes, I know. So he can own me. He doesn't seem to realize I'm not ownable, that I can't be bought at auction like one of his slaves."

"Of course he doesn't. And of course you aren't."

"Why do you know it when he doesn't?"

"He's a man, Charli, and not a very observant one at that, at least not when the truth in front of his face is not what he wishes to see." The truth in front of Lisette's face, however, was one that delighted her entirely. It told her that her son might very well have met his match at last. And she'd been dealt a hand in the game. She debated how best to play it so they could all come out winners. "What will you do if I do fire you?"

The answer was immediate and decisive. "Find another job."

"Difficult but not, of course, impossible, especially with your unique talents."

"Thank you," Charli said.

"You're entirely welcome." She stood. "And now perhaps we'd best both return to our customers.

I'll think over what my son has requested of me and let you know."

In the end, Lisette decided it would be much more interesting to stay on the sidelines and watch the show these two were determined to act out. She didn't fire Charli.

She didn't need to. Before the last of the customers either disappeared up the stairs or staggered out the door toward home, Charli quit. And she did it in front of Trey.

"Good," he said before she could even finish. "I'm glad you've decided not to be stubborn. Let's go." He grabbed Charli's arm. She pointedly lifted his hand and removed it.

"Go? Where would we go?" she asked with an innocent smile.

"Home," he replied, signaling to Jacob for his hat and coat.

She ignored him and turned to Lisette. "I'm sorry to leave you like this, and I hope you don't think I'm ungrateful. You helped me when I had nowhere else to go, and I'll never forget that. But it's not fair for me to make you choose between me and your own son. It's better for everyone if I leave. I'll go first thing in the morning."

"Of course I understand, my dear," said Lisette, taking her hand. "But where are you going?"

"I've been offered another job." She smiled at Lisette and Lisette smiled back and it was definitely a conspiratorial smile; the kind that only two women who understand each other share. Before Trey could get out a word, Charli turned and ran up the stairs.

But just as she closed her bedroom door and

bent over to ease off the silk slippers that were pinching her toes, the door was thrown open again and there he stood, so handsome in his anger that all she wanted to do was throw herself into his arms and relive the glory they had shared that afternoon.

Even as she savored that thought, he strode across the carpet, grabbed her up in his arms, and gave her a kiss that left her panting and trembling and wanting a whole lot more. Before she could stop herself, she was kissing him back.

His hands slid across the bare flesh of her back, smooth and warm as chamois leather, melting her skin beneath them, melting her resistance. . . . She pulled away. "No," she said softly. "No, Trey."

"You want me. You can't deny it. I can feel it in the heat of your skin, in the softness of your lips. You want me, Charlotte."

"Of course I want you." She leaned farther back, trying to create a safe distance. "What does that have to do with anything?"

He stared at her, confused.

"It doesn't matter that I want you," she went on. "I want to eat a hot fudge sundae every day of my life. I want to start smoking again. I want to lie on a beach in the tropical sun and bake until I'm the color of teakwood. But I'm not going to do any of those things because, as wonderful as they feel at the moment of doing, ultimately they are bad for me. And I'm not going to bed with you again for the same reason. You're bad for me, Trey Lavande. You mess up my mind so I can't think. You make me forget what's important. You make me lose control."

He pulled her to him again and nibbled at her ear. "Lose control, Charlotte. Lose control for me."

"No!" She pushed completely out of the circle of his arms and walked to the fireplace, staring into the glowing coals. "I've lost control of too much already in the past week. It's time I started *taking* control."

"Is giving up a good job the way to do that?"

"I told you, I've got another one."

He chuckled. "Who would give you a job? And doing what?"

She spun to face him. "Your confidence in me is touching. Thank God Mr. Sauvage has more faith in me than you do."

"Sauvage! Remy Sauvage? What's that rotter got to do with it?"

"He's offered me a job singing on one of his riverboats. I've accepted."

"Impossible! I won't allow it."

"That's a nasty habit you've got, telling people over whom you have no control what you will and won't allow them to do. Must make you awfully frustrated when they do it anyway."

"Why would you want to work for him?" There was an almost plaintive note in his voice.

"Because he's not you," she said, as gently as she could, "and he's not your mother."

"No!" he said, his voice nearly a shout. He strode to her, grabbed her, and pushed her till her back was against the wall. "No," he said, his voice now very quiet, menacingly so, and vibrating with determination. "You're not going to work for Remy Sauvage or for my mother or for any other damn person who wants you. You're coming home with me. You're mine."

And then he kissed her again, a determined, almost ruthless kiss, a demanding kiss, a kiss that shouted possession in its every nuance. A kiss she wanted, craved. A kiss she returned.

As he devoured her mouth, his right hand, just as determined as his lips, deftly reached inside the low décolletage of her gown, kneading her breast, not gently but oh so excitingly. When his lips left her mouth and made their way down to the exposed nipple, Charli gasped with pleasure.

"You see," he murmured, leaving the swollen little rosebud of a nipple long enough to smile at her. "You are mine."

The words were like ice water on her flaming emotions. "No, Trey, I am mine. Got that? No one owns me, and no one is going to. No one runs my life but me."

"Charlotte," he said softly, pulling her to him again.

She took a deep breath. Her voice steady, she said, "I should warn you, if you're planning to try to rape me, I'll stop you."

Rape! He had never in his life taken a woman who was less than eager for his touch. And she was! He knew she was. He could feel it in every panting breath from her mouth, every tremble of her flesh beneath his lips. He stared down at her.

"I know how to stop you," she went on, "and I promise it'll hurt like hell."

He straightened. "I seriously doubt you could stop me, Charlotte, but I've never had to force myself on a woman in my life. I'm not about to start now."

"Good, because you wouldn't like the consequences."

He turned and stomped to the door, anger vibrating through every muscle that moments before had trembled to his passion for her. Just before he left, he turned and faced her. "I wonder if Remy Sauvage will like them any better."

The next afternoon, Charli felt totally and comfortably in control for the first time since Rob Sams had fallen into the Mississippi. Here was a situation she was familiar with, one she knew she was the master of. She was in the middle of negotiating a contract with Remy Sauvage.

He was no more difficult than any of a dozen club managers she'd wrangled with; he was less hardheaded than any record-company exec she knew. Of course, she was in an enviable position, she thought with a chuckle. When it came to singing twentieth-century jazz and blues for passengers traveling on the Mississippi, she was definitely the only game in town.

They'd settled the issues of money, hours, and accommodations for her on board the riverboat that plied the Big Muddy from New Orleans to Vicksburg. She'd even managed to negotiate for herself a percentage of any increase in his business that could clearly be attributed to her.

"Great," she said as he wrote down the terms. "Now there's just one last item."

"What else could there be, *cher?*" asked Remy. "You've already got me to agree to terms no man could have got out of me or anyone else. Must be because you're such a pretty thing."

"Which is precisely my last point. I want it spelled out in words of one syllable that you agree not to give me a hard time, not to try to lure me into your stateroom, not to finagle me into dark corners. In short, Remy Sauvage, this contract will say that you promise not to even try to seduce me."

"Oh, *cher*," cried Remy, throwing down his pen, "you're not being fair, darlin'."

"It goes in the contract, *darlin'*." She drawled the final word with a grin. "One pass, one lewd suggestion, anything more than a wink, and I'm off at the next stop, and with two weeks' severance pay in my purse."

"C'mon, *cher*, look in the mirror. No sane man would sign such a contract with you."

"You will, if you want me to sing aboard the *Belle Brigitte* and make you an even richer man than you are already. I don't think I need to remind you that in the short time I sang at Lisette Lavande's her business increased threefold."

He stuck his cigar in his mouth and his hands in the pockets of his waistcoat as he tipped his chair back on its hind legs and glared at her through half-closed eyes. "You drive a hard bargain, *cher*. Never knew a woman with such a head for business. If I hadn't seen with my own eyes how gorgeous and sexy you are, I'd wonder if you were a man in disguise."

"Spoken like a true Victorian sexist," she muttered, then laughed at his confused look. "Do we have a deal?"

He sucked in a lungful of smoke, blew it out with a resigned *oooph*, and nodded. "Yes, darlin', we have a deal."

"Good."

He righted his chair, wrote the terms onto the contract before them, and signed his name. Then he handed her the plumed pen.

She dipped it in the inkwell, dropped a large black blot on the paper, made another when she attempted to scratch her name on the contract, and swore in a very un-Victorian, un-ladylike manner. "I can't seem to get the hang of this thing," she said as she threw the pen on the table and rummaged in the yellow tote bag at her feet. She came up with a black ballpoint, clicked it, and signed her name with a flourish.

Remy reached for the pen and examined it. "Clever," he finally said, after signing his name with it a couple of times. "I've never seen anything like it. Where'd it come from?"

"Woolworth's" she said with a laugh, knowing he wouldn't understand. She stood up and so did he.

"Well, *cher*, welcome to the *Belle Brigitte*. Your first performance begins in . . ."—he consulted the pocket watch he pulled from his vest pocket— ". . . twenty-two minutes."

"Right, boss," she said, shaking his hand in a businesslike manner that clearly surprised him as much as her contractual demands had done. "I'll be there."

She was there, looking regal and sexy and altogether desirable in one of the dresses Lisette had lent her—a violet-blue off-the-shoulder gown of crepe de chine edged with dove gray lace that had come straight from the new couture house of Worth in Paris. In her hair she wore a pair of glossy black coq feathers that swayed deliciously as she moved.

The audience, just as it had been at Lisette Lavande's house, was stunned—by her voice, by her songs, by her. They'd never seen or heard anything like her and they couldn't get enough. Even the women were immediately taken by this new sensation, even if she was a Yankee and far prettier than they would have liked.

Only two people in the elegant riverboat lounge were not bowled over, and then only because they'd heard her before.

Remy Sauvage stood in one corner, puffing on a cigar, very satisfied with his bargain and wondering how he could get her in bed without breaking their contract and having her walk out on him. Much as he wanted her, he wanted the money she would bring in even more. Still . . .

Trey Lavande watched Charli from a table at the back of the grand saloon. He'd chosen it carefully because it was in a shadowy corner, and he didn't want her to see him. Not yet. But he had to see her. He wanted to kick himself—he certainly laughed at himself—but he couldn't stay away from her. She was like a lungful of opium that had gone straight to his head—and another part of his anatomy that responded to her face and her voice and the creamy hills of her tantalizing breasts revealed in the violet gown in a way that made him even gladder he was sitting in the shadows.

Charli sang, and Remy counted his money, and Trey drank good French cognac and scowled as the miles swept past under the giant paddle wheel. Shortly after midnight, when they made a stop to take on firewood, Trey jumped ashore and hired a horse for the long and amazingly lonely ride back downriver to New Orleans.

Charli watched him go. She'd seen him the moment he entered the room. It was almost as if she'd sensed him even before her eyes found him, though of course she tried not to let him know it. And when he left without speaking to her, she felt something sink inside her. She sang "Smoke Gets in Your Eyes" with a special poignancy.

Why did this man bother her so? Why did she feel more alive when he was in the room, at the same time wanting him to leave, and then feeling totally bereft when he did just that? She hardly knew the guy!

But she did know him. She thought she'd probably known everything she needed to know about him the moment she first set eyes on him. And she liked what she knew. Besides being drop-dead gorgeous, he was smart. He was kind. He had a strong sense of who he was and what he wanted. She even admired his single-mindedness in going after Rive Douce, though she wasn't sure it was really the best thing for him. And he had a sense of humor; he tended to laugh at the same sort of absurdities of the world as she did.

She also knew he was dangerous. Any man who could make her forget herself so completely was a man she just couldn't afford to let too far into her life—especially right now when she needed to use all her energies to make her way in this strange world until she could figure out how to leave it and go back home. No, she'd been right not to accept his impetuous invitation to move into his house. He'd only asked her in the heat of the

moment anyway, in the afterglow of a passion she
had to admit had been pretty spectacular. He was
probably sorry now that he'd asked and relieved
that she had refused.

Suddenly she was exhausted. She sang one last
number—a hauntingly pure "Summertime" that
had the big saloon absolutely silent—then bowed
her way out of the room, applause and shouts of
"More!" following her through the door and along
the decks to her cabin.

It took fifteen minutes of struggling to get herself out of a gown that was designed to be worn
only with the help of a maid, then she collapsed
into a sleep full of shadowy dreams of Rob Sams
and muddy water and kisses that had her gasping
into wakefulness.

Chapter Seventeen

Two days later, Charli was back in New Orleans, having successfully completed her first trip for Remy Sauvage. She was a smashing success and word spread quickly. Tickets for the next day's trip were sold out while other boats went begging for passengers. Charli Stewart was the new star of the river.

Another aspect of her rapidly rising reputation also spread quickly. More than one gentleman had made incorrect assumptions about Charli on that first trip—the same assumption Trey Lavande had originally made—and had to be shown the error of their ways. With some, gentle persuasion and humor was enough to turn them off. But twice, she'd had to rely on more physical means to get across the point that she was not for sale, and her karate training had stood her in good stead.

A well-placed fist, a perfectly angled elbow, and the word went out—Charli Stewart was not a lady to mess with.

The minute the boat pulled up to the wharf, Charli went to visit Lisette. If she was disappointed not to find Trey at his mother's house, she didn't admit it, even to herself.

They sat over tea in Lisette's private sitting room, an airy upstairs salon all done up in pale mauve and moss green moiré silk against white walls. The furniture was light and delicate, though sturdy enough for Lisette's very solid form, and combined with the draperies and light Oriental carpet to provide a wholly lovely background for the woman Charli was quickly coming to love.

They talked of Charli's job and the river and Vicksburg, where Charli had spent a few hours before the boat headed downriver again. Trey's name only came up in the conversation about a dozen times.

"You would be very good for him, Charli," Lisette finally said as she bit into a praline.

"I doubt that," Charli answered. "And I know he wouldn't be good for me."

Lisette laughed, a rich, booming laugh that held nothing back. "Amazing, isn't it, how we women love to delude ourselves? He would be the best thing that ever happened to you, Charli, and I think you know it."

"How could you—" she began.

"And I think that is exactly why you are so afraid of him."

"I'm not afraid of him. I'm not afraid of anybody." She put her teacup down with a clatter.

218

All the Time We Need

"No? Then why do you run so hard and fast whenever he's within half a mile of you? You look to me exactly like a frightened doe running from a very large bear." Charli had to laugh in spite of herself. Lisette reached out and put a hand on her arm. "But he isn't a bear, Charli. Really, he isn't. And any woman would be fortunate to win him. He's a rarity, you know."

"In what way?"

"He likes women. Most men don't, you know. But Trey actually likes us. And even more important, he respects us. I imagine it has something to do with the way he was brought up." She laughed again. "I suppose it would be hard to grow up in a brothel and not like women."

"It would be hard to grow up with you for a mother and not like women," Charli added.

"Why, thank you, my dear, what a lovely compliment. The point is, he doesn't think us all empty-headed and vapid. He knows better. Though I shudder to think how close he came to actually marrying just such a creature."

"You didn't like Corinne?" Charli was surprised.

"There wasn't enough there either to like or dislike. She was just a pretty little parrot, one of those awful 'yes, Trey, no, Trey,' type of woman our society turns out by the bushel. Convent schooled to excel at dancing, drawing, and needlework and never even think about what goes on in the bedroom—even when she's doing it. Trey would have been bored to death with her within six months, but by then she probably would have been pregnant and he would have been stuck with her."

"He talks about her as though he loved her."

"He loved the idea of her—the right girl with the right manners from the right sort of family. Frankly, it surprised the hell out of me when her father agreed to the match. He's been one of my customers for years, you know." She gave a wry smile. "Amazing, isn't it, how 'uncouth' money suddenly loses its taint when you need it badly enough."

Charli looked at her intently. "He's still alive, her father?"

"Of course." She laughed again. "Jacques duClos owes me several thousand dollars. I couldn't possibly allow him to die with that kind of debt outstanding."

"Jacques duClos," Charli murmured, then frantically figured in her mind. "My great-great-grand—no, my great-great-*great*-grandfather."

"I beg your pardon, dear?"

"Lisette," said Charli, setting her cup down more carefully this time, "there is something I need to tell you about myself."

"How mysterious you sound."

"Well, it is rather unusual, to say the least."

"Good, I love mysteries." She picked up the pot. "More tea?"

"Yes, please. This may take a while."

That night, Charli attended the opera, escorted by Remy Sauvage after several stern reminders about their agreement.

New Orleanians took their opera seriously, she'd learned, especially the old-line Creole families, and Charli was not immune to the elegance and excitement that buzzed in the air. A deep red carpet had been spread over the banquette to protect the gowns of the ladies arriving in carriages. And what gowns they were! Miles of silk and tulle, acres of satin and lace, pounds of beads, fistfuls of diamonds and emeralds and sapphires. Even among her mother's circle, dressed up for the biggest charity ball of the year, Charli had never seen quite such a conspicuous display of wealth or an orgy of fashion.

At least she knew she blended in well. Lisette had lent her the most gorgeous dress in aubergine crepe de chine, its double skirt edged in deep rose silk. It was cut very low and bare at the shoulders. Lisette had also given her a pair of long rose kid gloves and shown her how to sprinkle them with talc so they would smooth on easily. A beautiful diamond spray held a pair of rose-tipped egret feathers in her hair, and she had dabbed a bit of Joy behind her ears—thankful that she hadn't sold the tiny bottle along with her Poison.

Remy escorted her up the carpeted staircase to the horseshoe-shaped second tier where he had a box. Charli didn't fail to notice that more than one woman turned a lorgnette in her direction before whispering to a companion. Already, she had become an item of gossip.

Charli looked around. Above her she saw a sea of black and brown and beige faces in the tier reserved for the free people of color, and above them, up in the gods, were rows and rows of black slaves. Below her, the orchestra section was clearly reserved for men only. The French opera house gave a definitive picture of the layers of New Orleans society.

Just before the gaslights dimmed for the opera to begin, Charli's eye caught something she would rather have missed. Directly across from Remy's box, Trey Lavande escorted a petite young woman in white ruffles and with roses in her blonde curls into a box. An elderly woman in black bombazine followed them. Trey seated the girl, offered her a program, and bent over her with a solicitous air Charli found disgusting. The girl flirted a lace fan at him and simpered. Charli was certain she could hear her giggling all the way across the vast space.

Charli turned to Remy and fluttered her own fan, an exotic bit of black lace and rose ribbon. His eyebrows went up and one hand fell to her shoulder. Immediately, she stopped the fan and looked pointedly at the hand until it was removed.

"Well, darlin'," he said with a shrug, "you can't blame me if you're going to flash those eyes at me that way. Give a fellow a chance, *cher.*"

He was right. She had to cool it, right now. What did she care if Trey Lavande chose to escort some little twit to the opera? She glanced back across the theatre just as Trey turned her way. He gave her a bow, polite and correct, and only she could see the mocking attitude it conveyed.

The overture began, and Charli forced herself to listen. Much to her surprise, the production of *Les Huguenots* turned out to be one of the finest she'd ever heard. The voices were magnificent, the orchestra superb, the acoustics perfect.

At the first intermission, Remy's box was thronged with visitors, both men and women, all wanting an introduction to New Orlean's newest sensation. She told herself she was not disappointed that none of them was Trey. Then she forgot about him entirely when one of her visitors, a portly, gray-haired man, was introduced as Jacques duClos.

He bowed over her hand, but his eyes stared into hers. "Amazing," he said finally. "I received a note today from," he paused, "from a mutual friend who told me we should meet, Miss Stewart. Now I see why. You bear a striking resemblance to my eldest daughter. Her name, too, is Charlotte."

Is, she thought. He said is. She's still alive. I could get on a train to New York right now and go see my own great-great-grandmother who died almost sixty years before I was born. Amazing! She looked at him more closely. This man talking to her at this very moment was her great-great-great-grandfather. Charli was seeing her own ancestor, in the flesh. She was astonished to realize that his eyes were the exact shade of turquoise and set at the exact same angle in his face as her mother's. And he had Grandmother Charlotte's smile. Silently, she thanked Lisette for sending him.

At the next break, more visitors came but still no Trey. It wasn't until the opera was over and Charli was being led back down the carpeted staircase that they met.

"Miss Stewart," he said with a bow. "May I present Mademoiselle Fourché?"

"*Enchanté*," said the young woman, cocking her head at a coquettish angle. She had a voice like a breathy music box with a squeak. Charli would be

Megan Daniel

willing to bet that she played the harp, badly, and did perfect needlework.

"*Enchanté*," Charli parroted in a breathy voice, cocking her head to exactly the same angle. Trey coughed, and Charli knew it was to cover a laugh. She had to bite her lip to keep from chuckling herself.

"Well, Lavande," said Remy. "Will we see you aboard the *Belle Brigitte* tomorrow? I always knew she was finer than the *Corinne*, but I didn't expect to see you admit it by riding her so often yourself."

"One should always keep an eye on the competition, Sauvage," he said to Remy, though his eyes remained on Charli. "No matter how minor a threat it poses." Then with a tip of his elegant silk top hat, he led the simpering Mlle. Fourché away.

Charli went back to her stateroom on the *Belle Brigitte* and punched pillows all night.

The next afternoon at precisely four o'clock, the *Belle Brigitte* pulled away from the New Orleans levee once more, belching clouds of billowing smoke and with a shrill cry from its whistle. And once again, when Charli sat at the piano that evening in the befringed and brocaded saloon, Trey Lavande drank cognac in the corner and watched and listened. Again, he got off at the first wood stop, and again Charli felt a deep pang of disappointment.

She had missed him more than she would have imagined possible in the last few days. There was so much she wanted to ask him about this world she found herself in. He was the only person who would understand her curiosity about it, her lack of knowledge, her feelings of awkwardness when she made some silly faux pas only because she didn't understand the rules of the time.

She sang her last song and wearily made her way back to her cabin. It was not empty.

"Oh!" said the young black girl, jumping up with a cry as Charli opened the door. "I'm sorry, miss, you frightened me."

"Who are you?" asked Charli, "and what are you . . . ? Wait, I know you, you're . . ."

"Dolly, miss," said the girl with a curtsy.

"The slave girl. From the auction. Trey bought you."

"Yes, miss." Another curtsy.

"But what are you doing here? Have you run away?"

The girl's eyes grew enormous. "Oh, no, miss. I'd never. Master Lavande, he sent me."

"Why? To spy on me?"

"No, miss." The girl seemed extremely nervous.

"I wouldn't put it past him. The guy has very strange ideas about what he has a right to know about me and what he doesn't. Why else would he send you to me?"

"Because . . . oh, here, miss. He said to give you this." She reached into the pocket of her immaculately clean and pressed gray skirt and handed Charli a note, then made another curtsy.

"Stop doing that," said Charli as she opened the folded letter.

"What, miss?"

"Bobbing up and down like a jack-in-the-box. You don't have to curtsy to me. You shouldn't have to curtsy to anyone."

225

"Yes, miss," the girl said in a frightened whisper as she started another curtsy, stopped herself, and almost lost her balance.

Charli opened the note.

> *"My dear Miss Stewart:*
> *"It occurs to me that you have no maid to tend you and, from what you've told me of 'modern' clothes, the gowns my mother lent you are not exactly what you are used to. I know from personal experience that they take more than a little effort to get into— and out of. Dolly will help you with them as well as looking after you in any other way you may need. Consider her yours, a gift from an admirer.*
> *Your most obedient servant, Trey Lavande"*

Consider her yours! Charli crumpled the note and threw it in a corner. How dare he! He was actually giving her a slave? Knowing how she felt about the whole institution—and about his purchase of this girl in particular!—he was giving her another human being, to own, to rule as her whim dictated? She wouldn't have it. She would not have it!

Angrily, she retrieved the note, smoothed out its wrinkles, and thrust it toward the girl.

"Dolly, have you read this?" she finally asked the girl, her voice like steel.

"No, miss. I can't read."

"Well, the way I read it, you're mine now."

"Yes, miss, that's what Master Lavande said."

"Good. You're free."

"Miss?" The girl looked totally confused.

"You're free. I'm setting you free."

"Oh, you can't do that, miss."

"Of course I can. This note says you're mine, you're my slave, my property. That means I can do whatever I want with you, right?"

"That's right, miss, but—"

"Well, I choose to set you free."

Tears formed in the girl's large, chocolate-brown eyes. She drew in a ragged breath. "You can't, miss," she repeated.

"Why not? Don't you want to be free?"

"Yes, miss," said Dolly, her voice barely a whisper. "It's what I want more than anything in the world. But it isn't possible. The law says so."

"The law? I don't understand."

"I guess that's 'cause you from up North. I hear they do things different up there. But here in Louisiana, it's real hard to free a slave, miss, takes years sometimes and a pile of money. Folks are scared of us, y'see, and the law, it's got a whole lot stricter the last few years, almost nobody gets freed no more. Maurice, that's Master Lavande's butler, he be freed last year, and he said it took the master 'most five years and thousands of dollars to get it done, and Maurice says he got a lot of people mad at him when he finally done it. Now he's working on freeing Margie, that's his cook, but it be a long time before it happens." She gave a sniff. "I'll be a old lady 'fore he gets to me, miss," she said, swiping at her tears with the back of one hand. "Now if you just turn around, miss, I get you out of that dress."

Numbly, Charli turned around and Dolly's nimble fingers quickly unfastened the long row of tiny hooks that ran down her back and were almost impossible to deal with alone.

Five years. Thousands of dollars. Trey had been willing to spend a great deal of time and money to free a slave, and in the face of disapproval from his friends and neighbors. And he was ready to do it again.

She remembered how she had railed at him the day he'd bought Dolly, how harshly she had judged him for buying a slave. She wished she could apologize for that. But except for those few cryptic words on the opera house stairs last night, it didn't seem like he was ever going to actually speak to her again. Maybe he'd just sit in the shadows and watch her forever. For now, all she could do was accept this very unexpected gift and be as kind to Dolly as she could.

"You're sure he didn't ask you to spy on me, to report back on what I do and who I do it with?" she asked Dolly, wishing she weren't standing there in her camisole and petticoats until she was sure whose camp the girl was in.

"No, miss," said Dolly, standing up straighter. "And even if he did, I wouldn't do it."

So, the girl had some spirit. That was good. Charli believed her. And unexpected though she might be, now that she was here Charli realized she did need a maid. More than that, she needed a friend.

"Okay, Dolly," she said. "You stay. But here are my ground rules. My name is not miss, it's Charli."

"Oh, miss, I couldn't . . ."

Charli held up one hand. "As my dad used to say, rules is rules, and that's one of mine. No curtsying to me, either. I'm no better than you are, and I don't want you ever to forget that.

Also, slave or not, you'll earn a salary as long as you work for me. Agreed?"

"Oh, miss," Dolly breathed, then caught herself. "I mean . . . Charli."

"See, that didn't hurt so much, did it?" She grinned and Dolly grinned shyly back.

"No, mi . . . Charli." Then they both laughed.

"Good. I don't know what's a fair salary around here for a maid, but I'll find out. What you do with your money is your own business, but I suggest you save at least some of it. You'll need it when we figure out a way to set you free."

"Free? But—"

"There must be a way, Dolly. Together we'll find it. That is, if you want to."

Dolly stood very erect and looked Charli straight in the eye. "I want to."

"Good," Charli said again. "We've got a deal."

Chapter Eighteen

This is ridiculous! Trey thought as he strode down Rampart Street toward home. His long legs fairly ate up the banquette in frustration. This obsession with Charli Stewart was beginning to make him angry. He wasn't sleeping well. His business was suffering. And he was handing a small fortune over to his worst competitor to ride the damn man's boat up and down the river just so he could sit in the shadows and watch her sing!

He'd tried not watching her, and that had only made things worse. Instead, he just sat at home imagining her—hearing her throaty voice, smelling that intoxicating perfume she wore, feeling the softness of her lips with his mind. Wanting her more than ever.

Seeing her at the opera on the arm of that bastard Sauvage hadn't helped either. It had been his

mother who alerted him to the fact that Charli
would be there—she seemed quite taken with
Miss Charlotte Stewart. He had thought to use
Suzanne Fourché to put her out of his mind by
reminding himself of all the things he wanted in a
woman that Charli Stewart was not. And she had
made Suzanne look like an empty-headed china
doll with a bent neck.

And if that wasn't bad enough, just now he
had been to visit his quadroon mistress, Justine,
for the first time since he'd made love to Charli.
Needing her badly, he'd walked into the tidy and
always welcoming little cottage only to walk out
again after no more than a half-hour and a pair of
chaste kisses. He just couldn't seem to muster any
interest in the dark-eyed, golden-skinned beauty
who in the past had always satisfied him in every
possible way.

He wouldn't blame Justine if she were livid
with him. She couldn't be any angrier than
he was growing with himself, he thought as
he strode down Dumaine toward the French
Market, ignoring two close friends who passed
not more than three feet away and stared after
him with offended looks.

He didn't want Justine. He didn't want any of
the girls in his mother's house who would have
been more than happy to have him. He most
certainly didn't want Suzanne Fourché. He didn't
want any woman, except the one who didn't seem
to want him.

But that wasn't true. She did want him. She'd
admitted it. And even if she hadn't, he would
know it was true. He could feel it in her touch
and see it in her eyes and hear it in her voice.

Megan Daniel

They were wonderful together. They made magic together, such magic as he had never experienced with Justine, or any other woman.

He tried to figure out why that was as he grabbed a cup of strong coffee that a street vendor sloshed into a cup for him. Still thinking of his mysterious Yankee girl, he gulped it so fast it burned his throat. She certainly wasn't the most stunningly beautiful woman he'd ever made love to, though he did adore the way she looked, with that disgracefully short hair and her cocky grin and her sultry smiles when she sang—or when he made love to her. She was completely outrageous, but it was in a way that made him laugh, once he'd gotten over his shock at the things she did and said. And the songs she sang. And the way she sang them.

She intrigued him, certainly. He believed now that, incredible as it might have been, she really was what she said she was—a woman from 135 years in the future. And he was full of questions, about the inventions she had described—motorized carriages and undersea boats and flying machines—about the buildings she said would one day be built in New Orleans, and the pictures that moved and talked, and lights that went on at the flick of a switch and stayed on till you switched them off again, and something called a telephone that meant you could talk to someone clear across town—or across the country. He stopped short, causing a woman behind him to nearly barrel into him. He stepped aside and gave her an absentminded bow, then looked around him, wondering what it would be like to live in such a world, with the cars she described roaring

232

up and down the streets, with colored lights in the shop windows, with women striding along in tight trousers. That was something he'd like to see, he thought with a grin.

But she had also told him about the war that was coming, very soon, and about the devastation it would wreak all over the South for many years to come. That he had no trouble believing, much as he wanted not to. The abolitionists in the North wouldn't rest till they had freed every slave, and the Southern landowners wouldn't give up the call of "State's Rights" till they were all dead.

She had told him something else, too, about the profound social changes in store—women voting and working at men's jobs, men taking care of babies, and men and women living together openly, without being married.

So damn! What did the woman want and why was she being so stubborn about it? What did he have to do to woo her back into his bed and into his home? For he realized now that that was where he wanted her. He wanted her not just at night but in the morning, too, at his breakfast table, in the afternoon on his arm as they strolled through the Vieux Carré, in the evening sitting in his box at the opera, laughing with him over a late supper, comparing opinions on everything. And then he wanted to feel her again, but in a soft feather bed beneath the sort of lovely damask hangings her warmth and beauty deserved, not on a narrow upholstered bench. He wanted her in his bed, responding to him as honestly and as sweetly as she had done that afternoon in his study, opening to him with such eagerness, accepting him with such passion. He wanted to

touch and taste and kiss every inch of her beautifully muscled body, so soft yet so amazingly firm
beneath his, so yielding yet so strong, so feminine
yet so sure. His body was trembling with the
memory of her as he walked through the streets,
and he was afraid he was about to embarrass
himself with his obvious need for her.

He climbed up on the levee and glared omi-
nously at the *Belle Brigitte*, one in a long line of
glistening white steamboats tied up at the wharf.
She'd come in again last night and would be heading back upriver in a few hours.

He punched his walking stick into the grass
atop the levee so hard it almost snapped. Damn!
When she sailed, he would be on her.

When Charli didn't see Trey sitting in the
saloon shortly after they pulled away from the
New Orleans dock, she was disappointed—far
more than she wanted to be, in fact. That made
two trips now when he hadn't come. Maybe he
would never come again. Maybe he simply no
longer cared. Her performance didn't have its
usual sparkle that evening.

When she finished, she dragged herself back
toward her cabin, exhausted and a little head-
achy. She never got there.

He was leaning on the railing, watching the
water, luminous in the moonlight, as it foamed
back from the sidewheels and away in a giant *V*.
He had a long, thin cheroot in one hand, its thin
line of blue smoke barely visible as it curled up
and disappeared on the cool breeze. She caught
her breath at the sight of him and he spun to
face her.

"I didn't think you had come," she said, pulling a gossamer-thin shawl closer about her shoulders.

"I didn't intend to," he said with a rueful grin. His voice was soft, as soft as the night air or the fall of a drop of Mississippi River water on fevered skin. "But I find I am unendingly curious to know more about the future."

"Oh," she said. Was that the only reason he came? She didn't want to think so.

"Walk with me a while?"

"Sure," she said, trying to sound nonchalant when she felt anything but. She walked toward him and he took her right hand and tucked it into the crook of his arm. It felt so at home there, so warm and safe. Her skin buzzed. Oh Lord, she thought, I shouldn't have let him touch me. She tried to take her hand back, but he held it firm, pressing it gently to his side with his elbow.

They strolled along the deck. As they passed under the hanging lanterns that were strung across the deck, the planes of his face became clear, then lost in shadow, then clear again. She loved watching the play of the light on those strong features.

He smiled down at her and she had to look away. She reacted to the man like she was some blushing teenager, for God's sake! She was all but digging her toe into the floor and sticking her finger in her mouth and saying "Aw, shucks."

"Thank you for sending me Dolly," she finally said for something to say.

"I had to do something with her. I don't need a young girl in my bachelor household, and I knew you would be kind to her."

"You also knew it would make me mad as hell to own a slave."

"Yes, and I knew you'd get over it."

She looked up at him. She didn't think she liked his knowing her so well already. No, she definitely didn't like it. She looked out at the water and the distant shore sliding by in the blackness. "Why didn't you tell me about the slave laws, about how hard it is to free them?"

He chuckled. "Well, I suppose I could give you an answer that makes me sound more magnanimous than I am, but the truth is it never occurred to me that you didn't know."

"Well, that's honest," she said with a light laugh. A bit of music floated down the deck toward them. "Anyway, I like Dolly. When she first came she was like a scared little rabbit, but she's okay now that she's not afraid she's going to be sold into the fields. She's really very intelligent. And you were right about these stupid clothes," she went on. "With their dozens of hooks and buttons and tapes and their layers and layers of underthings, they're more than impossible to get out of without help."

Her shawl slipped from her shoulders and he bent to retrieve it. When he wrapped it around her bare shoulders again, he left his hands there. "Not like a nice pair of trousers and a simple shirt and those almost invisible bits of lace you like to wear under them, are they?"

"Uh, no," she said, wishing he would remove his hands so she could breathe . . . and hoping he wouldn't.

"Does she know about you?"

"Dolly? Not yet, but I'm going to tell her. As soon as I think I can make her believe me. It's too hard talking around it all the time, and she already thinks I'm more than passing strange. She'll probably be relieved to have an explanation."

He chuckled. "Probably. You're impossible to figure out otherwise."

She joined his laughter. "And since you do know about it, does that mean you think you've got me all figured out?"

"I'm not idiot enough ever to claim such a thing."

"Good," she said. "I hope you don't mind, but I told Lisette."

"You told my mother? Did she believe it?"

"Yes. Unlike you, she believed me at once. Actually, she simply nodded and said, 'Well, that explains it, then.'"

He laughed. "My mother is an incredible woman."

"Yes, she is." She sighed and pulled the shawl closer, though she no longer felt at all cold. She looked up at the sky. The moon was just a shaving off full, casting a shimmering moon river on the water. "It's beautiful," she murmured.

"Yes," he agreed, but he wasn't looking at the moon.

"This is such a lovely way to travel, so slow and easy."

"Slow? It's by far the quickest way to get upriver."

She chuckled. "Well, it seems slow when you're used to hopping a jet and flying off at any moment to Paris or Los Angeles or even Podunk. It took

237

me less than four hours to get here from New York."

He shook his head slowly. "You're going to have to be careful what you tell me about this miraculous future of yours."

"Why?"

"Because since I've decided to believe you and virtually everything you say about it is unbelievable, I've had to make a blanket decision to simply accept it all. You could tell me you'd flown to the moon and back and I'd believe you."

She laughed. "We did."

"What?"

"Flew to the moon and back. In 1969."

He guffawed at that. "I've heard the phrase 'over the moon', and I think that comment just was."

"No, really, we did. I mean we will. Three men will go up in a spaceship, land, walk around a bit, plant a flag, do a couple of somersaults, and come back again. There will be a full moon that night, too, and millions of people will watch it on television."

He looked up at the silver circle in the ebony sky and shook his head, chuckling. "It rather takes the romance out of it, don't you think?"

She joined his laughter. "Perhaps you're right. I always did like a full moon."

"Me too." He leaned over and she knew he was going to kiss her. She knew she should stop him, because it was going to be awfully hard to stop at one kiss, but she didn't because she really wanted him to kiss her at that moment.

It was as soft as the moonlight on the water, as soft as his smoke on the wind or his voice when he said her name—"Ah, Charlotte,"—and then he kissed her again, more firmly, but not demanding any more. It was Charli's mind and body that were doing the demanding.

Her arms went around his neck; the shawl slid unnoticed to the deck. He threw his cigar over the rail and into the river and leaned into her until she could feel the railing at her back. She tilted backward over it, loving the slight edge of danger and the feeling that she was totally safe with him. He would never let her come to harm.

The thought shocked her. How could she feel safe with Trey Lavande? He was anything but safe. She had instinctively known it from the first. But now, with a blinding flash of clarity and even as he was kissing her so deliciously, she knew exactly why he was unsafe.

He was dangerous because he had the power to make her want to stay in the past. And she didn't want to stay in the past. She wanted to go home!

"Trey," she said, pushing gently away, but his lips captured hers again, and she seemed to forget for a moment what she was going to say as his fingers slid up her back and entwined themselves in her short curls, caressing the scalp she had never before known was an erogenous zone. But with Trey, she was afraid even her fingernails would be erogenous zones. She groaned and kissed him back.

"Charli, darlin'," came a voice from a few feet away, languid but steely, "you're on my time."

She tried to struggle up from the rail, but Trey held her too close. "Go away, Sauvage," he said. "The lady's occupied."

"I do believe, darlin'," Remy continued speaking to Charli, "that we wrote somethin' in that

239

damned contract of yours about not fraternizing with the customers?"

"Let me up," she whispered to Trey as she struggled to stand and wriggle out of the circle of his arms.

"For your own protection, you said," Remy went on, "but it doesn't seem to be working too well. And you made such a point about bein' able to protect yourself, too. Oh well, shall I challenge the fellow to meet me under the oaks at dawn?"

"Don't you dare!" Charli pushed away from Trey, though he still held her. "I'm perfectly able to handle my own affairs." As soon as she'd said that last word she was sorry.

"I can see that, *cher*, but would you mind not doin' it on my boat when you're workin' for me?"

"Look, Sauvage—" Trey began, but Charli cut him off.

"Shut up," she hissed and turned to Remy. "I'm sorry. It won't happen again." She twisted completely out of Trey's arms. "Gentlemen," she said with an elegant incline of her head. "Good night." She stooped to pick up her shawl, lifted the hem of her skirt, and walked away, stepping on her petticoats only once, and only a little.

The two men glared at each other. Trey took out another cigar, lit it with a sulfur match that flared brightly in the dark, then reluctantly offered one to Remy. He took it and the two of them stood there, wrapped in the rich scent of good Virginia tobacco and their own less mellow emotions.

"I could order you off my boat," Remy finally said. "I could have you thrown off at the next

240

wood stop and tell my people to see that you never set foot on it again."

"But you won't."

"No? Why not?"

"Because you know it would be a challenge I'd have to answer, and I'm a better swordsman than you are, Sauvage. Also a better shot. And you like living; you'd like to keep doing it a while longer."

"Are you calling me a coward, Lavande?"

"No, I'm calling you smart."

Remy looked at him a long moment, then burst out laughing. "How well you know me, Lavande. And besides, if I killed you I'd never be allowed past Lisette's door again, would I?"

"Not a chance, and the charming Felicité would be devastated."

"Can't have that. Got any other ideas?"

"As it happens, I do." He took in a mouthful of the cigar smoke, then let it out in a thin stream, watching it dissipate entirely before he spoke. "You're a gambler, Sauvage. So am I. We've played more than a few games together in our time. I propose another one."

The Creole's eyes lit up. "Poker?"

"If you prefer."

"And the stakes?"

"I think you can guess."

He also took a long puff, then said, "Charli."

"Exactly. You lose, and she's mine."

"Doesn't sound very fair to her."

"Let me worry about what's fair to Charli Stewart."

Remy looked over the man who had been a friendly rival for both business and women for

241

years. Trey was a good gambler, he knew from personal experience. He wasn't reckless except when it counted, and he never gave himself away. "And if I win?"

"You always had an eye for a beautiful woman, Sauvage. But I think you've got an even sharper eye for the bottom line."

"True, but with Charli Stewart I get both. She's been a gold mine. I'm booked solid for weeks, and they're spending hand-over-fist to hear her sing."

"I'm sure. But you could do even better if you had two *Belle Brigittes* instead of one, couldn't you?" His voice was seductively soft.

"What do you mean?"

"The *Corinne.*"

Remy stared at him, clearly flabbergasted. "You'd take a chance with the *Corinne?* She's your flagship and one of the finest boats on the river. She's worth a fortune."

"Win, and she's yours." *What the hell am I doing?* Trey kept asking himself, but he couldn't seem to stop. *This is insane!* his mind screamed, but the words kept coming out. *Stop!* his reason demanded, but he only added, "The *Corinne* against Charli Stewart. That's my offer. Take it or leave it."

Remy's eyes lit with avarice. "She won't like it," he said.

"You can let me worry about that too."

That was just fine with Remy because he stuck his hand out like a bullet and said, "Done." The two men shook on it.

"Cards, gentlemen?" said Jean Telle. The man in the immaculate white suit and brocade vest was a well-known riverboat gambler who just happened to be aboard the *Belle Brigitte* that night. Trey and Remy had enlisted him to act as dealer for their game. With so much at stake, a disinterested party seemed the best way to keep both players honest. A dozen other men stood around the table, watching with interest. The air was thick with swirls of blue tobacco smoke.

"Three," said Remy, throwing down his pair of discards with a confident flourish and smiling across the green felt at Trey. Telle dealt him three cards. He left them face down on the table.

"One," said Trey, his voice even and perfectly controlled. He wasn't smiling. Nor was he frowning. He was a good enough player that he never gave a hint to the cards he held, even when he was taking such insane risks as his request for one card entailed. He was a gambler, he knew better than to try to draw to an inside straight. Yet here he sat with a nine, ten, Jack, and King of Hearts in his hand asking for one card. But in the midst of the insanity that Charli Stewart engendered in him, it seemed like the thing to do. And so appropriate. The Queen. That was all he needed, and he would own Charli. The Queen of Hearts.

Telle raised an eyebrow and looked at Trey with a speculative grin as he dealt out a single card.

It slid smoothly across the felt surface; Trey fancied he could almost hear the silent *whoosh* of its passing. He stared at it, at its elaborately patterned red-and-white back, as it lay against the green tabletop.

He saw Remy pick up his two cards, saw the man flinch ever so slightly as he looked at them.

243

He saw his own perfectly manicured hand reach down. With one finger, he slid the single card toward him. If I were a more religious man, I'd pray right about now, he thought. His thumb flicked up one corner of the card.

The King of Diamonds.

He'd lost. The *Corinne* was gone. And Charli was out of reach. He might as well throw in his cards.

Then he heard Remy sigh. "I hoped the Queen of Hearts would call in all her sisters," he said. "She seemed so appropriate." He turned over his cards.

Trey looked at Remy's pair of queens, including his Queen, and felt like laughing and singing and getting drunk. As he turned over his own cards, he noticed that his hand was shaking. "Kings," he said, pushing them forward. Then he reached for the contract which lay in the middle of the table. "My game, I believe."

Chapter Nineteen

It was nearly four in the morning when he knocked on the painted door of Charli's cabin. It wasn't fair, he knew, but he needed her, he craved her, and when she found out later about the poker game, she was going to be livid. She might never speak to him again.

When she opened the door, she was so incredibly desirable in her tousled, half-awake state and dressed only in a filmy dressing gown that he swept into the little room, lifted her up into his arms, dropped her onto the bed, and began kissing her before she could even say a word.

She didn't want to say a word. For a minute, she thought maybe she was still dreaming. She had been dreaming of this very man doing this very thing to her, hadn't she? One thing was sure; if this was still a dream, she didn't want to wake up.

But it was no dream. A dream wouldn't set her on fire when his hands slid inside the silk of her robe and caressed her suddenly burning skin. A dream wouldn't take her breath away with a single touch of his lips to the hollow between her breasts. And a dream would not then struggle so rapidly to get out of his clothes so that he was as naked as she.

A bit of dim gray light filtered in through the cabin's small window, but it wasn't enough for Charli. She needed to see him.

Just as she had the thought, he fumbled in his coat pocket a moment. She heard the scratch of a match, saw a burst of flame.

"I need to see you," he said, his voice low and intense. He lit a lamp on the dresser, turned the flame low, and replaced the chimney. Then he looked at her and she looked back.

He was beautiful. That was the only word for it. Without benefit of Nautilus machines and personal trainers, he was more perfectly proportioned than any man that had ever worked out at her health club. And the evidence of his desire for her, standing huge and rigid and ready, made her grow excited just looking at it. She reached out and touched him lightly.

He groaned, then turned to fumble in his pocket once more. He brought out a small package and unwrapped it, and she realized it was a condom of some sort. She was touched at his thoughtfulness.

She put out her hand. "You don't need it," she said, grateful once more for her pills.

"I'll not give you a child, Charlotte."

"You won't. I'll explain later."

"You're sure?"

"Trust me."

And then neither of them gave another thought to anything but what they were doing to each other and feeling for each other, for they had wanted each other so badly for so long. They were frantic in their need. They wanted to look at, to touch, to taste every part of each other, and they did.

He made love to her breasts, worshiped her stomach, and glorified the hollow of her left hip.

She fell in love with the taste of his right nipple. She adored the dimple of his navel and celebrated the texture of the hair between his legs.

She idolized his feet. He made a shrine of her buttocks. No part of her body or his was left unworshiped. No part was found less than perfect.

Then his hand was stroking the most sensitive part of her while his mouth poured his feelings into hers.

When she could stand it no more, when she knew she would explode if he kept touching her that way and she didn't want to reach that height without him, she rolled over until she was on top of him. She bent and kissed first one nipple, then the other, then she raised herself and slowly slid down over him, willingly impaling herself on the beautiful scepter below her.

Within minutes—or seconds, or hours—they reached that magic peak together, crying into each other's mouths as the pulsing rocked them, clinging to each other so they wouldn't drown. Then they rode down the other side into a breathless peace.

Charli was rocked to her very soul. What had this man done to her? It was more, far more, than mere desire that had brought them together with such power just now, and she was too smart and too honest with herself to try and pretend it wasn't. She was afraid this man was becoming the most important thing in the world to her, and what was she going to do if that happened?

She remembered the offer he had made once before, to move into his house, and at this very moment, there was nothing she wanted more. She wanted to share his house and his meals and his bed, to wake up with him, to sit opposite him at breakfast, to ask him about his day. To lie in his arms at night and feel again that wonderful magic.

And how the thought terrified her! She was on the verge of giving up everything she had struggled so hard to achieve, of kissing good-bye to the independence she had wrestled from her mother with an emotional hammerlock and then clung to with the tenacity of a pit bull.

She felt a tear well, spill over her right eyelid, trickle down and drop onto his broad chest where her head rested. Don't hurt me, her heart cried. Please don't hurt me.

He felt the tear and wiped away another one before it could fall. "Don't cry, my love. I'll never hurt you."

She didn't answer him out loud, but the answer was, I'm so afraid you already have.

He rocked her in his arms until she fell asleep.

It was well into the morning when Trey slipped out of Charli's bed. She was sleeping peacefully with a smile on her lips. He felt such tenderness looking at her, and regret. He had said he would never hurt her. And yet he knew he was about to do that very thing.

But he couldn't help himself. He was so afraid of losing her, of having that damnably independent nature of hers take her out of his life, that he couldn't go back.

At ten, he knocked on the door of Dolly's tiny cabin. The slave girl was just tying a fresh *tignon* of blue calico over her hair.

"Go and pack your mistress's things," said Trey. "You'll both be going ashore with me in less than an hour."

Dolly looked confused. "Sir?" she said.

"Tell Miss Stewart she no longer works for Remy Sauvage. Tell her she works for me now and we are going home."

That made the little slave girl smile. This man was something of a savior in her eyes. "Yes, sir," she said.

"And Dolly."

"Sir?"

"Tell her if she wants to see me, I'll be in my cabin. Number twenty-four."

"Yes sir." Dolly bobbed another curtsy and closed the door.

He knew he wouldn't have long to wait for the explosion. In fact, it took all of five minutes.

She didn't knock. She threw open the door so hard the wood chipped. She hadn't even bothered to dress. She wore only the lavender silk dressing gown he had so enjoyed removing last night, knotted now at her waist and trailing behind her like the wings of an angry dove, revealing a beautifully muscled leg all the way up to midthigh. She was barefoot. She must have made quite a show striding angrily along the deck from her cabin, he thought. She made quite a show right now. In fact, he thought she looked magnificent. He had another pang of guilt at what he was doing, but it fled when she spoke.

"What do you mean giving my maid orders?"

"Good morning, my love. You look fetching."

"And what the hell do you mean by saying I work for you now? I certainly do not and I'm not going to. If you think that just because I made love to you last night I—"

"Oh, but you do work for me, my love." He cut her off. "You most certainly do." He picked up her contract and held it under her nose.

"What's that?"

"Take a look."

She grabbed the paper, recognizing it within seconds. "It's my contract with Remy," she said, confused.

"Smart girl. Read the addition at the bottom."

Her eyes flew down the page and read, "I, Remy Sauvage, do hereby give, without exception, all rights and duties assigned to me in this contract to Trey Lavande." It was dated with today's date, signed, and witnessed.

"Where did you get this?"

"Does it matter?"

"Of course it matters."

"I really don't think you want to know, Charli."

"Where did you get this?" The contract shook in hands that trembled with anger.

He shrugged. He really hadn't wanted to tell her. "I won it. In a poker game."

He expected her to explode, to rant and scream. Instead, she only glared, her breath coming in little gasps, too angry to speak. But that quick mind of hers was obviously working like mad behind those flashing eyes. "When?" she finally asked, her voice deadly quiet.

She would ask, he thought. He sighed. "Last night."

"Last night. Before or after?"

"Charlotte, please . . ."

"Before or after you made love to me?"

"Before."

He expected her to fly at him, to rake his face with her nails or pound on his chest with her fists. He didn't expect her to double over with a moan, as though she'd been punched in the stomach. He went to her.

"Don't touch me!" she screamed just before he reached her. He froze. Then, as he watched, she got hold of herself. She straightened, closed her eyes and took a deep breath, then let it out very slowly. Then another. When she opened her eyes again, he hated what he saw in them—a mixture of hurt and hate. "It can't be legal."

"Oh, it's legal, all right."

"Not if there's no contract." She turned the paper in her hand, and he reached for her just in time, just at the moment she started to rip it in half. His hands closed on hers, stilling her fingers with their strength until she dropped the paper.

He picked it up. "I'm sorry, Charlotte, but as of four o'clock this morning, I own you."

"Nobody owns me!" she shot back.

"This contract says otherwise."

"So sue me. Get yourself a lawyer. Take me to court. But if you think I'm working for you, buddy, you're crazy. You're not rowing with both oars in the water. You're two bricks shy of a load. Or, as my Grandmother Charlotte would have said, the butter has definitely slipped off your noodles."

He laughed. "I think I would have liked your Grandmother Charlotte."

"I will not work for you, Trey Lavande. I'll rot in jail first," she said, her hands on her hips.

"Or starve?"

"I'll find another job." She tossed her head like a defiant horse.

"No one will hire you."

"That's what you thought before. You were wrong then, too."

"I didn't have the power then to keep them from doing it. Now I do." He crossed his arms over his chest and leaned back against a bureau. His confident smile made Charli want to smack him. "I won't sue you, as you suggest, but I will sue anyone who tries to hire you away from me. Believe me, once they know that, they'll quickly find they have no job opening."

"You'd do that?"

"That and more, Charli." He reached out one hand and caressed her cheek, then slid his finger down across her jaw, past her collarbone, tracing the deep V of the neck of her dressing gown until his hand slid inside the loose opening and cupped her breast. "To have you, I'd do much more than that."

She closed her mind to the delight of his touch, armored herself with her anger, and shoved him away. "You manipulating bastard." As soon as the word came out of her mouth and she saw the look on his face, she knew she'd struck below the belt. But she was so angry and so hurt she didn't care.

He grabbed her wrist hard, hurting her. His voice was very low and very sharp and very angry. "Don't you ever call me that again."

"Oh, so sorry. Let me rephrase it. You manipulating son of a bitch!"

"Not very ladylike, are we?"

"Go to hell. And let go of me."

He released her. "As fetching as I find your present garb, I think you should go get dressed now. We dock in Natchez in half an hour. One of my boats will be stopping there just before midnight, heading back downriver. We'll be home tomorrow afternoon."

She turned to the door, looked back at him, and said, "At the risk of repeating myself, go to hell." Then she left, slamming the door hard behind her.

She didn't go to her cabin. Ignoring the scandalized looks of the other passengers strolling the decks as she passed in her bare feet and revealing gown, she headed for the owner's cabin. She didn't care that Remy Sauvage was still in his nightshirt. She ranted at him for a full ten minutes, barely allowing him to get a word in edgewise.

At least he had the grace to sound sheepish when he finally said, "I'm sorry, *cher*, but we have no choice, either of us. He won you fair and square. It's a debt of honor. As a gentleman, I have to honor it. I can't allow you to stay on board."

"A gentleman! You call yourself that? After what you did to me?"

He shrugged. "I'll find a way to get you back, darlin'. Maybe another game—"

"Don't bother," she said as she flung herself out of the room.

Back in her cabin, it only made her madder to see Dolly packing her things in the carpet-bag she'd bought in New Orleans. For the first time, Charli really knew what it meant to be mad enough to spit. And she had to stay mad. It was the only defense she had against the hurt that was tearing her up inside.

She had opened herself to Trey, she had let herself trust him, had believed him when he said he would never hurt her. And all the time he had known. He had known! He didn't care about her, not really. He just wanted to control her, to own her. He wanted to be sure she would be there, within reach of his bed, whenever he wanted her. Until he got tired of her and didn't want her anymore.

It hurt so much she was afraid she would throw up. Instead, she drew her anger around her like a bulletproof vest. The despicable, manipulative Trey Lavande was at the top of her hate list, with Remy Sauvage running a close second, but she was mad as hell at herself, too.

"How could I have been so stupid?" she railed at Dolly, pacing the tiny cabin as she spoke. "Me, who's had this very sort of thing happen to my own clients. I know better than anyone that a contract can be sold. How could I have been so dumb, for God's sake, when I always insist on a no-transfer clause?"

Dolly stopped folding a petticoat and looked up at her. "Master Lavande, he's a nice man, Charli, a kind man."

"Nice? Kind! He's a piece of bottom-sucking pond scum." She swept a green velvet gown off the bed and sat down. "And the worst part is, he's got me in a corner. Remy won't let me stay on board, and I've got almost no money left." She'd spent most of her first earnings on some clothes and other day-to-day necessities she'd badly needed, plus the suitcase to carry them in. She had last night's pay still coming—and she'd be damn sure she got it!—but it probably wouldn't be enough even to get her back to New Orleans, much less support her and Dolly there until she found some way around Trey's threat to keep her unemployed by anyone except him.

The obvious solution was to go home. She had to figure out how to get back to New York, back to the future. "Michael J. Fox, where are you now that I need you?" she muttered.

"Who?" Dolly said, looking up from her work.

"Never mind." She chuckled. Maybe when she did get back, she'd write a screenplay. This story could be worth a million bucks if she could find someone who didn't think it was too far-fetched, even for Hollywood.

The secret of getting back obviously lay in New Orleans, and it had to do with the river. If she was going to figure it out, she had to start there. All right, she'd go back to New Orleans with Mr. Trey Lavande. And when she got there, she'd find a way to leave again—straight for 1993.

Chapter Twenty

The trip back downriver was mostly silent as far as any conversation between Charli and Trey was concerned. She took her meals in her cabin with Dolly, she walked on deck with Dolly, and she slept alone, with her door locked. But the dialogue inside her head was incredible, a veritable cacophony.

I will not be manipulated this way, she told herself over and over. I will not be betrayed and then controlled and told what to do, like a puppet dancing on the end of a string. I've had more than enough of that in my life from my mother. Now I pull my own strings. And Trey Lavande can just stuff it if he doesn't like it!

She tried to make plans about what to do next. The problem was, she still knew so little about this foreign country called the past that she had to make her way in.

She still had no definite strategy in mind when they rounded the bend at Jefferson and the first few buildings of the Crescent City began creeping into view.

She stood on the deck in the late afternoon breeze, watching the city appear. Along the decks, dozens of others strolled, chatted, and watched the brick salt warehouses, the cotton buildings, and the sugar refineries come nearer, but Charli felt utterly alone.

And then she smelled him beside her. Lord, the man smelled good—a mixture of tobacco and lime and man. She saw his hands, long-fingered and capable, resting lightly on the railing beside her.

"Almost home," he said quietly. She didn't answer. "Are you ever going to speak to me again?" She thought his voice sounded almost, not quite but almost, sheepish. She thought, just maybe, there was the smallest note of apology in it.

"Probably not," she answered, finally looking up at him.

"Oh." He chuckled.

"I don't speak to despicable manipulators who make love to me knowing they have just taken away my choices about how to live my life."

"Even when they know better than you do what's good for you?"

She wheeled on him. "That is the most arrogant thing I've ever heard out of your mouth. How dare you presume to know what is right for me?"

"I'd dare an awful lot to have you near me, Charlotte." His voice was a caress and, much to her own annoyance, she was not immune to it.

"You've convinced me," she said dryly.

He looked out at the low skyline of the city. It was nearing sunset, that hour when the light was at its warmest and loveliest. The spire of the cathedral poked up through the trees of Jackson Square and glinted in the sharply angled rays. "We'll be home soon," he said.

But Charli wasn't listening; she was looking. She stared at the water, the ripples on its surface, the foam creaming out from the edges of the boat.

"Where was it?" she asked suddenly.

"Where was what?"

"The spot where you fished me out of the river? Exactly where was the boat?"

He looked around, judging their distance from the shore, trying to remember. "Right over there, I'd guess." He pointed. "Opposite Algiers."

"Midriver?"

"More or less. Perhaps a little closer to Algiers. Why?"

"It might be something in the water. The thing that pulled me back from the future. Some special current, an eddy, or vortex, or whatever you call it. Maybe if I could find the exact spot, that vortex would suck me back again."

He grabbed her shoulders and turned her to face him. "And maybe it would suck you back to 1532 or something. You could end up in an Indian canoe. Or maybe it'll just suck you under once and for all and you'll drown. Is that what you want? Are you so angry at me that you'd rather die than work for me, or spend time with me?"

"The idea did cross my mind," she said dryly.

"Well, don't even think about it. It is far too dangerous."

"Don't worry, my sense of self-preservation is stronger than my hatred of you. But I have to do something. I have to at least try to get back."

"Why?"

"Because I have responsibilities to my clients. Because my mother is probably worried sick about me. Because I don't belong here!"

He pulled her to him and looked deeply into her eyes. "Yes you do, Charlotte." He pulled her even closer. "You belong right here."

And Lord, if she didn't think for just the barest moment that he was right.

Warm in the circle of his arms, she thought about home. What had been going on in her absence? Did they think she was dead, drowned in the river that night? She realized it was very likely. Had her mother arranged the perfect, tasteful little memorial service for her? Had her clients started sadly looking around for other agents?

But . . . A new thought brought her up short. If she did find a way to get back to her own time, Trey would be dead. In 1993, he would have been dead for years, maybe a century or more. His great-great-grandchildren would be roaming the streets of the French Quarter.

The thought of his death sent a giant shudder through her body. Instantly, he removed his coat and wrapped it snugly around her shoulders. "You'll be in front of a warm fire in no time."

It sounded heavenly, but where was she to go? "I suppose I'll go back to Lisette's," she said, as much to herself as to him.

He moved back. "You could, of course. She'll take you in because she's kind and she likes you. But have you thought about what you'd be asking?"

"I beg your pardon?"

"My mother is a businesswoman. Her only assets are her brains and her girls and the rooms in her house, and it is extraordinarily expensive to maintain the sort of establishment she runs. She can hardly afford to give one of those rooms up for long while getting nothing in return."

That made Charli pause. "I hadn't thought of that. And she's been so kind to me already. A hotel, then."

"For how long? How much money do you have?"

The smirk on his face made her wonder if he had counted the pitifully few dollars left in her purse. "Enough for tonight, at any rate," she snapped.

"Come home with me, Charlotte." He caressed her elbow. "I promise not to lay so much as a finger on you."

She looked pointedly down at his hand, idly stroking her arm, then back up at him, one eyebrow cocked. He pulled his hand quickly away. "On my honor as a gentleman."

She laughed. "I've heard that before. But I've got to tell you, your Southern Victorian idea of honor is just a wee bit different from mine, suh."

"And your idea of what it means to be a lady is remarkably different from mine, ma'am." He grinned at her.

"I can imagine." She grinned back and they

shared a brief moment of harmony.

Then she left to get her things from her cabin. They had arrived.

As she gathered up her purse and a parasol and made sure Dolly had everything else, she wondered if she would eventually have gone to him willingly had he not used such heavy-handed tactics to force her. She wondered and was honest enough to agree that there was a very good chance she would. But the betrayal hurt so much. And the sense of powerlessness was intolerable. She had to find a way to break his hold over her, to break the contract.

The contract! Yes, there was a way, she realized. Quickly, she scanned the handwritten pages in her mind, recalled every detail of the day she had negotiated it with Remy. Yes. She knew exactly what she was going to do.

Caught up in the bustle of arrival, Charli and Trey didn't speak again until they were standing on the pier about to step into the cab Trey had hailed.

"Well!" he asked as her foot was poised on the iron carriage step. "Where's it to be?"

She smiled sweetly up at him. "Take me home, Trey," she said, then lifted her skirt and stepped up into the cab. He put Dolly and the luggage in a separate carriage, gave the driver his address, and jumped in beside Charli.

They hadn't clip-clopped along for more than two minutes when he put his arms around her. "Come here," he said, pulling her close.

"Trey," she said, snuggling under his chin. "There's something I have to ask you."

"Mmmmm," he murmured, burrowing in her hair with his nose.

"My contract with Remy, the one you won?"

"Mmmmm?" He kept burrowing and his hand stole inside her cape, caressing one breast lightly.

"Have you read it?"

"I glanced at it," he said without looking up. "Enough to know what I'll have to pay you to work for me. Don't worry. I can afford you." He began nuzzling at one ear.

"But did you read it all?"

"Not all of it. Why?"

"You didn't read the final clause, did you?"

"Should I?"

She chuckled, though it was hard to do when he was nibbling on her ear and sending such amazing feelings shooting right through her. "Oh, I think you should."

"You can tell me what it says."

"It says," she started, then gasped as his lips trailed down her neck and touched her collarbone. She pushed him away and struggled to sit up. "It says that if you seduce me—if you even try—the contract is broken."

"What?" he said, sitting up straight.

"Broken. Null and void, kaput, terminado. I'll be free as the proverbial bird once more." The carriage stopped in front of his house. "And you know what, big boy?" She ran her fingernail up one lapel and caressed his chin. "I intend to do everything in my power to see that you do make the attempt." The carriage door was opened and she stepped out. Looking in at his astonished face, she grinned. "Welcome home, Trey." Then she turned and swept up the walk and into his house.

After dropping her off, Trey left almost at once for destinations unannounced, and Charli knew he was simply eager to get away from her. She would always relish the moment she had dropped her bombshell. The look on his face had been priceless.

In his absence, she was made to feel immediately at home by Margie, Trey's cook/housekeeper, the slave he was working to free next. She showed Charli to a lovely room, all peacock blue and lilac with touches of white. It was a surprisingly feminine room and she said as much.

"Didn't you know, miss?" said Margie, a tall woman and almost painfully thin, but with a smile full of very white teeth in her eggplant-colored face. "Master Trey, he built this house for Miss Corinne, what was to be his wife. This would have been her room."

Charli looked around more closely, at the silver-backed brush and mirror on the vanity, at the delicate chaise longue placed before a window— perfect for reading on a sunny afternoon—at the Aubusson carpet on the floor, all woven in delicate shades of blue, gray, and rose. "It's lovely,"

"Well, I think so, but Miss Corinne, she thought it was too empty. Told me she planned to add more furniture and paper the walls with peacocks. Asked me not to say anything to the Master, though, said she'd suggest it herself, after the wedding." She flipped open a heavy drape to reveal crisp white undercurtains. The peach sky

Megan Daniel

of sunset glowed into the room. "Myself, I like it this way, miss."

Charli smiled back at the black woman. "So do I." She pointed to a door beside the fireplace. "Where does that go?"

"Why, to the Master's room, miss."

"I should have known." She walked over and opened it. "Does it have a lock?"

"Why no, I don't think so."

"Of course not," she said dryly. For this was to be his wife's room and in this world a wife had no right—legal or moral—to lock her husband out of a room. Though of course he had every right to lock her into one.

She looked into his room. It was as masculine as hers was feminine, done in charcoal gray and maroon damask on comfortable but not heavy furniture. An inviting wing chair sat before the fireplace, a full bookshelf within easy reach. And a huge, high four-poster bed dominated the room, a bed for more than one, a bed to make love in, to make babies in, to make a life in.

Quickly, she shut the door.

So, no way to lock him out. Never mind. If she needed to she'd just move a piece of furniture in front of it or something. Though she wanted him to try to seduce her so she'd be free of the contract, she didn't want him to succeed. She couldn't afford to have him succeed ever again.

Dolly bustled in then with a pair of hat boxes, followed by another servant carrying Charli's carpetbag. "Oh, Charli," cried Dolly, surveying the room and not seeing Margie's scowl at such familiarity between a slave and her mistress. "Just look at it! It's ever so much prettier than anything at Rive Douce."

Rive Douce. Charli knew, after several conversations with Dolly, that it was not a happy place, at least not since Trey's father died and his half-brother Laurence took it over. The field hands were whipped for the slightest infraction, or none at all. And Dolly had been treated most cruelly. Laurence's decision to sell her was the best thing that could have happened to Dolly, and the girl knew it. But it still rankled with Charli that anyone should have to put up with what Dolly and other slaves like her had to put up with. It was inhuman.

But now Dolly was here. Charli would take care of her.

She took off her hat and stretched her neck, circling it a few times to work out the kinks, and stretched her arms high over her head. It felt so good to stretch. "Boy, am I out of shape," she said.

"Miss?" said Margie, still moving about, setting the room in order.

"I haven't worked out in weeks," Charli explained. "I'm not used to it."

"Oh, never you fret, miss, everything will work out just fine in Master Trey's house."

Charli laughed, realizing Margie hadn't a clue what she was talking about. But the woman certainly had faith in her master. Everything would work out, she said. But how?

She wondered when Trey would return. She might as well get her campaign under way as soon as possible. But within that thought was a strange reluctance. To be honest, she didn't know if she would be able to withstand the man if he actually kissed her, if he touched her with those hands that were like stun guns, shocking her senseless. She didn't know if she was strong enough.

But she only had to manage it once. For once he even tried to get her into bed, the contract would be broken, and that was all she needed. It occurred to her that he had already done that, but it didn't really count. She couldn't, in good conscience, accuse him of seducing her on the boat last night when she had been as eager as he, as hungry, as much a participant. The next time, she would not be so easy, no matter how hard she had to steel herself against him. The next time would count. And then she would be free again.

But free for what? Free to get back to her life in New York, or free to build a new life for herself here? There was no way she could know that, but whatever the outcome, she was determined to be ready for anything. And part of that meant getting back in shape.

She had an idea. "Margie, have you got a couple of old sheets, something worn out that you wouldn't mind parting with?"

"Why, I suppose I could find a few, miss."

"Great. Would you send them up to me, along with some scissors and pins and a needle and thread?"

Margie looked confused, but she nodded her head. "Of course, miss. Right away."

When she'd gone, Charli turned to her maid. "Dolly, can you sew?"

"Of course," said Dolly, sounding offended at being asked.

"Great. Double great. We've got a project to attack."

A few minutes later a footman walked in with a pile of snowy sheets and the other things she'd asked for and dropped them on the bed, then withdrew.

"What's them for, Charli?" Dolly asked.

"I need a partner to keep in shape, and you, Miss Dolly, need to learn to defend yourself. We are going to make a *gi* for each of us and then I am going to teach you karate."

"Karate?" Dolly looked confused.

"The ancient and noble art of self-defense. Hand me those scissors."

Trey didn't go home that night. Instead, he spent the night on a sofa in his office.

He had so carefully planned what was to be a tender seduction scene once he got her home. His entire body had ached with wanting her. And then she'd thrown that unsavory bit of information about that damned contract in his face—ignore her and keep her, or seduce her and lose her. He didn't trust himself to be under the same roof with her without giving in to her wiles, so he had left. And spent the night tossing and turning and aching and thinking about her.

He woke up more exhausted than when he went to sleep, but when Robert Prideaux told him there was to be an auction with items from Rive Douce, he didn't hesitate. Off they went.

The auctioneer let his gavel drop with the ringing sound of wood on wood. "Sold to Mr. Lavande for four dollars." The wicker bassinet was taken away.

One more piece of Rive Douce was his.

To Trey, it mattered not at all that he had no need for a bassinet, wicker or otherwise, nor was he likely to need one for a great while. It was from Rive Douce. It should have been his. Now it was.

The next item up for bid was an exquisite humidor of ebony inlaid with mother-of-pearl. It didn't interest Trey. It was not from Rive Douce.

A porter picked up the bassinet he'd just purchased to take it away. Trey looked at the delicate thing, worn now with age—the last white baby born at Rive Douce had been his half-sister Camille, and she was married now, living up along Bayou Teche with three children of her own. The bassinet must have been hidden away in a corner of the attic, or Laurence would have sold it off long since. Now it would be sent to Trey's warehouse, to wait with all the other bits and pieces of Rive Douce, until he could return it once again to its rightful home—with himself as its rightful master.

As he saw it carried away, he had the oddest image. It nearly made him gasp. He saw the bassinet with a dark-haired baby in it, his baby, but with the laughing eyes and stubborn chin of Charli Stewart. He saw his own hand reach toward it and almost told the porter to wait, not to take it to the warehouse, to take it to his home. He had need of it.

Robert Prideaux, his colored business manager, broke that spell. "That's the last of his lots, I believe. We can go."

He turned to leave, but Trey stopped him with a hand on his arm. "I want to get the music box.

It's pretty, don't you think?"

Robert glanced in the direction of a dainty, porcelain music box, painted with lilacs and roses. An assistant to the auctioneer picked it up, wound it, and opened the lid. The delicate strains of "I Dream of Jeannie with the Light Brown Hair" tinkled up into the vast dome. Robert shrugged. "It's not his."

"I am aware of that, Robert." He smiled to himself. "I do occasionally buy things that do not belong to my half-brother, you know. I have a house guest who I think will like it."

Robert stared. "The odd Miss Stewart?" he asked. Trey simply smiled. Robert was his closest friend as well as his employee and privy to the entire saga of Miss Charlotte Stewart—except for the insignificant little fact that she hailed from the future. Trey was keeping that to himself for fear he'd be locked up in the madhouse if he tried to tell anyone.

Trey and Robert had met some years earlier in Paris, that beacon for New Orleans's favored sons, both black and white. Despite the obvious difference that was the first thing anyone in New Orleans saw, the two young men had a lot in common. They were both the bastard sons of rich white planters, both born to women not considered ladies by the "ladies" of the town—Trey's mother was a madam, Robert's a quadroon mistress. Both had grown up with fathers who visited when they felt like it, conveyed benefactions when they could, and made it clear their sons had no true claims on them. In Paris, they could be friends, sharing walks beside the Seine and talks in absinthe cafes and smoky bars. In Paris, they could be to each other what New Orleans wouldn't allow. In Paris, they were as close as brothers. In New Orleans, they had to work to remain friends. And they did work at it.

So Robert knew all about his boss's recent obsession with the outspoken New Yorker who was New Orleans's latest singing sensation. "So you actually got her to move in," Robert said. "How'd you manage it?"

"Let's just say I won her over," Trey answered with a grin.

He raised his hand to bid on the music box, won it in two minutes, and instructed the porter to have it delivered to his house. Then he and Robert left the St. Louis Hotel. A cold wind was whipping in off the river, carrying with it the smell of salt and fish. Trey turned up the collar of his caped overcoat.

"You're serious about her, aren't you?" Robert interrupted his thoughts as they strode down the banquette, their long legs matching each other's stride for stride.

Trey shrugged. "I don't know. I hardly seem to know anything anymore, except that I can't think about much of anything but her these days."

"So I've noticed," was Robert's dry comment.

"And now that I've finally got her in my house, I'm sorely tempted to lock the door and throw away the key."

"Is that the only way to get her to stay?"

"I'm afraid so. That or marry her." He almost jumped in surprise at his own words. Marriage? He hadn't even thought of marriage since Corinne died, and certainly not to an unconventional hoyden like Charlotte Stewart. She would not serve his purposes at all. Still . . .

"Marry?" Robert exclaimed, almost as surprised at the idea as Trey was himself. They turned the corner and Trey stepped off the banquette to cross Decatur Street, so lost in his images of having the lovely Miss Stewart as his wife that he was nearly run down by a dray loaded with heavy kegs of beer and pulled by a pair of enormous Belgian horses. Robert yanked him back onto the banquette just in time. He stared at his friend. "This is serious." Robert shook his black curls. "Justine won't like it."

"Justine will understand."

Robert laughed, though there was a bitter edge to the sound. "And I thought you knew my cousin. I just hope I'm nowhere in the vicinity of Rampart Street when you tell her you won't be back. I don't imagine she's let you see much of it, but she has the devil's own temper, our Justine."

"She has always known I must leave her one day, when I married. I have to provide heirs to take over Rive Douce once it's mine. And she certainly knows I can't marry her."

"Oh yes, she knows that," said Robert, the bitterness more pronounced. "All the quadroon concubines of rich white men know it, just as my mother did. But that doesn't stop them wanting it, Trey. That doesn't stop their crying when the men they've cared for and waited for and acted for leave them alone because they're no longer young and beautiful."

Trey felt a stab of guilt, but he said, "Justine is both. One appearance at the next quadroon ball and she'll be snapped up in moments."

"Suppose that's not what she wants?"

His guilt grew stronger. He hadn't told Robert, but he'd been feeling guilty about Justine for days. "Then she can stay at home. She knows I will always see that she is taken care of. She has the house I bought her. She'll continue to collect her allowance from me."

"And that's supposed to be enough, isn't it?" Robert's voice was tight with anger. He thrust his hands in his pockets and walked faster, his head lowered against the wind.

"She'll understand," he repeated mulishly. He wanted badly to believe it. "She'll accept it."

"She won't. You haven't seen her like I have, Trey. For you, she is all smiles and kisses and willingness. With me, with my mother and my sisters, she cries. She yells out her gratitude that she's barren so no daughter of hers will ever follow her to the quadroon balls at the same time that she cries because she will never rock your babe in her arms."

Trey suddenly felt very cold. He shivered inside his heavy overcoat. "I had no idea," he said, his voice almost a whisper.

"Of course you didn't," said Robert. They had reached the levee, and he looked up along its length. "That's part of the plan, too, you see." He turned back to his boss. "Do me one favor?"

"Of course."

"Tell her yourself. Don't write a letter. Don't send a message. Go to her and tell her yourself." Trey nodded. "And now, if it's all the same to you, or even if it's not, I'm taking the rest of the day off. You're my friend, Trey. I like and respect you, but right now I don't much feel like being around you."

"Robert, I—" He reached out toward his friend.

"Don't bother. Tomorrow, I'll be fine again. Tomorrow, I'll be able to smile and shake your hand and share your jokes and even drink with you. We'll laugh and remember Paris. I'll be able, once again, to accept the position your white world has decreed for my people and be grateful that I'm not a slave. But today I'm feeling just a little sick of it and you and everything." He turned and strode away. Trey watched him walk along the levee and disappear into a bar that was a favorite haunt of the city's free gentlemen of color. And he knew that he would never truly understand his friend's pain.

He turned toward Rampart Street. He would tell her himself.

Chapter Twenty-One

Much to Trey's unbridled relief, Justine was not in when he knocked on the door of the cottage he'd bought her in the traditional neighborhood for the quadroon mistresses of white gentlemen. It wasn't odd that she should be out, since he seldom called at this hour of the morning. Well, he had tried, he had to give himself that. It wasn't his fault the day of reckoning was to be postponed. He left word with her maid that he would return tomorrow, in the afternoon. It would be soon enough.

Feeling lighter, he turned toward his office. He would attempt, hopefully more successfully than most such attempts of late, to get some work done before heading home to Charlotte.

Home, to Charlotte. The words had a certain ring to them.

All the Time We Need

*   *   *

Justine had not been out when Trey called. She was upstairs in her bedroom, peeking through the curtain, her glorious ebony hair streaming down her back in tangled waves, her eyes puffed from crying. She knew why he was there and she couldn't bring herself to listen to the words just yet.

She'd had the first inklings of trouble the very night he fished Charli Stewart out of the river, for she had been dancing in his arms at his Mardi Gras ball aboard the *Corinne* when Charli appeared out of nowhere. She had seen with her own eyes the way Trey looked at the odd woman, cosseted her, and carried her ashore in his arms.

Within forty-eight hours, she'd known she had good reason to worry. Never, since the magical night four years earlier when Trey picked her out at a quadroon ball and made the arrangements for her *plaçage* with her mother, had Trey let more than two days pass without visiting Justine, unless he was out of town. Even when he was engaged to Corinne duClos, Justine hadn't worried. He still spent most afternoons in her bed, delighting her and being delighted in return by her endless inventiveness, and she knew that even if he left her for a while after the wedding— playing the good bridegroom—he'd be back in less than six months. The pretty, proper blonde would never be enough to satisfy the heightened sensual appetites of a man like Trey Lavande. Justine would have bet her house on it.

But this was different. This time Trey was exhibiting all the signs of a man obsessed, a man

275

enraptured, a man falling in love. And that terrified Justine clear to her bones.

She knew all about Charli Stewart now. In
fact, Trey would have been astonished to learn
just how much Justine knew about all his affairs
and always had. She made it her business to
know, and she had an elaborate network of
friends, relatives, slaves, and ex-slaves among
the colored community she could call on for
information—a group that had learned the sur-
vival value of knowing as much as possible about
the ins and outs of the white world that ruled
their lives.

She knew that Trey had taken Charli to Lisette's
house, that she had disappeared for three days
and that during that time Trey had not been seen
or heard from at his office. She knew about the
singing job with Lisette, and later with Remy
Sauvage. And she knew that Trey seemed to follow Charli about like a puppy dog.

When Trey had visited Justine for the first time
since Mardi Gras, she had rejoiced in her soul,
hoping his obsession with the Yankee was at an
end. But when he left without taking her to bed,
she mourned like one who had lost her core. It
was at that moment, when he kissed her at her
door and said good night, that Justine knew she
had lost him.

When word came that Charli Stewart was living
in his house, something in Justine snapped. She
would not give Trey up without a fight.

When he walked out of sight around the corner,
Justine rang for her maid. Quickly, she dressed,
put up her hair, and grabbed a cloak. She had an
important call to make.

* * *

Charli and Dolly finished sewing the *gis* by early afternoon, none too soon for Charli. She was feeling tired and irritable from lack of sleep. She had lain awake most of the night in her pretty room, listening for sounds of Trey next door, waiting for him to turn the handle on the connecting door, steeling herself not to feel anything when he touched her.

But he never came. She didn't know if she was grateful or disappointed. In any case, come morning she got up with a raging headache and a mood to match.

She knew from experience that the best remedy for her bratty mood was to get physical.

Ruing the fact that foam rubber hadn't been invented yet, she asked Margie to dredge up enough fabric scraps and feathers to make a solid, padded shield, useful for practicing punches and kicks without disabling your partner. Then she asked a couple of footmen to help her push the furniture back against the walls and roll up the fine Savonnerie carpet in the back parlor. It was the obvious choice for her impromptu karate *dojo*, since it had a huge gilt-framed mirror on one wall, and Margie told her the room wasn't used much.

Finally, she scrambled into her *gi* with relief.

What freedom! she thought, to be able to move again with perfect ease. Nothing got in the way. There were no steel bones, no hoops, no crinolines or starched ruffles, no shoes to pinch her feet, nothing to step on or snag or sway. Just freedom, perfect freedom.

It took Dolly a while to get used to the feeling.

"It just don't seem right proper," she said. "Not very ladylike."

"It is perfectly ladylike," Charli said, "and necessary if you want to be able to move. Now, come on." Shyly, Dolly agreed.

They began with a series of stretches to warm up reluctant muscles, then moved on to the basics.

"The word karate means open hand," Charli explained, "but you also have to know how to make a proper fist." She demonstrated and Dolly tried to copy her. "No, don't let your thumb stick out. It'll get broken off. Curl it around your knuckles." She did. Charli showed her the proper stance, her feet spread, toes turned slightly in and gripping the polished parquet floor. "Now, let the power start at the floor, move up the center of your body and outward toward your arms and legs."

They worked for well over an hour, until the sweat was pouring down both their backs, their hair was damp and sticking to their foreheads, and they were grinning like crazy.

Charli decided to end the session with some simple snap-kicks. She demonstrated for Dolly, then held the padded shield while the young black girl kicked out as hard as she could.

"Not so high," Charli instructed. "That can come later. Go for control first. The rule is control, power, speed, in that order. Again." Dolly repeated the move. "Better. Again." And Dolly kicked again.

"Better," said Charli, "but watch me do it. And listen." Dolly took the pad and Charli kicked, yelling a great karate yell that set the chandelier tinkling, and thrusting so hard that Dolly nearly went flying with the force of it. "Now you try it again."

Dolly took her stance, gripped her feet into the floor, took a deep breath and kicked, yelling like a banshee.

The momentum of the kick almost knocked Dolly over, but when she regained her balance, she was grinning from ear to ear. "I did it! I did it, Charli."

Charli grinned back. "Damned if you didn't." The two friends began to laugh.

Charli was still full of unspent energy, so she had Dolly hold the shield while she kicked. Again and again, her leg shot out, as she moved across the room, yelling louder with each kick.

Just as she let out a final mighty "Haaah!" the parlor door burst open. Trey ran across the bare wooden floor and grabbed Charli by the shoulders.

"Are you all right?" he asked.

"Of course I'm all right." She was smiling hugely. She felt great.

Trey was not smiling. He looked around at the room, at the rolled up carpet and the pushed back sofas and chairs. "What the devil is going on here?"

"A karate class," said Charli. "Wanna join us?"

He didn't smile back. Instead, he turned to Dolly. "Go clean yourself up. And prepare your mistress's bath."

Dolly curtsied, the action looking totally ludicrous in a sweaty karate *gi*, and skittered out of the room.

"Do you always order other people's servants

around?" asked Charli, her smile fading.

"Only when they are making complete fools of themselves. Now I want you to explain exactly what you were doing here."

Charli gave him a brief description of the noble and ancient art of karate, not bothering to explain that she was nearly a black belt or what that meant. "I've been getting out of shape. I need to practice."

"You mean you actually do this for sport?"

"Why not? You told me yourself you often go to the fencing academies in Exchange Alley to practice. And you spar at a boxing school."

"That is not at all the same thing."

"That is exactly the same thing. If you enjoy physical exercise and being able to defend yourself, why shouldn't I?"

The question took him aback. He didn't have a ready answer. Finally, he said, "You have me to defend you."

"Maybe it's you I want to defend myself against."

"Very funny."

"You don't think I could?" He smirked. "Okay, try me."

"Now, Charlotte—"

"Try to hit me," she insisted. "I'll bet you anything you like you can't do it."

"Anything?" His smirk grew.

"Anything."

"A night in my bed, with no canceling the contract."

"You got it," she said at once, not even bothering to state her own terms. "Come at me, any way you want. You won't get a hand on me."

She dropped into the basic fighting stance, centered, knees bent, the toe of the front foot directly lined up with the heel of the back one. Her hands moved rhythmically in front of her.

He lunged. She dodged. Surprised, he tried again. Again, he hit only empty air. She laughed, inflaming his masculine pride. He pulled off his coat, loosened his neckcloth and tossed it away. Then he turned back to her. She taunted him, knowing he was getting really angry.

This time he came in low in an attempt to bring her down by the legs. Her right leg swung across her body, then up and over his head, avoiding him completely, and he fell on his face. She helped him up.

"Give up?" she asked. He was panting and she wasn't even breathing hard.

"Not on your life."

She could read his mind as he fell back to reconnoiter. He'd underestimated her; he wouldn't do it again. He feinted left, then came in for a blow to her midsection. In one smooth, nonstop motion, she brought her arm up across her face then down in a circle across her body. He felt himself knocked away to the side, lost his balance, and sat hard on the floor. But he scrambled right up again. His face told the tale—he wanted to win.

This time when his arm came toward her, she didn't dodge it or block it. Instead, she grabbed his forearm with both hands, and before he knew what was happening, she had flipped him onto his back, stepped over him, and pinned him to the floor by sitting on his chest with one knee on each side of his head.

She laughed at his stunned expression. "That wasn't really kosher, I know. I used judo on you instead of karate. But it seemed to be the only way to get you to quit." He struggled to catch his breath. "Do you?"

"Do I what?" he managed to get out.

"Quit."

He looked up at her. Despite his frustration at being bested by her, he thought her even more beautiful in that white cotton thing she was wearing and with a tiny rivulet of perspiration running down her temple than she had been in a silken evening gown. He had an insane desire to kiss the sweat from her brow.

"Do you?" she asked again.

"If you'll pay a forfeit."

"Me? Hey, I'm the winner here, remember?" She looked at his grinning face. "What forfeit?"

"A kiss. A voluntary kiss."

"You can't possibly want to kiss me now. Good lord, look at me, I'm all sweaty."

He grinned. "I've never known a lady to admit to sweating."

"Oh, right. I remember my mother explaining it. Horses sweat. Men perspire. Ladies glow. Well, I'm glowing all over your nice parquet floor here. I need a shower. But of course, that is too much to hope for. A bath will have to do."

"First a kiss." He reached up and took her face in both his hands. Tenderly, he pulled her down to him. He brushed his lips across her forehead, licking away the salty taste of her sweat, loving it. He licked her eyes, her ears, the side of her jaw. Finally he approached her lips.

"You said one kiss," she said, her voice weak

with the sensations he so easily roused in her.

"This is one."

"Not the way I see it." Her voice was light as a feather.

"That depends on how you count." He rubbed a thumb across her lower lip, sighing when her tongue involuntarily came out to taste it. Then he pulled her to his mouth and kissed the resistance out of her.

She felt like she was dissolving in a puddle of her own sweat and sensation; she felt like she was melting. She felt like she didn't want him ever to stop.

But he did. "*That* was one kiss," he said, "and I suppose I'd better not push my luck."

"I suppose not," she said, disappointed. She got up and helped him to his feet.

As he brushed the dust from his pants, he asked, "Could you teach me? This karate, can you teach me to do it?"

Charli grinned, her equilibrium beginning to recover. "I could try, if you don't mind starting out with a few bruises."

"I think I've already got one or two. I suppose my backside can take a few more."

She laughed. "Yes, but can your ego?"

He laughed with her, richly and wonderfully. "We'll have to find out."

When Justine got to the little house in St. Ann Street it was crowded. There were whites and blacks, young and old, women in Paris gowns and barefoot slaves in homespun shirts and ragged trousers. Candles burned in the corners, and the smell of incense hung rich and heavy on the air.

283

Megan Daniel

Marie Laveau, the former hairdresser who was now New Orleans's queen of voodoo, sat in an enormous chair like a throne, its back and arms covered with *Xs* in circles and other odd signs and symbols burned into the wood. Beside her stood her daughter and heir apparent, also named Marie.

One by one, the supplicants approached the haughty woman with her coal-black hair piled into an elaborate coiffure above her exquisite mulatto face. Though already in her sixties, she looked no more than thirty-five. Some said she kept her youth by drinking the blood of fresh-killed babes, others that she stole it from the white women she prematurely aged with her hexes. At her feet rested a wooden box with small holes in the top. Every so often, a hiss could be heard from inside it.

A woman dressed in copper-colored silk and with her face hidden by a veiled bonnet approached and whispered to Marie, her hands fluttering like birds. Marie listened, her regal head inclined slightly, then reached into a drawer beside her and handed the woman an apple-sized ball of her own special *gris-gris*, an amulet made of salt, gunpowder, saffron, and dried dog dung with gaudy feathers pressed into its surface.

"Around your neck while in your bed is the place for it," she advised the woman. "And before your man come to you, drink this." She handed her a small vial full of a milky liquid.

"What is it?" whispered the woman.

"It is what you need. Drink it. A child will come."

The woman nodded, whispering her thank

yous. She drew some money from her reticule and handed it to the daughter, then glided swiftly from the house.

Suddenly, Marie looked up, stared straight at Justine, and beckoned her through the crowd.

"You come to me about a lover, is it not true, pretty?" Marie said to Justine, touching the quadroon's smooth cheek with one finger. "He wish to go and you wish him to stay."

"How did you know?" Justine asked.

"My business is to know. And you wish to peel another woman away from him too, heh?" Justine simply stared, and Marie nodded. "*Oui*, I will help you. I will give you powerful *gris-gris*."

Turning her back on all those waiting, Marie took Justine to another room. She made her remove her pantalets and tore a piece of lace from them. She pulled several of Justine's pubic hairs, pared her nails, and scraped a small piece of skin from her right breast. Then she shredded everything together with the leaves and yellow petals of the potent High-John-the-Conqueror root, pricked Justine's finger, and mixed in three drops of her blood. All the while she worked, she chanted softly, "*Canga bafie te, danga moune de le, canga do ki la, canga li.*" Finally, she put the mixture into a black silk bag and tied it with a red ribbon, sealing the knot with another drop of Justine's blood.

"Put it near to him, in his bed if you can," Marie told her. "Soon enough, he want no woman but you."

The second amulet she gave Justine was more potent yet—a "mojo hand" made of dried toad and bat wing, cat's eyes and owl's liver, the little

285

finger of a person dead by suicide, and hair from the head of a dead child. These ingredients had been ground to a fine powder and poured into a hollowed-out piece of bone—a sure and certain way to dispose of an enemy.

Then Marie went back to the front room and knelt by the box beside her chair. As she opened its hinged lid, the room fell silent.

Moving slowly, chanting no louder than a whisper, she reached in and lifted out a snake three feet long. She held it at the back of its head, just behind the jaw, whispered to it a moment, then kissed it on its nose. A soft gasp came from one corner of the room. In another, a woman fainted.

Squeezing gently, Marie opened the snake's mouth, held the "mojo hand" under one fang, and massaged the snake until a single drop of venom seeped out and fell onto the piece of carved bone. Then she lovingly laid the snake back in the box and closed the lid.

"Soon, pretty," she said as she handed the amulet to Justine, "soon the Yankee bitch be no more."

Many dollars passed from Justine's reticule to the hand of Marie's daughter, but she didn't care. She would pay any price Marie Laveau asked.

That night, Trey and Charli had their first dinner together in his home, and it was delightful. Margie was in heaven with someone besides just Trey to cook for, and she outdid herself with redfish soup, poached pompano in a white wine sauce, roasted woodcocks, lettuce in brown gravy, and the tiniest, tenderest artichokes Charli had ever seen. For dessert, she proudly carried out a citron soufflé.

"That was superb," said Charli as she pushed away her empty dessert dish, "but I may pop."

"I must admit I've never seen a lady eat with quite such obvious pleasure," said Trey, smiling. He had enjoyed watching her eat, unashamed of her appetite. It reminded him that she had other appetites he wanted to satisfy just as completely.

Charli smiled. "Right, I remember in *Gone With the Wind* that Mammy made Scarlett eat before the barbecue because God forbid anyone should actually see her put food in her mouth." He stared at her, his confusion obvious. "It's a movie," she explained, and this led to another discussion about movies and television and VCRs and satellite transmission. Trey was fascinated by every detail she could conjure up.

From there, the conversation somehow drifted to current literature—current being Alexandre Dumas, Balzac, and Dickens. *Madame Bovary,* she learned, had been published only the year before and was thought to be very daring.

"For my part, I thought Emma Bovary was a complete twit," said Charli. "I wanted to shake her."

Trey laughed. "Actually, so did I."

"There may be hope for you yet."

After dinner, they played chess. Trey won the first game, Charli the second. Then Charli sat down at the piano and began picking out a Chopin étude. Then next thing she knew, he was beside her on the piano bench and they were playing a duet. Without speaking, their rhythms matched perfectly.

By the time the evening was coming to a close, Charli was willing to admit that she liked this man, truly liked him. She couldn't remember when she'd enjoyed an evening more, the kind she had always imagined perfectly matched couples spent together all the time, an evening without pressure, without argument, a time of simply being together and enjoying each other's company.

And then it was time to go to bed.

Trey had given the moment a lot of thought all evening—in fact, he'd hardly thought of anything else, it seemed. And he had come to a decision. But he wasn't going to tell her just yet.

Instead, he picked up a branch of candles to light their way up the stairs and showed her to her room. "The *Corinne* sails tomorrow at four," he said. "Do you plan to be on her?"

Waves of disappointment flowed through her. Why did he have to remind her that she was an employee when they'd been having such a lovely evening? "Of course," she said. "It's my job."

"So it is, and I do have a contract, don't I? Good night, then." He left and walked down the hall to his own room.

The contract. The damn contract! She wished she'd never signed the stupid thing. And at the moment she wished she'd never put that stupid "no seduction" clause in it. Still, he could at least have tried. Didn't he want her anymore? Having had her, was he tired of her already?

Well, she had promised herself and him that she would make him break the contract, and obviously she was going to have to do just that.

Quickly, she undressed and slipped into an

288

almost transparent peach silk peignoir she knew was irresistible. She brushed her hair until it foamed up into a shiny black halo. She stroked peach blush across her cheeks and dabbed some Joy between her breasts. Then she got up and walked toward the door connecting her room to his.

Just as she reached it, it swung open. There he stood in a dressing gown of gold damask, and he was beautiful, so damn beautiful. God, she thought, I don't know if I can pull this off.

Trey walked straight to her, took her face in his hands, and kissed her with an aching tenderness. No fair! her mind screamed. He's not supposed to be nice and tender. He's supposed to be a bastard.

He went on kissing her, but without urgency, without demands. It was a true lover's kiss, and she wanted it never to end.

Feeling weak with the emotion of it, she backed up a step and reached for the bedpost to hold herself up. He came with her and gently eased her back onto the embroidered coverlet. He untied the sash at her waist and opened her robe. Then he just looked at her for a long time. She let him.

"You are very beautiful," he said softly. "The most beautiful woman I've ever seen."

She let out a long breath that was halfway between a moan and a sigh. "Do you know what you're doing?" she asked.

"Yes, Charlotte, I know exactly what I'm doing."

"And you don't mind that you'll have no hold over me afterward?"

He smiled. "Won't I?"

"The contract—"

He stopped her words with his lips while one hand went to his pocket. "Here," he said, pulling out a paper.

"What is it?"

"Nothing of any importance," he said, and he tore the paper in half and handed her the pieces.

She unfolded one of them. It was her contract. She looked at him in confusion.

"Please, Charlotte," he said, being careful not to touch her though his eyes burned into her. "Please stay, not because you have to, but because you want to, because I want you to."

As an answer, she untied the sash of his robe, opened the heavy fabric, and pulled him to her.

This time, their lovemaking was slow and sweet, almost as if they were moving in slow motion, or underwater. And so very tender. They took their time with each detail, each kiss, each patch of skin, drawing out each new sensation to its ultimate point, to the place where they could take no more, until finally control was no longer possible and they flew together to that magic moment of complete union.

When she could speak, Charli raised herself on one elbow and looked down at this man who had become so important to her. "What am I doing here?" she asked him. "What am I doing in this time, Trey, in this house? In your life?"

He touched her cheek. "I think . . ." He had to stop and take a deep breath. "I think you are making it complete."

"Oh," she said, overcome by wonder, and she snuggled down beside him again.

She could love this man, she knew. Maybe she

already did. But it was so scary. What if she let herself love him completely and then was pulled out of the past, back into the present? She had no way to control whether she stayed or left. She had no way to know if she was here for another day, a month, or forever. But could she face going back without him? She didn't know.

They dozed, woke to make love again, dozed some more. At one point, Trey lay awake, watching her sleep, breathing in sync with her breathing, wondering what he was going to do with this woman who had turned his life upside down. He had no answer except that he could no longer think of living without her. He finally drifted into sated sleep, holding her close beside him.

Chapter Twenty-Two

Justine had no trouble at all getting aboard the *Corinne* the next morning. It was still early enough that not many people were about, and she had disguised herself well simply by putting on the neat dress and apron of one of the female servants on Trey's boat and putting her glorious hair up inside a simply tied *tignon*.

She was taking a chance, she knew, because she had been on the boat more than once with Trey. There was always the chance that one of the crew members loading supplies, polishing brass, or mopping the decks would remember her. But she kept her head bent as she walked along the decks, heading for a linen closet she knew of. With a stack of snowy sheets in her arms, no one thought to question her at all.

Quickly, she made her way to Trey's cabin, a large and elegant teak-paneled room running clear across the rear of the Texas deck. She had spent many a night in this cabin, and she planned to spend many more. Wasting no motion, she flitted to the big brass bed and tucked the silken amulet containing her body's essence under the feather mattress just below the pillow. "Lie beneath his head, and make him dream of me," she said. Then she sang softly in Creole patois, *"Si to'tai zozo, et mo'tai fisi, mo tai tué toi, a fo'ce mo l'aimai toi."* If you were a bird, and I a gun, I would kill you, because I love you so.

Then she kissed the pillow, chanted softly, *"Eh bomba, canga li. Hen, hen, gris-gris!"* and left the cabin.

She scurried away from Trey's cabin. She spotted a cabin boy lazing by the rail and asked if he knew which cabin the singer was to have.

The boy grinned a big white grin. "Number eighty-two, biggest and best on the hurricane deck. Guess you got to make it special for her, eh?" he said, glancing at the sheets she carried. "I hear she's really somethin'."

But Justine had already walked away. She knew that cabin. It had been her cabin when she traveled to Natchez with Trey last year. She reached the hurricane deck in a few minutes. Luckily, the cabin doors were unlocked. She slipped into number eighty-two.

She had the "mojo hand" ready as she looked quickly around to make sure the room was empty. Then she darted to the bed, her skirt swishing softly on the thick carpet, and thrust the amulet under the mattress, not up beneath the pillow as

293

she had with Trey's, but lower down, at a spot where it could cause greatest pain, where its evil could seep up through the mattress and attack the most womanly part of the Yankee woman.

"Eh Bomba! Hen! Hen!" she chanted over the hidden amulet. *"Canga do ki la. Canga li. Hen, hen, gris-gris!"*

Next, she carefully peeled back the ruby red satin coverlet from the bed. She took a small metal box from her pocket and opened it. It was half-filled with salt. From the pitcher on the basin, she poured some water into the box and mixed it into the salt with her finger, all the while chanting the voodoo curse under her breath.

With slow, graceful movements, she drew a large cross onto the bedsheet with the salt. Then she stood back and smiled at her handiwork.

The Cross of Salt. Very bad *gris-gris*. It would tell the Yankee she had a deadly enemy. Then, while she was so frightened from the open attack, the even more powerful hidden "mojo hand" would do its secret work.

With great care, Justine lifted the satin coverlet back into place on the bed, being careful not to ruin the cross she had so carefully drawn. She smoothed it down and gave it a little tap like a lover's pat before she left, silently closing the door behind her.

Swiftly, she left the boat. She had to hurry home and lay the rest of her plans. Then she had to be back here by four. She planned to be among the passengers riding to Natchez today, so that she could personally see the results of this day's work.

* * *

Charli couldn't seem to stop smiling. From the moment she opened her eyes that morning to find Trey Lavande smiling down at her, her face had been creased in a permanent grin. She should have been exhausted; he hadn't let her sleep much during the night, making love to her again and again. But she felt wonderful! And for the next half hour, Trey proceeded to make her feel even more wonderful, kissing her senseless, sending her reeling up to the stars and over the moon before letting her come back to earth and finally get out of bed.

They lingered over their breakfast, talking about the sights they would see on the river later that day, and thinking about the delights they would share on the riverboat later that night.

By three-thirty, they were at the levee. The *Corinne* was just one of more than forty boats preparing to leave within the hour. Charli thought she would never tire of the great panorama that was the New Orleans levee at departure time.

Thick black smoke spiraled up from dozens of smokestacks, each topped with a decorative coronet, marching off as far as she could see and beyond. Flags flew at every jackstaff; windlasses whirred, lowering freight into every hold. Passengers swarmed thick as honeybees, filing up the companionways, surging along the decks, hanging over the gingerbread railings, calling, waving, shouting, laughing, complaining. Hand trucks and wagons, buggies, wheelbarrows, carts, and carriages jockeyed for position on the vast plain before the boats, piled high with goods going and coming.

Trey ushered Charli aboard.

She was standing on deck when she heard the Chinese gongs and the cry, "All that ain't goin', please to get ashore!" A few moments later, the captain blew a mighty blast from the *Corinne*'s whistle and the big boat slid backward into the river. The surge of the water slowly grabbed hold of it, the wheels worked against the current, and gradually the behemoth turned her nose upstream and they began moving toward Natchez, some eighteen hours away.

"Well!" Charli said to Trey, standing beside her at the rail. "It sure ain't the Staten Island Ferry."

"I've been to Staten Island," he said, surprising her. "When I was at Yale, I visited a friend in New York. We sailed over to the island one day and went duck hunting."

She burst out laughing. "Well, I know a lot of people go armed in New York, but I don't think that's their quarry."

It was a beautiful day, sunny and warm though cooled by the breeze off the water, and they stood at the rail a long time. Trey pointed out the villages of Jefferson, Harahan, and Kenner and the graceful riverside plantations of Live Oak Manor, St. Rose, and Destrehan. Charli thought of how much money modern tourists would pay to see these same sights in the future so they could take a look at history.

Finally, fatigue caught up with Charli and she decided to go to her cabin to rest. Dolly was there, hanging her dresses in the huge armoire, laying her brush and comb on the dressing table, arranging the makeup which she had finally gotten used to handling, though it was unlike anything she had ever seen.

It was a lovely room, with rosewood paneling and brass trimmings and a luxurious maroon carpet underfoot. Large windows faced the rear of the boat, and Charli opened them to let in the breeze.

"I'm going to sleep for an hour, I think," Charli said. "Would you wake me at six, please?"

"Of course," said Dolly, helping her out of her crinolines before reaching to pull back the coverlet on the brass bed.

And then she screamed.

"What on earth—" Charli began.

"*Gris-gris*, miss," whispered Dolly, staring at the Cross of Salt, slightly dislodged but still obvious in its malevolence. Before Charli could even ask what she was talking about, Dolly yanked the sheets from the bed, pushed open the door, ran to the nearest railing, and flung them into the river rushing past below. They floated away like empty shrouds.

When she came back, she was trembling. "The Cross of Salt. Someone hates you very much, wants to hurt you real bad." She looked around the room, as if she were expecting to see a snake slither out from under the bed or a frog jump out of the water pitcher.

"You want to tell me what this all means?" asked Charli.

"Voodoo, miss. It's voodoo. You got a hex on you."

Charli laughed. "Voodoo? Surely you don't believe in that nonsense. It's—"

"It's dangerous," came Trey's deep voice from the open doorway. "You may not believe, but others do, and their belief can harm you."

"Not if I don't choose to let it."

"Particularly if they are desperate enough to pull a stunt like this." He also looked around the room as if he could see her hexer hiding in a corner. "I want you out of here until I can have the entire cabin searched."

"Trey, don't be silly. I—"

"Now! This isn't something you understand, Charlotte. Maybe in 1993, voodoo has disappeared from your world, but it is very much a part of 1858. If any of the crew members finds out about this, I could have a major mutiny on my hands."

Charli could see that Dolly was very upset. Her eyes were wide in her face, and she was trembling. Charli took her arm and led her outside. "We'll walk a ways, shall we?" she said. Dolly just nodded.

As they strolled along the hurricane deck, Charli chatted in soothing tones, not mentioning voodoo at all, not saying much of anything really, but she could see that Dolly was growing calmer.

"And now, I think a cup of coffee is what's needed here. Much as I hate to support such a sexist idea, let's give the Ladies' Salon a try, shall we?"

They sat on a huge tufted and fringed ottoman covered in gold velvet, with a sort of upholstered pillar in the middle of it—a piece of furniture Charli always associated with the lobbies of slightly down-at-the-heels hotels. A young black woman in a neat uniform brought coffee on a heavy silver tray and placed it on the marble-topped table before them, giving Dolly a sidelong glance before she walked away. Charli looked around the room and noticed that none of the other ladies present had their servants with them. Well, tough, she thought. Dolly needed a cup of coffee and so did she, and if they didn't like it they could lump it!

By the time the cups were half empty, Dolly no longer looked nearly frightened out of her skin. But she did look confused.

"Charli," she finally said, "what did Master Trey mean when he said that about 1993 and there being no voodoo in your world? It don't make sense that I can see."

Oops, thought Charli, then she sighed. "Well, I guess this is as good a time as any to tell you. At least it's sure to take your mind off that nonsense back there."

She looked around the room where ladies chatted over tea or sat in comfortable chairs reading the latest issue of *Godey's Lady's Book* or even, in one case, snoring gently. No one seemed to be paying them the slightest bit of attention. So Charli told Dolly that she was from the future and as much as she knew about how she had arrived in New Orleans in 1858.

She tried to break it as gently as she could, but the girl was still shocked through and through. But as Charli added details to her story, reminding Dolly about the makeup she found so odd, about her wispy underwear, about all the little things that had made Dolly's dainty eyebrows go up in surprise, Dolly believed. Charli had become a heroine to her maid, and it never occurred to her to disbelieve anything her mistress said.

"So," Charli finished, grateful that Dolly was a much easier sell than Trey had been, "here I am. I don't know why and I don't know for how long, but while I'm here I plan to get as much as I can out of it—which when you think about it isn't a bad approach to life in general."

Dolly was still speechless, though Charli was sure she'd have plenty of questions later. "Let's go see if they're finished with my cabin. It must be almost time to start the unholy process of rigging me out for dinner."

As they left the Ladies' Salon, a woman rose from behind the upholstered center post that hid the opposite side of the large ottoman. She wore the trailing black crepe of a recent widow and was heavily draped in thick veils. No one could see the look of startled pleasure on the widow's face.

Justine stood in the middle of the room and stared at the door where the Yankee had just disappeared. The future! She said she was from the future. Believer that she was, Justine did not doubt for a moment that it was true.

And if Charli Stewart had been sent from the future by some strange force, she could be sent back.

She consulted the watch pinned to her bodice. They'd be docking at College Point in less than an hour. She could be back in New Orleans, at Marie Laveau's house, before midnight.

Charli didn't argue too strenuously when Trey insisted that she sleep in his cabin that night—for

300

safety, he said, since someone obviously wished her ill. She didn't really care what the reason was; she just liked the idea of spending the night in his arms.

The vicious and ugly "mojo hand" had been found under her mattress, nearly sending Dolly screaming in terror right over the side of the boat and into the river. And all evening, while Charli sang for her avid listeners, Trey kept a careful eye on everyone in the room. He was not going to let anyone suspicious-looking get any-where near her.

"But why?" Charli asked him as they lay in his big bed later that night. "Why would anyone in this place—or even in this century—want to hurt me? I hardly even know anybody here."

"But I do," he said, his voice tight. "And there are certainly people who want to hurt me."

"Well, why would they think that hurting me would hurt you?"

He brushed a wispy curl from her forehead and kissed the spot. "Because it's the truth."

"Oh." She turned her face into his chest and rubbed her cheek against the smooth, warm skin. "Who wants to hurt you, Trey?" she asked.

"Well, I'd say Laurence is at the top of the list."

"Yeah, I guess he would be." The thought of anyone hurting Trey made her want to hold him very close and not let go. "But if you weren't going after Rive Douce he wouldn't hate you, would he?"

"Probably he would. It's in his nature. But he'd have less reason to actually want to harm me."

"So, why not let him have it?"

301

He jerked so that her head came up. "What are you talking about? Rive Douce is mine."

"No, Trey, it isn't, and you don't need it. Can't you see that? Rive Douce belongs to the Campbells, and you're not a Campbell." He swung his feet over the edge of the bed and sat up. She laid her hand gently on his bare shoulder. "You're something better," she said. "You're Trey Lavande."

"Rive Douce is mine," he repeated, his voice low. "And I intend to have it." He ran his fingers through his hair. "I think it is past time that I had a talk with my half-brother. I'll make a point of it just as soon as we get back to the city." He lay back down and reached up to tangle a hand in her hair. "In the meantime, I'm going to make sure you are safe."

"Ummm, that sounds nice." She lay down beside him. "How do you plan to do that?"

"By keeping you very close to me." He pulled her close enough to feel the entire length of his body.

"Ummmm," she said again, and it was the last thing she said for quite a while.

An hour later, when they were both limp and smiling in the big brass bed, Trey said, "I don't want you making any more river trips for a while, not until we find out who put that thing in your cabin."

Predictably, she didn't like being told what she could and couldn't do. "You've got no right to tell me I can't work," she said.

"I have every right. It is my boat, and while you are on it, I am responsible for your safety, just as I would be if you were a porter or a wood stoker."

Damn him, he was right. He should be a liability lawyer, she thought. "Well, what do you expect me to do instead?"

"You will stay in my house until we know it is safe for you to leave."

"So now I'm going to be a prisoner?"

"Charlotte, be reasonable—"

"Giving in to stupid voodoo scares is not being reasonable." He gave an exasperated sigh. "Well, it's not!"

"Nothing about voodoo is reasonable. The trouble is that it sometimes works. Call it magic, call it faith, I don't know. But it is dangerous, Charlotte, believe that."

"And what will you be doing while I'm cooped up in your house?"

"Making certain that Laurence understands beyond a shadow of a doubt that you are out-of-bounds in this little tug-of-war of ours."

There was one other thing he had to do as soon as they got back to New Orleans, but Trey didn't tell Charli about it. He had to go see Justine. He'd been carrying that guilt around long enough.

Twice more he had knocked on the door of her house, planning to tell her that she was free to look for another *plaçage*, another position as mistress to a rich white man. Or not. But either way, that it would be without Trey in her life. He didn't have the least physical desire for the beautiful quadroon anymore. When he compared what he had experienced in her bed with what he had shared with Charli, it was like comparing grape juice to the finest vintage wine.

But she was never at home when he called—which surprised him, since Justine had always been scrupulous about being available to him whenever he might want her.

This time, he would wait, if necessary. It was past time the business was done. And then he could concentrate on what he was going to do about Charlotte Victoria Wainwright Stewart.

He didn't have to wait. Justine had been expecting him, watching at the window. She was ready for him this time. She opened the door herself when Trey knocked on it at noon the next day.

She put a sad smile on her face as she showed him into her tidy little parlor. She poured him a balloon of his favorite French cognac and rolled the glass in the palms of her hands to warm it before she handed it to him. Then she opened a silver box and took out one of the small, thin cheroots he liked, lit it in her own mouth, and gave him that as well.

Then she sat on the ottoman at his feet and let a single tear roll from each eye as she looked up at him.

"You already know, don't you?" he said kindly. She nodded. "How?"

"There are no secrets in New Orleans," she told him, "especially among the free people of color."

"You knew it would come, Justine."

"Of course." She smoothed the cranberry silk of her skirt. "Will you marry her?"

"I don't know." He sipped some of the brandy. "I'm not sure she'll have me."

Justine laughed then, one short, sharp burst, before catching herself. "Oh, Trey, of course she will have you. Who would not?"

"Several thousand women, I should think," he said with a chuckle.

She laid her hands on his knees and slowly let her huge dark eyes slide up to his. They were brimming—but not spilling over—with tears. "I will wait, you know."

"Wait? For what?"

"For you. Perhaps you will tire of her. Or she will tire of you. You will need someone who cares about you then. I will be here."

He reached down and took her hands in his. "No, Justine. Don't wait. You deserve to have someone of your own. You are very beautiful, and very loving. Any man would be proud and happy to have you for his own."

Any man but you, she wanted to scream, but she only smiled bravely.

"You will be taken care of, of course," he went on, "until you find someone else. My business-man will be happy to go over the particulars with you whenever you like."

"You have always been extremely generous, Trey. My friends have always been jealous of me."

"It was never more than you deserved." He gulped the rest of his brandy. "Well, I think I should go." He rose. "I will always be grateful to you, my dear, for some very lovely memories." Then he lifted her hand and kissed it. When he saw another pair of tears spill down her caramel-colored cheeks, he reached up and wiped them away. "Good-bye, Justine."

At the doorway, she helped him on with his coat. "Remember, Trey, I will be waiting."

He faced her and paused. "As you wish, but I will not be back." Then he went out the door and down the little path to the street.

She stood in the doorway and watched him go. "Oh yes, my darling, I will wait," she said softly. Her smile was no longer sad or brave. It was triumphant. "But I will not have to wait long."

Well, that's over, Trey thought. There was a spring in his step as he left Rampart Street. All in all, it had gone off much better than he could have hoped. Not a pretty scene, of course, nor one to be looked forward to, but it certainly hadn't been anything like the nightmare Robert had envisioned. It seemed he knew Justine better than her cousin did after all.

And now it was done. He could turn his attention to dealing with Laurence, deal with this vicious voodoo business. And then he would deal with Charli.

Chapter Twenty-Three

"Difficult," Marie Laveau said to Justine, tapping the manicured nails of one hand against her cheek while the other stroked the fur of a pure white cat in her lap. "*Oui*, a challenge." She lifted a glass beside her and took a long drink of dark rum, licking the last drop from her lips. "Me, I like a challenge, but it will cost."

"I will pay," said Justine.

"Yes, you will, pretty." She reached out and stroked her fingertips across the quadroon's ebony hair, down her cheek, across her lips. "Oh yes, you will pay."

She stood up suddenly, disturbing the cat into a screechy *meow* as it fell to the floor. Marie laughed. She picked three white hairs from her skirt and carefully laid them in a box on a bureau, then turned back to Justine. "And now I tell you what we do."

Charli paced her room in Trey's house. She was bored and she was worried.

They had finished the Natchez run that morning. Trey brought her home, told Dolly to make sure she stayed there, and left again, saying only that he planned to pay a surprise call on Laurence that night and not to expect him home until late.

She had managed to entertain herself for most of the day by giving Dolly both a karate lesson and a reading lesson, showing Margie how to make a proper egg cream, and working on some new material at the piano. She was getting tired of singing the same old songs all the time—even if they were the same new songs to her listeners. She had re-read the beginning chapters of *A Tale of Two Cities* and played three hands of solitaire.

But now it was going on two A.M., and he still wasn't home.

Stop worrying about him, she told herself sternly. Why, you'd think I was married to the guy!

She stopped pacing, caught by her own thoughts.

No, not married. You'd think I was in love with the guy.

She stood very still, barely breathing. I am in love with the guy, she realized. God help me, I really am.

How could this have happened? How could she be in love with someone who shared none of her modern interests, someone who thought a woman who wanted to work had to be crazy, someone from another century! How could she be in love with a man who she had no reason to believe loved her back?

But she was, and far from feeling the panic or confusion her brain told her was reasonable in this situation, when she looked in the tilted cheval glass she saw that she was smiling hugely, her cheeks were glowing, and there were tears in her eyes.

She walked to the French doors that opened onto the iron-railed gallery overlooking the street. It was quiet at this hour. There had been a drizzle earlier, and the cobblestones still glistened under wisps of fog rolling in from the river. A crepe myrtle, bare and bony, cast weird shadows on a wall across the street. The air was heavy, humid, pungent with the scent of the just-blossoming honeysuckle climbing over a trellis below. At the end of the block, a Charley, one of the night watchmen who patrolled the city, paused under a gaslight, struck a match to a cigar, then moved on.

Charli took in every detail, seeing it more clearly than she'd ever seen anything in her life. She rested her hands on the cold iron railing.

"Come home, Trey," she whispered to the night. "Come home, my love."

Trey found his half-brother exactly where he expected to find him, at Helene's, one of the most notorious and high-rolling gambling houses in New Orleans. If it hadn't been for Helene's, Laurence might not be quite so near to losing Rive Douce.

What Trey hadn't expected to find was Remy Sauvage, sitting opposite Laurence at a card table.

"Well, Remy, I see you've switched to gin rummy," said Trey, pulling up a chair. "Good thing. Poker hasn't been your game lately."

"Nothing has," the Creole muttered. "And now that you've taken the lovely Miss Charli away from me, my business is off by fifty percent." He picked up a glass of bourbon and drank deeply. "You owe me, Lavande."

"We'll discuss it later, Remy." He turned to the smaller, paler, weaker version of himself. "Right now, I need to speak to my brother." His slight emphasis on the last word did not go unnoticed.

Laurence slammed his own glass on the table, sloshing whiskey on its green felt surface. "I haven't got a brother, only a nuisance of a bastard buzzing around me."

Trey clenched his teeth, but his voice stayed calm. "At least my bastardy is honestly come by." He lifted a finger and ordered a glass of Madeira. "And I plan to go right on being a nuisance. And if anything, I mean anything, happens to Charli Stewart, I'll be an even bigger nuisance than you can ever imagine. Your fight's with me, Laurence, not her. Stay away from her."

"Charli who? I don't know what you're talking about."

"Then I suggest you go right on not knowing, and that you forget anything about her you just happen to remember."

Laurence pouted. "You're just trying to confuse me. I know you want Rive Douce. You already bought my furniture, you bought my slaves, you

310

even bought the portrait of my father."

"Our father." He sipped his wine. "And that's not all I've bought. I also hold two thousand dollars in outstanding mortgages on Rive Douce."

Laurence jumped up from the table. "You bastard!"

"I thought we'd already established that."

"You'll never get Rive Douce! It's always been Campbell land and it always will be. My next crop will pay off those mortgages, and I'll buy back every single thing you've stolen from me."

"Stolen?" said Trey, one eyebrow raised. "Why, Laurence, how could I steal what you have so willingly sold?"

Laurence glared at the half-brother whose very existence he had always hated. Then he turned to Remy. "Are we playing or not? Deal the cards. I'll be right back." Then he walked off toward the back of the room.

When he was gone, Remy chuckled. "Such fraternal affection is always a blessin' to witness."

"Stuff it, Remy," said Trey, leaning back in his chair. Laurence's words were spinning in his head. It was true that next year's cane crop would pay off the mortgages, if Laurence didn't drink or gamble the money away first and he hadn't gone that far yet. Oh, he'd do it eventually, but Trey was getting impatient. At the rate things were moving, it would be a good three or four years before he owned every meadow and canebreak, every creek and valley, every sugar house, grinding shed, slave cottage, all of Rive Douce.

And according to Charli, he didn't have four years. In four years, they'd be at war. He had to have Rive Douce before it started, early enough to make arrangements to protect it. He had to speed things up. He just didn't know how.

"Y'know," said Remy, interrupting his thoughts, "I meant it when I said you owe me. At the very least, Lavande, you owe me a chance to win somethin' back. Oh, I don't expect you to give up the divine Miss Stewart—any fool with eyes could see she's meant to be yours, however undeservin' you might be."

"Yes, she is." As he said it, he knew it was true. She *was* meant to be his. He would have to convince her of that fact.

"But some other arrangement . . . ?" Remy went on.

"What did you have in mind?"

Remy pulled a cigar from his pocket, sniffed it, licked along the length of it, bit the end off, and finally lit it. When the smoke had made a cloud around his head, he spoke again. "I've ordered two new boilers for the *Belle Brigitte* from Pittsburgh, the finest in the country."

"Congratulations."

"They're being installed right now. Take another week."

"I imagine you're getting to the point here?"

"They'll make her the fastest boat on the river."

"How nice for you."

"And when I prove it to everyone by beatin' the *Corinne* in a race from here to Natchez, everyone will want to ride the *Brigitte*."

"Ah, I see."

"What do you say?"

Trey slowly shook his head. "I don't think so, Remy, but thanks for the offer."

"Dammit, Lavande!" Remy struck the table with the flat of his hand. "Why won't you race her? Are you afraid you'll lose?"

"Who knows? We'll never know, because racing is a form of gambling, and I never risk a gamble unless there's something at stake I want." He drank some of his wine. "You don't have anything I want, Remy."

"I've got river business, damn you."

"I already have more than I can handle."

"How can you—"

Laurence cut him off. "Are we playing gin, Sauvage, or shall I move to another table?"

Remy scowled. "We're playin'." He started angrily shuffling the cards. Trey watched the little pasteboards slide across the table. Then he got up and turned to go.

"Wait!" Remy said, his hand frozen mid-deal. Trey turned back to him.

Slowly, Remy laid down the deck of cards and folded his arms on the table. He stared at Trey. Slowly, he turned his head and stared at Laurence. Then he stared at Trey again. And then he smiled a slow, triumphant smile. "You're right, Lavande. I don't have anything you want." His smile grew. "But Laurence Campbell sure does."

Slowly, Trey sat down again, staring at Remy a long moment. Then softly, he said, "Damned if he doesn't."

A half hour later, when Trey stepped out into the damp night, the terms were set. One week from tomorrow, the *Corinne* would race the *Belle Brigitte* to Natchez. If the *Brigitte* won, Remy would have a lock on passenger business on the river, business worth a fortune—

and Laurence Campbell would get back every piece of Rive Douce he'd lost, as well as the mortgages Trey held.

But if the *Corinne* won the race, Rive Douce would belong to Trey Lavande, every stick, stone, and square acre of it.

Charli had fallen asleep in a comfortable chair pulled up before the fire, her feet tucked up under the skirt of her light blue taffeta dress, waiting for Trey to come home. The grandfather clock in the hall chimed half past two, its echo faded away, and the house was very quiet again.

Something woke her, she didn't know what. A sound? Then she heard it again. Something rattling against the window, like gravel. Then again.

She was definitely awake now. She got up and opened the French doors and stepped out onto the gallery.

A young slave boy, dressed all in black so that she could barely see him in the shadows where the gaslight didn't reach, beckoned to her.

"What do you want?" she called, not too loud.

"Come down, missie," he said, also softly. "I got a message for you."

She remembered Trey's warnings. It could be a trick, she thought, someone wanting to plant some more of that stupid *gris-gris* on her, or worse. But the kid was about the size of E.T. He wasn't likely to give her any trouble she couldn't handle.

"Just a minute, I'll be right down," she called. She hurried out the door and down the stairs.

She had to fumble with the lock on the door a minute before it opened, then she stepped out onto the banquette. "Well, what is it? What do you want?"

"You be Missie Stewart?"

"Yes."

The boy thrust something at her, a lump of fabric. She took it and examined it. It was one of Trey's silk shirts—she recognized the monogram—and it was covered with blood!

"What have you done to him?" she cried, clutching the shirt and lifting one hand as if to strike the boy.

"I ain't done nothin', missie." He flung his hands up in front of his face and cowered. "I ain't! He sent it to you. He be hurt, missie, hurt bad, he wants you. He sent me to get you. You gotta come."

She dropped her arm and clutched the shirt tighter, holding it to her breast. "What's happened? Where is he? What's wrong with him?"

"I don't know, missie, he just said to get you, to bring you. He be hurt bad, missie. Better you come right now."

"Yes, yes, let's go." She didn't even turn back for a cloak against the rising mist. She didn't care. "Hurry," she told the boy. "Run!" And she followed him down the banquette.

From the window of her tiny room on the top floor, Dolly watched Charli and the little slave boy. Though she couldn't make out their words, their voices had awakened her. Now full wakefulness and alarm sprang up in her as she saw Charli hurry down the street after the boy. Where was she going? Master Trey had specifically told Dolly to take care of her mistress. She was responsible. And here was Charli running off in the middle of the night with a slave boy Dolly would swear she had never seen before.

She stuffed her feet into her shoes, grabbed her cloak from a peg by the door, threw it on over her nightdress, and ran out the door. She almost tripped running down the stairs. Then she was out the door and running in the direction she had seen Charli go.

Please God, she prayed, don't let the watch get me. A slave on the street alone in the middle of the night without a pass could be arrested, and then how could she help her mistress, her friend?

Already Charli and the boy were out of sight. Dolly ran as fast as she could until she finally saw the moving blur of Charli's light blue dress. They had turned the corner into St. Philip Street and were hurrying towards the river. Panting, she ran after them.

They turned again at Decatur, ran past the French Market, past Jackson Square. Dolly kept losing sight of them as they moved in and out of the black shadows that the hazy yellow halos from the gaslights couldn't reach. Toulouse Street, St. Louis, Conti, Bienville, Iberville, she sped past the cross streets as she ran, pressing her hand to the stitch in her side and gasping for each breath.

Brick warehouses loomed all around them now, casting even larger and blacker shadows. She saw the boy emerge from one of them with Charli right behind him and begin climbing up the levee. Dolly was still half a block behind them when she felt a hand on her shoulder.

"Hold it, girl. Where you running to in such a hot foot hurry?"

The hand spun her around. It was a Charley.

She gasped out the words. "My mistress." She pointed after Charli. "Have to get her. Help. It's dangerous."

The watchman looked in the direction Dolly pointed, but Charli and the boy were already out of sight further down the levee. "No one there, and no pass in your pocket neither, I'll wager," he said. "C'mon, it's a night inside the Calaboso for you, girl, and lucky it's nothin' worse. If your mistress wants you so all-fired bad, she'll pay your fine in the morning."

"No!" Dolly struggled. "She needs me. You can't—"

"Here! Stop that!" He grappled with her while he tried to get his stick free to fight the little tigress.

She had to get away. Her mind raced over what Charli had taught her. She hadn't had many karate lessons, but she had to do something. Now.

He had his arms around her from the back in a sort of bear hug. She pulled her arms together, crossed them, then flung them up and out in an arc, breaking his hold. As he staggered backward, off balance, she spun, bent her knees, tried to grip the ground through her shoes, and kicked like the devil himself was in her face while she shouted "Haaaah!"

Whether it was the minimal power of her kick or the sheer surprise of her attack, the little Charley didn't have a chance. He went flying into a brick wall, slid down to the ground, and sat there, too stunned to move.

Dolly was gone before he knew what had happened.

She couldn't find them. She climbed the levee and looked down the other side. They weren't there. She ran along the top of the levee, away from the lights of the Quarter. Farther and farther until the wharves and docks thinned out, then disappeared, to be replaced by fishing boats, flatboats, rowboats, and rafts pulled up onto the grassy slope of the levee or anchored in the shallow water.

There! As a cloud rolled away from the moon, Dolly saw Charli's blue taffeta dress glowing like a beacon. She was standing in the prow of a rowboat that had just been pushed into the water about a couple of hundred yards away. As Dolly scrambled down the levee and across the broad flat expanse to the water, the little boat moved farther into the river. A pair of oars bit the water, powered by some strong arms invisible in the dark, and the boat cut straight across the current. By the time Dolly got to the water's edge, the boat was halfway to Algiers.

She called Charli's name, but the boat never slowed and Charli never turned around. Dolly collapsed on the ground with a sob. She had failed. Charli was in dreadful danger—she just knew it— and Dolly had failed to help her.

She heard a sound behind her and spun around. The little slave boy who had guided Charli here stood there, watching her. She jumped up and ran to him, grabbed his shoulders. "Where they taking her?" He just stared up at her with big eyes, so she shook his shoulders until his head flopped. "You tell me, boy! Where they taking my mistress?"

"Home."

"What you mean, home? You just brought her from there."

"They say they take her home. They say the bad hoodoo brung her here, and they say now the grand *zombí* gonna take her home again."

A shiver rippled through Dolly, and she dropped her hands from the boy's shoulders. He scampered out of reach, ran up the levee, and was gone.

The grand *zombí*, the voodoo god. His name had been used to frighten her and the other children in the slave cottages into good behavior ever since Dolly could remember. The very word froze her into immovable panic.

She looked back at the river. She could no longer see the little rowboat or the beacon of Charli's blue dress. Her mistress was being taken to the *zombí*, and she didn't know what to do.

She had to think. What would Charli tell her if she were here? She'd say something like, "Well don't just stand there. Let's do something, even if it's wrong."

Do something! Yes. She had to get Master Trey. She had to find him. He'd know what to do.

She turned and started running back toward the house in Chartres Street, glancing back over her shoulder every few minutes. She couldn't afford to be caught again by the watch.

Chapter Twenty-Four

On the opposite shore, the rowboat approached the levee. In the glimmering moonlight, Charli could make out the shapes of trees growing right to the water's edge: huge live oaks, cypresses, sweet olive, all draped with Spanish moss swaying in the breeze, its fingers clawing across the river's face.

Frantically, Charli scrambled out of the boat even before it stopped moving, sloshing into two feet of icy water, running up onto the grassy banks.

"Where is he? Is it far? Take me to him, please," she begged the huge black man who had rowed the boat across—he had been waiting for her at the levee on the New Orleans side.

Silently, the man pointed her toward the trees.

"There?" she said uncertainly, moving toward

the darkness. The man waved her on.

As she moved into the all-enveloping blackness, Charli knew the first moment of fear for herself. Up until now, all her concern had been for Trey. But what would he be doing in this black, remote spot?

He'd said he was going to see Laurence, to stop the threats to her, and maybe to taunt his half-brother with the inevitable loss of Rive Douce. Could there have been a duel? she wondered. What she knew about duelling would fit on a microchip, but she'd heard enough references to it in the past few days to know that it was common among New Orleans's planter class—which certainly included Laurence. But were duels fought in the middle of the night? Charli had no way of knowing, but it would explain the bloody shirt.

Remembering the sight of all that blood, determination pushed her fear aside and she walked farther into the trees. She had to find Trey.

Suddenly she heard a snap, like a twig breaking underfoot, followed almost immediately by a bright light shining right in her eyes. Instinctively, she flinched and squeezed them tight. When she opened them again, she saw a man with a lantern. She realized that it must have a shuttered side that he had opened abruptly. Before she could figure out anything more, something fell over her head, a cloth, snuffing out the light, smothering her with its thick, burlap smell.

Instinctively, she dropped into a fighting stance, but karate wasn't designed to be used with a bag over your head. Her arms were useless; she couldn't see her enemy. Strong arms came around her, lifting her up like a sack of potatoes.

Her struggles made no difference at all as she felt herself being carried off.

Within minutes she could tell, even through the rough weave of the bag, that the light around her had brightened. She could hear murmurings, shuffling feet, crackling sounds. She felt heat. Then she was set on her feet again.

Suddenly the bag was pulled off. She flinched and squeezed her eyes shut against a brilliant light. When she opened them again, she saw that she was standing near a raging bonfire. Beyond it, the river glimmered in the moonlight.

She turned in a circle. She stood in a large clearing surrounded on three sides by high, thick trees. And all around her, seated on the ground, sat black men and women, their faces shining in the fire's dancing glow.

At one side of the circle, facing her, a woman sat on a wooden throne. She was enveloped from her neck to the ground in a voluminous white robe covered with odd symbols embroidered in red.

This has got to be a bad movie I've fallen into here, Charli told herself. This cannot be real. It's too scary to be real.

But she jumped when a drum sounded a single beat behind her, loud and sudden as a cannon shot. That was certainly real. It sounded again. Then a steady rhythm. A second drum, lower pitched, joined in, then a third. Several of the men on the ground began beating drums of wood or bamboo they held between their legs, slapping them with their fingers or the sides of their hands.

A young man started strumming a long-necked

instrument that looked something like a banjo. Another hit on a large, metal-studded gourd with what looked like two thigh bones, while others shook rattles made of gourds.

She took in the odd jam session, or whatever it was, noting the exotic details even as the sound grew in intensity, the rhythm building until it felt like it was pounding inside her head. Shadows danced across the faces, glistening with sweat from the fire.

Suddenly, Charli was very frightened.

She took a deep breath. I will not panic, she chanted to herself, I will not panic. She remembered *Sempai* Joe's words—"Show weakness and become prey; show strength and become master." She would not show weakness or fear. She would be the master here.

Quick as thought, she spun around the circle, flung up her hands, palms facing flat out, and shouted at the top of her voice, "Stop!"

To her surprise, the rough music ceased instantly. Every face turned toward the seated woman in the white robe, calm but expectant.

The woman smiled. "Welcome, Yankee," she said in a dramatic Haitian Creole accent. "Welcome to our circle."

"Where's Trey?" Charli asked, forcing herself to face the woman without flinching. "Is he all right?"

"There be no reason to think he is not."

Relief flooded through her; she sagged with it, murmuring, "Thank God." But anger rushed in as soon as worry dissipated. "You mean it was all a lie? A trick?" The woman shrugged slightly. "Why have you brought me here?" Charli demanded.

"What do you want from me?"

"Only to help you."

"Help me? I wasn't aware I needed any help." Except to get out of here, she added silently.

"Do you not, little Yankee? Do you not wish to go home, back to the future you come from?"

Charli gasped. "How do you know about that?"

The woman smiled even more, but it was not a friendly smile. *Je suis Marie Laveau,*" she said with dramatic flair.

"I take it that is supposed to mean something to me?"

The woman's dark eyes flashed. "I be the voodoo queen, lover of the grand *zombí* who knows all secrets." Her insinuating smile crept back. "There be no secrets between lovers."

"And you've brought me here to send me back to the future with your voodoo rites?" She almost laughed, but she thought better of it. She didn't see a lot of humor in the faces around the fire and especially not in their "queen." "What makes you think I want to go back?"

"You do not belong here. It be our world, not yours. It will never be yours."

Charli realized the woman was only saying what she herself had spent a lot of time thinking ever since she'd arrived in the past. But voodoo as a means of transportation? It seemed more than a little ridiculous.

Of course, she had already been forced to believe the unbelievable; why not go the whole nine yards and decide that this grand *zombí* of theirs just might get her home if he felt like it? It was a temptation, anyway.

The woman stared at her and Charli found she

could not look away. It was as though she were hypnotized. Her fear vanished; instead, she felt a strange exhilaration—a mixture of awe, curiosity, and total amazement at where she found herself. The cool, calm part of her mind was saying, "Remember this and you'll dine out on it for years; not one of your friends has ever seen anything remotely like it." The less rational part of her was completely dazzled by the show.

"You miss your world, heh?" Marie went on, her voice low, insinuating. "You wish to return to family, friends. Only the power of the grand *zombí* can help you. And only now, only here, tonight, when all the forces are right. Refuse and you never see your home again."

That thought, too, had haunted her for days. Never to see New York again, or her clients, her friends, the apartment she loved. Never again to ride a bike through Central Park when the fall leaves were thick on the ground and the air was crisp or fly off to Paris for an April weekend. Never to sit in a smoky jazz club and listen to music that touched her soul.

Never to see her mother again.

Marie Laveau seemed to read her mind. "*Oui*, you see? You wish to go and there be nothing to hold you here."

Oh, but there is, Charli's mind shouted. There is Trey, and the thought of leaving him, of never talking to him again, never laughing with him or fighting with him or kissing him, never again feeling him inside her, was more than she could stand.

"You hesitate, Yankee," Marie said. "The grand *zombí* knows why. Now he help you decide."

Marie clapped her hands and another woman emerged from the shadows. She, too, was dressed all in white, but it was a fashionable evening gown of heavy satin embroidered all over in silver thread. It was beautiful, but not half as beautiful as the woman who wore it, with smooth skin like creamy coffee, hair like polished ebony shimmering in thick waves down her back and across her shoulders. She had a figure like a goddess, the waist tiny, the magnificent breasts large and lush and proud.

She looked familiar. Charli was certain she had seen her somewhere.

Before she could ask, the woman spoke. "Oh, yes, Yankee, we know each other. In a way, we are sisters. I am Justine." The name meant nothing to Charli, but unlike Marie Laveau, the woman didn't seem to mind. "You saw me the very night you came to this time, on the boat in the river." She paused. "I am the lover of Trey Lavande. I have been for many years."

Charli's stomach clenched, as though she'd just been punched in the gut, and she doubled over.

But Justine went on relentlessly. "It is not you he wants. You have been but a diversion, an amusement. He laughs at you."

"He doesn't!" He couldn't; the idea hurt too much.

"Oh, yes, we have laughed together, Trey and I, over your odd ways. And over your skinny body. He said that bedding you was like bedding a boy."

The remark struck a nerve. Charli had always been sensitive about what she thought of as her too-small breasts. "Then why did he?" she managed to ask.

Justine shrugged. "Novelty, variety. I do not begrudge him these. As you know, Trey is a man of strong appetites—perhaps the result of his upbringing? He is a magnificent lover, is he not?" Justine's eyes glittered in the flicker of the fire. "Trey beds many women; he returns to only one."

There was no doubt which one she meant.

"Yes," she repeated, "we laughed about you tonight."

"Tonight?" While Charli was in his house, waiting for his return, realizing she loved him, had he been with this woman? The thought cut like a knife.

"He left my bed not an hour ago." Justine closed her eyes and ran her hands down over her breasts to her waist. "My skin still burns from his kisses." Her hands slid down in a V across her stomach to her groin. "His seed rests inside me still." She breathed deeply. "Look!" she demanded as she reached inside the neckline of her snow-white gown and scooped out one magnificent breast. "His mark is fresh upon me!" Proudly, she thrust the breast forward. The nipple was large and dark and hard as a nut, and just above the areola was the unmistakable mark of an ardent lover, brilliant red against the creamy flesh.

Charli had a similar mark on her stomach. Trey had left it there last night—unintentionally, he claimed—and she had been foolishly proud of it.

She didn't want to believe what this woman was saying. She wanted to believe she was simply facing a jealous woman willing to stop at nothing to keep her man. She wanted to believe

327

that Trey's kisses and gentle words to her had been real.

But there was one thing she could not deny, however hard she might want to. The only way Justine could know that Charli was from the future was if Trey had told her.

Marie had said it. "There are no secrets between lovers." The grand *zombí* certainly hadn't told them about Charli Stewart; only Trey Lavande could have done that.

Which meant he was capable of betrayal, and betrayal was the one thing Charli could not forgive in anyone.

"Decide, Yankee," said Marie Laveau. "The time is now, the only time. The grand *zombí* comes tonight. Later be too late." Her eyes pierced into Charli's. "Now," she repeated. "Now."

All around them the black faces softly chanted. "Now, now, now."

Charli was so confused. She ached for Trey even as the anger grew within her. She wanted to believe in him, but the evidence of the woman Justine, so proud and beautiful and confident before her, was overwhelming. He didn't want Charli; he didn't love her. She had been foolish to think he might. She was just a novelty. Well, he got that right. How many Victorian men got the chance to go to bed with a liberated, twentieth-century woman with a black belt in karate, anyway?

And now the novelty had worn off. Or, worse yet, maybe it hadn't and she still had that to look forward to—the moment when Trey would tell her to hop on her broom and fly back to 1993.

"So, Yankee," said the voodoo queen. "We

begin? You need but to clap your hands for the grand *zombí* to enter our circle."

She looked through the flames, back across the water at the dimly flickering gaslights of old New Orleans. He was there somewhere. Still feeling, perhaps, the glow of making love to Justine? Would he have come straight from Justine's bed to hers? she wondered. Would he have carried the smell of Justine's perfume to leave on *her* sheets, the imprint of Justine's breasts in his hands to lay on *her* body?

A tear spilled from one eye, but she dashed it away with her hand. There was no point in crying; it was over. She had gone crazy for a time, lost control of her life and her heart. Now she would do anything to get it back—even if voodoo was what it took. What did she have to lose? Right now, she didn't think dying could possibly hurt any more than this pain inside her.

She had to escape it, and that meant escaping New Orleans, escaping 1858. If voodoo would do it, great, but just to help the process along, she offered up a prayer to her own, more benevolent, deity. Then slowly, she pivoted, looking at each face in the circle. She looked back at Marie Laveau. She raised her hands.

With no idea of what—if anything—to expect, she clapped twice.

And the circle erupted. The drums began again, but twice as loud, twice as fast. The rattles shook. All around the circle, men and women leaped to their feet and flung themselves in a spinning, writhing dance.

Marie Laveau rose from her chair. She lifted her arms in a V above her head, arched her back, threw back her head. "Hear and come, oh grand *zombí!* Hear and come to work your magic."

Then her fingers untied the ribbon at the neck of her robe and she threw it off to reveal a gown of brilliant red silk, the color of fresh blood. It was cut so low in front that her breasts thrust out completely above the silk. The nipples were rouged a startling vermilion. On her chest rested several necklaces of snake vertebrae, alligator fangs, and tiny bones like those in the fingers of dead children.

Charli saw two people approach the fire and kneel to light cones of incense on the ground. Almost at once, the sweet, pungent aroma wafted up to surround her. She looked down and noticed something she hadn't seen before— a square drawn on the ground with white chalk. A woman came and set a burning candle in each corner. Hands at Charli's back pushed her to the center of the chalk square. At least a dozen people brought torches dipped in pitch to the fire, lit them, and added their dancing light to the growing frenzy circling the fire. "Come and hear, come and hear," they chanted. "Come and hear, oh grand *zombí.*"

Shifting shapes danced round and round her. The flames burned scorching hot on her face. Marie appeared again, her hands thrust into the air once more. But now they held a snake, stretched out to its full length of more than three feet.

"*Bomba zombí!*" she chanted. "*Bomba zombí! Danga le, canga li, bomba zombí!*" Making a wide loop with one arm, she threw the hissing snake into the fire. It writhed a few minutes before disintegrating into a shower of crackling, spitting sparks that floated high up into the black sky, and the sound of the voices seemed to rise with it. A smell of burning oil and charred meat mixed with the heavy odor of the incense to permeate the air.

Still, Charli was not afraid. Appalled, but not afraid. Maybe that explained why she didn't flinch when Justine handed her an elaborate goblet made of coin silver and said, "Drink it."

"What is it?" she asked in a dull voice, mesmerized by the noise, the flames, the smell, the whole damned pageantry.

Marie laughed. "Water, Yankee. Only water, drawn from the river at the exact spot where you traveled here. The magic is in the water as well as the moon and the secret forces. Drink it and it will take you home."

Charli looked into the goblet. The liquid was clear as crystal. She sniffed it; it had no smell. She dipped one finger and licked it; it had no taste. Water—she believed that was exactly what it was. Of course, in 1993 she wouldn't consider drinking Mississippi River water. Probably had hepatitis and mercury and PCBs and God knew what else floating around in it. But she supposed they hadn't managed to screw it up quite so much yet in 1858. And if Marie Laveau and the others had reason to believe that drinking water from the spot that pulled her into the past was likely to send her back home, she was willing to try it. Actually, she didn't know why she hadn't thought of it herself.

She closed her eyes and drained the goblet.

The volume and frenetic quality of the music

increased yet further until the whole world was full of sound, until it echoed as though it were coming from inside Charli's head. The voodoo revelers, all except for the drummers, were on their feet now, dancing, calling on the grand *zombí* to heed their cries and take their new daughter back, back to her home.

She stared into the raging flames. She felt heavy all over, as if lead were pouring through her veins instead of blood. Her neck would barely support the weight of her head; her eyelids seemed to have bowling balls attached to them.

"Believe, Yankee," Marie said, her voice very close beside Charli's ear. "You must believe for the grand *zombí* to do his magic. He require your faith."

Right, Charli thought. You gotta believe; you gotta believe. She'd believe anything they told her; it was easier than trying to think when all she really wanted to do was curl up by the fire and go to sleep. It occurred to her to wonder if something had been added to the water after all.

Trey—his name eased through her mind. Trey, come take me home. But Trey wouldn't do that. He didn't want her. And this wasn't her home.

Her feet started tingling and her fingertips began to feel numb. She felt hot all over and not just from the fire. The heat came from inside her.

Suddenly something in the distance caught Charli's eye and she stared, through the flames and beyond, across the river floating past black as night, to where New Orleans shimmered. She saw something red, like a light but very dim and hazy. It seemed to hover above the horizon, flickering into focus then disappearing again, blocked out by the flames.

It twinkled into sharper focus just for a split second, but it was long enough to tell her what it was. It was the red *H* atop the Hilton Hotel on the levee near the Riverwalk Mall.

But the Hilton wasn't there in 1858; it was there in 1993!

"*Oui*," said Marie, close beside her, "it begins."

Good God, Charli thought. Was it really working? Was she really leaving this time, this place? Instinctively, she cried out, "Trey!" But Trey wasn't there. No one who cared about her was there. Marie was right; this was not her place.

Over the roar of the fire, she heard another sound. Instinctively, she looked up. High above her, she saw what she was sure was the blinking light of a jet moving high across the sky through a break in the clouds. Involuntarily, her hand went up as though to reach out to it.

"You want to go," Marie chanted in her ear. "You want to go back, to your family, to your world. Go back. Go back. Go back."

Someone took Charli's arms. As she concentrated fiercely on the red *H* across the river, they led her around the fire and down to the water's edge. The whole crowd took up the chant as they followed, their torches dancing wildly, sending gleaming tongues of reflection across the water. "Go back. Go back. Go back!"

She was dimly aware of someone kneeling before her, lifting her feet one at a time, removing her slippers. The grass was cool beneath her stockinged feet and damp from the river mist that still hugged the ground in patches.

Across the river, she could see more lights now—vague, almost dreamy flickerings where the windows of modern skyscrapers would one day glow brightly through the nights. She felt a hand at her back, nudging her forward. She walked toward the lights.

The river licked at her feet, cold, but she didn't stop. She glanced down. Her body seemed to be shimmering, almost as though she were becoming invisible.

"Go back," the crowd chanted, on and on. "Go back, go back."

She took another step into the water. Already, she could feel the inexorable tug of the mighty river's current.

There was a final fierce volley of drumbeats, and suddenly the drumming, the banjo, and the voices stopped. The world fell silent except for the lapping of the river against the shore, the call of a night bird, and the crackle of the fire. She would return to the future in silence.

"Charlotte!"

Her whole body flinched as Trey's voice sliced through the night. He was here! With every ounce of her being she wanted to turn, run out of the water, hide in the safety of his arms.

But he didn't want her. He didn't love her. And there was no safety there, only pain and humiliation.

But why was he here? she wondered. To laugh at her? To gloat over his easy conquest? Maybe just to be entertained by the voodoo spectacle of her return.

"Charlotte," he yelled again. But there was no Charlotte there; there was only Charli. Charlotte

was the woman Trey had made love to, the one
who had let herself grow weak with wanting him,
the one who gave up all control to him.

Now Charli was taking it back.

"Charlotte, stop!" he called once more, his voice
closer now. Against her own better judgment, she
turned and looked over her shoulder. He had just
emerged from the trees and was running toward
her, but he stopped when she turned, his eyes on
her face.

They stared at each other a moment, frozen in
their separate and private emotions. Then she
looked up at the sky. Hurry, she prayed. Please
hurry and get me out of here. I can't bear to see
him laugh at me.

She took another step into the icy river.

Chapter Twenty-Five

Why doesn't she stop? Trey wondered, as he watched Charli turn and walk farther into the water.

What he saw on her face in that moment when she turned to look at him chilled him through to his soul. She looked hurt and frightened and so terribly sad. She looked like she was dying inside. And seeing her in pain hurt Trey more than he would have imagined possible.

For long moments, he couldn't move. He watched her slowly shake her head, turn away from him, and walk into the Mississippi.

It was as though he himself felt the icy sting of the water on his skin, and the sensation jolted him into action. He ran toward her, past the staring faces of the slaves and the glaring face of Marie Laveau, past Justine, who had dropped to

336

her knees to sob on the grass. He sloshed into the river, his powerful thighs pushing against the current that immediately clutched at him.

Charli was still walking away from him, steadily but slowly, moving like a sleepwalker. He quickly caught up with her, grabbed her shoulders, and turned her around.

She felt like air beneath his hands, as insubstantial as a cloud. Where he touched the bare skin of her arms, they tingled and tiny sparks glittered there in the dark night.

He looked down at her, at that body he had kissed with such passion, loved with such thoroughness. She was disappearing beneath his fingers!

"No!" he cried. "I won't let you!" He shook her shoulders, but she barely moved in his grasp. He tried to make her look at him, but she kept her head turned away, staring across the river as though she saw some magic beacon there in the empty blackness of the night.

He glanced toward Marie Laveau, who stood tall and calmly proud at the water's edge. "What have you done to her?" he shouted, his voice frantic.

"I only tell her her own desire, monsieur," said Marie, "and give her the chance to act on it. She want to go home, so I help her."

"Home! Do you know what you've done?" He spun back to Charli. "Fight it, Charlotte. Whatever she did to you, whatever she gave you, you've got to fight it." He tried to pick her up, to carry her from the frigid water, but there wasn't enough of her left to lift. She was becoming a chimera before his eyes. He was losing her!

337

"No, Charlotte, please!" he cried.

Charli barely heard him. She barely felt his hands on her arms. Part of her mind knew Trey was there, but he was like a lovely dream she'd had and was now waking up from. She fixed her stare harder on the lights across the river, growing brighter and clearer by the second. She could see the streaky headlights and taillights of cars moving along the road atop the levee, the Jax Brewery sign, the skyscrapers. Chains of lights twinkled in a string across a cruise ship, laying brilliant tracks on the water.

She was going home.

"Charli! Don't leave me!"

Suddenly, his words pierced the fog around her, coming loud and clear. Charli. He had called her Charli. And he was calling her back.

Reluctantly, she let her eyes leave the talisman of the lights to look at him. His face was close and, even as he became hazier with each second, she could see that it wore an expression of anguish. Don't leave me, he had begged. She tried to ask "Why?" She moved her mouth, formed the words, but no sound would come out.

She could see tears in Trey's eyes. She could see them as clear as anything she'd ever seen. And then he said, "Please, don't leave me, Charli. I love you."

The words poured into her like honey, warming her despite the icy cold of the river. She felt a tug toward him, as strong as the tug of the lights across the river. But could she believe him? She was so confused. She turned back to look at the lights.

"No, Charli," he cried, forcing her around again.

338

"Don't look at the future. Look at me, only at me."

"I don't belong here," she said, and this time the words, though soft as a breeze, were audible.

"Yes, you do. You belong with me. I need you."

Need? Did he really need her? Did he really love her?

She turned her head to look at Justine. The woman who claimed that Trey loved only her was bent over in a heap on the ground, sobbing into the hands that covered her face. She was a vision of defeat.

"I love you, Charli," he said again, his mouth close to her ear, but the words sounded like they came from very far away.

And then he kissed her. She could barely feel his lips on hers. She couldn't feel their warmth, their softness. But she could sense the need in his kiss, the tenderness, the yearning for her to stay. He hadn't lied. He did want her; he did need her. He did love her. She believed.

And so she had to choose. To stay—if it wasn't already too late to stop the process. Or to go home. If she stayed, she would stay forever. She felt that as clear as anything. She would never see her mother, her home, her friends again. And if she left, she would never see Trey again. She had to choose. Now. The moment was now, for with every second, her vision of Trey grew dimmer, the lights across the river grew brighter and beckoned more fiercely. A sob shuddered up inside her.

"Fight it, Charli!" he cried again, the catch of tears and fear thickening his voice. "Look at me, only at me. Focus on me. See my love. Feel it. It is stronger than their evil, stronger than the future, stronger than anything. Only look at me."

And she did. She focused on his beloved face, staring into his dark, frightened eyes. And she knew that Trey Lavande was her future. She loved him. And he loved her. She could not leave him.

But she was going, disappearing back into the future. And she knew it was only by her own strength of will that she could stop the process. She closed her eyes, breathed deeply. Trey, she said silently. Trey. Trey is my home. Trey is my future.

A shock, like a jolt of electricity, shot through her. She could hear it crackle in the night air. She could smell the burning wood of the bonfire.

When she opened her eyes again, her vision of him was clearer. "I love you," she said, the words floating out through her frozen lips like tiny birds.

He pulled her close in a fierce, protective hug, and now she could feel his arms, feel the warmth of his strong body seeping into hers. She could feel the rough wool of his cape beneath her cheek, growing more solid with each second.

And he could feel it too. Her slender body grew more substantial with each heartbeat as he held her close. "Yes, Charli," he whispered into her ear as he brushed the hair back from her forehead. "Come back to me. Come all the way back."

Gently, he lifted her in his arms, and now she was solid enough for him to do it. He carried her from the river, up the grassy bank, toward the trees. Beside the bonfire, he paused long enough to look down at the beautiful woman sobbing on the ground.

All the Time We Need

"This is your doing, Justine," he said, his voice as icy as the river. "Don't think I don't know that. I'd advise you to find a reason to leave New Orleans, my dear, because I never want to see your face again—and if I do, you won't like the consequences."

Then he turned to Marie Laveau. "And you, you evil bitch. I'll see you flogged from one end of Jackson Square to the other."

Then he carried his precious burden into the trees.

It wasn't long before Trey carried Charli into his house in Chartres Street. She protested that she could walk, but he wasn't letting her out of his arms for even a second. He carried her directly to her bedroom, and refused to leave her even for Dolly to help her with her bath.

"Go, Dolly," he said as the cans of hot water were brought in. "I'll act as the lady's maid tonight."

Dolly blushed all over her round, brown, smiling face and curtsied herself out the door.

Lovingly, Trey undressed Charli. Using every ounce of restraint he could muster, he barely kept himself from taking her instantly to bed and instead helped her into the tub. With gentle hands, he washed her smooth skin, massaged her shoulders, poured the steaming water over her back and breasts.

They barely spoke, except with their eyes, which communicated volumes—of tenderness, need, desire, love.

Gently, he lifted her to her feet and helped her from the tub, then tenderly dried her muscled body with the thick towel. Finally, he carried her to the bed.

"I love you," he breathed as he kissed her.

"And I love you," she answered as she kissed him back.

"Forever," he added.

"Yes, forever."

Quickly then, he stripped off his own clothes. He lay naked beside her on the bed, pulled her close, and held her so tight she could hardly breathe. But she didn't mind. She was so happy she didn't think she needed to breathe.

For a long moment, they just lay that way, rocking slightly, feeling their heartbeats synchronize until they pulsed as one. Then he slid his hands down her spine, across the small of her back, to cup her buttocks. Almost of its own accord, her body opened to him, one leg coming up and over his, and his hand slid lower, to stroke that part of her that made her a woman.

As she gasped, he slid one finger inside her welcoming warmth. She felt like she was back on the brink of the future, feeling the electricity shoot through her, but this time there was only pleasure, exquisite pleasure, and not a trace of fear.

He brought his lips to hers and kissed her with his whole soul as his hand brought her body to the edge of ecstasy. Between kisses, he whispered her name, over and over, matching the rhythm of his fingers. Her heart and her body both responded to him so forcefully she nearly cried.

Just when she thought she could take no more, he removed his hand, leaving her bereft. But only for a moment. Instantly, he slid his magnificent body down hers, trailing hot kisses as he went, until his mouth replaced his hand, until his tongue took up the rhythm begun by his fingers, keeping it up until the pleasure built to a crescendo and detonated inside her, bursting through her whole body like a mushroom cloud and she cried out his name.

Before she could even descend again from her mountaintop of pleasure, he pulled himself up, poised a moment above her, then drove into her and sent her instantly spiraling over the edge once more.

On and on it went, wave after wave of pleasure engulfing her as she felt herself closing spasmodically around him and clutched at his buttocks to keep from flying away completely. She was soaring, she was disintegrating into total sensory response, maybe she was dying. And then he joined her. She felt him go rigid inside her as he, too, called out her name.

Time disappeared. There was no 1993, no 1858, no yesterday or tomorrow. There was only here, now, this very moment. And it was the only time they needed.

The first thing Charli was aware of the next morning was Trey kissing her awake. She smiled up at him; he smiled back. Before she could even say "Good morning," he was devouring her mouth, running his hands over her body, as though to reassure himself that she really was still there, still with him in 1858.

There was little preamble to their lovemaking this time—none was needed, for they were like two starving people at a banquet. He entered her quickly, and they both responded as if they'd been kissing and stroking each other for hours. And this time, as they brought each other once more to the edge of delight and beyond with a force that took them both by surprise, Charli laughed out her pleasure, joy flowing through her with every wave of sensation, leaving her breathless with happiness.

When they were done, she gazed at Trey with something like awe. His handsome face was lit up with a smile like a Bourbon Street bar sign, circa 1993. Together, they laughed out loud.

A half hour later, while doing perfect justice to Margie's enormous breakfast of coddled eggs, sausages and gravy, red beans and rice, and fried okra, washed down by large gulps of delicious coffee, Trey told Charli about the upcoming race between the *Corinne* and the *Belle Brigitte* and what was at stake.

Charli was alarmed. "Trey, what if you don't win?"

His mustache lifted in a smile that was insouciant, but with a definite edge of determination to it. "Haven't you noticed? I'm on a winning streak, lately. I think you've brought me luck."

"Oh, no you don't. I refuse to take responsibility for this. And if you ask me, it's one of the dumber ideas to come down the pike. You could lose everything you've worked so hard to get."

"Or win everything," he said softly. "This is my chance to have Rive Douce. I'm tired of waiting." He calmly cut into a boudin sausage and took a bite.

For the next half hour, she tried to dissuade him. She knew in her gut that owning Rive Douce was not the answer for Trey. He needed to find his own place, make his own way, not take his brother's away from him. She wondered, briefly, if this was why she had come to the past, to keep Trey from ruining his life by ruining Laurence's.

Charli knew what it was to fight against a private demon. She had battled her own—had, in fact, kicked and punched the hell out of them all the way to a black belt. Trey still had his demons to wrestle. She wanted to help.

But he had dreamed too long, wanted too badly, missed out on too much to give up when the goal was finally in sight. She couldn't talk him out of the race, even though losing would be a devastating blow to his plans as well as his fortune.

She watched him for a moment. "You've got the soul of a gambler, haven't you?" she said. "You'd do great on Wall Street."

He grinned. "Where do you think I made my fortune in the first place?"

"I assumed you got it the same way you got me, at a poker table."

"Only the first few thousand. As soon as I had enough to invest, I decided to gamble a little smarter. Unless you know how to cheat and not get caught, poker's a fool's game, even when you play it well."

She gave him a teasing smile. "Does that mean you cheated when you won me away from Remy Sauvage?"

"Miss Stewart! If you were a man I'd have to call you out for that insult."

"Would I get the choice of weapons?"

"You would."

"Then do it. I choose karate *gis* at two paces. You won't have a chance."

Megan Daniel

"You've already made that particular point, thank you very much." He put down his fork and gave her a comic leer. "Besides, I can think of much better ways to get my hands on you."

"Don't I know it!" She poured steamed milk into yet another cup of coffee.

"Actually, I'm coming to prefer those other ways myself."

"I sort of thought you might," she said.

"In fact, what I really want to do is take you upstairs and get my hands on you again right now. Unfortunately, I've a race to prepare for."

Charli felt a sting of disappointment, then marveled at herself. They had made love for most of the night, then again this morning. How could she want him again already? But she did. She most certainly did. "What's involved in getting her ready?" she asked.

"The key to winning is to make the *Corinne* as light as possible, so I plan to strip her down to the bare skeleton."

Charli grinned. "You're good at stripping ladies, I've noticed."

"Only ladies I love."

"Hah, pull the other one! I know a man of experience when I see one."

"Experience with women, perhaps," he admitted, "but not with love, Charli." He reached across the table for her hand. "I realize now that I have never been in love before. I never even knew what the word meant."

His touch was like warm velvet against her skin. Odd, then, that it should make her shiver. "Me neither," she whispered.

"Last night, when I saw you disappearing right

346

before my eyes, I felt like I was disappearing too, right into a private hell that would never stop." He stroked the back of her hand with his thumb, then squeezed it hard, as if afraid to let go. "Never leave me, Charli. Please."

She lifted her other hand to his cheek, smooth and cool below his mustache. "Never," she agreed.

He leaned forward and gave her a long, warm, coffee-flavored kiss. Then he reluctantly pulled himself away, grabbed his hat, and left to begin preparing the *Corinne* for her great moment on the river.

Later that morning, a note was delivered to Justine's house in Rampart Street. Enclosed was a generous draft drawn on Trey Lavande's bank and a one-way train ticket to Philadelphia, leaving that very afternoon. Trey was taking no chances of a repeat of the strange voodoo rite that had almost taken Charli away from him and back to the future.

Justine knew better than to ignore the message. By midafternoon, Trey had confirmation that the beautiful quadroon was gone and her house was on the market.

Chapter Twenty-Six

Word of the upcoming race was soon all over town. Everyone wanted to be on board one of the two boats, but both Trey and Remy were strictly limiting the number of passengers they agreed to carry. Every extra ounce of weight could slow a boat down; every body meant less room to carry the massive amounts of firewood necessary so the boats would not have to stop to take on fuel.

Bets were being placed in every saloon, gentlemen's club, and beer joint, as well as many a genteel drawing room. Perfect strangers stopped Charli in the streets, begging her to intercede with one owner or the other for permission to ride along.

To add to the general excitement, the *Corinne* and the *Belle Brigitte* had been docked next to each other at the levee while crews worked around the clock to ready them for the race. Both boats were stripped of every ounce of extra weight, all the fancy trim that might add wind resistance was removed, every engine tuned, every boiler cleaned, every hinge and valve oiled. The rival crews could hear each other calling their singsong chants as they worked in rhythm, and soon the chants became a sort of contest in their own right, bouncing back and forth across the narrow gap dividing the two boats.

"Lift the wood, haul the load, bring it, 'board an' get it stowed," chanted the *Brigitte*'s crew, passing enormous logs from hand to hand from the levee onto the lower decks.

The *Corinne*'s crew answered. "Load 'em up, we gonna win the race; other man loses, other man pays."

Trey worked side by side with his men, urging them to a faster pace, building enthusiasm in his team for the upcoming race, encouraging them with his confidence that they would win. He hauled furniture, carried off carpets, oiled valves. He pored over charts of the river and talked at length with a dozen riverboat pilots, memorizing every turn, snag, and sandbar, every change in the river's texture in recent days and weeks.

He would not let one single thing, one tiny detail that might give the *Corinne* the advantage, slip past him. This race was too important. This race was perhaps the most important event of his life.

While Trey worked on the *Corinne*, Charli was on her own. The first morning, she'd assumed she would simply go to the boat with him, help him with whatever was to be done.

Trey refused to hear of it. She didn't belong in the middle of a work crew, he explained. She would be in the way. He didn't want her there.

If she hadn't heard the first reasons, she heard that last one, and she took herself off in a huff.

But unused to having so much time on her hands and no work to do, she was hard-pressed to amuse herself. Charli was not easily bored, but she'd always been a working girl. She intended to go on being one, though she could see it was going to be a job-and-a-half convincing Trey to let her keep singing for her supper, so to speak. But she'd be damned if she'd sit at home all day, waiting like a dutiful Victorian wife for him to come home.

Wife! The word was causing her increasing fidgets. She felt certain Trey was going to ask her, and she didn't know what answer she would give him.

She loved him. God, how she loved him. And if they were together in 1993, she'd marry him in a New York minute, she knew. But could she marry him in an 1858 New Orleans minute?

All the rules had changed, and she didn't know if she wanted to play that particular game by the old rules. As Trey's wife in the nineteenth century, she would be his property, as much as Dolly was hers. She would be his chattel—God, how she hated that word. She wouldn't even have the option of keeping her own name if she wanted to, as she would have in 1993. She would have no rights to own property of her own, to live where she chose if it didn't match where he chose. In fact, she would lose all legal right to be her own person, to control her own destiny.

And yet . . . The idea of being his in every way was achingly sweet. And what if there were children? Her birth control pills wouldn't last much longer—she didn't even know if she wanted them to. The idea of holding a tiny baby in her arms, perhaps with Trey's magnificent eyes and hair like coal, filled her with a glow of happiness even greater than she had felt last night when she really, truly knew that he loved her. And she could never, would never bear Trey's child without first bearing his name. It was the one thing he would never forgive her for—to make a child of his a bastard.

In her world, the word was just a word, though not a nice one. But in Trey's world, it defined everything he had fought against his whole life. And once applied to their child, it would stick like Krazy Glue, no matter how much they loved this creation of their love. She couldn't do that—to Trey or to their child.

Well, he hadn't asked her yet. Maybe he wouldn't, though she didn't seem to like that idea any better than worrying that he might. So okay, for now she'd take a leaf out of Scarlett O'Hara's book. She'd worry about it tomorrow.

In the meantime, there were things she could do—things she was uniquely qualified for, in fact, that no one else in 1858 New Orleans could accomplish. She could continue teaching Dolly to read as well as to defend herself. She could help Lisette prepare for the Civil War that would be coming in just a few years.

My God, she thought as she walked toward Lisette's house. I'm going to live through the Civil

War! What an incredible and awful realization.

Well, perhaps at least she could help once the awfulness began. She knew CPR and the basics of first aid, though if *Gone With the Wind* was any guide, the scale of casualties was going to be way beyond any help she could provide. She shuddered at the thought. She vaguely remembered reading or hearing about shortages due to the Union blockade—she wasn't sure where; maybe on the PBS series. After she explained what little she knew to Trey and Lisette, they could at least be prepared: stock up well in advance on medicines like quinine—weren't people always calling for quinine in those old Civil War movies?—and morphine and chloroform and . . . well, Lisette would know. And coffee, and tobacco, and staple foods, candles, oil, fabric—she didn't want to have to make a gown out of the living room drapes!—and anything else vital that was likely to be hard to come by. And Trey and Lisette could move their money and investments off-shore—or whatever it was called these days.

Her steps quickened with new energy. The war might still be a couple years off, but there was no time like the present to get busy with plans.

By the second day, Charli was a mess from idle fretting. Making plans with Lisette had helped, but Charli had always needed to be part of the action. She had to be on the *Corinne* with Trey.

Just after noon she showed up on board, dressed in her breeches and shirt, the knot of her cravat somewhat improved with practice. Instead of Trey yelling and throwing her off the boat—which she half feared but was prepared to refuse to accept—he merely laughed at the sight of her and told her that since she was dressed for it she could carry the coil of rope lying at her feet to the dock.

Before long, her coat, like Trey's, was lying on a pile of boxes, her cravat was draped across a railing, and her shirt sleeves were rolled up. For the rest of that day and into the evening, she and Trey worked side by side, as torches and lanterns lit the now stripped bare decks of the *Corinne*.

It was well past midnight when they returned to Trey's house, sweaty, tired, and sore-muscled but satisfied that they were on schedule and everything would be ready when the whistle blew for the race tomorrow at noon.

For now, all they wanted was a hot bath—and what Charli wouldn't give for a giant, steaming Jacuzzi!—and then to fall into bed and sleep in each other's arms for what was left of the night.

Their hopes were not to be met.

The house was dark, just as they'd expected, since Trey had told the servants not to wait up for them. But up they were, every single member of the household, sitting around the big kitchen table with the corners of the room lost in the shadows cast by the feeble light from a single oil lamp.

The minute Trey and Charli walked into the house, Margie ran from the kitchen, her nightrobe flapping around her ankles and a frizzy gray-black braid hanging from under a white cap. Maurice, the butler, was right behind her, his formal black coat looking ludicrous over his nightshirt and carpet slippers.

"Oh, Master Trey," Margie cried, though in a sort of stage whisper. "Thank God you've come home." Then she unceremoniously took his hand and dragged him into the kitchen. Worried, Charli followed.

"Margie, what the devil . . . ?" Trey began, but the cook plunked him down in a chair. Charli looked around at the circle of faces, all of which seemed to be looking at Trey with expectation—or hope. "Very well," Trey said as patiently as he could, which was not very. "Now that I am sitting down, will you tell me why everyone is sitting up in the kitchen at this hour?"

Something struck Charli as wrong. "No, not everyone," she said. "Where's Dolly?"

"In the attic, miss," Margie answered. "Under some drapes I found. I didn't rightly know what else to do with her."

"The attic? But . . ."

"We was afraid, miss," Margie went on, "afraid the Charleys'd come for her. I knew you'd want her kept safe till the master could get here. I knew he'd know what to do."

Trey spoke then, his voice grim. "What's she done?"

"Just about the worst thing she could do," said Maurice, " 'sides running away, that is." He puffed out his cheeks with disapproval. "She hit a white man."

"She what?" Trey exploded. "The girl's got more sense than that."

"Well, she did, sir," said Margie. "Admitted it. Come home not half an hour ago with her dress all tore up and blood on her cheek and admitted it straight out. Said she was defending herself," she said, then added half under her breath, "as if black folks had a right to go 'bout defendin' themselves from white folks."

"Damn!" Trey exclaimed, running his fingers through his thick hair and muttering, "What a mess to have to clean up just now. Couldn't she at least have waited until after the race?" He turned to Maurice. "Who'd she hit?"

Margie and Maurice looked at him, neither of them wanting to speak. Finally, and with great reluctance, Maurice said, "Laurence Campbell."

"My God," said Trey, sitting down. "Why would she do such a thing?"

"Wait!" Charli cried, throwing up her hand to stop anyone from speaking. "Dolly's got a right to tell her own story. I want to hear this from her personally."

She picked up the lamp and headed up to the attic, taking the stairs two at a time and silently thanking the freedom of her breeches. Trey was right behind her with Margie huffing along after and Maurice bringing up the rear at a more sedate pace, carrying a branch of candles.

They found the young slave girl cowering under several pounds of dusty brocade and yellowed lace in a cramped trunk in a dark corner. When Charli lifted the lid, Dolly shrank down even smaller. A tiny whimper escaped her.

"It's all right, love," said Margie in the soothing tones of a born mother. "It's the young miss and Master Trey."

With that, Dolly leaped from the trunk, tossing curtains every which way, and threw herself at Charli. "I'm sorry, Charli, I didn't mean to cause no trouble. I just did like you taught me, and I . . .

355

I . . ." Her words dissolved into sobs as Charli held her close.

"It's okay, Dolly," Charli soothed. "Just tell us what happened. It'll be all right, I'm sure it's nothing we can't fix."

Suddenly, Margie slammed the shutter over the window and ran to blow out the candles Maurice held, plunging the attic into deep shadows with only the small oil lamp still burning. "Master Trey," she whispered harshly, "it's the watch; they're comin' down the street."

Trey hustled Charli and Dolly toward the stairs. "We'll go out the back way." He turned towards Maurice. "Tell them you haven't seen Dolly—act angry about it—and say we haven't come home yet . . . you don't know when we'll be back . . . I told you not to wait up. That, at least, is the truth. Send them down to the *Corinne* to look for us if you can. That'll give us a little time."

"I don't understand," said Charli. "Where are we going? And why? If she was only defending herself . . ."

"We'll talk later," he said, urging them through the door and down the stairs, "unless you want Dolly to spend the night in the Calaboso."

They reached the foot of the servants' stairs just as the pounding sounded on the front door. Through the kitchen and into the courtyard they scurried. Trey stopped at a small gate that opened onto an alley. He held up his hand for them to wait, eased open the gate, which creaked with alarming volume, and looked outside. "It's all right," he whispered after a minute, motioning them through. "Hurry." When Charli would have spoken, he laid his hand over her mouth—none too gently, she thought—and nudged her down the alley. Dolly was too frightened to even try to talk. She merely went where she was led.

Finally, after three or four blocks of scurrying through alleys and shadows, Charli whispered, "Where are we going?"

"To my mother's," Trey answered.

"Won't they think to look for us there?"

"It won't matter if they do." He looked down at her, his hand still on her elbow to hurry her along. "In a house such as my mother's it is often convenient to have a secure hiding place."

"Oh," she replied and kept walking.

They reached Lisette's house within minutes. It blazed with lights, and music poured from an open parlor window—but it was not, Charli noted with satisfaction, a modern jazz singer. She and Dolly huddled in the shadows near the garden gate while Trey entered boldly through the front door.

Five minutes later, his face appeared at the gate, and a few minutes after that Lisette was unlocking a small door at the back of a third-floor closet. It opened to reveal a tiny, windowless chamber, not more than five feet by eight, with a small bed and an even smaller night table, a washstand, and a chair—nothing more. With four adults crowded into it (one of them in an exceedingly large hoopskirt), there was scarcely room to breathe and none to turn around.

"She'll be safe here until you decide what to do with her," Lisette said, setting a lamp on the little nightstand.

"And now," Trey said, sitting Dolly on the one chair and standing over her, "we'll have the whole story, Dolly. Why, in God's name, did you hit Laurence Campbell?"

It took more than a few minutes, between her sobs and hiccups and hesitations, to get the story out of Dolly.

Excited about the upcoming race and eager to be part of the hubbub of preparation—and unbeknownst to Margie or Maurice—she had headed down to the levee around eleven o'clock that night with a stone jar full of hot coffee and some sandwiches for Charli and Trey. But before she even reached the levee, she encountered Laurence, her former—and to his mind still her rightful—owner. He was on his way home from the *Belle Brigitte*.

"He grabbed me, Miss Charli," Dolly explained. "Said one more day and I'd be back at Rive Douce, I'd be his just like I always been, and he could . . . he'd do what he damn well wanted to with me." She sniffled. "And then he said as how he didn't see why he should wait till tomorrow to use what was his anyway."

She told how Laurence had grabbed her then, pushed her against the wall, and tore the top of her dress open.

"I tried to push him away and he . . . he called me a little bitch and he slapped me, but he took time to turn that big ring of his around first so as it'd cut my face." Her finger went to the blood that had dried on a long, nasty scratch on one cheek.

"The bastard," Charli hissed.

"Then he said he needed some place more private like for what he had in mind, and he started to drag me toward a carriage that was there."

358

That was when Dolly decided for the first time in her life to fight back. Emboldened by her karate lessons—both physically and mentally—and by her success at getting away from the watch two nights earlier, she threw a stiff-armed punch that landed right in Laurence Campbell's gut.

"I just wanted to get away, Charli," she explained between sobs, "to make him let me go. I didn't hit him hard, not really, not enough to hurt him. But I guess he lost his balance or something. He went down real hard and hit his head on the brick curb of the banquette. He was out just like that. And I ran home."

Charli put her arms around the now sobbing girl. "It's all right, Dolly," she soothed. "You did the right thing. No one will blame you for—"

"You said," Dolly went on, "you told me, Charli, you said I didn't have to, not no more, that no man could make me—"

Trey spun toward Charli. "Do you mean you told her it was all right to hit a white man?"

"I told her she had a right to defend herself."

"Against a white man?" he asked again.

"Against anyone who tried to hurt her."

He ran his hands through his already thoroughly disheveled hair. "My God. How could you do something so incredibly stupid?"

"Stupid! Is she just supposed to let herself be raped again?"

"Again?"

"Yes, again. Trey, your brother raped her at Rive Douce, not once but many times."

"Oh, dear," said Lisette quietly, effectively breaking into what was becoming a shouting match. "Laurence always was a wild child, and

359

with a definite streak of cruelty. I don't know where he could have got it; Arthur was such a good man."

Trey spoke again, but more softly this time, his anger controlled. "Laurence is a pig, but Charli, Dolly is a slave and at the time she was his slave. He had the right."

"Right? No one, *no one*, has the right to do that to a woman. Not any woman. Ever!"

"The law disagrees."

"A law written by white slave-owning rapists!"

"And because you don't like the law you encouraged her to break it?"

"What does defending herself have to do with breaking any law?"

"How the devil . . . ?"

Lisette stopped him with a hand on his arm. "Trey, remember, this is all still new to Charli. She doesn't know our ways or our laws."

He looked at Charli a moment, his eyes wide, and finally shook his head again. "That's it, isn't it? You have no idea what you've done, though Dolly certainly should have known better. Don't you know that if Dolly or any other black, free or slave, so much as touches a white person without their consent, even in self-defense, even if her life is at risk, she can be arrested at once? That as punishment, she could be publicly whipped—or even confiscated from you and given to Laurence if they knew you encouraged her?"

"That's ridiculous. Everyone has the right to defend herself."

"Not a slave. Not even a free man of color. Not against a white man."

Charli stared at Trey, then at Lisette, then back

at Trey, not wanting to believe what they were saying. "Do you mean to tell me that if Robert, that black man who works for you, was being robbed at knifepoint by some drunken white sailor, he wouldn't have the right to fight the bastard off?"

Trey's mouth firmed into a grim line. "That's right."

"That stinks!"

"Perhaps, but it is still the law, and you've encouraged Dolly to think she has the right to break it."

"You're damn right she does if the law is wrong."

"The jail cell will be just as small and the whip just as painful, whether she was right or not."

Dolly started to sob again, and Charli sat on the bed beside her and put an arm around her shoulders. "She's not going to jail! And no one is going to whip her; not while I'm alive."

Trey sighed; Lisette was her usual brisk self. "Well, not tonight, at any rate," she said. "She'll be safe enough here for a day or two." She turned to her son. "Trey, go home. Even if Maurice managed to convince the Charleys to look for Dolly on the *Corinne,* they'll be back at your house soon enough and full of questions. They might even have Laurence with them. You'll need to convince them that Dolly didn't come home after the attack, that she has, in fact, run away."

"You're right. And then, perhaps, we can get some sleep. We'll need it for tomorrow." He reached out a hand to Charli. "Come on, love. Dolly can stay here until we get back from

Natchez. Then we'll decide what's best to do. Let's go home."

Charli started to get up and go with Trey, but as soon as she let go of Dolly, the girl began to whimper once more, fear shivering through every cell. Charli took her hand again. "You go on, Trey. I'm going to stay with Dolly tonight."

"But—"

"Go," she said more firmly, then softening, she added, "I'll see you on the *Corinne* well before the race starts."

He protested a bit more, but already Trey was aware of Charli's strong protective instincts toward those she cared about, and of her distinct stubborn streak. Without too much complaint, he left.

After two cups of tea—with some drops of laudanum added to the second—Dolly finally fell asleep, and Charli and Lisette retired to the private sitting room. There, Charli sat, rocking in a comfortable damask rocker, sipping good whiskey and wondering what to do.

"I don't know how you can avoid eventually having to hand her over," said Lisette, "either to the police or to Laurence. I can't keep her here forever."

"No," said Charli with firm conviction. "That I will not do." She sipped her drink and rocked silently a moment. Then, as an idea struck, she stopped rocking, stared intently at Lisette, and then slowly set her drink on an end table.

Finally she said, "Lisette, what do you know about the Underground Railroad?"

Chapter Twenty-Seven

By race time the next day, Charli was a mishmash of exhaustion and exhilaration. She'd been up all night making plans for Dolly's safety, then hurried down to the levee at nine to help with the last-minute preparations for the race.

The police were waiting for her. And the first question out of their mouths was, Where is the slave known as Dolly?

She was ready for them. "I certainly do wish I knew that," she said in her best huffy manner, with just a trace of a drawl thrown in to convince them of her trustworthiness. "Why, just look at me! I had to manage without her this morning, the ungrateful little wretch, and I look a regular fright." She was beautifully put together, thanks to Lisette's maid, in a gown of rose-colored dimity sprigged with red roses and green leaves, a huge,

Megan Daniel

drooping shawl of pale ivory cashmere, and a ruffled parasol hanging off one shoulder. But she grimaced as though she looked like a hag. "She's run away. Can you believe it? And after all I did for her, too. I'm going to put out a big reward for her, you watch. I'll have her back, and I promise I'll see to it she won't run away again. Why, I'll whip her myself so hard she—"

"Thank you, ma'am," the man in charge interrupted. "If she comes back, you'll let us know, ma'am. There's a warrant outstanding, and . . ." His words drifted off as Charli batted her eyes at him. Shortly afterward, they left.

Trey told her they had searched the *Corinne* that morning, at Laurence's insistence, just as they had searched his house the night before. "Laurence is threatening to put the dogs out after her."

"Dogs! He wouldn't!"

"He would. But fortunately the race is taking up most of his attention right now. But later, after he loses, I think he'll be so angry that getting Dolly might become an obsession. She'll be his only way to hit back, you see."

"But dogs! Trey . . ."

He put an arm around her shoulders. "We'll take care of Dolly later. She's safe enough for now."

Charli shuddered and resolved once more that Dolly would be safe from Laurence Campbell as Trey went on talking.

He had rather enjoyed having Laurence in his house last night while the police searched, he said. "The look on his face when he saw our father's portrait in my library was priceless—a

364

moment I've waited a long time for."

Charli cast him a worried glance, so quickly he missed it, and stared out at the crewmen swarming over the boat's decks, moving various items from place to place. "I'm glad you had that moment, then," she said softly. Then she took a deep breath, put a briskly efficient tone into her voice, and said, "Now, what's left to be done?"

"Not much. We're doing the final trimming to even up the weight. She makes her best speed drawing exactly five-and-a-half feet fore and five feet aft. And that's what she's going to draw, not an inch more, if I have to shave my mustache and throw your hoop overboard to lighten her up."

Charli grinned. "Well, I'm all for kissing the hoop good-bye forever, as you very well know, but if you shave off your mustache, Trey Lavande, I may never speak to you again." He gave her a speculative look, and she added, "And I certainly will never kiss you again, at least not until you grow it back."

"In that case, my dear, the mustache definitely stays. But perhaps," he said softly, his fingers toying with the lace at her throat, "we can find something else to eliminate."

She let her own fingers stray to the knot of his cravat. "It's been known to happen."

He chuckled deep in his throat, then patted her bottom—less than totally effective through her layers of hoop and petticoat. "You know, I think I'm almost getting to prefer you in breeches."

"I'll go change!"

"I said almost."

"Well, I have to admit there are times when looking like a belle comes in handy. I don't think

the cops would have believed me quite so easily
if I were in pants."

"Not a chance," he said and laughed. "And
besides, if you were in your trousers, I couldn't
kiss you in public." He leaned down and did just
that, a light brushing of lips that made Charli want
much more.

"Why, sir!" she drawled when he finished.
"Right here in front of God and everybody?"

"In front of God and the devil and my crew and
anyone else who cares to watch," he said, and
gave her the kiss she'd been wanting, a thorough
joining of lips and tongues and hearts and souls.

It was broken by Lisette. "I hate to interrupt,
my dears, but where can I put this?" she asked
calmly.

Trey looked at his mother, then down at the
medium-sized crate a stevedore had just set at
her feet.

"You can put it back on the dock," said Trey.
"Whatever it is, you can't bring it aboard, *Maman*.
I don't want the extra weight."

"But darling, I must, or how else will we have
it when we need it in Natchez? It's my contribu-
tion to your victory celebration, you see. Three
cases of champagne—enough for every man and
woman on this boat to get more than thoroughly
giddy."

"I appreciate your confidence in me, *Maman*,
but absolutely not."

"But Trey, it's French!"

"But the weight, *Maman* . . ."

"Of course, if you lose, I'll have to pour it all
into the river, and that would destroy my hedonistic soul. Such a waste."

He sighed. "Then I suppose I had better win, hadn't I, ma'am?"

"Indeed."

Shaking his head, he signaled a crewman to take the crate down to the galley. Then he went below to do whatever was necessary to balance this new weight. Charli and Lisette were left alone on deck.

"Is everything arranged?" asked Charli.

"It was a bit difficult on such short notice," said Lisette, "but yes, everything is arranged."

"Good," said Charli on a sigh. "I'll miss her."

"She'll be fine."

"I hope so. I don't understand this world where people can go to jail for defending themselves or be hunted down with dogs when they disobey."

"I don't always understand it myself," said Lisette. "But now, let's talk of better things. You love my son."

"Oh boy, do I," Charli admitted. "More than I think I want to sometimes."

"Not an unusual emotion for a woman," Lisette said dryly. "But he loves you, too, you know. I've never seen him look at a woman the way he looks at you, like he wants to eat you and protect you at the same time."

"Funny, I feel the same way about him."

"Good. That's settled then."

Charli laughed. "Is everything so easy in your world?"

"Of course not, my dear. Life is seldom easy. That's why whenever we're given a great gift such as you and Trey have been handed, we have to grab it with both hands and hold on for dear life. Don't let go, Charli. Don't ever let it go."

Megan Daniel

"I don't intend to," she answered, as much for her own benefit as for Lisette's.

By eleven o'clock, the levee was lined with throngs of people, for a race between two good riverboats was an event, a holiday, a treat not to be missed. Men, women, and children watched, yelled, waved flags and flowers, speculated on the outcome, and placed bets. Vendors circulated among the crowd, selling *calas*, boiled shrimp, sweets and strawberries, cool lemonade and beer. The more innovative sold hand-colored etchings of the two riverboats, ribbons embossed with their names, and even a few photographs—expensive as they were.

More people perched on the rooftops of every home and warehouse lining the river, sat on top of carts and carriages massed in the roadway, jockeyed for space at the railings of dozens of nearby boats and ships and dinghies.

The two great steamboats, side by side and bobbing gently on the river's current, looked sleek and ready in the morning sunlight. They'd each been pared down to the bare bones—spars gone, derricks missing, all the gingerbread trim moved to warehouses ashore. The decks were stacked with cords of firewood, ready to be hauled down to the giant furnaces to feed the insatiable fires that kept the steam pouring through the valves to power the mighty wheels. Few people lined the railings, since extra passengers only added extra weight. Some two dozen of the chosen few glared or grinned or challenged each other across the narrow space separating them.

All was in readiness. The crews were massed

on the forecastles, waiting for their orders, ready to swing into action at a blink, loading wood and coal, shifting weight, doing whatever was necessary, as eager as their masters to win.

By eleven-thirty, the air was thick with the black smoke pouring from the chimneys as steam built up in the boilers below. Bands played on the shore. Flags flew.

Trey was positively vibrating with energy and excitement, Charli thought as she walked into the wheelhouse. She imagined that if she touched him just then she'd get an electrical shock. His face held the grin of a child on Christmas morning, of a groom on his wedding day, of a man on the verge of achieving every dream in one fell swoop.

A sharp pang of guilt sliced through her. She was about to destroy that excitement, to wipe away that grin. Or to make him do it himself— which was even worse. She shook her head. It was right, she was doing the right thing. But she'd tell him about it later—much later.

He was conferring with George Macintosh, his chief pilot. Trey was all but dying to pilot the boat himself, but it was a luxury he wouldn't allow himself. He wasn't about to let the *Corinne* be handled today by anyone but the very best, and Macintosh was known up and down the river as a "lightning pilot."

At ten to twelve, the two great steamers backed into the stream and edged up to each other until they were side by side, jockeying for position like two racehorses fidgeting in the starting gates. For a few minutes then, everything felt suspended, Charli thought, as if the boats and everybody on them had stopped breathing. The bands stopped playing in midsong, their last notes floating off on the warm air. The people on the shore grew silent, waiting. For several moments, the only sound was the shriek of the pent-up steam escaping through the safety valves.

Then the bells of St. Louis Cathedral struck twelve, a cannon boomed, and all hell broke loose.

Tall columns of thick white steam burst screaming from the pipes of the two steamers. Whistles blew. The crowd roared. The crews set up a cheer, handkerchiefs waving. One huge black crewman, standing on the capstan on the *Corinne*'s forecastle, waved a red flag. The steamboats surged up the river, leaving a stream of churning foam in their wake.

Charli knew the best thing she could do right now was to stay out of the way. All Trey's energy and attention was concentrated on the race. But she wanted to be near him, so she stayed in the wheelhouse, listening as he conferred with the pilot, interested in every detail of shepherding the giant steamer up the mighty river. And thrilled because every few minutes Trey came and gave her a quick hug or a kiss, his face alight with the excitement of the challenge and the anticipation of knowing that he was on the threshold of having everything he ever wanted.

And Charli knew there was a good chance she was going to ruin it all. Well, maybe not. Maybe the *Brigitte* would prove to be the far faster boat, leaving Trey and the *Corinne* so far behind that there would be no decision to make.

The *Corinne* took an early lead, churning

through the water almost as if she were flying, as if the water had no resistance at all. Indeed, she was so light and so shallow that she barely cut the water, almost floating along the surface like a feather under power. The lead wasn't much, not much more than a few furlongs, but encouraging. All along the riverfront, crowds waved and yelled as the boats passed by, doing close to fourteen miles an hour. But by the time they'd reached Harry Hills, an hour out of New Orleans, the *Brigitte*'s new boilers had started showing their stuff. By Bonnet Carre, she had closed the gap and was threatening to pass the *Corinne*.

"More steam," Macintosh called down the pipes. "Give me more steam." Then he turned to a fretful Trey. "Not to worry, lad, she's got more in her, and so do I."

By the time they reached Plaquemine, shortly after seven, the wood they'd stocked on the deck and in the holds was running low. But they soon met up with a pair of the thirty-cord wood-boats Trey had arranged for. Slowing so little it was barely perceptible to Charli, they hitched the two boats alongside the *Corinne*, working by dancing torch and lantern light in the evening dark. Immediately, they picked up speed again. Crewmen swarmed down into the barges, passing wood up in a daisy chain so quickly that the wood-boats were emptied faster than Charli would have believed possible. Just as quickly, they were unhitched and left in the *Corinne*'s wake as she steamed on up the river, her belly full of fresh wood to feed the furnace's hunger.

Through it all, Lisette sat calmly in the Ladies' Lounge, knitting, of all improbable things! To

Charli, a pair of knitting needles in the hands of Lisette Lavande seemed about as much in character as a feathered headdress would be at a Quaker meeting. Then there was the fact that the garment spooling out from beneath her clicking needles looked suspiciously like a baby blanket. Charli decided not to ask.

By the time they swept past Baton Rouge, it was full dark, but the *Corinne* was nearly half a mile ahead and Trey was breathing easier. The darkness and dropping temperature didn't deter the crowds of watchers and cheerers. The riverbank was alight with torches and a band played "Hail Columbia" from the shore. Trey sang along, waving gaily from the wheelhouse door.

It was well past ten and growing quite cold. Charli had long since changed into her breeches and coat so as to be more comfortable roaming about the boat with Trey as he checked on this and that, leaving no detail to chance. They were still ahead, but not by more than a quarter of a mile. They could see the sparks floating up from the *Brigitte*'s stacks as they went into a bend below Bayou Sara.

"You're exhausted," Charli said to Trey as they stood at the aft railing, looking into the night. "Why don't you go rest for an hour or so? Macintosh can sail this thing without you for a little while." She brushed her hand across his cheek, feeling the stubble there. Her own eyes felt sandpapery—she'd had no sleep at all the night before—and she gave them a rub. "A nap?"

"Only if you'll join me," he said, caressing her cheek.

"Gladly, if you promise to let me sleep."

He turned toward his cabin, taking her arm and leading her along the deck. Once there, he took her in his arms. "No promises," he said softly, and kissed her so completely she thought she'd melt.

"Sleep," she protested rather feebly. "We need sleep."

"True," he said, nuzzling her neck, "but there's something else we need even more." His hands slid up to cup her breasts. Already, he knew so completely just how to touch her, just how to set her on fire.

"True," she agreed as he pushed her gently back onto the bed. "How true."

In their exhaustion, their lovemaking took on a slow-motion quality. Their exhausted brains turned off and their hands and lips and hearts took over, knowing exactly where to touch, how to kiss, when to wait and when not to. Their clothes disappeared as if of their own volition. Their skin meshed into one unit—Charli no longer knew where she ended and Trey began.

Breasts to breasts, breath matching breath, they held, they kissed, they touched. They loved. His mouth found her nipple and loved it until she thought she'd scream. Her fingers found his sex, so firm and full and heavy in her hand, and loved it until he begged her to stop.

His lips moved unerringly to that central spot at her core and soon sent her spiraling into the heart of her need and her love for him. Her hand infallibly guided him up and into her, joining them completely until he, too, was soaring, calling out his love for her that the whole world might know it.

Then together, they floated gently back to earth and lay in each other's arms.

Exactly an hour and a half later, Charli's little travel alarm sounded its soft electronic *beep-beep-beep, beep-beep-beep.* Trey stirred but did not wake. Charli lay there watching him sleep for a long while. It was time, time to tell him, to make him choose, and she wanted to put it off just a few minutes longer.

She felt in her soul that what she was about to do was best for everyone concerned—as much for Trey as for Dolly—but she also knew he would not agree, at least not right away. He would feel she had betrayed him. She didn't want to see the look in his eyes when she told him, when she made him choose.

She leaned over and gently kissed him awake. He returned the kiss in full measure and then some, but she pulled back. She couldn't let him make love to her again, it was too unfair for both of them.

"Trey," she said softly, "I have something to tell you."

"Ummmm," he murmured, nuzzling her breast. She jumped out of bed and threw on her shirt, feeling a strong need for some armor between them. She stood at the big aft window, hugging her arms close. In a moment he was beside her, arms around her, warming her even when she wished he wouldn't.

"Damn," he said, stiffening slightly.

"What?"

"Look," he said, motioning out the window. They had just rounded a bend, and as they straightened out they could see that the *Brigitte* was less than fifty yards behind them. While they slept she had closed much of the gap.

Trey reached for his trousers. "What the hell is Macintosh doing up there?" he muttered.

"Trey, wait. I need to talk to you."

"Now?" he said, pulling on his boots.

"Yes, now. I need to ask you something very important."

He stopped and looked at her. "Ask."

She took a deep breath. "What will you do if you lose this race?"

He laughed. "Probably kill myself."

"Trey, I'm serious. I need to know."

His face took on a look of grim determination. "Start again. Even if Laurence gets back every bit of Rive Douce I've managed to collect, he'll only squander it away again. I'll be waiting to pick up every piece of it he throws away."

She sat beside him on the bed and took his hand. "Trey, I've come to realize the last few days that you're a very wealthy man. Isn't that right?"

"Aha! So you're in this for my money, are you?"

"Please, be serious. You could buy another plantation, couldn't you, one ready to move into, ready to put your heart into making a success of?"

"It wouldn't be Rive Douce. I've told you that before."

"But you could do it?"

He shrugged. "I suppose there are at least a dozen plantations I could buy between New Orleans and Baton Rouge."

"Some even better than Rive Douce? With more productive land, in better condition?"

"Some, but what does that matter? I don't want

them. They're not mine; Rive Douce is."

"No, Trey, it's not." She took a deep breath. "And I'm about to ask you to let it go."

"Let it go? What do you—"

"Yes, my love, let it go. Let go of a dream of revenge; let go of the need to lash out at your father and your brother for an accident of birth that was not their fault; let go of trying to prove to the world that you're as good as they are when the real truth is that you're better—and most of them know it."

He stood up abruptly. "I don't understand what you're asking."

"I'm asking you to save Dolly's life."

He spun around. "Dolly! What does Dolly have to do with me or this race or Rive Douce?"

"She's here, Trey."

"What do you mean, she's here?" he said, looking around as if Dolly were about to spring forth from under the mattress or pop out of the woodwork.

"She's on board the *Corinne* right now."

"Nonsense, she's at my mother's."

"No, she's here."

"I would have seen her come aboard."

"You did." He looked mystified. "She was in a crate."

He stared at her a minute and then the penny dropped. "My mother's champagne," he said.

"That's right."

He wasn't smiling anymore. "I imagine you're going to get around to telling me why."

"If you'll sit beside me," she said, patting the rumpled bed.

"Charli, I want to know."

But she reached out and pulled him down next to her. "Trey, did you know your mother has occasionally used her house as a station on the Underground Railroad, to help runaway slaves escape to the North?"

"What?" he said, jumping up, but she pulled him down again.

"She knows many people who are involved in the Railroad. She knows who to contact when a runaway needs help."

"Dolly is not a runaway."

"She is now. Oh, Trey, you know as well as I do that Laurence is not going to let this thing rest. We've only kept her safe this long because of the race. As soon as we all get back to New Orleans, he's going to go after her. She did much more than cause him to hit his head on the sidewalk; she wounded his pride, and she did it publicly. Laurence isn't the type of man to take that. He lashes back. And he won't give up; he's going to get Dolly unless she's safely far away before he starts seriously looking for her."

"And my mother has agreed to help you do that."

"Yes. We spent most of the night making plans and sending messages. It's all arranged."

"Do you plan to share these arrangements with me?" he asked. Every trace of his earlier warmth had deserted him now.

"Yes, but only if you promise to listen and not interrupt until I'm done."

He stared at her a moment before nodding curtly.

"Dolly is to be picked up by a conductor of the Underground Railroad just below Bryaro. There's an oxbow there where the river's made a cutoff. Remy will go through the cutoff, of course, since it's ten miles shorter, but if you tell Macintosh to take the *Corinne* around the oxbow, we can stop and let Dolly off there without anyone knowing we've done it. Someone will be waiting to meet her and lead her to the first safe station along the way. Trey, they'll never find her. She'll be safe."

"And I will have lost the race," he said, his voice like ice. "Ten extra miles!" He jumped up and paced the small space. "Sauvage doesn't need half that much to pass me and gain enough of a lead that I'll never catch him before Natchez. And you very well know that."

"Yes, I know that."

"So you know what you are asking me to do." He stopped pacing and stared at her.

"Yes, I know that too." The look on his face was cutting her in two. He looked angry, and hurt, and confused. But most of all he looked betrayed.

When he spoke again, his voice was low, controlled. His whole body was taut, like a panther on the watch. She could feel his strength coiled within him, ready to spring. "Knowing what this race means to me, you are asking me to willingly lose it so that one slave can get to freedom."

She nodded.

"Is this some sort of a test, Charlotte, a way to prove your influence over me? Because I warn you, I don't take well to being tested."

"No! It's nothing like that, Trey, believe me." Her hand automatically reached out for him, but he pulled away, grabbed his shirt and stuck his arms into it, then went to the window and turned his back on her. "I don't want you to do this because of me, Trey. I want you to do it because it's right. And I think you know that."

"Right," he murmured. "Was it right that I should be born a bastard?" he asked, almost as if he were talking to himself. "Was it right that my father left me nothing but a boat ticket to Paris while my legitimate brother got Rive Douce?"

"No, it wasn't," Charli said softly. "Is it right that Dolly was born a slave instead of a free woman with the inherent right to choose what to do with her own life? Is it right that Laurence is allowed to beat her, rape her, kill her even, with total impunity?" She rose and went to him and laid a hand on his shoulder. When he didn't immediately push her away, she was encouraged. "Life isn't always fair, Trey. And we don't always know why things happen the way they do. I don't know why I'm here, in 1858, instead of in my Greenwich Village apartment running my business in 1993. Maybe it was to find you; maybe it was to find myself. And just maybe it was to save you from making a terrible mistake as well as saving Dolly's life." She moved to stand in front of him, forcing him to look into her eyes. "Trey, if you don't turn this boat into that riverbend and stop it, Dolly will be dead within weeks, maybe days."

"She could die on the way North. It happens all the time."

"She knows that. She also knows that if that happens, she'll die free. Frightened as she is, she's willing to take that chance."

"The implication being," he said with a grimace, "how can I do any less?"

379

Megan Daniel

Charli shrugged. "We all do what we have to, Trey. I believe you're the sort of man who makes right choices. Maybe I'm wrong, but I don't think I would have fallen in love with you otherwise."

He turned away again, toward the window, and gripped the curtain hanging there so tightly that it came crashing to the floor, its brass curtain rod clanking loudly. Trey scarcely seemed to notice. All his attention was focused on the lights of the *Belle Brigitte* not far behind them. Charli thought she saw moisture gathered in one corner of his eye, but she couldn't be sure.

Finally, he dropped the rumpled piece of curtain he still held; his whole body sagged. Slowly, he turned and looked at Charli's little glow-in-the-dark clock. "We'll be at the bend in less than twenty minutes," he said, his voice and body the very image of defeat. "Go get Dolly out of that crate and get her ready."

"Oh, Trey," Charli cried, throwing her arms around him. But he grabbed her hands and threw her away from him.

"Don't touch me. Don't talk to me. Perhaps later, when this is over, we can try to recapture what I thought we had, until half an hour ago. But right now, I don't want you near me."

With that, he stuffed his shirt into his trousers, grabbed his coat from the chair, and strode out of the cabin.

Charli never knew what Trey said to Macintosh, how he explained that they were taking the bend instead of the cut, adding an impossible-to-make-up ten miles to their route when the *Belle Brigitte* was less than ten minutes behind them.

But her body relaxed somewhat when she saw the nose of the big steamer turn into the oxbow.

They stood at the rail—Charli, Dolly, and Lisette. Dolly was wrapped in a long black cloak, a hood covering her head. She carried a small valise filled with an extra dress, food for the journey, and as much money as Lisette could give her without causing suspicion. She also carried a set of papers identifying her as a freedwoman—hurriedly done in the small hours of the night, but still good enough to pass all but the most careful scrutiny.

Not far ahead, just at the apex of the bend, Charli could see a faint light. It flashed twice—on-off, on-off—then a pause and the same pattern repeated again.

"That's the signal," Lisette said, as calmly as if she were asking one of her customers for payment. She edged Dolly closer to the railing. The Underground Railroad conductor was waiting.

"Here," said Charli as she felt the giant paddle wheels begin to slow. She handed Dolly a letter. "You can read well enough by now to read this address."

Dolly looked at it. "Charlotte DuClos," she sounded out the letters.

"My great-great-grandmother," said Charli. "Give her that letter and then give her this." She slipped Trey's silver and amethyst ring from her finger. "Explain to her who I am and what's happened to me. She might not believe you— I'm not sure I'd believe you myself—but from what I've heard of the old gal, she's just enough of a renegade to buy the story. I'm sure she'll help you."

Megan Daniel

Just at that moment the boat bumped against the darkened and seemingly deserted dock. At the last moment, the lantern flashed on again. A bearded man in a black coat buttoned high stood there. He reached a hand up toward Dolly.

"I'm scared, Charli," the girl whispered.

"I know. But it'll be okay. You've got a whole life waiting, Dolly. Go grab it." She gave the girl a hug. "Grab it and squeeze it and get every drop of living out of it before you let it go. Promise me that."

"I promise," said Dolly. Then she let go of her friend and benefactor, turned toward the man on the dock, reached for his hand, and jumped toward her new life. Almost at once, the lantern flicked out and Dolly disappeared into the darkness. She was gone.

The *Corinne*'s paddle wheels churned as she nosed away from the little dock. In the stillness of the night, Charli could hear Macintosh's voice bellowing from the wheelhouse. "Lay it on, lads. Give me everything you've got!"

Steam screamed through the safety valves and the *Corinne* shot forward.

In minutes, it seemed, they were turning out of the bend and back into the river's main channel. Up ahead, maybe two miles, maybe three, but certainly not as far ahead as Charli had expected, they could see the lights of the *Belle Brigitte*.

Charli walked toward the wheelhouse. She would stay out of Trey's way—he deserved that much, at least, however much it hurt—but she needed to know what was going on.

"More steam!" Macintosh cried. "Give me more steam! We can catch her."

Incredibly, over the next half hour, the distance between the two boats gradually narrowed. By the time the eastern sky had lightened to a rich rose color, the *Corinne* was less than two hundred yards behind the *Brigitte*.

Trey, excited again by the possibility that it might not all be over after all, ran back and forth between the wheelhouse and the boiler room, exhorting his crew to greater effort. He rolled up his sleeves and tossed wood into the roaring furnaces. He was like a man possessed.

Dear God, Charli thought, he wants it so bad. Maybe he should have it. Allowing herself to be caught up in the electric atmosphere of the challenge, as well as in Trey's burning need to win, Charli found herself running back and forth, carrying buckets of coal oil and stacks of wax candles to the boiler room, anything to add to the fires to make them burn hotter. She even threw a disposable lighter she'd been carrying in her pocket into one of the furnaces. It exploded with a loud pop and the fire whooshed, creating more steam to push the *Corinne* harder still.

The boat shuddered with the enormous effort being demanded of her, but she was up to the task. By the time the buildings of Natchez came into view, warmly lit by the emerging sun, the two steamers were side by side.

Scarcely fifteen feet divided the railings of the two boats; their noses were dead even. Charli could see Laurence Campbell on the deck of the *Brigitte*, ranting at Remy Sauvage and his pilot, screaming that they had to win, that he'd see them in hell if they didn't, that he'd kill them himself if they lost. Charli knew the same sort of melee had to be going on in the *Brigitte*'s boiler rooms as the one that had turned the *Corinne*'s into a scene from hell.

Back in the wheelhouse: Macintosh yelling, Trey pacing, Charli fretting. The paddle wheels churned for all they were worth; the cocks on the steam valves screamed. Voices from the *Brigitte* carried across the small distance: Laurence screaming, Remy exhorting.

Closer and closer to the Natchez docks the two great boats moved. The *Corinne* nosed ahead by a foot, two feet, three.

"We can do it," Trey shouted. "We're doing it! We've got her!"

Macintosh shook his head, looking troubled. "Listen to her scream," he said. "They've disabled the safety cocks; you can hear it. She's going to blow if they're not careful."

Even as he said it, an explosion rent the air. A ball of fire blossomed out from the *Brigitte*'s stacks, the brilliant orange of a nasturtium. A blast of heat nearly knocked Charli off her feet, and she grabbed the railing. Another explosion sounded, and the *Brigitte* was engulfed in a cloud of flame and dense black smoke.

"Turn her! Turn her!" shouted Trey as Macintosh wrestled with the wheel, trying to turn the speeding *Corinne* away from the inferno the *Brigitte* had turned into.

The ball of fire was coming straight at them.

"Trey!" Charli called just before it hit. He grabbed her hand at the moment of impact.

The crash was deafening. Wood splintered; brass tore away from its screws; people screamed.

Charli felt herself tossed through the air. Trey's

hand no longer held hers. She hit the water with a stinging smack.

Cold! It was incredibly cold. And familiar. She'd been here before, not so long ago, drowning in the Mississippi. She was sucked under by the current. The thought passed through her mind that perhaps it was still Mardi Gras, 1993, and none of the past few weeks had even happened, that Trey was not real, that it had all been a death's-edge dream. That now she would learn what lay beyond that dream, on death's other side.

She surfaced, gasping for air, her eyes open. The ball of fire that had been the *Belle Brigitte* was still there, still burning. And the *Corinne* was still afloat. She could see Lisette standing on the listing deck, looking in her direction, calling something, though she couldn't hear it.

So it was real, after all. She was glad of that, comforted by the fact that she had at least known true love once in her life, if not for long enough.

She was sucked under again. Something brushed against her legs. She grabbed for it and opened her eyes.

There was enough light for her to barely see through the murky water, but she would have recognized him anywhere. It was Trey, and he seemed to be unconscious. The knowledge gave her new strength. She didn't mind dying—well, not too much—but she'd be damned if she was going to let Trey Lavande drown while there was a spark of life left in her body.

She kicked hard, spiraling her body and his together up through the water toward the surface. The current had carried them closer to the shore, a rocky levee that sloped up out of the water. With one hand under Trey's chin, she used the other to stroke hard for that shore.

It seemed to take forever. Finally, though, one foot touched mud. She sank in up to her ankles trying to drag Trey out of the river, but she reached the dry levee. With her last strength, she turned him onto his back and felt for a pulse. It was there, but weak, and he wasn't breathing. She started giving him mouth-to-mouth resuscitation.

"Don't you die!" she cried between breaths. "Don't you dare die, Trey!" Breath. "Not now, just when I've found you." Breath. "I won't let you die!" Breath.

After what seemed like hours, but was probably two minutes, he coughed. Immediately, she turned him on his side, and water ran from his mouth. He opened his eyes. "I don't plan to die anytime soon, so you can stop," he whispered. He had heard her pleas. She collapsed onto the gravel of the levee beside him.

They must have lain like that for a long time; perhaps they slept, or even passed out. When Charli opened her eyes again, the sun seemed to be higher in the sky. Trey stirred in her arms and opened his eyes, too.

"Can you walk?" she asked.

"I think so. Can you?"

"One way to find out."

They helped each other up, a little unsteadily, but once up they managed to stay on their feet. Charli turned toward the river. And froze.

"Oh, my God," she whispered. An oil tanker, big as a sideways skyscraper, was passing up the river. On the opposite shore, buildings rose dozens of stories into the air. A light pall of smog hung low above them.

From behind her, and not far away, Charli heard music—a chorus of children singing "Everybody's beautiful, in his own way...." Then came the unmistakable squawk of a microphone over a loudspeaker. She turned toward the sound.

"What is that?" asked Trey, still not too steady on his feet.

"C'mon," said Charli, taking him by the hand and walking toward the sound.

Within minutes they reached a blacktopped area lined with cars and trucks. A large crowd of people, dressed in jeans and work shirts, suits and ties, polyester pants and bright spring dresses, stood facing a bandstand, its front edges draped with red-white-and-blue bunting. A small, well-dressed black woman of perhaps sixty years had just stepped up to the microphone.

"Charli," said Trey, his voice steadier now, and definitely confused. "What is this? What's going on?"

"Shhh," she said, as the black woman started to speak.

"I was born a free woman," she began. "My great-grandmother was born a slave, on a plantation not far from where we stand today. She would have died a slave had it not been for some caring white people who, at great cost and danger to themselves, helped her escape from Louisiana on the Underground Railroad. Other people helped her too, both black and white, men and women, Christians and Jews.

"My great-grandmother lived to be a hundred

387

and four. She taught me many things before she died. She taught me that we are one people; she taught me to be proud of who I am, to value freedom above all things; to help those that need my help. And she taught me that it is only when people work together that great things are accomplished.

"And so my mission, as the first female African-American governor in the United States, is to bring people together, to create a state in which every person—man and woman, black and white, the disabled, the young, the unempowered—knows he or she is an important and valued part of this society. With that promise in mind, I dedicate my term as governor of Louisiana to the memory of a slave, my great-grandmother—Dolly Lavande Stewart."

Trey and Charli looked at each other, knowledge dawning, wonder and fear and excitement mingling inside them both.

"Charli," Trey whispered. "Are we where I think we are?"

"Oh, Trey," she said, beaming up at him with a hundred-watt smile. "Have I got a world to show you!"

Dear Reader:

Thank you so much for coming with me on this journey through time——and through the complex highways of the heart. I hope you've enjoyed spending time with Charli and Trey as much as I have. I hated to say good-bye to them.

I hope you'll share your feelings with me. I love hearing from readers. Please write to:

Megan Daniel
Aldama #1
Box 19L
San Miguel de Allende
GTO 37700
MEXICO

P.S. If you enjoyed *All The Time We Need*, I hope you'll watch for my story, "The Christmas Portrait," a time-travel novella in Love Spell's *A Time-Travel Christmas*, to be published in November, 1993. Come with Cass and Nick to Gilded Age New York—— and see what's in a window.

LOVE SPELL

THE MAGIC OF ROMANCE PAST, PRESENT, AND FUTURE....

Dorchester Publishing Co., Inc., the leader in romantic fiction, is pleased to unveil its newest line—Love Spell. Every month, beginning in August 1993, Love Spell will publish one book in each of four categories:

1) *Timeswept Romance*—Modern-day heroines travel to the past to find the men who fulfill their hearts' desires.

2) *Futuristic Romance*—Love on distant worlds where passion is the lifeblood of every man and woman.

3) *Historical Romance*—Full of desire, adventure and intrigue, these stories will thrill readers everywhere.

4) *Contemporary Romance*—With novels by Lori Copeland, Heather Graham, and Jayne Ann Krentz, Love Spell's line of contemporary romance is first-rate.

Exploding with soaring passion and fiery sensuality, Love Spell romances are destined to take you to dazzling new heights of ecstasy.

COMING IN NOVEMBER!

TIMESWEPT ROMANCE

A TIME-TRAVEL CHRISTMAS
**By Megan Daniel, Vivian Knight-Jenkins,
Eugenia Riley, and Flora Speer**

In these four passionate time-travel historical romance
stories, modern-day heroines journey everywhere from
Dickens's London to a medieval castle as they fulfill their
deepest desires on Christmases past.
_51912-7 $4.99 US/$5.99 CAN

A FUTURISTIC ROMANCE

MOON OF DESIRE
By Pam Rock

Future leader of his order, Logan has vanquished enemies,
so he expects no trouble when a sinister plot brings a mere
woman to him. But as the three moons of the planet Thurlow
move into alignment, Logan and Calla head for a collision
of heavenly bodies that will bring them ecstasy—or utter
devastation.
_51913-5 $4.99 US/$5.99 CAN

LEISURE BOOKS
ATTN: Order Department
276 5th Avenue, New York, NY 10001

Please add $1.50 for shipping and handling for the first book and
$.35 for each book thereafter. PA., N.Y.S. and N.Y.C. residents,
please add appropriate sales tax. No cash, stamps, or C.O.D.s. All
orders shipped within 6 weeks via postal service book rate.
Canadian orders require $2.00 extra postage and must be paid in
U.S. dollars through a U.S. banking facility.

Name _____
Address _____
City _____ State _____ Zip _____
I have enclosed $_____ in payment for the checked book(s).
Payment <u>must</u> accompany all orders.☐ Please send a free catalog.

COMING IN SEPTEMBER 1993
TIMESWEPT ROMANCE
TIME REMEMBERED
Elizabeth Crane
Bestselling Author of *Reflections in Time*

A voodoo doll and an ancient spell whisk thoroughly modern Jody Farnell from a decaying antebellum mansion to the Old South and a true Southern gentleman who shows her the magic of love.

_0-505-51904-6   \$4.99 US/\$5.99 CAN

FUTURISTIC ROMANCE
A DISTANT STAR
Anne Avery

Jerrel is enchanted by the courageous messenger who saves his life. But he cannot permit anyone to turn him from the mission that has brought him to the distant world—not even the proud and passionate woman who offers him a love capable of bridging the stars.

_0-505-51905-4   \$4.99 US/\$5.99 CAN

COMING IN AUGUST 1993
HISTORICAL ROMANCE
WILD SUMMER ROSE
Amy Elizabeth Saunders

Torn from her carefree rustic life to become a proper city lady, Victoria Larkin bristles at the hypocrisy of the arrogant French aristocrat who wants to seduce her. But Phillipe St. Sebastian is determined to have her at any cost—even the loss of his beloved ancestral home. And as the flames of revolution threaten their very lives, Victoria and Phillipe find strength in the healing power of love.

_0-505-51902-X $4.99 US/$5.99 CAN

CONTEMPORARY ROMANCE
TWO OF A KIND
Lori Copeland
Bestselling Author of *Promise Me Today*

When her lively widowed mother starts chasing around town with seventy-year-old motorcycle enthusiast Clyde Merrill, Courtney Spenser is confronted by Clyde's angry son. Sensual and overbearing, Graham Merrill quickly gets under Courtney's skin—and she's not at all displeased.

_0-505-51903-8 $3.99 US/$4.99 CAN

LEISURE BOOKS
ATTN: Order Department
276 5th Avenue, New York, NY 10001

Please add $1.50 for shipping and handling for the first book and $.35 for each book thereafter. PA., N.Y.S. and N.Y.C. residents, please add appropriate sales tax. No cash, stamps, or C.O.D.s. All orders shipped within 6 weeks via postal service book rate. Canadian orders require $2.00 extra postage and must be paid in U.S. dollars through a U.S. banking facility.

Name_____

Address_____

City _____ State_____ Zip_____

I have enclosed $_____in payment for the checked book(s).

Payment <u>must</u> accompany all orders.☐ Please send a free catalog.

COMING IN AUGUST 1993
TIMESWEPT ROMANCE
A TIME TO LOVE AGAIN
Flora Speer
Bestselling Author of *Viking Passion*

While updating her computer files, India Baldwin accidentally backdates herself to the time of Charlemagne—and into the arms of a rugged warrior. Although there is no way a modern-day career woman can adjust to life in the barbaric eighth century, a passionate night of Theuderic's masterful caresses leaves India wondering if she'll ever want to return to the twentieth century.

_0-505-51900-3 $4.99 US/$5.99 CAN

FUTURISTIC ROMANCE
HEART OF THE WOLF
Saranne Dawson
Bestselling Author of *The Enchanted Land*

Long has Jocelyn heard of Daken's people and their magical power to assume the shape of wolves. If the legends prove true, the Kassid will be all the help the young princess needs to preserve her empire—unless Daken has designs on her kingdom as well as her love.

_0-505-51901-1 $4.99 US/$5.99 CAN

LEISURE BOOKS
ATTN: Order Department
276 5th Avenue, New York, NY 10001

Please add $1.50 for shipping and handling for the first book and $.35 for each book thereafter. PA., N.Y.S. and N.Y.C. residents, please add appropriate sales tax. No cash, stamps, or C.O.D.s. All orders shipped within 6 weeks via postal service book rate. Canadian orders require $2.00 extra postage and must be paid in U.S. dollars through a U.S. banking facility.

Name _____

Address _____

City _____ State _____ Zip _____

I have enclosed $_____ in payment for the checked book(s). Payment <u>must</u> accompany all orders.☐ Please send a free catalog.

A TIMESWEPT ROMANCE
TEMPEST IN TIME
EUGENIA RILEY

"Eugenia Riley's romances are sumptuous reads!"
—*Romantic Times*

An assertive, independent 1990's career girl, Missy Monroe is having second thoughts about marrying gentle Jeff Dalton.

A timid Victorian virgin, Melissa Montgomery is terrified at the thought of her arranged marriage to domineering Fabian Fontenot.

But when the two accidentally switch places—and partners—on their wedding day, each will have to discover for herself whether she is part of an odd couple or a match made in heaven.

__3377-1 $4.50 US/$5.50 CAN

A TIMESWEPT ROMANCE

Timeswept passion...timeless love.

REFLECTIONS IN TIME

ELIZABETH CRANE

When practical-minded Renata O'Neal submits to hypnosis to cure her insomnia, she never expects to wake up in 1880's Louisiana — or in love with fiery Nathan Blue. But vicious secrets and Victorian sensibilities threaten to keep Renata and Nathan apart...until Renata vows that nothing will separate her from the most deliciously alluring man of any century.

_3254-6 $4.50 US/$5.50 CAN